BORDERS

Also by Roy Jacobsen in English translation

The Burnt-Out Town of Miracles (2007)
Child Wonder (2011)

Roy Jacobsen

BORDERS

Translated from the Norwegian by
Don Bartlett and Don Shaw

MACLEHOSE PRESS

QUERCUS · LONDON

First published in Norwegian as *Grenser*
by Cappelen Damm AS, Oslo, in 1999
First published in Great Britain in 2015 by

MacLehose Press
an imprint of Quercus
55 Baker Street
7th Floor, South Block
London W1U 8EW

This translation has been published with the
financial support of NORLA

A CIP catalogue record for this book is available
from the British Library

ISBN (HB) 978 0 85705 306 0
ISBN (TPB) 978 0 85705 307 7
ISBN (Ebook) 978 1 78206 957 7

2 4 6 8 10 9 7 5 3 1

Designed and typeset by Libanus Press in Scala
Printed and bound in Great Britain by Clays Ltd, St Ives plc

To Anse

The Miller's Bridge

By the River Our – between Luxembourg and Germany – there is, on the German side, a mill barely a kilometre south of the village of Dasburg. It is known as Frankmühle, but the owner, Johann Holper, lives on the Luxembourg side, in the village of Rodershausen.

In late summer, when the water level is low, he can wade across the river – and the border – on his way to work, which takes him five minutes. In the winter months, when the river is high, he has to walk up to Dasburg, cross the bridge there and walk back along the German bank, which takes him about an hour. By horse and cart it takes the same time, because then he can't use the tracks through the forest.

As Johann Holper doesn't live a great deal further from his workplace than many a farmer does, he sits down at his desk on 26 November, 1893 and writes a letter to the *Bürgermeister* in Daleiden, the closest district to his home on the German side.

"... as I live in Rodershausen but own a mill on the German side, Frankmühle, and have to make a detour of about an hour to get there, I hereby most respectfully beg permission to make a path and construct a small wooden bridge by the mill in the Our Valley to fulfil my needs ..."

Since Johann Holper was born on the border and had learned at his mother's knee that national borders are not something to be taken lightly, he assures the *Bürgermeister*, twice in fact, that he is requesting only a "very small bridge", in other words not a major road between two nations which may be used for importing or exporting goods, for commercial ends, that is, which necessarily would require a customs office; nor was it to be built for wheeled vehicles, thus allowing it to be used for military purposes, which would necessitate a border-control point: all he wants is a footbridge, the sole function of which is to keep the feet dry of those who are already legally entitled to cross the border in the summer and to save them two, otherwise wasted, working hours in the winter.

The next day he takes the letter with him on his way to Frankmühle and posts it on the German side, so that it will only be en route two to three days up the mountain to Daleiden, rather than sending it from home, in which case it would have to go via Luxembourg, the capital city, constituting a detour of around 140 kilometres, which with checks and transport time would have meant a journey of at least seven days. It is tricks like this that Johann Holper has learned over a long life by the border, so he has German stamps in his desk drawer and in this way also saves on postage. Now, he reflects with a certain pleasure, his letter is taking the same welcome shortcut he himself has hopes of taking in the future, without breaking the law.

The *Bürgermeister* of Daleiden is also a seasoned border fox, who immediately recognises that this is far too big an issue for his office, so he passes the letter on to Kreis Prüm. But even this regional authority is not high enough, so the miller's application is passed up a level, to the provincial government in Trier. Here the matter is dealt with according to the usual procedures for bilateral state affairs and a copy is sent to the government in the Grand Duchy of Luxembourg, to the miller's own government, that is, with a request for comments and views.

The Luxembourg government is somewhat bemused that one of their subjects has taken the long way round the river with his application, instead of going straight to them, this approach only delays proceedings, but that is the miller's business. After the turn of the year a delegation, together with the corresponding authorities from Trier, is commissioned to examine the feasibility of coming to an agreement with regard to the "Frankmühle Case".

A number of points have to be clarified first. *Who* can use the bridge, apart from the miller himself? And as "use" is to some degree reflected in the size and design of the construction, a decision is taken to demand binding guarantees from the miller that the bridge will only be utilised by people travelling on foot.

And now the miller replies through "the official channels", for he has also Luxembourg stamps in his desk, and he repeats that of course it will be a very small bridge, a footbridge, as stated in his application, and since the River Our is so shallow that you can wade across in the summer and winter, such that the proposed construction could not possibly have much effect on any undesired or unmonitored crossings, which are hardly likely to be determined by whether one would get one's wet feet or not, I cannot see that there are any reasonable grounds for *not* allowing a bridge to be built . . .

The officials dealing with the case in Luxembourg detect a tone of irritability in this letter but choose to ignore it. In the meantime their German counterparts suspect that with his private bridge initiative Holper is only trying to avoid paying the toll that a pedestrian has to pay to cross the official bridge at Dasburg. To which the miller responds that he does not pay a toll as he has land on each side and accordingly does not represent a source of income for either part under the present arrangement and so would not constitute any loss under a new arrangement.

The officials accept this too and can eventually get to grips with the main problem: who will have *jurisdiction* over the new bridge? Germany or Luxembourg?

This is a tougher nut to crack.

Ownership of – and therefore responsibility for – the other bridges over the Our is regulated according to a bilateral agreement, and even though there is nothing in principle to prevent the status of these bridges acting as a precedent for the miller's bridge, this would not solve the question of financial responsibility as neither the German nor the Luxembourg public can commit themselves to this kind of project since the construction will be of no benefit to anyone other than Johann Holper and his small family, who are the very people who made this unorthodox application in the first place.

Whereupon Johann Holper sits down and pens yet another letter, or rather two identically worded letters, one to Trier and one to the capital of the Grand Duchy, in which he unconditionally assumes responsibility for the bridge, both financially and in all other respects.

This proposition is accepted, with reservations, whereby in truth both parties sweep the legal complications under the carpet, concomitant with a private citizen not only owning property on two sides of a national border but also "owning and having responsibility for" the link between them, as it is well known that there are farmers along the Our with land on each side who wade over or cross by horse and cart when they have to mow or milk rather than using the official crossing points, but then the authorities have turned a blind eye to these goings-on from time immemorial.

So on 22 July, 1894 the authorities in Trier, in conjunction with the government of the Grand Duchy, "grant permission for an extremely small bridge – of wood – to be constructed over the River Our at Frankmühle . . ."

By this time, however, Johann Holper has lost patience, or else assumed it would never occur to anyone to refuse him this bagatelle of a bridge, or couldn't care less, no-one knows, so he has already set to work erecting it, six pairs of oak piles are rammed into the river bed to hold two support beams to which Holper nails a few rungs, it looks like a horizontal ladder which neither beast nor vehicle can use to cross the river.

The authorities in Trier, though, have – after the decision to grant permission was taken – sent the case to the National Building Council with a stipulation that plans for the construction of the "Frankmühlerbrücke" should be drawn up and approved.

In late autumn that year, on October 17 to be precise, Land Surveyor Krebs, who has just returned from a trip to the Our Valley, personally informs the *Regierungspräsident* in Trier with consternation in his voice that a "Frankmühlerbrücke" has already been built.

In German official circles it is felt that Holper has possibly been a little too quick off the mark, but of course it can't be proved just like that and permission has after all been granted.

But then Krebs comes to the rescue of his superiors by suggesting that the tricky "question of responsibility" cannot be said to have been resolved after all, as the case is in *his* hands now, and he – without breaking the laws of the land – cannot give his technical approval to the shoddy work that has been perpetrated at Frankmühle – nor "take responsibility for the safety and durability of the hastily assembled collection of poles and planks", as he put it.

With a certain relief, the German authorities thereby note legitimate grounds for suspecting a breach of building regulations and refer the case to Das Königliche Forstamt – the Royal Forestry Commission – in Kreis Prüm for further action, who in turn assign the case to their man on the spot, Jakob Hemmerling, a forester living in Dasburg, less than half an hour's walk from the disputed construction.

Like Holper, Hemmerling is a border fox, inured to this nonsense from birth, so he takes his time over the investigation and the following March sends a report to his superiors in Prüm, who are then able to read in black and white:

"There is no bridge at Frankmühle."

Das Königliche Forstamt hereby declares the case closed and commits it to the archives.

Jazz

At the crack of dawn on 16 December, 1944 General Hasso von Manteuffel's Fifth Panzer Army broke through the Allied lines along Skyline Drive, as the Americans called it, or the Siegfried Line, as the British called it, or *Westwall*, as the Germans called it, Hitler's border with Luxembourg and Belgium, thereby starting the Ardennes Offensive: the last convulsions of the Third Reich, as everyone agreed.

The Germans had managed to assemble close on 300,000 men and more than 900 armoured vehicles behind the front without these movements being spotted by Allied aerial reconnaissance. In the forward deployment area the 2nd Panzer Division crossed the River Our at Dasburg, having first hastily constructed a new bridge as a replacement for the one they had blown up when they retreated three months earlier, and advanced into territory defended by the American 110th Regiment under the command of Colonel Hurley E. Fuller, an outstanding officer who had made a name for himself and been decorated in the First World War, and who at this moment was at his H.Q. in the picturesque medieval town of Clervaux, thirteen kilometres further west in the heart of the Grand Duchy of Luxembourg.

Despite determined resistance from the American border forces, who had been caught off guard, 2nd Panzers rolled through the Ardennes in massive numbers and on the morning of the 17th reached the outskirts of Clervaux. Fuller had billeted his staff at the Clervalis Hotel in the middle of town – which lies in a deep valley – and had absolutely no idea what was going on. Manteuffel had persuaded Hitler to allow him to deploy his infantry before the tanks, to secure bridges, clear the roads, disrupt communications and prevent sabotage by the fleeing Allied forces, for Manteuffel was a German to his boots and knew that when all hope was gone, when all roads were closed, when all resources were exhausted, when all lives had been sacrificed and the skies were laden with soot, there was only one thing to do, to invade the Ardennes, for that is what no-one expects, however often it happens, this fur-coated, sleeping miracle, which through the ages has lain here between the sea and the Reich with its unanswered questions and winding side roads, with its shadows and farmers and forests and dwarfs and its enticing steep hillsides, its mysterious castles and its unendingly depressing rain trickling down over the most sorrowful stories that no-one can be bothered to tell any more.

Colonel Fuller's communications with the rest of the world were effectively severed on this strange Sunday morning in December 1944 when all the whole of Europe was waiting for was peace. The American was left to try to get an overview of the situation by means of intelligence reports which were in effect little more than rumour supplied to him by a civilian population fleeing in panic. Through the hotel window he could see women and children and the elderly pouring through the streets, horses and domestic animals, carts and tractors and rickety vehicles in improvised columns, while the sounds that reached him through the majestic beech treetops, the inexorably swelling song of the forest, was unmistakable: full-scale war once again.

Fuller had dug in on the high ground around the town, but he had no more than twelve Sherman tanks (as opposed to the thirty Tigers which the Fifth Panzers powered in with, as well as twice as many Panthers), and all twelve of them were knocked out in the course of the morning. By half past eleven the Germans were beginning to encircle the town, and minutes later the bombardment started; the medieval chateau was one of the prime targets, the highest point, where Fuller had established his quarters.

But a little later – at 12.34 hours according to records – he miraculously managed to get through to the staff H.Q. in Wiltz, a town fifteen kilometres south-west of Clervaux, under the command of Major General Norman D. Cota. Colonel Fuller gave his superior as precise a description of the situation as possible and asked "in desperation" – his own words – for artillery and tank support.

Cota answered:

"I can send you a battery of S.P. guns, but that's all. I've got two other regiments which need help." (These were busy resisting – also in vain – Manteuffel's

Panzer Lehr Division, which had broken through the lines south of Dasburg, between Gemünd and Vianden.)

Fuller:

"I've got twelve Tigers on my back." (The correct figure was in fact thirty.) "They've moved into position on the ridge east of town!" (They were in the process of encircling them.)

Cota:

"I can't – with the best will in the world – give you more than one battery. And don't forget the orders. Hold out at all costs. Yield no ground! Every man at his post."

A few seconds of silence followed at Fuller's end of the crackly line.

Cota:

"Are you there, Fuller? Did you get that?"

Fuller:

"Yes, sir. Every man will remain at his post."

At 3 p.m. Clervaux was, to use the German word, *eingekesselt* – "kettled in". All Fuller's strongpoints were in enemy hands. The German tanks advanced on the town from three sides. The G.I.s put up doughty resistance, but were still losing ground. And shortly before the onset of darkness Fuller gave his surviving company commanders – by telephone (another miracle!) – "strict orders to fight to the last man!"

A second later the line was cut, a deafening explosion followed, floors and walls shook, the roof was holed and on the verge of collapsing, the lights went out, and through the shattered window Fuller caught sight of a German tank, at a distance of fifteen metres, pumping shell after shell into the old hotel. "The Colonel decided to regroup", as the *Time Life* report the following spring phrased it, which more accurately meant that he jumped out of a window at the rear of the hotel with the raggle-taggle remnants of his staff and then managed to climb up a ladder leaning against a cliff, with a blinded comrade clinging to his belt. Five men reached the high ground between two German panzer positions more or less in one piece, where they hunkered down on the snow-covered forest floor, exhausted; it was the hardest winter in the Ardennes for decades, huge falls of snow, on some nights down to minus twenty, all of which Hitler had been counting on, or at least had hoped for (there was some disagreement among his meteorologists); the offensive had in fact been given the code name *Operation Herbstnebel*, Operation Autumn Mist, amongst others.

After regaining his composure – and breath – Fuller raised his head and looked down at the town: "Clervaux was like an inferno", he later reported. "The Panthers roared through the ruins and fired at close range into house after house, where a few scattered and desperate G.I.s were still offering resistance. Above the burning buildings there was a dense cloud of smoke, as if from burning oil, occasionally rent by flares and searchlight beams."

With his comrades, Fuller managed to struggle the fifteen kilometres through the forest to Wiltz, while the remnants of his troops barricaded themselves in the old chateau and held out for another twenty-four hours beneath a massive bombardment from all sides (including phosphorus shells), but when that too was over the Germans stormed the building to find only dead and wounded, except for in the chateau's smouldering ballroom, where a solitary G.I. was playing the piano – jazz.

2

All this happened a long time ago, but jazz and the war and Clervaux have pursued me for twenty-five years; the soldier at the piano was eventually to father one of the main characters in this novel, although the child was conceived under such enigmatic circumstances that it took me quite a few years to identify him as the perpetrator. When the Germans attacked the battered chateau they were so astounded to find a man absorbed in Scott Joplin amidst the hail of bullets that they quite forgot to kill him. Instead they took him prisoner and dumped him in a jeep with two wounded German soldiers, after which the men were sent behind the lines to Germany. But the Dasburg road was blocked by advancing panzer columns, so they had to take forest roads and here they were in unknown territory, both the attackers and those under attack, on top of which, after nightfall, the vehicles broke down in mud and slush.

The trio had to set off on foot – a musical G.I., a German officer with one arm in a sling and an infantryman with one mangled eye and the other covered by a blood-stained bandage (fortunately with his pockets full of amphetamines, though) – as best they could, and they ended up – literally – following Colonel Fuller's footsteps to Wiltz, which was now also in Wehrmacht hands; however, it took them more than two days to cover the fifteen kilometres, and by then Fuller and his sorry crew had fallen into the clutches of the Germans out of sheer exhaustion; Cota had had to abandon the town, more or less in a state of panic.

As a result, the Pianist once again came face to face with his superior officer, Fuller, who demanded a correct military salute before giving him a brief embrace, also in the correct manner, and informing him that: All life has to offer is a deferment of the inevitable, young man. We're going to die here, since we didn't do so in Clervaux.

Wiltz had to be held at all costs (Hitler's orders), so they had rigged up a kind of prison area, a combination of torture chamber and field hospital, I later learned (possibly from a not entirely reliable source, the mother of one of this novel's main protagonists), where the prisoners were alternately given beatings and medical treatment behind the thin partitions; the Germans were primarily interested in discovering the location of the Allies' fuel supplies in the Ardennes; indeed lack of fuel was to prove fatal for Manteuffel.

As a result of a beating, the Pianist lost his hearing in one ear and the use of his left hand. But five days after his arrival he escaped with the help of a Belgian nurse, one of the civilians in Wiltz who had been ordered to serve the Germans. She was a couple of years older than he was, tall and slim and blonde, like in a fairy tale, intelligent, headstrong and romantic. Her name was Maria and she fell head-over-heels for "this odd American" who with "his crazy good humour" managed to keep up the spirits of his fellow prisoners ("and me") even here "in the depths of hell", as she was later to confide to her closely guarded diary.

And they became a couple.

He simulated an epileptic fit which was so like the symptoms described in the medical manuals that the "idiot" in charge of the field hospital transferred him to a more humane department where supervision was slacker. Shortly afterwards the guards held an improvised party, thanks to the confiscation of a stash of Letzebuerger Kirsch (it was the fall of St Vith that was being celebrated, somewhat prematurely, it turned out), and the Pianist got up, sneaked out unseen into the latrines, removed the window from a wall using a screwdriver and crept out naked into the snow. The Belgian angel was waiting for him, her eyes filled with love and panic and her arms holding enough underwear to equip an army through a Russian winter; she put several layers on him and draped a German uniform over the top; they strolled out past the guard (who saluted), arm in arm as young lovers do, left the road as soon as they were out of sight, cut across a white field and were swallowed up by the forest.

So as not to leave a trail behind them they followed the farmers' footprints, zigzagging back to Clervaux, of all places, where they sought refuge on the outskirts of the ravaged town at an abandoned farm in the valley near Abbaye St Maurice, the childhood home of one of Maria's student friends, a farm, by the way, which this friend had no desire to see again after the war – she lost several of her nearest and dearest there – and which therefore in due course she would let Maria takeover for a nominal sum. But here, in a deserted farm behind one of the war's least clearly defined fronts, the Belgian woman and the American pianist spent the next month in total isolation, or "in each other's arms" as she expresses it in her diary.

But then peace came, it didn't arrive as suddenly as the offensive, but came in fits and starts, and the Pianist became more and more restless as the Allied planes droned overhead in thick swarms on their way into the Reich bringing death and destruction together with civilised hopes of creating calm in Europe once and for all. And when, towards the end of January, some passing civilians – on their way home – told the couple that Manteuffel had run out of fuel before Christmas, had suffered bloody defeats at Bastogne and Celles and had not managed to reach Maas or Antwerpen, the Pianist hastened to join an Allied unit rumoured to have established itself in the border town of Vianden, about thirty kilometres south-east of Clervaux, making his way there, once again, on foot.

The two lovers looked into each other's eyes, promised eternal fidelity and went their separate ways. "It was something he absolutely had to do, which could not on any account be postponed," Maria writes bitterly in her diary, in English, in upright handwriting. For that was the last she saw of him. The Pianist deserted her. Or the war took him. He deserted both her love and his redeeming angel. Or the war destroyed everything. But not before he had become father to one of the main characters in this novel – Maria's son, Robert.

Later, incidentally, she found out that the Pianist might have been a Canadian, that he had been living in the Luxembourg capital when hostilities broke out, as a kind of bohemian who entertained at cafés and cabarets for tips and other handouts. Thereafter he threw himself into the war against Hitler, like so many others in this courageous little country, which he eventually identified with, seeing himself as much more than a polite guest.

But there were only very few and very vague indications to support this Canada theory: "something he had said", she argued without being very specific, "some place name", and a certain knowledge of French that pointed to Quebec, but with her weakness for tragic heroism and her inability to distinguish her life from others' she could just as well have exaggerated these details. Earlier that autumn (1944) – before Wiltz, that is – she had, you see, served at a field hospital on the outskirts of Antwerp, when the Canadian First Army, showing almost complete disregard for their own safety, wrested control of Scheldemunningen, opening the port of Antwerp to shipping, in the Battle of the Scheldt, as it is called in her encyclopaedia of World War Two, an engagement that has, incidentally, been described as "the worst ever theatre of war" – albeit in Allied military history – in which both the Luftwaffe and the Royal Air Force bombed the dykes and submerged the battlefield in water, with the result that those who were not killed in the fighting most likely froze to death in the icy water. In South Beveland Maria had some family who survived by hiding under a sail in a rotting boat for days. The nightmare lasted an eternity, and Maria may have suffered a spiritual cataclysm as she spent day after day and night after night stooped over Canadian soldiers who were dying in her hands; and this turmoil may have later caused her to risk her life for a total stranger (the Pianist, because she thought he could have been Canadian) and also to confuse the two experiences, at any rate subsequently, when she had to fit the pieces together to find an explanation, the strangest of explanations.

For a long time after the war she corresponded with several of these "Canadian saviours of ours", or with their surviving relatives, and contributed in this way to making an interest in Canada, of all countries, one of this tiny family's many quirks. When her son grew up, hers and the Pianist's that is – he will soon be introduced – he got to know more about Canada, for example, than her own country, Belgium: the names of towns, climatic conditions, its history and the depth of Lake Huron – 228 metres.

But none of these theories about the origins of the Pianist could ever be confirmed. Or refuted. So for the son – and presumably for his mother, too – he will forever be "some *sort* of American" who in all probability made his living as a cabaret artist in various European towns in the years leading up to 1940 – it is at least not wholly impossible, an artist on the run from his own roots – until his conscience and the seriousness of events caught up with him, the war and a Belgian nurse.

"There was a freedom about the war," Maria was wont to exclaim at emotional moments, "which I have never experienced either before or since."

One might wonder whether the word "freedom" was well chosen, but this was a basic concept in her religiosity, the way other Catholics adhere to *Mutter Gottes*, Ave Maria and Lourdes. And it is an irrefutable fact that the whole of Maria's existence (and thereby also her son's) revolved around this one incomprehensible winter month of 1944–45, the quiet month of conception, peace in the eye of the hurricane, and that everything related to this was collected in photo albums, boxes, voluminous scrapbooks on bookshelves, and was read, studied, checked and scrutinised until, at the beginning of the 1970s, large quantities of the material ended up in the War Museum, founded in the meticulously restored chateau at Clervaux. In addition, the only thing that gave her childhood any meaning was that it led to that same climax, 1944, while the years after (when her son was a child) were a source of shame since they allowed the golden apogee to slip further and further behind her and everyone else. One might well say that time was her bitterest enemy. And the situation did not improve when – some time in her fifties – she began to say:

"Yes, those were the days." A sentence she articulated with the same heartrending valour with which intelligent women throughout history have always contemplated their fading beauty.

3

But she did have one palpable memory, the living proof that the whole thing had not been a dream: a son, whom she bore one beautiful October day in the greatest year of peace ever and whom she immediately named Robert after his absent father; he was his spitting image, he didn't look like her at all, nor anyone in her family, the boy was a "*sort of* American" (him, too) and she was not ashamed to admit it, to have borne and raised this war child, there were enough other births in the region with a far more dubious origin.

The first ten years of peace passed with a receding hope, in the mother (and to a certain degree also in the son), that the Pianist would return – people don't vanish into thin air, she would often say, not even in a war, at times there are the most incredible family reunions. (She was much mistaken with regard to the former: in the Ardennes Offensive three times as many American soldiers went missing in action as fell in combat). Moreover, the Pianist didn't only owe her his fragmented life, she insisted, he also loved her, as she loved him, so he wasn't staying away out of choice; this love was a credo in her and her son's home, their vespers and catechism.

"He loves me," she would say again and again, always in the present tense and especially after a couple of glasses of wine, like a staccato incantation, with hope and supplication in her faltering voice, though on occasion also with great conviction.

Thus the two most obvious explanations for the man failing to return were not even touched upon: either he had been killed on the dangerous journey to Vianden (there were mines and unexploded shells everywhere, and Vianden was not liberated until well into February, which meant that he could easily have walked straight into a German foxhole); or else, of course, he had fabricated the whole Vianden story in order to cover his tracks: for the things he "absolutely" had to see to, which "could not be postponed", might have been something as mundane as a family, wife and children.

Robert himself – as he gradually began to get these matters clear in his mind – opted for the first explanation, a sudden death in a chaotic war zone, but he couldn't ignore the fact that the Pianist didn't actually need any family or any other external reasons as a pretext for staying away; Robert's mother could be very demanding, especially in terms of love and idealism, and what man in times of peace can live up to a myth he has created in war, show me a man who wants to spend the rest of his life feeling "rescued" in the company of his rescuer, a woman, moreover, to whom he owes an eternal debt of gratitude and so on . . . ?

The son was never sure which theory gave her the consolation she craved.

But from her behaviour he presumed she must have concluded something along the lines that the Pianist was still looking for her, feverishly but blindly, due to memory loss, shell shock or as a consequence of a regular war neurosis. On several occasions she remarked that she had found herself in a coma-like condition from February to late autumn that year, throughout her pregnancy that is, with the consequence that all these months had completely vanished from her memory, the happy and unhappy times as they must have been, all in one tangled mess.

As Robert Junior grew up, and whenever the subject was not completely taboo (it was at times), he would ask her what the two of them had talked about during the month or so they were holed up, an ocean of time really, if you tot up the hours, the days and weeks that form a whole month for two lonely people – what clues might the Pianist have given her about himself and his background in that period?

But the pickings must have been lean because she always became vague and guilt-ridden when he broached the subject, and it would have come as no surprise to him if they had just spent the time fooling around and doing all the other things life offers two young people who want nothing more than to shut out the insane world around them. Later she must have regretted this frivolity, but of course she didn't have the slightest inkling that her man would suddenly be gone, this woman who had now found a meaning in her life here in the midst of war, regained her hold on life after South Beveland, she trusted her love, and his, though neither spoke the other's language very well – French was his preference while she did not acquire a good command of English until later.

When eventually she did, however, she made several attempts to contact the Pianist's superior officers. She wrote letters to Colonel Fuller and Norman D. Cota, who both survived the horrors and returned home as highly decorated war heroes. She didn't hear a word from Fuller, while Cota wrote semi-psychotic letters in which he asserted that "Europe is now in the midst of a difficult period of reconstruction that will claim further victims among an already hard-tried population, but the cradle of civilisation has survived crises before . . ." and so on. And only as an afterthought did he mention that unfortunately he had no knowledge of any pianist. Maria should also remember that Fuller was the commanding officer in Clervaux and there were not many survivors . . .

She wanted to reply at once and point out that there was no doubt about it, the Pianist had escaped, it was beyond discussion, she described his brief imprisonment in Wiltz, together with Fuller, furthermore, and afterwards the scramble back to Clervaux. But at this point she suddenly broke down, tore up the sheet of paper and scattered the pieces around her with a wail of despair: "Have I dreamt all this up? I can't remember a thing!!"

That was the first and only time Robert saw his mother so overwrought. And it didn't last long. The very next evening she sat down and composed a new letter to Cota, with a detailed description of the whole course of events, almost identical to what the son would later find in her diary. But this letter did not lead anywhere either; she didn't even have the Pianist's full name (it was her desperation about this that had caused the anguish the day before); she had just called him Bobby (a name her son refused to let pass his lips and which even today he is reluctant to use), but of course it was a short form for Robert, and there were many Roberts in the Allied ranks in the Ardennes, though no musicians or pianists who had been in Clervaux, or none of his age . . . for she had noted his date of birth on the G.I. tag he wore around his neck, 12–1–1919, because on that day – his 26th birthday, 12 January, 1945 – she had surprised him with a roasted goose she had managed to purloin from one of the evacuated neighbouring farms.

This roast dinner, which Robert Junior on one occasion in his adolescent thoughtlessness had called "The Last Supper" (earning himself a stinging slap), was incidentally one of the many war memories that gave rise to rituals in the humble existences of the mother and son which were preserved long into peacetime. Roasted goose was their favourite dish, it was often on the menu, especially in the winter, and always frugally prepared like a kosher meal in the desert. And for Junior to intimate that he wasn't particularly keen on poultry or that he forced it down so as not to hurt her feelings was not an option – that would only have hurt her more. In this way she was allowed to persist with her misconception that he loved goose as much as the piano lessons she sent him to three times a week, with one of her colleagues at the secondary school in Clervaux, where she taught classical languages – nursing was something she had learned in a hurry when the war broke out.

This was how they lived their lives, mother and son, each with their own philosophy, slightly out of sync with one other, each with their own awkward sensitivities. When he objected to something or was rebellious, then Our Lord (almost) always managed to get him to link this behaviour with things that had no direct connection with the war or the Pianist. As mentioned, he never complained about the piano lessons or the goose – nor about the Canada theory for that matter – but he did complain about drawing at school. Robert hated drawing, drawing and painting, and he produced no more than a handful of pathetic sketches in all the years he was there.

"You're a strange lad," she said, "not liking drawing. All kids like drawing."

"Not me."

But she could accept this, regard it merely as an idiosyncratic flaw in a delicate child's mind, which it is a good mother's duty to temper, with patience.

They had an old well in the yard, which was no longer in use, but which they left uncovered, and one evening when her son was romping around with a friend of the same age, she came running up and shouted:

"I hope you're not going to jump in!"

She had got it into her head that he was going to commit suicide and could not see that nothing could be further from his mind, could not see that he was having such a good time that he didn't even understand what she was talking about, now they were off to the forest to shoot wild boar with a bow and arrow.

Every so often she would discover that he was allergic to certain food: white bread, apples, marzipan . . . At other times she would stop him from going to school, it might have been due to something she had read in the papers, a murderer on the loose in Hunsrück or in the Moselle region, or an epidemic which had broken out in Holland, and probably she just needed to have him safe and sound in bed on days that were a little darker than others.

Any other child – who did not have a missing pianist as a father – might perhaps have demanded an explanation for these incidents, especially if the child was approaching puberty. But not Robert. He considered any mysterious behaviour on his mother's part a consequence of the cold handshake of war. In some way he was also conscious of the terrible miracle that meant he – despite everything – could thank that same war for his very existence. The trials and tribulations documented here do not mean that Robert felt he'd had an overprotective or unhappy childhood. Only much later in his life does his childhood become a problem, when he realises it won't let go of him.

It should be added that Robert Junior had a serious failing, inasmuch as, like his father, he was in the habit of running away from home. He started doing this when he was only five or six years old, he would suddenly disappear into the forest and had to be found by neighbours and teachers and friends. As he grew older these excursions became longer, they took him up to the surrounding villages, occasionally over the borders into Germany and Belgium, he cycled, went on foot, caught the bus, it happened about once every six months, always without warning, and neither mother nor son could come up with a satisfactory explanation, other than it had to be the hand of fate, the boy didn't actually belong here in Luxembourg, he too was a guest, like the Pianist.

However, none of the scant information Maria had managed to note (or remember) about the Pianist could bring him back. He was and remained a phantasm, with all the qualities and shortcomings of phantasms. Cota sent a Christmas card for a number of years, pleasant and impersonal cards where he expressed his pleasure that reconstruction work was in progress in Europe, that Robert Junior had begun school, played football and especially that he had joined the Scouts (the aged officer espied the beginnings of a military career here, unaware that the Scout movement in the Ardennes has a much stronger affiliation to the Virgin Mary than to Baden-Powell).

One year he also sent a large package containing chewing gum and cigarettes in abundance, and mother and son had a good laugh at that because rationing had long ceased.

"Poor old man," she smiled. "He's living in the past."

But at that moment the fateful idea of sending him a photograph occurred to her – of Robert Junior. No one can resist the pleading eyes of an eight-year-old who has lost his father. And Robert remembers this photo session – which took place in the rooms of a court-accredited photographer and which must have cost his mother a fortune – as the single most excruciating episode in all their endeavours to trace the Pianist.

They caught the train to the capital city, the boy was seated in a fashionable studio on the rue du Cure, beside a piece of Flemish oak furniture and a resplendent display of flowers which his mother had hired, and was forced to listen to an endless squabble between her and the photographer about how he should be dressed – as a ragamuffin, in his school uniform, in his Sunday best or perhaps with a football under his arm – and especially about the expression he should wear to best motivate the retired war veteran to start tracking down his father.

Should he be smiling at all? Maria wondered.

This question was resolved to her satisfaction by the boy's terrible mood, and by the photographer, who was given permission to take as many pictures as he wanted, whereafter Maria could choose the one showing the boy's saddest mien. As for his garb, he was dressed in sports clothes (her idea) and really did have a football under his arm (the photographer's idea).

She learned only many years later that Americans don't have any interest in European football, and then she burst out laughing again, with the same ambiguous indomitability with which she had received the cigarettes and chewing gum.

"To think we could be so naive!" she said. "Think of all those things we did to find your father. We were so desperate . . ."

"We?" the boy might have answered, but he didn't, and after he himself had a son, he realised that the football idea was not such a bad one. He just shouldn't have looked so miserable. An open, friendly eight-year-old with a football under his arm has a much more alluring effect on a runaway father than a miserable wretch who weighs like a boulder on his father's conscience as soon as he casts his eye on his son, no matter whether the father has any interest in sport or not – strange actually that Cota didn't send them any more Marshall Aid.

Robert shared the view (in puberty and later) that Cota's friendly lack of interest – which was not changed by the photograph – derived from the desperate telephone conversation he'd had with Fuller at 12.34 on Sunday, 17 December, 1944, when he made the perhaps militarily correct but nonetheless very unpleasant decision not to go to the aid of his subordinate officer with more than a single lousy battery of S.P. guns (which by the way never arrived, nor is it even certain they were ever sent). Robert could well imagine that some of the same resentment which came in the wake of the recapture of Scheldemunningen – between the Canadians who froze to death in the icy waters and their allies, the British, who bombed the dykes – must also have arisen between Fuller and Cota. With this in mind Cota would hardly be keen to get into contact with Fuller again, ask him stupid questions about a soldier in *his* – Fuller's – regiment who was supposed to have played the piano in Europe's hour of destiny when everyone was under "strict orders" to fight "to the last man", an order given by Cota himself. Yes, Robert Junior could well imagine that contacting such a haunted subordinate would contravene Cota's military good sense, perhaps his whole way of thinking with regard to waging war and concluding peace.

However, he never mentioned to his mother this possible explanation for the lack of response from America. And, as already intimated, he gradually became fairly sick of all the searching and did what he could to cope with, undermine, obfuscate or ignore the project as sensitively as possible. The loss of a father is something mothers know little about. A small boy's loss of a father is far from identical to a woman's loss of a man. These two entities have nothing in common. They cannot work together. They need to be kept at a distance from each other. An intelligent distance. But this, then, is how they grew up. Maria and that American son of hers, each on their own side of an unanswered question.

4

Further north in the same small valley, a short stone's throw away, lies another pink-walled farm from the golden 1800s, on an idyllic beech-clad slope of the type the tourist authorities like to use to convince the rest of the world that the Grand Duchy has more to offer than a shady banking system and a blossoming steel and porcelain industry. Here lived Markus and Nella, a middle-aged couple whom Robert from the age of two or three referred to as Uncle and Auntie, despite the absence of any blood ties between them. However, Markus was his godfather and he carried a "terrible secret", as he himself put it. His wife, Nella, on the other hand, had no need for any secrets at all, she could dress as she pleased, wash her hair or not, eat titbits all day long despite a growing weight problem, or pick her nose for that matter, at will, because Markus was blind. The "terrible secret" was that he wasn't.

He was Belgian by ancestry, as was Maria, from a small village near Stavelot in the Ardennes, and by virtue of his being "*neu-deutsch*" was enlisted in the Wehrmacht in the late winter of 1941. He was sent to the Eastern Front that same spring and served in the signal corps – with the rank of Leutnant – in General Manstein's Eleventh Army during the invasion of the Crimea in the autumn of 1941 and through to the raid on Sebastapol the year after. He was wounded in the final stages of the Battle of Stalingrad, lost his sight for a day or two, but then saw it was of benefit to him to have lost it for good and was sent home well before the collapse in the east. He spent the last two years of the war on Nella's father's farm on the outskirts of Clervaux and even though she was a good and kind person, she was not much good at keeping a secret when a suitable opportunity to reveal it presented itself; as a result Markus chose to be blind at home as well – "for the time being", as he called it, or "I'll open my eyes again when the war is over", which he told himself, and later Robert, for no-one likes to dupe their nearest and dearest. However, we cannot ignore the fact that it was his blindness which saved him, after peace was declared, from a couple of years in Allied captivity in England, a fate which so many of his "*neu-deutsche*" Belgian brothers were subjected to.

But Markus never did open his eyes again, although he had a clear view of how it should happen, preferably on a summer's morning, he sits up in bed and stares at the window and bursts into hesitant jubilation: "I can see shadows, Nella! Shapes! I can see light! Is that the window . . . ?" After which he would simulate a slow, incredible recovery of the world of the sighted. Instead, though, he accustomed himself to the blind man's protected existence as a spy. "No-one has a better life than blind men who can see. They have had the veil drawn away from their eyes; the curtain goes up to reveal real actions and people, with all their faults and charming secrets. It is of course sad to see all these things, but I wouldn't have been without it for a day."

This optimism was not always quite so convincing; in particular it lost its shine when the German troops passed by for the second time during the Ardennes Offensive, and it was left to Nella to draw up an escape route through the snow-covered forest, this girl who had hardly ventured beyond Clervaux's steep slopes. But the couple's youngest daughter, Marion, a Girl Guide, had. And when the young girl was unsure which path to take, Markus tapped her hip with his white stick, raised his face like a hunted animal scenting the wind and said:

"Are you sure it's this way, sweetheart? I don't seem to recognise this . . ." Or he feigned the blind man's panicky intuition: "No, no, not down there, I can feel it in my bones, we have to go up . . . The wind's coming from the north, isn't it? So, it's this way . . ."

By means of this fine interplay between father and daughter, the family had by morning reached the safety of a relative's house in the village of Boevange, where they lay low for a week before they had to move further south towards Enscherange, which the Germans called Enscheringen, staying at the homes of various forbearing families until the offensive collapsed – that is, in the same month as Maria and the Pianist were holding the fort in Clervaux.

Even after the war Markus' blindness was sometimes put to the test. For example, whenever he read a newspaper he had to be constantly on the alert, and not only while reading it: when he was talking to the family he also had to be careful to keep the information he had gleaned by his own efforts separate from the extracts that Marion had occasionally read out to him.

"It's just a question of tactics," he told Robert Junior, who as time went by was to become his confidant, and the kids gradually got used to having a father who asked intelligent and leading questions about what was going on in the world, a subject that never failed to interest Markus, about politics, affairs of state and industrial development, not to mention the tribunals that followed in the wake of the war, and which as far as his commanding officer, General Manstein, was concerned, extended into the 1950s.

None of the family members thought it remarkable that Markus never dirtied his clothes, tripped over furniture that had been moved, or showed any indecision regarding the weather. Blind people have exceptionally good hearing, they sense everything that we others are dependent on our sight to know – in fact, the blind don't actually *need* sight; in addition, once in a while Markus threw in the odd stumble when he realised that it was a long time since he had last tripped, or he feigned surprise when someone addressed him out of the blue. In order to avoid direct eye contact with the people around him he also always wore dark glasses.

But after his daughters moved out he came up against another problem, as Nella liked neither the news nor reading aloud, and on top of that was mean, and so she often "forgot" to buy useless items like papers, magazines and books. And this is where Robert Junior came in, Markus' godson and closest neighbour. It was the boy's job to get hold of suitable material and read aloud to his friend whenever Nella was around. And the reason why Markus eventually let him in on his "terrible secret" was simply the boy's poor reading skills; the little American was just seven when this not entirely straightforward collaboration began, and doubtless the old man also needed a break from his blindness, a place where he could be himself and enjoy the company of a fellow conspirator. In this way it was actually Markus who taught Robert how to read, in the brief period they had to themselves every day between the end of school and Nella's return from the draper's shop she managed in town.

Markus had trained as an electrical engineer in the Belgian Military Academy, the only form of training that was available to him, he claimed, and in the pre-war years had built up quite a name for himself as an inventor, not least of a vulcanisation process – or a kind of adhesive – which proved very useful to the Belgian army, and later also the Wehrmacht. He helped Robert with his maths and physics homework, he knew Latin, he could reel off the names of all the Catholic saints, and was furthermore a rich source of dramatic tales and curious observations. Being with Markus was therefore no sacrifice for Robert, and he was more than pleased to read aloud everything except the reports of the war tribunals. But he liked their walks even more, especially those in the woods, where Markus could behave more spontaneously, there was no end to his quirky stories, a veritable circus unfolded in the woods, a narrative with many beginnings, digressions and, as a rule, a happy ending, for a child's credulity can be man's most effective weapon.

Every Saturday afternoon they strolled around town like father and son, sat on a park bench or in a brasserie, where Markus drank beer and schnapps while Robert had an ice cream and cakes and read from the daily papers. And on these walks, in full public view, Markus always moved stiffly and awkwardly, almost like a newly blind person, he walked with his right hand on the boy's shoulder, making remarks about their surroundings in wry, grouchy terms, the reconstruction work, new fashions, people he knew more about than they did themselves, and tourists who had begun to return, the Germans attracting his attention in particular. And even though Robert thus got to know two people instead of one, he never slipped up and gave away his friend, not even when his mother gave one of her most compassionate sighs and said: "Poor Markus. What a pity he'll never be able to see the autumn colours again or how beautiful Marion and Josephine are now."

"He *feels* it," the son said, unruffled, perhaps because of all the simulated interest for the Pianist she had forced on him; moreover, Robert had an increasing sense that something was not quite right about these American origins of his. And in this way he learned to look upon Markus as his only *true* friend, the one he knew everything about and could therefore tell everything, without reservation, including his growing unease regarding the Pianist.

5

Markus had a dog, a mongrel he had acquired on an impulse, as if to put the finishing touches to the "blindness" artifice. But after only a few days he named it Delilah, after Samson's treacherous inamorata, because she was a contrary and uncontrollable dog who had no wish to be the master's eyes; she was ill-tempered, scabby, and as mangy as a well-thumbed atlas, and she went her own way – at any rate she avoided everyone else's. So after a year Markus gave her away, or rather he sold her for a nominal sum to a butcher who claimed he needed a watchdog, to Robert's great sorrow.

But one day, walking through town, they saw the butcher beating Delilah with a stick. The dog whimpered and squealed and blood ran from both ears. "It's my dog," the new owner said in his defence when Markus intervened. "I've paid for it and I can do what I want with it."

Markus said a dog was a living being which you cannot treat like an object, life sets limits to the use of force and the rights of ownership.

This nugget of wisdom had such an effect on the butcher that he offered to rescind the deal, to which Markus reluctantly agreed, after intense pressure from Robert.

The boy was ecstatic, and once again impressed by Markus' wisdom and eloquence. On the way home, however, the blind man insisted that the butcher had not relinquished Delilah out of the goodness of his heart, which had been opened by some well-chosen words on Markus' part, but because Delilah was as worthless a watchdog as she was a guide dog, she was downright useless for everything except living her own life.

Robert said this was a depressing interpretation. But Markus disagreed:

"If someone does a good deed," he said, "you don't start asking what the motives are, it's enough that the deed is good, you can't expect any more than that unless you want to be racked by disappointment and bitterness."

Robert said that this too was a depressing way of looking at life.

"Well, in that case, you will find most explanations of human motives depressing," Markus said. But from then on Delilah lived by their side, at times of her own accord, she lived in Markus' house and did as she wished, like a human being, or like a cat – she also had nine lives.

"She's a clever dog," Markus said. "She's seen through me."

At school Robert learned about the Grand Duchy's motley past, the way it had belonged to Spain and Austria and Holland and France and Germany, just as all schoolchildren first learn about their own country before others. It was Markus who revealed to him the true nature of the Ardennes forests:

"They are a mystery to those who don't live here, and a blushing beauty to those who do, a green cushion in the middle of Europe whose shifting borders we cross without moving so much as a millimetre – that's why we speak several languages, to be on the safe side. It is also strange to reflect that no war has ever started here: it is war that comes to the forests, again and again, usually without warning."

Through chatter and play and grandiloquent lectures Markus introduced his young companion to life's banalities, as well as its less obvious sides, he whispered and spoke aloud, declaimed and illustrated, ordered, pleaded and persuaded, and he it was who was able to present the boy with the definitive explanation of Clervaux's divine location at the bottom of a dark well: St Bernard had founded its namesake, Clairvaux in France, a good eight hundred years ago and made God aware of Clervaux's existence; St Bernard was the founder of the Cistercian Order of monks who, unlike the Benedictines, did not allow themselves to freeze on bare rock and barren slopes in order to come closer to their Creator, but instead preferred gorges and deep valleys where they could be in intimate contact with the inner being of all things, of the earth.

Bernard extolled not only spiritual exercises but also the mortification of the flesh – hard work, to put it plainly, from which everything is derived, both the physical world around us and our clear insights, whatever good they might be.

"The greatest wisdom is to be found in the legends of the saints," Markus said. "And as for our own patron saint, Hubertus, the apostle of the Ardennes, he has more to offer the younger generation than any political party, because it is the same with politics as it is with borders, you can't be in two parties at once, that is the truth of the matter; moreover, politics makes people bigger than is good for them, it gives them power. Remember that, Robert. Actually we're only tiny. In every respect. That's also the first thing we forget when we grow up."

He would sometimes ask:

"Have you noticed that, in some respects, we not only resemble each other but are *identical*, not only in a chemical sense, as those new books of yours tell us, but inasmuch as we all, in certain situations, will try to act in the same way? We are equipped with an ability to imitate each other, Robert. That's why we feel sad and lonely when we're *not* like someone else; without a mirror we lose our understanding of who we are; our sense of security does not lie in independence and individual traits but in there being many others like ourselves."

His inventor's instinct also lived on in the dark, even though for obvious reasons the practical manifestation of it had been put on ice, and Markus was a true master at repairing toys, in all secrecy, adapting them and devising new ones.

"It's all about having an eye for what's missing in this world," he said. "It might be a pair of newly polished women's boots which still let in water – in which case you improve the waterproofing – or it might be a bike that you can always get to go that little bit faster than it does now."

Just seeing someone *standing* on the pedals of a bike going up a steep hill, let alone getting off and pushing, was enough to start his mind working.

"All it needs is a single mechanical modification – it's only a matter of gearing – for any child to be able to make it up the hills to Reuler while *sitting*. Yet it can take years and a day before anyone can be bothered to invent such a device. The discomfort of modern-day bikes, you see, is not significant enough, which means the profit made from inventing a new one is not significant either, even though we cannot rule out the possibility that one day laziness might turn out to be the decisive factor.

"Nor is there such a big difference between getting a bike to go faster and inventing the bike itself, even though many like to think there is. For the bicycle did not suddenly appear out of nowhere It is constructed on the basis of more simple bikes, or carts, and a primitive mechanical knowledge of the wheel and the principles behind the balance nerves, just as the compass presupposed a knowledge of magnetism and the nature of the world, likewise the sailing ship was based on a centuries-old awareness of the simple fact that even a sail-less boat drifts in the wind. So man is not so clever, Robert, he is minuscule, he imitates his predecessors and moves much, much more slowly than even the greatest pessimist can imagine on a dark day."

Markus continued:

"At school when they start telling you stuff about great progress, about tech- nological wonders and political miracles, keep it in proportion, think of it as very minor, especially as far as man's thinking capacity goes – do you remem- ber William of Orange?"

Yes, yes, Robert did remember William, who is a central figure in Markus' wax cabinet, which he used to illustrate the principle of imitation – the fact that human beings have a limited range of movements at their disposal, and they repeat these movements, they fine-tune and improve them until they become identical with those others have performed. This is called both inheritance and tradition. What you call it is of no significance.

In fact, for Robert's first communion Markus gave him a biography of the Prince of Orange, as well as a children's illustrated encyclopaedia of saints in which it was said that St Vitus – one of the great figures from the Ardennes – was tortured to death by his heathen father, and lucky is he who does not have a father like that, it is better to be fatherless.

For Robert's second communion he was given a facsimile edition of the life of St Malachy, an Irish monk who, eight hundred years ago, breathed his last in the French Clairvaux, as well as a classic edition of the Old Testa- ment, containing a dedication written by Markus to the effect that it was the Old Testament that had significance and power, because God hadn't decided yet whether He should invest in man or not; and, as we all know, He still hasn't.

Maria was a little uneasy about this last present, not so much because of the unusual theological message but because the book was very valuable and had belonged to Nella and Markus' son, Peter, for which child they'd had

33

similar aspirations, but whom they lost on the Eastern Front before he could live up to any of them. Maria was worried Robert would not only be raised and adopted by the neighbouring couple but also be transformed into a substitute for the child they had lost, and thereby become an even greater phantasm than he already was.

6

At this time mother and son had other problems to contend with. Robert was lonely at school, and outside too; his peers were either too young or too old, he made a friend and lost him again. He took up an interest, engrossed himself in it, then it became as boring as clearing the table and he dropped it. He took Delilah for walks or went alone, then he disappeared again, wandered around in the borderlands, crossed the River Our and exchanged small talk with the local farmers, and this time he wasn't found by nightfall, he didn't come home of his own accord either, he was on his way south.

"How can he do this to me?" Maria complained to Markus, who placed both hands on top of his white stick and answered consolingly:

"He isn't doing it to *you*, Maria, and he'll get over it. Look how calmly *I'm* taking it, even though I love him like my own son."

"But what if the Knife-Thrower gets him?"

"There is no Knife-Thrower, you know that."

"But why doesn't he stop doing it?"

That is a question her son has to answer for himself, so Markus says nothing, and Robert is found the next day. He had slept on the slopes above Gentingen, on the Luxembourg side, it was bright, early summer weather, warm, and he had wanted to listen to the Our's tinkling, silvery voice and watch the sunrise above the Rhineland, he is a dreamer, there is no more mystery to it than that.

"But can't you just stop doing it?!" Maria exclaims to the person in question. To this he just smiles and asks if he can have a budgie, a new book, a Thermos flask, or a mudguard for his bike. He is beginning to get a name for himself as a schemer, but Maria is not having any of this, so he doesn't get the budgie, or the Thermos flask, but he may be given an edifying book a little later, and his attempts to run away are gradually demystified, they suddenly stop for a while, and there appears to be an external cause:

The world has moved into the 1960s, and Maria has a year's sabbatical from school to put the finishing touches to a work she has been struggling with for as long as anyone can remember, at any rate since she herself was a schoolgirl: a new Latin primer for use in the top classes, a book which aims to reveal the ancient language's true beauty in an attractive and engaging manner.

Robert cannot quite see what is wrong with the old book, except that it is old, and of course producing something new is always a worthy motive, whether there is a need or not. This is her life's work, a task which calls for both idealism and endeavour, presumably it is also the gateway to a new era, an ambition she has nurtured for so long it is now impossible to lower her sights.

But a paid sabbatical to work on this pie in the sky is out of the question, so mother and son have to live on their savings, which are next to nothing, since Maria in the post-war years "was fortunate to have full-time employment", as she used to say, and "fortunate to live in the large house she had paid almost nothing for", and therefore had acquired the habit of giving away everything she could dispense with to those "who were even worse off than us": pupils she had for some reason taken an interest in or felt sympathy for, poor wretches from the sleepy villages on the surrounding hillsides, for education is that gift of God – next to love – which we must do our utmost to make ourselves worthy of; so they decide to take in a lodger.

The first to arrive is one of her young colleagues, a maths teacher and a bookworm from the capital, who is out of place up here in the north, in Ösel, at any rate, he can't talk about the weather, the war and growing potatoes in a natural, chatty way, he demands a territory of silence around his person, requires hot milk every morning and wants his dinner served in his room in order to avoid the ridiculous and incomprehensible conversations between the mother and son. This lasts for approximately three weeks. Then that is the end of room service and silence; Maria ensures the former, and Robert the latter. And they have to look for someone else.

There are even greater problems with the next lodger, however, as in

Robert's eyes he is as unbearable as the first, while Maria is transformed into a foolish young girl the moment he appears. His name is Albert, a farmer's son and a real ruddy-faced son of Ösel, bursting with energy and the possessor, furthermore, of a heroic war record: when he was only sixteen he joined the partisans and fought the Germans tooth and claw and was later duly decorated when the country's rightful government returned from London. Now he is working on the railway, which creeps through the valleys in this rugged little country like a slow-worm through a quarry, and is in permanent need of repair and maintenance: trees that fall on the lines, landslides, bushes and shrubs that grow where they shouldn't. He is in his early thirties, with a body that youth will not relinquish, energetic from morning till night, also in his free time at home on his host's badly neglected farm, chopping wood, doing garden work and making repairs here and there which Markus, because of his blindness, cannot help him with – new tiles on the roof, a broken attic window, that type of thing. And Robert particularly dislikes the lingering gazes his mother casts like a veil over those broad, brutal shoulders. So he does what he can to sour the atmosphere in the home by means of moodiness and backbiting. But it has no effect, neither on the new Adonis nor on his beloved mother, especially not on her.

"Why are you behaving like that?" she says. "Anyone would think you were jealous! As if I will ever find a new husband . . ."

Her words are not without a tinge of sorrow and regret, her intonation in particular is revealing, and her sitting at home all day, lonely, dwelling on all the things she hasn't got contributes further to Robert's annoyance. In the end, the boy has to turn to Markus once again:

"Yes, I see the problem," the blind man says. "And it shouldn't be too hard to solve . . ."

But then he has second thoughts, and mumbles something to the effect that the solution may be beyond them, or beyond Robert at least, who is only fourteen . . . But this is not what Robert wants, he nags Markus until he gives in:

"First you've got to realise it's no use criticising or maligning him to your mother. It's better to make friends with him and make him your new idol. But – after a month or two – express your disappointment with him, she won't be able to take that."

Robert immediately recognises that this plan is a stroke of genius and cautiously begins to change his sullen manner, as though reluctantly falling for the same charm that has so dramatically cast his mother at the interloper's feet. And it is a surprisingly painless transition, it is a sheer relief to call off this self-destructive tactical warfare, and Albert doesn't object to Robert chopping wood alongside him or talking about girls and football (he supports Standard Liège), or school for that matter. He teaches Robert how to work a draisine, shows him how to shunt a train onto another track, and Robert begins to value his opinions, including in those areas where earlier Markus had reigned supreme.

One Sunday in autumn he also goes with Albert to visit his family, who live in the village of Boennange in the hills to the west. They have just got their electricity back, so Robert is present at the solemn presentation of an electric coffee grinder and a hairdryer to Albert's younger sister, who giggles and hardly dares show her face until the guest has talked Letzebuergesch long enough to prove that he is normal. A wonderful meal is served, they talk about the weather and the war and the crops in a natural, chatty way, and afterwards Albert shows Robert his medals and an album of photos taken during the darkest days of the offensive, and he lets Robert hold a gun he seized from the Germans and later kept as a trophy – it is things like these that tell a man where he belongs and who he is, Albert says pointedly, and Robert feels the scales falling from his eyes, bred as he has been on Markus' much more chaotic war, and on his mother's, which he will probably never ever make sense of.

On the way back, the old jeep has a puncture and they find themselves with an unplanned walk of more than two hours, but the weather is magnificent, the autumn as clear as water and the silence as immense as it can be around the screeches of distant buzzards flying above unchanging forests. Robert, in other words, begins to suspect that "being disappointed" by this man is not going to be an easy task. So he postpones his plan, some flaw will crop up, no doubt, even beneath such a hale and hearty exterior, if it makes sense to speak in such paradoxical terms. But as a result they become even closer, so Robert decides at length to forget the whole project. And he does. Until Markus brings up the subject again as they are walking home from high Mass on Christmas Day, a few steps behind the rest of the party.

"Well, how's it going with Albert?" the blind man asks, and he does so because it is obvious that he has already seen how it is going. "Not so easy, eh?" he concludes before Robert has time to cough up an answer.

"No," Robert is forced to admit, and suddenly realises – seeing his own reflection in the dark glasses – that this was in fact the plan, Markus' plan, from the outset, to ensure that his dear friend and neighbour, Maria, didn't get her much-needed romantic pleasure spoiled by a pampered whelp. Robert was stunned.

"Your mother's still a beautiful woman," Markus says. "In these past few months she's been more beautiful than ever."

After a moment's thought, Robert feels a kind of relief at this development, despite everything, even though the purely aesthetic side of the matter still disgusts him, the thought of this bundle of energy from the woods, ten years younger than her, uninterested in anything bookish, an impossible constellation even in his darkest fantasies, but if the worst came to the worst, what would his family relationship be with Robert? Father? Big brother? Or a constant reminder that he wasn't either?

But just into the New Year, Robert comes home from school and finds his mother in quite a distraught state, similar to when she received a letter from her saviour Cota.

"Albert's gone," she says bluntly, without giving any further explanation, just shaking her head in despair (too theatrical, the son thinks) – Albert who had promised to extend her kitchen garden in the spring.

Robert realises that something has happened in this house during the last few hours, which has nothing to do with him and which he doesn't *want* to have anything to do with either, he is content to miss the railway man in silence, he is used to this, missing a man in silence, and afterwards Albert is never mentioned again, except for once when Maria, in reply to Nella's impertinent question about what had become of the war hero, mumbles with an apologetic blush, there was nothing wrong with him, no, there wasn't. But, as already mentioned, Robert's disappearances have come to an end. He hasn't run away for more than eight months, hasn't even considered it.

7

Maria was tetchy and absent-minded for a month after the break with the flawless Albert. Work on the Latin primer came to a standstill, and now and then her son heard her groan in anguish that she had absolutely no talent for writing: "At my age it's sad to have to admit that my time has gone . . ."

But the new lodger is accepted precisely because of this inertia. She is a former pupil of Maria's, her name is Leni and she comes from the tiny village of Dorscheid, south-west of Clervaux; she is one of the gifted poor children who have benefited from Maria's small-scale philanthropy. Now she has completed her studies in Germany and returns just at the right time: her primary reason is to take a job at the school in Clervaux as Maria's closest colleague, but she needs a place to stay and accordingly joins Maria in writing the Latin primer.

It is a lively and constructive domestic arrangement, for as long as it lasts, because Leni soon falls in love with the energetic gymnastics teacher, gets married and moves into his house in the early autumn of the following year. But before that she manages to get the primer moving. She is a sleepy, intelligent and ironic person who can paint the world around her with such incisive language that Robert sees it in a different light. She has wide hips, great ambitions in life (with regard to what never becomes clear), she is hard-working and lazy by turns and not afraid to tell Maria that such and such chapters are "too boring", "too weak", "have to be reworked", and Maria takes on board the criticism to such an extent that when the book is finally finished, Leni's name features on the title page as co-author.

If there is anything wrong with her at all it would have to be the overwhelming erotic force she fills the small home with – she lives a grammatically correct life and is, as mentioned, ready to start a family. Robert falls profoundly and slavishly in love with her, peeps through the keyhole when she is having a bath, which she often does, for Leni is scrupulously clean; he listens to the creaking of her bed, greedily sniffs the air where she has been and scowls at her guests – especially the males – who now make their way to his home in great throngs, threatening to transform it into a self-important academic common room.

Maria is slightly uneasy about all this vitality, but only slightly, because the railwayman is forgotten, and she enjoys walking along the street with her new lodger, arm in arm, they are two young friends, sitting in cafés and attending the concerts that are occasionally held in the restored chateau – and Robert has his own ideas about what is going on in her mind; or the two ladies take part in meetings of the local history society, an organisation consisting of war veterans, historians and ordinary people with the Ardennes Offensive on the brain, who never tire of discussing its minutiae and its significance for world history, and especially the battle's moral implications, an activity which may well be justified, since the man who was behind the carnage here, General Manteuffel, stated, as late as in 1974, that the offensive was based on a correct analysis by Hitler: "Neither Hitler nor his Chief of Staff could shut their eyes to this last throw of the dice . . . "

Included among Leni's chattels was another sensation, her brother Léon, nine years older than her, whom the war had treated exceptionally badly. Before Léon made his first entrance, Maria drew her son to one side and whispered in his ear something about a war neurosis, but Robert never detected a sign of any mental afflictions in Léon apart from a permanently vacant smile, long periods of silence and a tendency to say: "Remember: I was never afraid!" as soon as the subject of war was broached, and it sometimes was, in a natural, chatty way.

But this was all Léon had to say about this European Calvary. And one of the reasons Robert got on with him so well was doubtless Léon's scorn for the Americans and the British and the Germans (and the Canadians!), and the fact that he viewed his own tiny little country with great disquiet, especially this new idea of having a radio station broadcasting in English, the only language uglier than German. Léon spoke only Letzebuergesch and French in emergencies – if he had to ask the way, confess to Father Rampart or read Les Oiseaux du monde, a ten-volume work about birds, his great and quite possibly only passion apart from Leni and her career.

Léon drove round with a wheelchair in the boot of his car, which he had no need for, as far as Robert could see, and he walked with a stick which, likewise, he didn't appear to need, even though he had a bad limp or else couldn't really decide whether he had one or not. He still lived on his family farm in Dorscheid, which he ran with a previous house help – "the lovely Agnes", as

Leni called her – and with whom – it was rumoured – he lived in sin. While Léon's explanation of the arrangement was that he didn't love her and therefore could not allow her to enter holy matrimony.

Agnes and Léon didn't have any children, but she had two sons from an earlier marriage, two boys it was claimed Léon didn't notice, or if he did he brought them up with strict discipline and self-denial. But to Robert this seemed more like a confused love of isolation; Robert was the only person who was allowed to go to Dorscheid and study this half-family from the inside and he was therefore asked many questions about them, which he soon learned to answer with: "I don't know."

Agnes' sons were called Max and Remo, they were born in the prosperous years after the war and were in their early teens when Robert got to know them. They were talented at sport and very popular with the girls at school, moderately endowed in academic respects and in many ways enclosed in their own inseparable world, like twins.

Leni said that Léon didn't exchange a word with the boys for the first three years they lived in his house. But when they were seven or eight years old they suddenly exhibited an interest in birds. Léon took them into the fields and pointed at the sky and told them the birds' Latin names, which they retained in their small heads, to Léon's cautious delight. He showed them how to take photos with a sophisticated camera, taught them how to identify rare species and to hate the Belgian bird-catchers who sneaked across the borders every spring and autumn to do whatever they wanted in our forests.

"The birds don't recognise any borders," Léon said. "They have the same name everywhere. We have to respect that."

As a result of an affair – or a connection – which no-one mentioned by name, he had managed to acquire a small car, a Triumph, in which he increasingly often drove to Clervaux to visit his sister and her interesting hosts, his sole friends if the truth be told, apart from Father Rampart, the priest in Rodershausen, who hasn't been introduced yet but soon will be.

Sometimes Léon also crossed the border, especially into Germany – to revisit places he had seen in more challenging times, as he put it – and once he took along one of the "twins", Remo – there was only room for one passenger in the car so they had to toss for it. They visited a wetland by the Rhine and studied herons. They splashed around in a public swimming pool, camped in a tent and wandered around the large meadows with binoculars and a camera. The trip passed without incident, but on the way home Léon stopped at the memorial cemetery at Daleiden. Here, in an out-of-the-way wooded area with a wonderful view of the Our Valley and the Luxembourg forests, the Germans can in embarrassed silence honour their comrades who died in the offensive of 1944–45. This is where Léon is said to have fallen to his knees by one of the graves – bearing the inscription "Jochen Berl" – and, sobbing with emotion, pleaded with both God and the devil to expel the insanity that still raged in his wretched head.

This scene had given Remo such a shock – he told his brother about it as soon as he got home – that a new silence ensued between Léon and his stepsons, a silence which remained unbroken until they started at secondary school, when he gave them each a racing bike superior to any others, on which they won many trophies, in Luxembourg, Belgium and the Netherlands.

People said that Léon had been very bright as a child, that ever since his birth he had been attended by hopes and privileges, but that the war and "the war neurosis" had destroyed all this brilliance, so it was left to Leni to become the first academic in the farming family. However, Léon accompanied her along the way, helped her through her studies with encouragement and small amounts of money on the few occasions he had any, he pushed and pressurised her and learned enough about what she was doing to be able to keep up a kind of dialogue. In this way, not only Leni but Léon, too, became involved in Maria's *Latin Primer for the Upper Secondary School*.

This was their rallying point, a shared interest which did not focus on themselves. They argued most about the choice of texts. Maria had a soft spot for Caesar, Cicero and Tacitus, arguing that the pupils could learn a little bit of history alongside the magical language, because the past is indubitably longer and more important than the future. Leni, for her part, wanted a greater proportion of holy scripts – the Jews and the Greeks can say what they like, Latin is the language of God! – Clervaux's namesake is moreover the seat of an age-old clerical tradition. Léon and Robert, on the other hand, were novices who wanted to translate cartoons *into* Latin: *Donald Duck* and *Tintin* – an idea that was later realised, though unfortunately not by our heroes, and which made no contribution of any value at all. Robert probably only took part so that he could sit next to Leni at the large dining-room table when the editorial team held meetings, which often ended with a few glasses of wine at which time his right thigh could rest against Leni's left thigh for half an hour of bliss without anyone else noticing.

"Latin is the mother of all languages," Maria pronounced, while Léon in a moment of clarity opined that it was a dead language and should be taught for that reason – the language of the dead must be respected and kept alive. Before blushing deeply.

Father Rampart held his trembling, alcohol-afflicted hands over the whole project, as its spiritual custodian. He had been an army chaplain – or maybe it was called a padre – in General von Vietinghoff's Army Group until he had to lay down arms in northern Italy at the end of April 1945. But Rampart spent fewer than two weeks in Allied captivity, as so many soldiers on the victorious side could testify that he had interceded on behalf of, and presumably saved the lives of, a large number of Allied P.O.W.s in the course of the Italian campaign. It was also said that it was his idea to evacuate the art treasures from Monte Cassino (and put them in the Vatican for safekeeping) before the monastery was razed to the ground by the joint action of the attacking and defending forces, even though there are many others who claim credit for this act. As a token of gratitude for his efforts – if we are really to believe this story – he was allowed to seek refuge in Reims during the summer of 1945, on a study tour financed by the Vatican.

Father Rampart was originally from Paderborn, a German in body, but not necessarily in soul, and he didn't want to go home again after the war and his stay in France, what suited him was an irregular white spot halfway between: Luxembourg. Now he resided in Rodershausen, a small border town in the Our Valley where Robert had got to know him on one of his excursions. There were more of these again now, but they had changed character and all of them ended up in Rodershausen, at Father Rampart's, it was as if the priest was also working as a border guard, much to Maria's relief.

"I don't have a father," Robert once gave as a vague reason for his sudden and irresistible desire to roam the forests.

"We all do," Father Rampart purred. Then instead they embarked upon a subject Robert didn't wish to discuss with his mother or Markus, or with any of his classmates: the other sex, which was a mystery to both of them.

Father Rampart never talked about the war, but liked talking about politics and national affairs and especially about everyday and spiritual matters, baking cakes and the Holy Trinity, which he loved to discuss using baroque metaphors. He drank his wine, and also beer and schnapps when Markus was around, he read the scriptures and forgave sinners with great forbearance in accordance with his own take on the poet's precept: "It does not behove a priest to accuse and persecute but to defend the guilty once they have been sentenced and are atoning for their sins." His sermons were often slightly wide of the mark with regard to both the occasion and the theme, and there was something improvised and very un-German about them. Occasionally there were complaints about him; after all, he was German, and who knows whether he was in hiding here? But he had many supporters and Father Rampart's position was as secure as a man's can be, knowing as he did every single stupid little secret that exists in such a small community. And he supported Leni's view of the texts the primer should contain.

8

The only person who didn't participate in the production of this book was Markus, which was strange because he was the best Latinist of them all, with the possible exception of Father Rampart. When he was asked for advice he declined to get involved in even the most trivial discussion of the matter, giving his blindness as a pretext. Robert soon suspected this had something to do with Léon. Markus was always absent when Léon was present, and if they happened to be in the same place, Markus immediately *scented* the presence of the stranger and discreetly slipped away while Léon for once lost his inscrutable war smile and became sheepish, like the time when he came up with a profundity about the Latin language. Robert once confronted Markus with this, but the blind man gave him short shrift:

"Don't waste your time thinking when you've got nothing to think with."

Maria, for her part, had a perfectly rational explanation for this mutual antipathy.

"Some people simply don't like each other. Just think of us and Alois" – this was the lodger who wanted hot milk every morning and had nothing but contempt for the intellectual life of the house.

Actually, no real problems arose because of the bad blood between Markus and Léon, except of a practical nature, such as at Christmas or at birthday parties, or when, finally, they marked the completion of the manuscript, not to mention when it was accepted after a relatively lengthy correspondence with a French publishing house – the happiest day of Maria's life (except for when she met the Pianist!). It was duly celebrated with a brace of geese, gallons of wine and a reluctant piano recital by Robert, with Markus sitting silent and withdrawn at the centre of the noisy assembly, entrenched behind his dark glasses, with Delilah at his feet growling and irritably gnawing at a bone.

There were never any problems with Nella in this regard. She viewed the whole book project with supreme scorn and preferred to bring the conversation down to a more sensible level:

"Why don't you ever bring that Agnes along, Léon?" she asked. "They say she is so pretty."

This was a subject they never discussed, so Léon hadn't devised an appropriate response, which meant that Leni had to come to his rescue.

"We're all very fond of Agnes . . ." she mumbled evasively.

"Yes . . . we are," Maria said, without adding anything further.

"So perhaps we could say hello to her one day?" Nella continued.

"I've been thinking about this, Maria," Father Rampart broke in, "and I'm glad we included the bit about Varus, the Prussians would like that, because it's going to come out there too, isn't it?"

"Mm, I suppose so . . ."

"Perhaps we can go and visit you both," Nella persisted. "Marion could drive us, we never go anywhere . . ."

In situations like this Léon goes bright red in the face, he stammers something incomprehensible, and after a cue from Father Rampart the others start discussing the weather and the crops and the war in a natural, chatty manner while Markus dons an enigmatic smile.

As mentioned, Leni moved out at roughly the same time as the manuscript was completed and took with her the greatest life-giving force Robert and his mother had experienced since the war. Then came an absurd decision by the staff at the school – Maria's own colleagues didn't want to have her primer on the list of approved books, the old one was good enough.

The decision exploded like a bombshell in their depleted home; a Latin book is surely the least controversial thing in the world one could imagine, a secret mission for the modest and the cautious, and carefully chosen for that reason. Maria might not have believed it, but she could not accept it either.

"You have no idea what this book means to me," she said. "It *has* to work, otherwise it's the end of everything."

Robert looked at her in surprise. She went on:

"Why is he doing this to me? I don't understand – why is he doing this?"

It was the school principal she was referring to, who had most of the staff in his pocket and with whom she had never had any differences, as far as she could remember.

Robert became very depressed about all this, first the loss of Leni to a gym teacher, "a baboon with a hairy back", then his indomitable mother going to pieces. Obviously he gave her his wholehearted support, but only when they were alone together, because he was at an age when it is not that easy to fight a battle on behalf of a spurned mother. And he became even more concerned when she suddenly felt a need to revisit her childhood home in Wallerode in the Belgian Ardennes. She had left her village "for good" as a teenager, when her parents died, and all she had left there now were two old aunts and a niece, whom she visited every third or fifth year, with or without Robert, and almost always because of a funeral, even though it was less than thirty kilometres away. But there was a border in between, and borders are like habits.

She went there in the middle of the school year – she had begun to work again – in Léon's Triumph, leaving Robert in Nella's care – and to his youthful notions that a catastrophe was imminent, the feeling that lies in wait in the surrounding forests and flourishes unseen, even *between* the blows of fate. And he became more and more annoyed with Markus, who hadn't done anything to help in this matter, because he could have done, that miracle man, with his connections both high and low; it wasn't only war veterans and historians who came in small delegations to visit him and talk about the past, he also had a finger in many a pie and on the pulse. But he didn't want to have anything to do with this book.

"I'm not risking it," he said cryptically one evening when Robert went at him hammer and tongs. Whereupon he mumbled: "There is nothing I can do. Nothing would come out of whatever I might do. I'd just mess things up . . ."

But now Robert had a glimpse of the strength which must have kept his mother going at the field hospital in South Beveland, or when she so resolutely snatched the Pianist from the clutches of the Germans, for after her pilgrimage to Wallerode she returned with renewed drive. She immediately sat down and drew up an in-depth analysis of the two competing primers, proving point for point that hers was superior, not least with regard to the pedagogical strategy which was necessary to combat the younger generation's misconceptions about the past in all its shapes and forms; and to his relief Robert heard that the letter was not laughed out of court, in fact it made quite an impression on both colleagues and the principal. She also wrote to the Ministry of Culture in the capital, to national and local school authorities, to the mayor in Clervaux, and in addition wrote articles in newspapers and magazines – the cuttings from which fill a small shoebox in her loft – which sparked a debate on the whole educational system.

She got plenty of plaudits and declarations of support. But the principal – on Maria's own home ground – continued to turn a deaf ear and didn't say a word about the case, maybe because Clervaux wasn't actually her home ground, she began to wonder, she was a foreigner here, a Belgian.

But when push came to shove it was perhaps an advantage that the principal hadn't tied his colours to a public mast, for now Markus threw his hat in the ring after all. He was sick and tired of listening to the whingeing of mother and son, he said one evening after he'd had an earful of it, and agreed to go and see the principal, whom he knew from meetings at the local history society, and to plead for Maria's book, on one condition, he added – that from now on she would keep quiet, inside and outside the home, whatever the outcome.

She said she couldn't promise, this was her life's work, it was the last thing she would do . . .

"OK, well, let's say six months then?" Markus suggested as a compromise. "You stay quiet for six months. You must be able to manage that?"

She wriggled and squirmed, but then promised, at least she said she would do her best, God knows whether she would manage it.

"And Robert comes with me," Markus said.

"Robert?"

"Yes."

"Why?"

*

Markus picked him up from the school playground one day just after Christmas and they went together to see the principal, a tall, bony figure with a legendary bowed neck which had earned him the nickname "Crookneck". And here Robert witnessed a conversation of which he understood not a single word. The two old men talked about the war for almost two hours, about tanks and the fighting around Mon Schumann – "Hill 490" (a particularly dramatic event in the country's history) – about concentration camps – the principal had spent more than a year in Natzweiler and was well-known for his vehement and irreconcilable hatred of Germans, he even sabotaged a student exchange arrangement with schools in Trier and Prüm. And they ended up with a lengthy discussion of elderberry wine, food, horses and the need to preserve the oak forests in the areas where expansive farmers wanted to dig them up and plant spruce instead, as they did on the German, the enemy's, side . . .

Maria's textbook wasn't mentioned at all. But Robert was there, fidgeting in his chair, and was doubtless an irritating reminder of what the conversation *should* have been about, and when Markus eventually stood up, he did so with a specific reference to "the young man", who was getting impatient, he could *feel* it, heh-heh . . .

"You managed to control yourself, well done," he said as they came out. "I couldn't have done at your age."

As Robert still had no idea what this was all about, he said they had both acted like cowards, they had come to get things sorted, to restore his mother's honour . . . But Markus smiled at that and said the boy should be proud of himself.

"As I said," he repeated, "a young man who can control himself beats an old man who can."

However, there was no progress in the "primer affair", except that Markus intervened a couple of times and ordered Maria to ditch a new newspaper article she was preparing, which irritated Maria beyond words, she wasn't a patient person – nor should she or anyone else be, patience is a weakness, it is cruelty's wicked stepmother . . .

"You have to be able to vary your tactics now and then," Markus said drily, and wanted nothing else to do with the matter, he didn't want to talk about it or hear about it, and Maria followed his advice, with visible reluctance.

But she used her own book in her lessons, to the principal's annoyance, but they don't like trouble in this peaceful country, so he bit his tongue. And in the exams she achieved better results than her colleagues; she always had done, but now they were even better and this time, for once, there were tangible reasons for the difference, which could not be overlooked when the staff met again the following summer to discuss course books. However, they weren't able to agree, several meetings had to be held, and finally there was a ballot, which Maria won by one vote. The four who voted against her were the same four who had opposed her the previous year, while the ones who didn't express their opinions the previous year, but who were also against her then, had changed their minds. The principal didn't vote on either occasion. This was a time when Robert was becoming politically aware and viewed – with exuberance – the result as the power of democracy – *one man, one vote* – where those who don't dare, or are unable to, or don't wish to state their opinions still make their voice heard.

But the whole affair was so odd it stuck in his mind for a while after, more as an anecdote than proof of this slogan. As Maria's book was so much better than the old one, one might well presume that it was *this* that made the difference, her colleagues just needed more time to see this, or to abandon old habits; indeed, several of them would perhaps have accepted the book at the outset if she hadn't smacked down her palm on the staffroom table with such a triumphant flourish (actually an expression of childish pride) prior to the decisive meeting.

Or one might think that her book *wasn't* any better but was accepted because her colleagues no longer had the heart to hurt her, she being the minor war hero in Clervaux that she was, even if she was a Belgian, though now they were beginning to get heartily sick of this war, it has to be said.

Maria's explanation, on the other hand, was this: My book was better, but the world is full of idiots who don't realise they are idiots, and that is why it took some time.

This is the romantic version, and it befits her, truth wins out in the end, but God knows what it would be like if you don't have a tactician like Markus on your side. And what was the opinion of the principal, Crookneck, who had acquired his wisdom in Natzweiler, and knew that all this was just tedious, depressing nonsense? He thought there was little difference between the two books. That was his view. And now, at least, there was peace.

9

But no sooner had the Latinist battle been brought to a happy conclusion than a new mystery struck our little circle of friends. Father Rampart had been thoughtless enough to help a young history student at the university in Leuven, Belgium, with what he knew about the Vatican's connections with the Nazi regime; he did this as a matter of course, even though his account was flawed in places through loss of memory and his very complicated view of humanity. In the process he lost much of his trust in the student and, in a violent exchange of words intended to guide the student towards a greater insight, he served up the following bold assertion:

"I don't mind telling the truth as long as nobody hears."

Nobody but God, he had intended to add, but in his excitement he forgot, and this sentence came to embellish the title page of the finished dissertation, almost as an ironic slogan, complete – unfortunately – with an acknowledgement.

The blunder might not have caused such a stir if the dissertation had been gracefully allowed to join the millions of files which gather dust in Leuven's cool, sedate archives, but the Belgian-language dispute also casts its Babylonian confusion over Leuven, which meant that a Flemish journalist got his hands on the dissertation, with the result that the matter landed on the front page of *De Standaard*, beneath the exultant headline SUSPICIONS OF VATICAN COLLABORATION CONFIRMED BY SERVANT OF CHURCH.

Father Rampart had his recreation in his valley-bottom sanctuary rudely interrupted and was harassed round the clock by both friend and foe of the true faith, the former under the cover of darkness, the latter in full daylight, but the Vatican, as always, was adept at dealing with hot potatoes, so Rampart was granted a new study tour, which he was to use to purge those aspects of his teaching that did not accord with that of the Church – local parishioners had frequently complained about his sermons. He was delighted to move out of Rodershausen, which was in uproar, and first stayed for a few months in secret with Robert and Maria, in Leni's old bed, thereafter with Markus and Nella.

But now the residence and the pulpit and the confession box were unoccupied, and people don't only need the Word of God and forgiveness, they also have to be buried and christened and joined in holy wedlock, and they are not keen to go to Daleiden – on the German side – for these purposes, nor to Hosingen or Clervaux, where you are on foreign soil in your own country, and deputy priests are as they have always been: their souls are elsewhere.

The unrest turned to a sense of loss and eventually to vocal dissatisfaction, and strident voices were heard demanding an immediate reinstatement of Father Rampart, a request which was also put to paper in two languages by the village mayor and sent to Rome, and after some closet discussion it was decided to grant their wish. At the end of his study tour Father Rampart could, in other words, move back to his valley and on this occasion hold his most memorable sermon; he was so moved by all the support and affection – he had finally found a home, on both sides of a border – that he wept through the Kyrie Eleison and the Gloria and didn't recover again until a good way into the Proprium Missae, the part where they collect the money, his usual star turn, and many in his flock wept with him.

However, people in this area are not only Catholics, like the average Portuguese, they are also down-to-earth border folk who have to keep all their options open, so when they emerged into the dazzling sunshine and their heads were cleared by the River Our's earthy sighs and rushing waters and the sobering moo of a cow, they began to wonder what kind of priest this actually was. They'd had their doubts about him before, they now remembered, there was some truth to them, but when all was said and done it was the Vatican – some claimed it was the Pope himself – who had sent him here, this German priest, so they would have to put up with him, he was better than nothing.

But, in the name of all that is holy, it has to be admitted that there were those who said the complete opposite, such as: "We couldn't have got a better priest," or, "We've got the priest we deserve," or, "We've got a priest who deserves us." For there are all sorts of people, that is what Father Rampart has realised, and there is only one earth, but that is how it is.

10

After Léon's arrival in Clervaux the relationship between Markus and Robert cooled. They saw each other less and less, and their conversations increasingly took the form of irritable debate.

"What is it with you?" Robert asked, annoyed. "Why can't you stand the sight of Léon? He's a war hero, you know?"

"Yeah, yeah, there are a lot of strange things going on in our country right now," came the enigmatic response. "It's haunted, heh-heh. And I've got quite different heroes."

"Oh yes, who then?"

"My heroes are German, Robert, if you really want to know, and the reasons are quite complex . . ."

"What rubbish. We hate the Germans!"

"Well, yes, but not everybody does."

"What do you mean by that?"

"There are some people who can pull off unimaginable feats, no matter where they come from, Germany or Luxembourg or Canada . . . both in war and in peace, there are people who are better than us, Robert, and they don't come from any particular place, we have to accept that, believe me, they come from the strangest places."

"Rubbish . . ."

"One day I'll tell you about a general in the Wehrmacht no-one has ever heard of and no-one ever will. Not only was he on the wrong side, he didn't save any Jews or Cossacks or gypsies either, only his own people, and he didn't even manage that properly, anyway that won't interest you . . ."

"Markus!"

"I've never met him, but I can still hear his voice saying, 'Panzerlage 0/4/2/0/1, Hauschild destroyed, no further use possible.' That kind of thing. Does it annoy you?"

"What do you think?"

"You're growing up, Robert, but don't forget, this is the time when we begin to believe we're not as small as God made us."

Yes, Robert had slowly started to view himself as bigger than he actually was, not only that, the final exams are approaching, he is above average on the football pitch, well above average in the classroom, he enjoys a large degree of freedom thanks to his own efforts and suddenly he has a sense that he is not so weak-kneed and aggressively neurotic in his thoughts and behaviour as many of his friends who have a father to help them, the St Vitus brothers as he calls them, St Vitus' father was his bitterest enemy, as we know, which is the reason why the saint has lent his name to those twitchings and tremblings of the body – St Vitus' dance – which extreme unfortunates are afflicted with, that at any rate is Markus' explanation, and it is not his most outlandish notion either, for, while there is a certain disagreement among believers about whether St Vitus was beset by these twitchings or whether he was able to cure them, Markus believes that one possibility doesn't rule out the other, illness can be a gift of grace, just like lameness or blindness.

In addition, Robert, after three failed attempts, has finally managed to start a relationship with a girl, a bright spark from the hills in the north who lives in a bedsit in Clervaux in the winter and must be able to avoid milking and digging when she is at home in the summer because she has such soft hands. Her name is Brigitte, she has feet like petals, milky white skin with invisible freckles and a slight squint, which means Robert sees two versions of himself in her eyes when he confesses his love for her. His mother knows her as a "quiet, gifted child" from school, but now, when Robert takes her home and makes the relationship official, Maria says:

"Ah yes, love, it's an impossibility, my dear, but come over here and I'll show you the family album."

And these are big words since this family consists of only her and Robert, he is frozen in all the brief stages of childhood, sometimes supported by his mother's hands, or wearing Markus' glasses or sitting on Nella's ample lap holding a sunflower the size of his own head. In one of the photos Marion and Josephine, their summer dresses fluttering in the wind, are holding a hammock between them, which is actually a sheet, and in it Robert is sitting with a catapult, wearing an American beret he was given for Christmas by the American war hero Cota.

Maria sits with a seraphic smile on her face as these photos are being admired, but it loses its glow as they approach the present, and the album is always closed well in advance, as though she hasn't got the strength to reveal the end of a complicated tale.

But there is limited scope for developing the relationship with Brigitte, seen through Robert's eyes; he can't reap the rewards today of his renunciation yesterday, as it were, in matters of the flesh for example; the same has to happen over and over again, i.e. nothing, otherwise something is lost. Change and innovation impoverish and confuse, bleed you white almost, Brigitte says. But a young man in this situation is more patient than an old one, so Robert strolls through the streets with her for weeks on end, hand in hand, murmuring words which are alien to him. He hears her calling his name from the stands (only just) when the school team hammers the village teams, and she always has to have *reisfladen* when he takes her out, what else, and Pepsi Cola. And he starts wondering how she ever manages to rise through the school without breaking down, not to mention what it must have cost her to leave home and move to town, a small town but a metropolis compared with where she comes from, a cluster of six houses around a crossroads, so there must be *something* in her, apart from this fragile light she carries around with her like a halo, he is sure of that, but less and less sure as the days and weeks repeat themselves.

Irritation begins to build up in Robert, impatience, and this results in a short conciliatory kiss in the wake of a tiff, whose cause neither of them can identify, but the argument is there and creates an atmosphere, and again the next time they meet, perhaps they are not suited, but a break-up now would be sad when we love each other so much, and so on. And Robert has to consult Father Rampart and listen at great length to his tortuous thoughts until the priest breaks off and says:

"I truly don't know, but perhaps you should say straight out that you want her, and now, and then at least there is no doubt concerning which question she is answering?"

This is strong stuff from a man of the cloth, but Father Rampart has lived for many years, heard a lot and understood most, so Robert follows his advice, but would you believe it, she manages to wriggle out of it again. And afterwards she withers before his eyes; he is struck by a sense that he has offended his own *mother*, it is a familiar feeling, but in his youthful exuberance he thought he had got past that, now it tells him he didn't deserve Brigitte, she is too pure, so he stops seeing her, his feet won't take him there, and she stops seeing him. They cast stolen glances at each other, thinking the other doesn't notice, but this is nothing to build dreams on. Thank God I escaped, Robert thinks, all of this has really been the complicated conquest of a different woman, a woman he already has a relationship with.

Leni is ten years older than him, she teaches aesthetics and literature at the school where he is a pupil himself, and her gym-teacher husband hasn't lived up to expectations; he has given her two children in quick succession, a boy and a girl, whom Leni has named after her father and mother, but that is his sole contribution if Leni is to be believed – he has no language, by which she means he has neither anything to say nor any interest in listening to what she has on her mind, to words which can change the world if only you believe in them – but you are so young, Robert!

Yes, he's not very mature but he is tough and knows what he wants and there is no stopping him anymore, and from the fiasco with Brigitte he has also learned that when love fails, half a person is lost, at least, life becomes a lie, unreal and meaningless when first you have loved and no longer do. And Leni yields slowly and calmly to the overpowering pressure, then one day she takes over and leads him by the hand along life's meandering paths of bliss, elegant circumlocutions of which Father Rampart listens to in the confession box every Saturday between five and seven. They meet in the forest, or at her house on Sunday afternoons when the kids are resting and the gym teacher is conducting training sessions with the local gymnastics club on the sports field. Or they sometimes bump into each other when Robert visits Léon in Dorscheid and Leni just happens to be at home in the room she slept in as a child, the room which has been untouched since then, with all its memories, both good and bad.

Léon doesn't see through much of this, but his non-wife, "the beautiful Agnes", does. She smiles and sees to it that Leni's tiny tots have their own room, because she nurtures high hopes for this passion that has invaded her arid home, we all have our problems, and Agnes' two teenage sons are no blinder than Markus, they nudge each other in the ribs and act like the unbearable interlopers they have always been.

But it is not these few knowing onlookers who complicate the relationship, it is Leni herself.

"I daren't imagine what your mother will say if she finds out about us," she says one day, when they have been walking in the forest around Dorscheid to admire a sundial which Léon has erected on a solitary hill with a fine view of everything that means anything in this world, and she says it with an ambivalent curl of her mouth, as if she meant to say "*when* your mother finds out about us." For Leni is waiting for an opportunity to inform Maria, she says without articulating the words, since Robert has everything the gym teacher lacks, both language and a lingering embrace, she says bluntly, so she is never going to let go of him – never!

These prospects fill him with a hitherto unknown panic; it is one thing not being able to live without Leni (and thinking about the curves of her hips at all times of the day and night, also when he is asleep, and about her hands and her sea-green eyes and her utter contempt for all and sundry – there is a vitality in Leni, life and action), and quite another the thought of his mother getting to hear about the arrangement, this must not happen, and on the horizon there are exams looming, which he won't be able to concentrate on.

Robert has plans to sort out all this mess. Things don't go well, and this time he can't visit Father Rampart, who has been Léon's failed spiritual adviser for ten years and knows both him and Leni a little too well – and not least Maria – to be able to act with the necessary objectivity, Robert feels, so it will have to be Markus once again, the only person who really knows how to keep a secret.

II

Robert arranges a time with Markus, which isn't normally necessary, but it is now, and the following Saturday afternoon he goes over to his house. Nella is alone there and says that Markus has gone on ahead, and adds with a peculiar smile:

"But you can shout. His hearing's fine." Robert nods and sets off up the hill behind the houses, along a path they call Via Dolorosa because it is steep and invisible and the thoughts people think while walking along it are painful, and here it is more like summer, the earth is steaming even though the foliage has already shut out the sun, the crystal drops drip from the trees, and the ground squelches beneath his feet. He spots Delilah, Markus' indomitable dog, sniffing around in her own world, but she walks a few steps alongside him and then leaves him, and Robert has a sudden insight, he knows what answer Markus will give him:

"Even an idiot can see there is only one option. Keep your indiscretions to yourself for three years. By that time Leni will be sick of you or you will be sick of her or else neither of you will be sick of the other and you can get married without Maria batting an eyelid."

"But by then I'll be twenty-one and she'll be thirty," Robert might protest, deep in thought, wary of being persuaded once again to adopt a strategy which is not to his benefit but his mother's.

"So?" Markus will answer. "You can't be young and old at the same time, no more than you can be both here and there. Leave the rest to God and Leni, if she's as smart as you believe . . ."

That is how the conversation will go. No doubt about it. Robert has found a solution on his own, he's pleased with it, even though it only means that he already knows, without asking, what Markus will answer, if he answers at all. He senses there is something false and unreal about all this, as though he is still a jumble of other people's opinions. But so what? He sits down under a hazelnut tree with newly sprung leaves on its gnarled branches and knows that he will soon be visiting Leni, even if it is in broad daylight and the middle of the afternoon when she has two friends visiting her to make arrangements for a charity bazaar to fund new floodlights for the chateau, and that he will get her away for a private tête-a-tête, where he will present his plan, three years, it is a long time to wait, probably longer for him than for her, but she will quickly consider it and see from his face that he means it and is serious, and she will agree without a second thought.

But now he walks on, with Delilah, who has reappeared, and down in the next valley he meets his old friend by a stream where in an earlier life they had fished for trout; the blind man is sitting on the remains of a stone wall by an old mill, and Robert sees that he has been crying.

"Is that you, Robert?" he mutters, staring into space, a completely unnecessary precaution, for no-one ever comes here. Robert sits down next to him and listens to yet another depressing monologue about the war:

"What's happened to them?" Markus wonders out loud. "Where have they gone, all the armies? This is the most inexplicable of all mysteries – they are still out here, or they are living somewhere else, if they ever existed at all, I mean, propaganda is not exactly an unknown phenomenon in war, nor mass graves or the destruction of rolls of men – for *no-one* disappears, Robert, without a hefty dollop of magic, but no event in our country's history has been scrutinised more closely than this, and we are talking about six to ten divisions. They are still wandering around in our forests like flickering images in the minds of those they left behind; they are the ones I talk to when I'm sitting here on a day like this, it has been heart-rending . . ."

Markus says no more, leans back and stares up at the sky, and there – above the massive oak crowns in the north – a gigantic orange sun is rising with a small grey tassel beneath, a wicker basket, they now see, the sun is a hot-air balloon, and there is a man on board, a black silhouette darting to and fro in a desperate attempt to manoeuvre it. It clears the ridge of the hill by a hair's breadth and sinks slowly but surely like a stone in honey to the valley bottom, where the basket makes a controlled landing on the banks of the river, without a sound. A man in a pale khaki uniform, leather helmet and flying goggles jumps out and runs round a beech tree with a rope to moor it, then turns to the onlookers and says:

"*Treibstoffmangel*," out of fuel, and grabs them by the hand with what seems like flustered relief. He is a university lecturer in Bonn, that is where he is heading, from Bastogne, trying to beat a distance record set by a colleague who covered the Aachen–Trier stretch in the same balloon, which of course they built themselves, the wind has let him down and, on top of that, he has eaten all his provisions . . .

The two dumbstruck eyewitnesses see immediately that Markus has given himself away to such an extent that now he cannot become blind again, which means that he cannot accompany this man to town and help him to buy whatever he needs – it will have to be Robert, while he and Delilah guard the craft?

The pilot nods his approval and on the way to town expounds on the laws of thermodynamics, which get up to such strange antics here above the Ardennes, he is working on some mathematical models which in time will be of benefit to the burgeoning aircraft industry and is trying out his ideas himself, as people used to do in the olden days, so the idea and the inventor can be obliterated at a stroke if they are no good, heh-heh.

Maria is not at home, so Robert grabs some food without having to answer any awkward questions while the pilot fills his jerrycans in Markus' stable, after which they hurry back to where the blind man is waiting, impatient and ill at ease, anxious to get the madman off again before the enormous balloon attracts too much attention. But the German is in no hurry at all and what is more the hot air burner is in no hurry either, and it takes time to fill a whole gigantic fabric bag, so Markus says they will have to be getting home, but as the pilot is about to take off he asks them if they want to go with him.

"Won't we be too heavy?" Markus asks, suddenly a different person.

"Not at all. I have several hundred kilos of sand on board. All I have to do is chuck it out."

"Er, well . . ." Markus says. "What do you think, Robert?"

Roberts looks at his old friend, sends Leni a warm thought, and they clamber aboard, they rise from the ground while Delilah runs around below in circles, growling, and has no idea what has become of them because dogs never look into the air; the three of them slowly ascend in the swaying gondola, while the professor empties the sandbags over the treetops as if from Our Lord's own salt cellar and sings pop songs at the top of his voice, they soar like birds to dizzying heights, down on the left the outskirts of Clervaux appear, and Robert sees the rooftops and the crooked walls, the road to school and the school, the chateau which looks like a large fox trap, cars which hardly move, and people out for a Sunday walk, who stop one after the other to lean back casually in mute wonderment.

The gentle breeze turns west, and they pass Vianden after half an hour, but as they glide into Germany and Schnee-Eifel, Robert notices that Markus has lost interest in the professor's lectures.

"What a wonderful view," he mumbles with the same soul-shaking awe that must seize a blind man when he regains his sight, as once had been his plan, let there be light and there was light. And this awe is transmitted to his young friend, Robert, because everything is changed for him too, it is now of absolutely no consequence to him what his mother might be hiding with regard to true or untrue secrets about his origins. Who doesn't fabricate an image of their own life, and of others too? Who doesn't cling resolutely to the world we can live with? And the next moment Markus comes out with what is on his mind:

"Even though we never talk about this," he says, glancing warily at the professor, who has taken a break from his sermon and is smoking a pipe while navigating with a steady hand, "you know, don't you, that we lost a son in Russia. A couple of days ago we received another letter, informing us that he was alive, somewhere in the Eastern Bloc, not far from Dresden. Nella doesn't know I've read it. She hasn't shown it to me yet. She doesn't think I can take it as we've received letters like this before, from people who think they know something. There's no truth in what they say, of course, but it's always me it hits harder, that's what she thinks anyway . . ."

Robert can see Nella's expression – "His hearing's fine, anyway" – accompanied by a scornful smile, or gloating, from a woman he considered had no more substance than the clothes she wore.

"He was registered as '*Vermisst*'," said Markus, "missing in action, like so many others. That's what has been going through my mind for all these years in the shadows, two questions I must have an answer to: Could I have done anything for him? That's how parents think. Could his superiors have done anything? That's how the courts of law and God think. Two small questions, these are what I have been grappling with, day and night, in the dark, since the sun doesn't shine on me, I don't know whether it does on you?"

All of this happened early in the summer of 1963. And for the first time Robert began to doubt whether Markus was of this world, but this was not the reason they called him "The Wizard of Clervaux". The Wizard of Clervaux sits, blind and happy, on a chair in the midst of a crowd of kids telling Ardennes folk tales, sometimes about the mysterious and dangerous "Knife-Thrower" whom no-one knows but who is still there, it is said, just like the bridge at Frankmühle. In the most boring scenario he regales them with a parable, at great length, about St Hubertus, the apostle of the Ardennes, who saw a deer on the crest of a hill in the morning mist bearing the cross of the Lord, or often also the whole of His head, with the crown of thorns, in the antlers; they can't hear the soft patter of the falling rain, so he makes the sounds himself.

Shark

In the 1570s Prince William of Orange sat ensconced in his castle at Dillen-burg, near Wiesbaden, fervidly fantasising about driving Philip II and his energetic general the Duke of Alba out of the Netherlands. The Spaniards were plundering the region and taking anything of value, everything it produced and owned, art and crops and goods and gold, not only that, they had even levied a new tax on real estate, a transfer tax, to get their hands on the dust which God enhances a commodity with just by letting it pass from hand to hand.

It made William ill. He not only saw himself as the legitimate heir to several thrones but also as the incarnation of the true faith's conception of justice and law, a man who could not sit still while the earth was groaning and panting, so he concocted plans and schemes to combat the Mediterranean oppressors, only to drop them just as quickly, in the name of common sense, as he put it, made new ones and ordered mass dismissals of "useless staff", a term he virtually made synonymous with the court's honourable, to varying degrees, administrative apparatus.

He couldn't find a solution. He found – if the truth be told – nothing at all, nothing he could call his own, a new idea to point the way forward, even the army he had so painstakingly assembled was modelled on the enemy's princi-ples, on Alba's, and consisted mostly of mercenaries, poor young men who harboured neither affection nor a sense of duty for the lands they would hope-fully conquer one day – and could they focus their disparate emotions on something as passionate as a war of liberation?

Doubts gnawed at William.

But one day the solution came, it struck Dillenburg like a thunderbolt, a matter of four small sentences in a dispatch which on first reading seemed both trivial and incomprehensible, but which William's "useless staff" immediately recognised as being perhaps the Prince's only chance, the chance a great man must see and grasp without hesitation, for it will never return!

When the Spanish conquered the Netherlands, sections of the most rebellious Dutch citizens fled to sea and became pirates, known as the Sea Beggars: William himself had equipped them with Letters of Marque and Reprisal to help them survive in exile, and of course also to have them ready and waiting to keep them loyal to him.

Between raids, the Sea Beggars usually laid up in English harbours, but now the dispatch which arrived in Dillenburg reported that the English had had enough of this "pack of robbers" hugging their coastline and incurring the hostility of the Spanish, and had chased them out to sea again. This fragile armada sailed away from the British Isles, but was met by a terrible storm, and it was a much depleted fleet that drifted in towards the Dutch coast. There the squadron commander had the – to put it mildly – remarkable idea of ravaging the coast while they happened to be there, and pillaging. And they discovered to their surprise that the Spanish outpost was much weaker than they had imagined, and indeed that the occupational forces might possibly not be so superior and invincible as hitherto thought.

The Sea Beggars built a bridgehead by a small fishing village by the name of Brielle and managed to hold their position in the face of sporadic attacks, and, inspired by this success, revolts broke out in other towns, in Rotterdam and Vliessingen, by the seaward approach to Antwerp.

"Brielle could be your chance," William's staff said to the demoralised Prince as they wafted the dispatch in front of his nose. "Brielle or nothing. We'll have to go to the town's rescue!"

But William's veins were hardened by five years of inactivity, the flesh hung loose around his hips and his brain had grown sluggish and hazy from birdsong and heavy wines and fruitless speculation. So, on their own initiative, his "useless staff" published a manifesto proclaiming him as the Stadholder of Holland, Zeeland, Utrecht and Friesland. And slowly but surely he came to life. He sought advice from his brother, Louis of Nassau, who had a post in French government circles, and he put him in touch with the leader of the Huguenots, Admiral Coligny, who himself was an ardent supporter of the war against Philip II.

Coligny and William met and devised an intricate plan of action. The

Prince was at last able to mobilise his newly created army, the mercenary army. First he rode south, with his head held high and his heart pounding beneath his uniform, because, as mentioned, he hadn't done this for a while – mobilised an army – then he turned west, but as he was about to cross the border into France he was "struck by a new calamity", as it is termed in one of his many bombastic biographies: his fellow-in-arms, Coligny, had perished in what was later known as the St Bartholomew's Day Massacre, and with him was lost, in William's view, the only key to the liberation of the Netherlands.

Thus once again he was rendered powerless by events he had no control over, but the thought of returning to his idle existence in Dillenburg repelled and embarrassed him. Yet he couldn't advance deeper into France now that the Calvinists had been defeated, nor, with such a weak army, could he move northwards along the planned route towards the Spanish. But as he lay there languishing in the French–German border areas, reports came in that the towns of Leiden, Alkmaar and Haarlem had risen up against the Spanish. On top of that, the energetic Duke of Alba had for some reason fallen into Philip's disfavour and been replaced by a pious weakling by the name of Don Luis, who in his eagerness to show initiative had besieged the rebellious towns while also demonstrating indecision by sending William an invitation to negotiate peace terms!

Encouraged by these small glimpses of hope, but mostly by the fact that an army has to be moving so as not to starve to death, William decided to launch an attack of his own, and cautiously they headed for the Dutch plains.

Meanwhile the Spanish continued to burn and ravage and put down one rebellion after the other, except in one town, Leiden, where the population held out with a tenacity no-one thought possible. After no more than a quick glance at the depressing maps constantly placed before him, William realised that it would be there and nowhere else, at Leiden, that the final showdown would take place, one that would decide his future and the future of the Netherlands, and that of the Spanish too, Leiden was the operation's strategic centre of gravity, as Clausewitz would one day call it.

On his way north William received constant reports about the wretched conditions in the town; the people were eating rats and sparrows, they made bread with ground timber and refuse, drank urine and sewage water when it didn't rain, and they had been doing this for several months, in those times

63

armies didn't move quickly, furthermore there were many trials and tribulations to contend with along the way, and it was well into the summer, six whole months after the Spanish had surrounded the town, before the Prince of Orange could ride into position along the dykes outside, only to have his doubts confirmed at once that he didn't have sufficient forces to break the Spanish siege.

Again William found himself in a quandary. Night after night he paced restlessly along the shore with his second-in-command discussing and rejecting untenable solutions. Once again he was waiting for the decisive strategy. But this time it didn't come from events he didn't have any influence over or from his "useless staff" but from an inner light, perhaps lit by the Lord himself, even though William, in order to gain support from the population in the north, had converted to Calvinism, but the truth was the solution had been staring him in the face, had been all around him, only he hadn't seen it.

At cockcrow the following day he summoned his general staff and held a short briefing which would link his name for all eternity with one of the most curious chapters in European history. The soldiers were to collect all the flat-bottomed boats they could find in the area and drag them up the grassy mounds behind their positions, and three days later – when the job was done – the Prince, with a proud grin, dispensed his orders: the dykes were to be blown up so that the sea could wash in over the fields. By the grace of God – he announced to his open-mouthed officers – the flood waters would reach the town walls and rise, thus allowing them to sail to the gates, *through* the Spanish lines, which would succumb to the force of the water.

The order was carried out, and later in the day all the officers stood on a mound above the demolished dykes surveying their military gains, the deadly salt water that flooded in over thousands and thousands of acres of cultivated land until it sank to its natural level once again. But Leiden still lay a good way off, on dry land, with the Spanish siege intact. The water rose a few inches before subsiding again in the evening. At the next tide the same thing happened and they all began to realise that William had sacrificed large tracts of fertile Dutch land to no avail.

The Prince went into a deep trance once more, resumed his sullen, uncommunicative Dillenburg attitude and again began to dismiss staff; otherwise he restricted his activity to sitting inside a tent with his hands folded, imploring

Our Lord to send a storm and, if possible, a storm surge, which in one concerted effort would force the waters the last kilometre to the town walls. But Our Lord wasn't listening, presumably because William in his political pragmatism had turned his back on him when he converted, He sent windless days all through the spring, and all through the summer too, it had never been so calm along the North Sea coast, now and then a gentle easterly wafted over the land, it was enough to make you weep, while the townsfolk of Leiden continued to starve and die.

Then William fell ill. He had delirious bouts of fever and lay sweating in the field hospital like a second Job, talking to himself and calling for his eleven-year-old son, whom the Spanish had kidnapped in France and sent to Madrid, where according to rumours they had tortured him to death. Now William could feel his son's mutilated body beneath the blood-soaked clothes, heard his pleading voice and gazed at the sea, which would not rise but only poison the land, return it to its barren origins, the primeval realm, where neither man nor beast could exist.

The Prince's second-in-command sat around for several weeks waiting for the physician's final bulletin to confirm that the commander of the armed forces had breathed his last, so that this idiotic campaign could be called off and a new, more promising one launched.

But in the middle of September William's health suddenly picked up, to the extreme consternation of his retinue, it was as if he had risen from the dead, with new blood in his veins and a host of new ideas in his head; he was cheerful and friendly, full of vim and vigour, he ate and drank, talked and did not betray the slightest doubt that this crazy venture would soon be crowned with victory. And on the night leading to 2 October, 1574 – exactly one year after the siege had been laid – a violent storm blew up from the west. What was more, it was a full moon and hence a spring tide, and at the sight of a sea so tempestuous that no vessel could stay on an even keel, William, with great conviction, gave the order to man the armada, load the boats to the gunnels with soldiers and weapons and food and water. His men jumped to it, scrambled on board, cast off and held up cloths and bits of tent in the raging wind, or they sailed with bare rigging, and in less than half an hour of sailing at breakneck speed the whole fleet arrived unscathed at the town walls, where large sections of the Spanish positions, weapons and tents were submerged and panic soon broke out. After a short and frenetic clash the enemy signalled *sauve qui peut*, and William was able to blast open the town gates; those townsfolk who could still stand rushed out and threw themselves around the necks of the soldiers and over the food and drink.

But when that same night a thanksgiving service was held in Leiden's largest church and the sound of hymn-singing rose like clear water up the tall stone walls to form a quivering veil beneath the vaulted ceiling – and when at that very moment the wind dropped – many of the survivors broke into convulsive sobbing; a procession of unbearable laments wound through the streets, people banged away on drums and pots and pans and wailed and screamed like demented souls.

William asked what on earth this was all about, and an emaciated monk was dragged before him and forced to give an answer. He explained that his faith forbade people to eat their dead, after which he held an eloquent silence before asking the uncomprehending William whether he believed that he himself would be able to look the Lord in the eye after eating his own children – after perhaps killing them first to spare them further suffering?

There is a famous picture of William, painted at that precise moment as he sits on his Gobelin-clad folding chair, his General's Seat, staring at this monk with the watery eyes who is uninterested in either the siege or the dearly bought freedom; it is a snapshot or a psychogram of the commander's final years, a coloured cardiogram that stretches from the time when, ensconced in Dillenburg, he made the great decision – which was actually made for him by his "useless staff" – via the doubt that gnawed at him on his trek northwards when he had to keep his army moving like a shark, so that it wouldn't become extinct, until the night leading to 2 October, 1574 when he sat on his famous folding chair and talked to a liberated Calvinist monk and realised that this was only the beginning: outside, the fields were under water, the people were starving, emaciated, some of them insane, his country consisted of seventeen states, three languages, two incompatible faiths, so William bad-temperedly swept the monk aside, rose to his feet and went to his quarters to drink himself senseless with his staff, and to plan his next move . . . Who is it that drives history? Who the hell is it that makes decisions here on earth? Not to mention – what is it that keeps a shark alive?

The William Tell Formula

An old circus artiste from Siebenbürgen wandered around in the Ardennes forests, a knife-thrower, a scrawny sickle-shaped figure who dragged his tattered garb from one village to the next and received alms from people who covered their eyes and ears, it was an act of remorse and penance, and no-one could say for certain if he was a human or a fairy tale or just his own bad reputation. But none of the children in the area suffered any harm at his hands, they could move about freely and without hindrance, the knife-thrower had other matters on his mind.

He had thrown his razor-sharp knives in a succession of legendary circuses and during the Second World War entertained bleeding and mutilated Wehrmacht soldiers in various field hospitals and camps in Russia, Italy and France. But long before this he had devised a "law" which he called "the William Tell Formula"; he had noticed that the most famous of his predecessors, those artistes whom folklore and literature and also the occasional nation-builder had been most fascinated and inspired by, often used their own sons to stand with an apple or a balloon on their head, or with a target attached to their stomach, or lying spread-eagled against a wooden board with the knives quivering between their limbs, but they never used a daughter.

By employing an assistant who was a relative of the knife-thrower, his own flesh and blood, not only was the fear-infused pleasure of the spectator enhanced but also the concentration of the thrower, with the consequence that the risk of an error was actually reduced; and a son is not only far more robust than a daughter, he is also the natural extension of the father, so in a way it is himself the father injures if things go wrong. Whereas no-one has ever been able to accept – or pardon – a father who exposes a daughter to the same danger: she would not enhance his concentration, she would damage it. This is the William Tell Formula.

Now his wife had borne him both a daughter and – a year and a half later – a son, and the knife-thrower's urge to follow in the steps of greats like William Tell was becoming an obsession; bringing his son into the act would increase the appeal of his already acclaimed performance and also his fame and, not least, his fee, and wasn't he living in an age that craved groundbreaking, spectacular shows?

At first he was met with outraged protests from his wife, but now at least the idea was out in the open and had been spoken about, also by her, and she had never seen him miss and furthermore she was as vain and money-grabbing as he was, so she gave in. When the boy was six and able to stand stock-still for the few seconds it took the father to concentrate and throw, they began to train together, at first with dummies, soft rubber replicas of the same size, weight and length as the knives. They all reassuringly hit their target just above or below the boy's outstretched arms, between his open legs or close to his protruding ears. Not once did the knife-thrower miss.

But when the moment came to take the knives from the suitcase he had inherited from his father, who in turn had inherited it from *his* father, his hands began to tremble. He tried to summon up the great artistic calm, he went through his lengthy preparatory ritual, mumbled his incantatory formulas, said his prayers and steeled his gaze the way he had been taught by his father and grandfather, but all that happened was that he began to adjust the vertical movement of his throwing hand, the surest factor, indeed, the most fundamental element, the nerve centre of a throw: the right arm that follows the pendular movement at an angle of precisely ninety degrees to the horizon, as sure as an amen in a church, such that no matter what goes wrong at the moment of release, with the timing, that is, the knife *cannot* land too far to the right or left of the vertical line which the arm movement traces over the target; a person with his arms squeezed into his sides, standing to attention, as the son was in this introductory phase of the training, is in other words as safe as a child in the mother's womb. But it was this very basic factor in the knife-thrower's lifelong training that failed him. He couldn't throw. After a gigantic effort of will he did throw, but the knives were so far from the boy's body that several even missed the green wooden board he was standing against. And this happened again and again, it didn't get any better, the knives whirled past, too far to the right or too far to the left.

But instead of calling this experience by its rightful name, a defeat, and admitting that he was no William Tell, and reverting to assistants of a somewhat lower sentimental value, the knife-thrower took to brooding about his son's remarkable ability to disrupt the nerve centre of his life. If only it had been the timing the boy had disrupted, the golden moment when the thrower relaxes the muscles in his wrist and releases the shiny steel from his fingertips, the function, to put it simply, which decides whether the knives land too high or too low, which of course is of vital importance for spread-eagled assistants, not to mention assistants who have an apple or a balloon placed on their heads – a tiny delay in the moment of release will, with something like a 100 per cent certainty, result in the knife finding its way into the assistant's skull; just as a slightly *premature* release will send the knife *above* the apple, or balloon, and spoil the show. A premature release is therefore the most common consequence of nerves. But it is also the reason why a show like this can be perfected by training: first of all you train the vertical arm movement until it is mastered, preferably in your youth. Then, when you practise timing, you start at the top, deliberately releasing the knife too early, and work your way downwards towards the imagined hair roots of an imagined assistant, to the horizontal plane of the throw, until, *consciously* and without deviation, the knife has lodged itself in the board a centimetre or two above this plane several thousand times; then a good knife-thrower has full control of his nerves and can perform his spectacular act as naturally as ordinary people taking out their bikes when the spring sun prompts them and going for a ride, as he did last year; once you can cycle you can do it forever because this type of movement is not governed by those parts of the brain that are sometimes subject to the ravages of forgetfulness, those parts that manage words and memories and knowledge of mathematics and Catholic saints. But forgetfulness had now afflicted the knife-thrower nonetheless. He couldn't ride a bike anymore. It wasn't the secondary variable that failed him, the ability to find the correct moment for release, which throughout a knife-thrower's life has to be rigorously nurtured and is subject to the same fine-tuning as a delicate guitar string in a musician's hands, but the very foundation of his work, the balance nerve, if we keep to the bike analogy, it was ruined.

Like almost everybody who finds themselves in a serious existential crisis the knife-thrower took to drink and kept going with tears and fights and prodigality until his wife begged the circus director to threaten him with removing his livelihood unless he came to his senses. But it took time, more threats were necessary, and more fights, and it was only when he had dug himself such a deep hole that the only way was up, that he resumed his training. This is when he discovered the cause of the problem, it was to be found in the subtlest nuances of his feelings for the two children; he loved his son in a different way from his daughter; his concern regarding the boy's future and career, if one can talk about that, was greater than it was for his daughter. The boy's naivety and trusting admiration deceived the father, it might have had something to do with seeing himself there somewhere, with sentimental memories of the innocence he had once left in such haste; the son was not only an extension of himself, he was also his previous and next life, his connection with the heavenly powers.

On the other hand, the daughter filled him with confidence – she'll manage, he thought – she is determined and dogged and, quite frankly, not as innocent as the son, not only that, another man, as strong as myself, will one day take care of her; and all of this was in total contrast to what he had previously believed about having a daughter and a son when he had devised the William Tell Formula.

The knife-thrower didn't mention any of this to his wife, but now he began to drop hints about including his daughter in the act. This didn't go down well, either, but once again his wife gave in. And everything went fine with the dummies, both the vertical movement and the moment of release were spot on. But the girl couldn't stay still. "What do you mean! Of course she's standing still." "No, she's moving." His wife watched their daughter carefully, and now she too could see the child was moving, swaying from side to side.

"Perhaps she's too old," the knife-thrower wondered. "After all, this is an art that has to be learned from the earliest age."

She was shown how to concentrate and did stand still now and then, but then she had to move again, she would move a limb into the danger zone without thinking, or sway slightly, not enough to cross the imaginary border her father had traced around her slender body, but enough to put *him* off, because she didn't trust him, that was obvious, she was frightened of him . . .

But then the knife-thrower realised that these movements didn't make her any taller, only broader sometimes, so they continued to practise, she stood still, full of fear, he reassured her and urged her to trust him, and they were making progress, even when they trained with real knives.

The stunt eventually became part of his repertoire and was an eye-catching addition to the poster they stuck to walls and telegraph poles when the circus came to town, with the trapeze artists, elephants and jugglers. But things went wrong, terribly wrong, the sixth time he performed the number, in front of 500 horrified spectators, and without the knife-thrower knowing how it had happened – he hadn't done anything wrong!

Thereupon he had a nervous breakdown and had to give up his career, his wife left him and disappeared with his son, so there was only one thing to do, return to his father's farm in the run-down village of Siebenbürgen in Romania, where he made his living selling eggs, chickens and other poultry.

But it would be wrong to say he was well received, after all he had entertained the Nazi scum with revolting experiments using his own children – even though the rest of this country had been on Hitler's side too – but enough is enough, the village had not only supplied the German armies with a considerable number of young men but also lost many of their women and children, and now they had their hands full mourning them and licking their wounds, as well as trying to make ends meet, so why should they have any sympathy with this cynical child-killer.

The knife-thrower had to take to the road again, everybody could see that. He left on foot with as little as possible, through a devastated Hungary and an equally devastated Slovakia, and ended up in a completely devastated Germany, where he deceived himself into thinking he was searching for his missing family, like so many others at this time. He drank all the spirits he could get his hands on, he worked for crusts and potatoes clearing ruins and ploughing fields for crippled farmers, mumbling to himself between sobs that it was only after he had killed one of his two children that he realised he loved them both equally, that there was no William Tell Formula, and, yes, that he was also too slow-witted to understand how it had happened.

As a result he became thinner and thinner while Europe slowly but surely rose from the dust and the tragedies and its own memories. The knife-thrower walked over a narrow, rickety bridge into the Ardennes forests, where time stood still, and he worked with a wheelwright, for whom there was no longer any need either, apart from on remote farms where cartwheels and millwheels were still in use and needed repair and maintenance. If people didn't find out on their own what a terrible tragedy he carried around with him, he made sure they were told, so that they could chase him away again, he deserved no less, he didn't belong anywhere, now he was going round in circles, he came to a village where a baker gave him a job delivering bread to the local community in an old van, or else he would idle his time away or work for the local forestry commission looking for shrapnel with a metal detector in the trees wood-cutters were about to fell.

The great tragedy in the knife-thrower's life did not fade so easily into the mists of oblivion as the war, neither in his own mind nor in the minds of others. People whispered and gossiped and shuddered in cowsheds and living rooms, around the kitchen table and the fireside and of course at Früh-schoppen and in the school, where the Siebenbürger had now become the big bogeyman.

But the fact that this man – who never talked and was never seen with anyone – drove around year in, year out, delivering bread, so necessary and trivial, yet so heavily laden with holy parables and symbols, must nevertheless have helped to wrap him in an aura of reconciliation, those wonderful, rounded *Graubrot* loaves with their crispy crusts, which all children in this region will think back to with longing in their hearts wherever their adult lives may take them, to the Tuaregs in Africa, to Regent Street to study optics or to Karelia to shoot bears, the loaves will accompany them on their journeys like rising suns, the way they are produced in the old brick ovens in a small, mealy-white house next to the cemetery, situated in the leaden peace up on the hill where only the buzzard distinguishes the ridge from the sky.

And suddenly all is quiet.

For even if there is a lot of malice in a small village, it also holds some tiny secrets; it contains more than one sinner when all is said and done, and one morning there is a notice hanging from a telegraph pole outside the school on which an unsteady hand has written: "I wish I were one of you."

It's not long before the words are read and reflected on and make their way into the houses in the village, and people slowly begin to greet the knife-thrower, not only when he arrives with the bread but also when they bump into him in the narrow streets or in the forests, where he still rushes about with his metal detector to protect the woodsmen from the long fingers of the war. And the knife-thrower tentatively returns their greetings, shame-faced and humble, relieved but also greatly surprised, because it wasn't him who wrote the notice and hung it up – he hasn't even read it – it was the parish priest, Father Rampart, and where people can't see a mystery, they don't look for an explanation.

Léon the Angel

I

At noon on 27 May, 1944 eighteen-year-old Léon V. was lying full length on the hayloft floor at home on the outskirts of the sleepy village of Dorscheid, spying on three girls who were bathing naked in the stream which wound its way through his father's lush fields; they were his two sisters, thirteen-year-old Gertrud and little Leni, who was nine, and the third was Agnes, the house help on the farm, a mature twenty and God's Revelation to Léon's sharp eyes. He had dammed up the river at this point to entice them into the trap.

But this is a black day for Luxembourg, it is not called Luxembourg anymore but Gau Moselland and is to be brought back "home to the Reich". The River Our has not changed its course, it is standing its ground, but it has lost its meaning and identity. Léon has been called up by the Wehrkreiskommando in the capital to be fitted out for a German uniform. So, lying there in the hayloft, he is ready to depart and is taking such a solemn farewell of the only world he knows and especially the woman who breezed into his life when his mother died three years ago and erased the bitter sorrow with stardust and bright laughter.

Quite a number of his countrymen have been called up, all too many, and again people have begun to mutter about boycotting these occupation troops and seeking refuge in the forests or staying at home in their houses and seeing to their civic duties, such as looking after children, animals and the land we all live off, and Léon – who also possesses a streak of heroism – is in no doubt about what a decent person should do, he is a resistance fighter and an anti-Nazi, lived a secret life in the depths of the forest with others of his age for the whole of last year, they have an old radio set, they smuggle Belgian army guns across invisible borders, speak in code and wave semaphore flags from rooftop to rooftop in the cold Ardennes air, all of this incidentally kept well hidden from his father, who Léon suspects might be doing the same, on a larger and more significant scale.

But when he aired this possible "boycott" with his family he began to have doubts; his sisters and Agnes wanted him to stay at home of course, the countryside is full of hiding places and it is only a question of time before Hitler is brought to his knees. His father, however, had been silent while the girls were there and was reluctant to commit himself when Léon got him on his own, so the boy had drawn his own conclusions: if he bravely went ahead with a boycott he would endanger not only his own life but also the lives of his family, his father did not want to admit this straight out and force him to make a sacrifice, so Léon made the decision himself, in deadly earnest.

He got up and brushed the hay off his Sunday suit, cupped his hands round his mouth and yelled at the top of his voice:

"I can see you! *Everyone* can see you – the whole *world* can see you!"

The sisters let out some delightful squeals and made clumsy attempts to hide behind clothes and close-cropped beech hedges while Agnes threw up her arms and laughed in delight and was as naked as anyone had been, at least around these parts. But then she saw from his suit he was leaving and pulled her dress over her head and strode resolutely towards him through the ankle-high grass.

"Where do you think you're going!?" she shouted angrily up to the hayloft. Léon climbed down the ladder to meet her.

"To the capital," he said brightly and stared at the black hair which clung to her marble-white skin, her neck, shoulders and – as she turned for him to button up her dress – her back which arched down to her hips and resembled the curve of a swan's wing or something that cannot be described by an earthly being.

"You're not going!" she said, the white arch of her back pressing against his burning fingertips. "You're going to do your exams and become a lawyer. All of us here are agreed on that."

"Not Dad," he laughed. "Who would take over the farm then?"

"If doctors can run a farm, so can lawyers."

She was referring to a retired village doctor in her home town of Hosingen who ran a farm alongside his practice, or at least had done so until the war broke out and he was needed on all fronts. Doctors and lawyers were princes and kings in Agnes' eyes, so it went without saying that in her self-appointed role as mother she was behind Léon and his sisters with a whip to make sure they worked hard at their studies.

"Shall we make a deal?" he asked, without managing to do up a single button. "I go. I come back. I promise to become a lawyer – and I take over the farm. And you wait?"

"You're just a boy, Léon, you can't make a promise that not even God can keep."

He had to accept that if he continued to fiddle with these buttons his heroic journey would soon be at an end, so he let go and, still caught in two minds, turned to the barn door, scanned the fields and forests down to the neighbouring village of Munshausen, and a moment later saw the figure of his father come round the corner and stop suddenly when he saw them: Agnes still had her back to him, either waiting or wise, Léon hesitant, as a quiver ran down his spine. His father nodded and withdrew, and Léon put a hand around her neck, the first touch, but now it was time, and he let it slide down between her cold shoulder blades where the drops of water glistened on the tiny hairs, then turned again and walked towards the car.

"We're going too," he heard. "Come on, girls, we're going with Léon to the station!"

"Oh no, you're not," his father cut in sharply, and Léon turned and saw the girls bounding towards him, Agnes a little way behind, her arms crossed, her body bursting with spring promise, one single touch, nothing to write home about, but God help me, it was more than enough for someone going to war, it was much too much, so he had to scan the fields again and blink a few times.

"Léon's going, girls," his father shouted through the open car door as he twisted the ignition key, with his suitcase on the back seat, the cows mooing, the mist rising from the fields and the dog in the neighbouring house barking. "Give him a kiss and say goodbye. And get started on the food. We've got visitors this afternoon."

Léon hugged them in turn and pinched them and made them laugh and flashed a quick smile to Agnes as he got in. They were on their way before he managed to close the door.

"It's not good to remember a tearful farewell on the platform when you're in the thick of it," his father mumbled after a few minutes of concentrated silence behind the wheel. Then he added with a cough: "There's something I have to tell you."

"O.K.," Léon said, when nothing more was forthcoming.

"I got out of it," his father said at length. "In 1941 – because of a knee injury. They've been terrible years."

"Oh, yes?" Léon said, when it went quiet again and no more was added. "Was that what you wanted to tell me?"

His father nodded. Thought for a moment, came to a decision and said:

"You're going to come back. Remember that. And remember one more thing – it's you you're fighting for, not them, whatever happens, it's your right."

2

Everything follows a pattern, it has been documented, because it has been done before and because some remember, and because people lack imagination, and here is Léon on the train, watching fields and forests and platforms passing by, with German checkpoints, military vehicles and uniforms, and he thinks about what his father said in the car, about how "terrible" it was not to go to war, perhaps it meant he *wasn't* in the heroic resistance movement after all, and Léon feels uneasy because he can't see that fate spares none of us, that those who escape don't, in fact, because they are doomed to suffer vicariously, to feel guilt and self-contempt, if they are decent people, that is, and not just donkeys with only grass on the brain and therefore derive no benefit at having escaped. This is why Léon also thinks – after arriving in the capital and hearing the Wehrkreiskommandant's angry outburst that only fifty of the eighty conscripts in this quota have obeyed orders and reported for duty – that in this way they get their hands on the best of us, while the cowards and those without families, the egoists and the donkeys escape, survive and perpetuate their inferior blood line. But he soon begins to wonder if this is such a big disadvantage as the war is not yet over, it depends on how it progresses and how you look at it, well, does it really, he thinks, because there was no clarity in his mind that day, to be frank it was all one great big mess.

*

Léon knew none of the other conscripts, but that same evening he met two young boys from the Ösel area in the north, strong, naive farmers' sons with flitting eyes and uncertain smiles, with whom he could discuss the situation in their own language, their common fate, for as soon as his uniform was on he felt an urge to take it off again as soon as possible while the reason he had reported here at all, for the sake of the family, faded with every kilometre that passed between himself and home. And there was only one thing to do now, his thoughts were beginning to take shape, both in him and his comrades, plans to desert, they would have to wait for an opportunity, they would have to have something of their own to fill out this alien uniform.

They were transported east, by train, to the Protectorate of Bohemia and Moravia, where the three comrades ended up in the same camp and were given weapons training – and stuck together in their own small enclave speaking a different language. But after a month they were separated, and Léon was assigned to the 82nd Panzergrenadier Replacement and Training Regiment, a motorised unit in the hastily formed Panzer Division Tatra, where after only two days he heard rumours that the Americans had landed somewhere in France, but had been pushed back into the sea by Rommel's impenetrable *Atlantikwall*, the fortifications along the western coast of Europe and Scandinavia. And then there were tales about how the Americans, far from being repulsed, were storming eastwards, there were all sorts of stories going around although nothing was confirmed, but since they weren't sent west to defend the Reich against the Americans and British but east to Slovakia to stem "the communist tidal wave", both Léon and his fellow soldiers assumed there couldn't be any truth to the rumours about an Allied landing.

Here in the east, during the summer and autumn months, Léon discovered to his surprise that it didn't bother him so much to fight in a German uniform, perhaps because the ordinary German soldier treated him like one of them, on the whole; he had even made friends with two of them, a terrified lad from Westphalia who was no less press-ganged than Léon himself, and a war-weary thirty-year-old from Dresden who had "wasted his whole life" on the Eastern Front and who because of his very clear stance on things no longer felt at home in the uniform he wore, him too. It probably also made a difference that Léon was fighting for his life now and not some airy-fairy principle or abstract sense of nationhood, or for his family, not directly anyway, and was happy to have as many soldiers as possible at his side in the same position, no matter where they came from.

The battlefield also made him feel unreal and unconnected; he did what his officers and his body told him, and was pleasantly surprised to find that he didn't go to pieces – he was on a high, he was alive and was living while soldiers around him fell like flies, the war-weary thirty-year-old was shot to ribbons at a machine-gun post close to his own, the young Westphalian just disappeared, during a night op, "*Vermisst*", as it was called, and Léon felt a strange tremor steal into his high, it would not go away, the question of who he was and where he came from was of absolutely no significance to him, for God was holding his hand over him, it was his war, God said, not Europe's nor Hitler's nor Luxembourg's, for the simple reason that it was his life.

The week after Léon's young friend "went missing" there was a pause in the fighting, and in this period he discovered what pleasure his comrades' grudging acknowledgement gave him. But then a new rumour did the rounds: the Allies had not only established a bridgehead on Rommel's impregnable coastline but also liberated Belgium, Luxembourg and parts of Holland; apparently in his home country this had been quick and painless, it had taken only a day or two according to the rumours, but this was not confirmed by their superior officers nor by the signals section, who occasionally shared their valuable knowledge. Nonetheless, a strained atmosphere arose between Léon and his comrades, for which he considered there was no cause: after all it wasn't him who had liberated his country but the Americans, while he had been striving to purge his heart of this hope and had tried to be as good a German as any of them, an endeavour they surely ought to respect . . . ? It was almost with a sense of relief that he returned to the battlefield, where everyone was equal, God's errant children and not the stigmatised sons of individual nations.

3

After two months at the front – his training presumably complete – Léon was withdrawn from the lines without warning and assigned to the 2nd Panzergrenadier Regiment, part of the 2nd Panzer Division. Not long after his transfer, 2nd Panzers, which had escaped from France without a single tank to its name, was incorporated into General Hasso von Manteuffel's Fifth Panzer Army and – this too without any explanation – then loaded onto a night train north, it seemed – to Poland? Well, after three days on the move, with a lot of stops in the middle of nowhere and only at night, the train pulled into a dilapidated station with a rusty, illegible nameplate, then it was off into the dark; there was troop assembly and then a half-hour march through flat, wooded terrain before they arrived at the village of Mötsch, and the village of Mötsch was in Rhineland, there is no doubt about that, not far from Bitburg. A low buzz of voices ran through the lines, for this was surely the definitive confirmation of an Allied landing, the Fifth Panzers was to be given the task of reinforcing *Westwall*, the front against France, Luxembourg, Belgium . . .

They slept on the floor of a schoolroom and had no contact with the civilian population, they received their provisions as usual and did some drill, but spent most of the time playing cards and waiting. Meanwhile Léon resurrected his desertion plans, he had become strong, but it was the dream of home which suddenly struck him with full force, the peaceful life, and especially Agnes's body, white as marble, which on some nights took his breath away, soon he would he be getting up early and going over to one of the local houses and saying in German that he needed some clothes, because he intended to ditch his uniform and make off; but he is on his own and *"non est bonum esse hominem solum"*, he has known this all his life, and he prays a lot and thinks about Agnes, unless it is her thinking about him, for he is haunted by these images, time is going backwards, why did they waste it back then, circling around each other like moths around a glowing cowshed lamp, or lying quietly in their separate rooms and allowing their lives to go in their different directions, Dear Agnes, now it is far too quiet here, if things carry on like this I'll go crazy, if I have to be away from you then I have to be fighting, in the lines, there are other things to think about then, in fact nothing goes through your head at all out there.

Then the Regimentskommandeur issued new marching orders, to Metternich, which didn't mean much to Léon, but he heard that this too would involve manning a defensive line along *Westwall*. But in Metternich another week of inactivity ensued, in another schoolroom, until late on the evening of December 15, Alert Level 1 was raised at the very moment Léon, lying wrapped in woollen blankets, decided that the time for desertion was nigh, Dear Agnes, I'm coming now, alone or not, actually I'm not alone anymore, there are a few Luxembourgers here, I just haven't had an opportunity to talk to them, but it is good to have them here . . .

They struck camp and marched west to Arzfeld, where the regiment took up positions of readiness in a dense spruce forest, but Léon noticed that there was straw on the roads, to muffle the rattle of the tank tracks and that the Luft-waffe was flying low sorties in a north–south direction, presumably to drown the same sound, and now smokeless coal was being handed out for them to cook with, so he couldn't sleep and lay listening to a conversation between an officer and the first gunner in the M.G. Kompanie section of his regiment, Jochen Berl, a madman from eastern Prussia who saw Hitler as his great liber-ator and now thought it would be hazardous to send Luxembourgers, Lorrain-ians and Alsatians to the front line, whereas his superior officer brusquely dismissed this as nonsense, claiming he knew Luxembourgers from Slovakia and was convinced they would do their very best here too.

It was only then that Léon realised he was on the point of invading his own country, the country that the Americans had freed a couple of months ago from the German yoke, an event which for obvious reasons he was unable to celebrate then, and he couldn't do it now either, for different reasons, which perhaps were also obvious, what does he know, he doesn't know anything anymore, and the irrevocable order was given well before dawn, as well as a detailed plan of advance, the Regimentskommandeur had barely uttered the last word of the order when the heavens were filled with lightning and light and awesome thunder, the like of which Léon had never seen or heard before, Lord God above and Dearest Agnes, it is as bright as day and the earth is shaking.

But then Léon's company was held in reserve, and at three or four in the morning of Sunday, December 17 he was clinging – as an assistant L.M.G. gunner – to a Panther tank racing at top speed over the straw-covered, muddy and by now churned-up, country road, with six other soldiers. In the sea of fog on the left he saw the road sign to Daleiden pass by, not only did he have to invade his own country he would have to do it via Dasburg, en route to Roder and Clervaux. They were already in the valley, crossing the Our on a makeshift bridge and continuing up into the Luxembourg Ardennes, and Léon told his "friend" Berl all about it, how he used to pick blueberries and enjoy the view on school trips or under the peaceful auspices of the Scout movement, he had to say that, he felt.

"Stick close to me," the First Gunner said with a short laugh. "And close your eyes."

The crews were ordered out of the tanks and into a wood, where they were given a short briefing and led on foot towards Marburg. They met a column of American prisoners of war, who were being marched back into Germany, passed two artillery posts and walked straight into some American crossfire, had to peel off and seek refuge at the double in nearby scrubland. Helmets, gas masks and battered weapons were scattered across the ground, Léon saw several dead soldiers, all German, shot in the head, and that stupid tremor set in again, Dear Agnes, I don't know what is causing it, but I am not afraid, you can have no idea how cold I am, it is not my war even though it is my life . . .

The Kompanieführer called them to a halt and detailed the attack position for the surprise afternoon assault on the village of Munshausen, which was only a couple of kilometres from Léon's Dorscheid. In the morning hours there had been two attempts to take it, first using tanks and then with tanks and infantry, now the 2nd Panzers had to finish the job.

But that was the last thing the Kompanieführer said, for a moment later he handed over the command to a Stabsfeldwebel and withdrew to the artillery post they had just passed. Berl wouldn't answer Léon's persistent questioning about what this meant – had there been an argument between a senior Unteroffizier, who was now setting an example, and the Kompanieführer about how the assault should be carried out? – but Léon heard the First Gunner mumble about the new commander – "That man's an idiot" – before repeating with a wry smile: "Stick close to me, boy, and close your eyes."

A reconnaissance patrol which had been sent ahead earlier in the day reported back that the Americans were leaving the village, heading north-west, towards Clervaux. Only minutes later the new commander gave the order to attack.

Léon had a last look around, "I'm cold," slung two cartridge belts around his neck, grabbed an ammo box in each hand and ran bent over through an ocean of swaying gorse, on the heels of Berl, a Lorrainian and a sobbing sixteen-year-old from Berlin, whom Léon with his great war experience had

had to console with reassurances like "It'll be fine", "Soon be over" . . . until they reached a low hill barely a kilometre from the village, where Berl surveyed the scene through his binoculars, but there were no vehicles in sight; there was no life, not even smoke from the chimneys, a low, freezing mist hung over the countryside, and the silence was as deafening as it can only be in the Ardennes.

New orders to advance, in battle formation, to a ditch close to the most northerly farm, but at that moment artillery began to shell the village, frozen earth, wooden splinters, slate chips and something Léon vaguely recognised as the remnants of a domestic animal rained down on him, he saw from Berl's grimaces that the gunner was cursing and observed from the corner of his eye the commander's desperate rush towards the communication equipment. "That's *our* artillery! The idiot has sent us into our own fire!" But before the clouds of dust had settled the orders to advance were repeated, into the village, where Léon – in the farmyard among the first ruined buildings – caught sight of an American soldier sitting on some hay, as helpless as a stray lamb, without a helmet or boots, poking the ground with a stick. The commander approached warily and shoved the gun barrel into his shoulder.

"Where are your comrades?" Léon heard.

"In the cellar," the American answered, nodding apathetically to the closest house before switching to broken German: "*Nicht schiessen. Nicht schiessen!*"

"What do they think we are?" the commander grinned, looking around with a triumphant expression, then grabbed the man by the shoulder and dragged him backwards while signalling to the rest of the unit to withdraw.

Berl and the young Berliner took up position behind a bullet-pocked oak to the north of the closest ruins while Léon and the Lorrainian lay on the ground twenty metres ahead, with a clear view of the cart track to the village centre, where he could make out a water pump and the turret of a Sherman tank protruding between two houses.

He crawled over the top of a collapsed wall, and down into a mud-filled ditch to join Berl. To the right he saw the commander behind a cart, with his ear to a field telephone again, but immediately he began to gesticulate wildly, and Léon saw two Americans come round the corner with rifles over their shoulders and their hands in their pockets chatting and in a different world from this one. He saw Berl mount the M.G. on the tripod and attempted to shout to him: "The sights! They're set to a thousand metres!" but his voice didn't carry and the tracers flew *over the heads of* the Americans, who crouched down and disappeared among the houses just as the second round of shelling rained down over the village and a deafening barrage filled the space between the German positions, Léon heard a hollow cry and was sprayed with hot, thick liquid, then he heard the yells, from Berl and the commander.

"Léon! Ammo! Ammo! Léon, where are you?! Léon!"

Léon was going nowhere, he was clawing the ground to get deeper, but the commander came and hauled him away, but no more than a couple of metres before they had to throw themselves down again.

"Stick with the gunner! That's an order!"

But Léon didn't leave this spot either – I can't get away, Agnes, that's the truth, the earth is shaking, and it's terrible, but I can hear Berl, and I won't die, I know, I am immortal, so now I'm getting up, I run across the open ground with the boxes and throw myself over the splintered tree trunk, Berl grins, but at that moment a salvo hits the foot of the tripod and I feel a jerk in my left knee, then I see what remains of the lad from Berlin, and that Berl is injured too, blood is streaming down his leg, Agnes, his right arm is dead, but he doesn't notice and he fumbles open the ammo box, I see him cursing, I can't hear a thing, you see, now he is loading and shooting wildly at everything in sight, this is just ridiculous . . .

"*That's* where they are!" he says suddenly like a fool, because the Americans have barricaded themselves in the loft of the nearest house and Berl quickly raises the barrel and sends all he has into the smouldering roof, I can feel the pain now, Agnes, and the nausea – "Léon, you idiot." "Yes, yes, I'm here," Léon does what he is told, I always do what I'm told, my hands feed his gun, but now the enemy in the loft has been wiped out, or it has been evacuated, just some strange screams, and on the ground between the commander's position and the demolished house there are two G.I.s writhing in agony.

"Berl!" I shout, and point, but he tells me to shut up, and to the right I notice there is something going on between the commander and an American position behind the two closest piles of rubble, some kind of negotiation, so it seems, at any rate the terrified American we found on the hay in the heap of ruins stands up, puts his arms in the air and moves towards his wounded comrades, not a shot is fired, and drags them, one by one, back to the German position while Berl signals to the commander that we are wounded, a medic appears as the American eases the last man over the pile of earth, but then they open fire again and he has to run for cover.

There are more negotiations, but the shelling continues, and lasts, you have no idea how long it lasts, Agnes, but you don't notice, because now the American prisoner gets up again and waves a white rag in the hail of bullets and charges towards us at top speed, obviously having been threatened by our commander, and screams something we don't understand, but we realise that he has orders to take us back to the commander's position.

"No chance," Berl decides, and the American puts on a horrified expression, apparently our commander has threatened to execute his wounded comrades if he doesn't return with us, I tell Berl, but I am just brushed aside.

"I'm not risking my life for those bastards! And you're not, either!"

The American becomes hysterical and collapses, and I continue to feed the gun, there is a steady flow now, Agnes, so I don't think it is an artery, it is running down his wrist and making the grip slippery, but it is worse with his leg which is bent at an impossible angle to the ground, I think he is dead, but he is alive, he had been on the Eastern Front for more than two years, and now he is looking straight at me:

"Do you speak English?" Berl yells at me.

"Bit . . ." I say, but of course I can't speak any English, I simply don't know what I am saying.

"Tell the idiot to fetch medical equipment, morphine, bandages – anything, just send him!"

I do the best I can, but the American starts sobbing again and I can't bear to see it, so I shout:

"We're sending him to his death!'

But Berl yells back:

"Fine by me."

And now he has run out of ammo, but he takes the gun from his belt and jabs it in the American's face:

"Go! Or I'll kill you. *Bei Gott, das schwöre ich.* I'll kill you."

The American sniffles like a child, and when I look at him I see how stupid he looks as he gets up and runs to the commander's position, the fool, and Berl gesticulates and is answered, and then the American is back, with a first-aid box in one hand and a rucksack in the other, he is walking more slowly this time, but again he makes it, and I hear Berl say:

"It's obvious who the Lord is protecting."

"All of us," I say with a smile, at which he asks:

"What do you mean?"

I can't answer that, so he says: "Don't get clever with me, you *Scheiss Letzebürger*, I know what you're thinking!"

I take the box from the American and bandage Berl's leg, but as I straighten it, blood surges over my hands, it is an artery, Agnes, it is his life, but at least I manage to get my belt off and tighten it round his thigh, and he shouts "Jesus, I'm dying!", and I say "No, no . . . you're not," but, Agnes, now I see the Sherman – which has been stationary between the houses for the whole battle – turn into the road and rotate the turret and head straight for us, so I take a deep breath and I see a flash of flame and throw myself to the ground even though I am already lying; but the shell passes *above* my head and hits a tree trunk behind me, I have to laugh as the tree hits the ground, it is snowing, snow and splinters, but now it is quiet, you can't imagine how quiet it is.

"Léon!"

"Yes, I'm here."

I was there, and I saw the commander and my comrades leave their positions and race towards the ruins, two didn't make it, then it was really quiet, the Sherman turned its back on us and slowly trundled out of the village towards Drauffelt, and Berl ground his teeth so loudly that I could hear it, and he was fumbling with a morphine syringe which I had to take from him by force.

"Are they retreating?"

He didn't hear.

"I survived Hünersdorff," he said to the sky. "And then there's this hell *here* as well!" I drove the syringe into his thigh, and he said: "Give me another," so I gave him another, and said: "They're retreating. It's all over now, Berl. You're going to pull through. Nobody's going to die." "What are you talking about, you idiot? We're all going to die . . ."

A few shots rang out from the village, but the artillery was quiet, and then I saw that Berl had drawn his revolver again and was pointing it at the back of the American, who had been sitting for the last half an hour with his head in his hands rocking backwards and forwards like a sleeping dove, but I must have turned as the shot was fired, I have to admit I did nothing to stop it, what should I have done, I wasn't at Munshausen, I rubbed my face against the tree trunk, and when I opened my eyes again the place was crawling with medics, Berl was lying on a stretcher covered with a blanket and being given something to drink, two men were also examining my leg, there can't have been much wrong though because they turned with a contemptuous snort and went away while the others finished treating Berl. I heard them say that someone would see to us before they too left, and I thought it was over, it was dark and biting cold, Berl regained consciousness and said: "I'm alive." I didn't answer, I'm sure of that, the pains in my leg were unbearable and my teeth were chattering, but he said: "I'm hungry. I need something to eat. The rucksack, Léon . . ." So I crawled over and fetched it, rifle ammunition, half a loaf and a bottle of brandy, I heard Berl laugh and took a swig myself, but he drank the rest, and I remember that when I awoke he was looking at me through red-rimmed, feverish eyes.

"You know this area," he mumbled. I must have nodded and said yes because he continued: "Get yourself home and find some civvies. I know that's been playing on your mind."

But I shook my head and said I had nowhere to go, "I'm a German," I said, and added in that case Berl would have to die here on his own, because no-one was coming, and he yelled: "That's an order!" He had his hand around his revolver and said "*Herrgott*" and pointed the gun at me, so I got up and rolled over the oak trunk and down into a ditch, where I found what was left of the Lorrainian as I heard the shot, and when I turned, Berl was lying across the tree trunk as though crucified, that was what happened, I don't remember anything else, I can testify to that, I won't put my name to anything else, as God is my witness.

4

Léon saw light. At first it was warm, then it went white and slowly sparkled into life, he dragged himself eastwards, found a branch and managed to walk a few metres, had a rest and went another hundred metres, stumbled through the night and home to Dorscheid, where three of the farms lay in ruins, one was still smoking. But his home was still standing, the windows in the end wall had been blown out, two cows were lying next to the stream, blasted to pieces by shellfire, but he couldn't see any people, dead or alive, Dorscheid had been evacuated, or wiped out, no lights and no sound.

Léon walked the last steps up to the farm building, through the washroom and into the kitchen where dinner was on the table, the sitting-room door was open, a chair had been overturned and the stove was cold, the yellowing potatoes and coagulated gravy on the plates, a day-and-a-half old because there were the remains of some meat, too, and that was what they had on Saturdays, and the table was set for all four of them.

Léon shuffled round the house and noticed that the bedding and the family's winter clothes were missing, that the binoculars he had got from his father on his eighteenth birthday had gone, as had two pans and some cutlery, and not least the horse and cart and the other animals, which suggested it had been an evacuation. But to his surprise he saw that several of the family photos were missing, as well as his father's Bible and Leni's favourite doll, while his gun was hanging in its usual place in the washroom.

He struggled up the stairs to his room, stuffed a pillow in the smashed window and slept in the bed he had slept in every single night up to May 27, Dear Agnes, there is fresh bed linen here, where on earth has it come from?

For four or five days, it isn't so easy to know, because Léon doesn't count, he lies there wondering who he is, or rather, who others will think he is, and he arrives at the wrong answer, at any rate an answer which no-one can agree with, since he puts off going to meet his family and friends on the old familiar paths, while the grandfather clock in the sitting room continues to tick and the time to make it back to his German regiment is running out, but he is not going back, that is for certain, though he can't stay here either, even so he doesn't go, the wound is not deep, but something must be broken in his knee joint, that is why he doesn't go.

He reckoned no-one would notice the smoke in the sea of mist outside and lit the stove in the kitchen. He burned his uniform, cut up part of one of the cows and hung the meat in the washroom, and went on a few short recce expeditions in the neighbourhood, in a vain search for a human being or at least a radio, he heard the drone of planes and thought he heard the clanking of tank tracks down the road to Neidhausen, but then it went quiet again, he ate some tough meat, wolfed down Agnes' jam, crusts of cheese, baked some bread and drank all of his father's modest stock of wine. But his leg wasn't getting any better, half a metre of snow fell and then the weather cleared up, and he still couldn't decide what to do.

But then he heard the sound of voices and saw from the window that two civilians in a horse-drawn cart had stopped at a neighbouring house, it was his next-door neighbours, father and son, his best friend and playmate, who went in and carried out two suitcases and several sacks and were gone again. While Léon crouched at the window, unable to make his presence known, he was wearing the wrong uniform, even if he had burnt it long ago, and late that night he went out under the starry sky to see whether it was safe to light the fire, and outside he saw his own tracks, the tracks he had made that morning and realised that his neighbours would also have seen them and known he was there, and then they had chosen to leave again. That decided it.

Where should he go though, it must be December 23 by now, or maybe Christmas Eve? He followed his neighbours' tracks, but they disappeared in the churned-up main road through Neidhausen, and he couldn't see any smoke or light there, so he hobbled on westwards, sometimes through the forest, but no innocent civilian had any business there, so he took to the road again, down to Drauffelt where he walked slap into a column of prisoners, forty, fifty raggle-taggle zombies in American uniforms, under German guard, the motorcyclist at the front stopped, whereupon Léon took a deep breath and said unbidden in his best Letzebuergesch:

"I've just come from Hosingen and I'm looking for my family . . ."

As the Americans marched grimly past, the officer measured him with a sleepless gaze, but did not dismount from his motorbike.

"Your papers."

"My mother has them. I was at work in Wahlhausen and we lost contact. They said in Bockholtz that they might be in Drauffelt . . ."

"Enscheringen," the officer said after a short pause and suddenly lost interest. "There are some civilians there, also from Hosingen."

He revved up and rejoined the front of the column while Léon waited until the procession had passed, a heavy lorry carrying wounded prisoners brought up the rear and a battered tank with "Hünersdorff" painted across its turret in yellow letters.

Léon waved briefly at the soldiers sitting on top and limped on, in the middle of the road now, like a man who has passed muster, he'd had enough credibility to deceive a German, the credibility only a truthful lie could lend him, and as he was approaching the River Clerve he bumped into two elderly women and a girl who said they were going "home" to Munshausen and that the Germans were in Drauffelt, he also spoke to them like a real local, he deceived them too and realised how simple it was as he gave Drauffelt a wide berth and made his way south through the forest, waded across the Clerve late in the evening and gave Enscherange a wide berth as well, in order to enter the town from the west.

In a bar he was told which people had taken in evacuees and was received with open arms at the very first house by a stout elderly couple by the name of Elsen, who had over twenty evacuees under their wing, on mattresses and camp beds. His host showed Léon around as if he were a guest of honour – eight children between the ages of three and ten were romping about on the sitting-room floor, a middle-aged couple from Clervaux were sitting on a bench by a majestic cabinet, him blind, her with downcast eyes and a rosary on her lap, and two girls, presumably their daughters, with their dainty heads bowed over their knitting, arms tucked into their sides; in the kitchen two girls from Hosingen were making a racket, to the enormous irritation of an old man from Wiltz, whom the host maintained they'd had to constrain by force because he wanted to "go home". The other part of the house had been requisitioned by three German officers, so Léon repeated the tale he had told the officer on the motorbike, but this time he replaced Hosingen with Stolzembourg as his hometown.

He was given a hot meal and a glass of wine, and when silence had settled over this wartime Noah's Ark, he told the farmer his story, that he was who he was and therefore didn't know what the hell to do, and the man became both pensive and annoyed, especially when Munshausen was mentioned, whereupon he took his guest down to the cellar, through the damp stench of mould and cheese and earth and in behind a potato bin where all types of discarded agricultural implements and old tools were piled up on wide shelves, swept one of them clean and turned it into a pallet with blankets and mumbled something about it being a pity the others in the house had seen him, but tomorrow he would have to get up before daybreak and move on as though he had never been there.

Léon thanked him and went to sleep. But he didn't wake until well into the day, with one leg just as stiff although the pain had eased, and upstairs in the house all was quiet, he heard someone moving about in the attic, but didn't see anyone, neither there nor in the kitchen nor in any of the other rooms, except for the blind man, who started in surprise when he went in.

"Who's that?" he said, craning his head.

"Just me," Léon said evasively in an attempt to merge into the background, for blindness affects not only the person who has lost his sight, but also those the blind cannot see, so Léon blushed at having been caught red-handed and gave up any idea of creeping out unseen. Instead he asked:

"Where are the others?" and scuffed his feet so that the blind man would turn his face in the right direction.

"At Mass. The Wehrmacht, too," he added with a wry smile. "It's Christmas . . ."

"Ah, I see . . ."

"You didn't know that, did you? I thought not."

"What do you mean?"

"Nothing. There's a medicine cabinet in there. I think you might be able to have a bath here, too."

The blind man flared his nostrils and laughed affectedly. Léon stared at his black pilot's goggles, or tank goggles, and wondered why he didn't think of washing in the days he was in Dorscheid, then he began to laugh as well, but this was a harrowing experience, so he stopped and went to the kitchen to wash and bandage his wound, but he was filled with a mounting unease, the blind man had spoken High German even when Léon answered in Letzebuergesch, he had to continue on his way towards his undefined destination, to heaven, there was no room for him on earth, but God led him back to the blind man who was sitting in the same chair, his face turned towards the sunlight which fell through the window on the south-facing wall, still with an enigmatic smile on his deeply lined features.

"It's a nice day," he said immediately after Léon had scuffed his foot. "The Allies have full control of the skies, so it won't be more than two or three weeks, four maybe? You were in Munshausen, weren't you?"

Léon started.

"Can you see things?" he asked.

"No, but what I have seen has made me blind. I'm Belgian," he added, as if to explain his High German and his psychic powers, and Léon was only just able to compose himself sufficiently to pose an important question:

"What happened in Munshausen?"

"Surely you know, don't you?"

"No, you don't see anything in battle, not that I was frightened, but I didn't see anything, we fell into an ambush, I reckon . . ."

The blind man smiled again.

"Something happened which neither the Germans nor the Allies are very proud of. But I think all the civilians were evacuated . . ."

"The Kompanieführer handed over the command to a Stabsfeldwebel," Léon mumbled.

"This is not a war they're going to win. I think it's best if you go now. The girls here are partial to the German officers."

Léon got up. He heard the roar of cannons.

"I have to find my family," he said distractedly.

"They're safe," the blind man said. "On your way now, before anyone starts asking questions . . ."

"I saw a tank east of Drauffelt," Léon said. "With 'Hünersdorff' written on it . . . what does that mean?"

"Good in the service of evil," the blind man muttered, turning his face to the sunlight again. "The last hope gone. It's not a good sign. Or maybe it is a good sign, I don't know, be off with you now."

A door slammed, and the host came in, red-faced with cold.

"Are you still here?" he said petulantly. "I told you to get going. Come back tonight if you absolutely must, but it would be best for you to find somewhere else. Look, I've scraped a few things together for you."

Léon put on his coat, grabbed the shabby suitcase and had a canvas bag thrust into his other hand. He crept out the back of the house and made his way across the neighbouring garden, to the south, in the opposite direction to the church spire, without meeting a soul, and took a path up the hill, west towards Eschweiler, but he had no more reason to be there than here, so he left the path and sought the cover of the forest, stopped and stared disapprovingly at his tracks, gave a shrug and continued until he reached a ridge with a view of Enscherange, his starting-out point.

There he lit a fire beneath a towering beech tree which had kept enough of its rust-brown foliage to make him invisible from above. The pounding of artillery came from every direction, but how would the Americans receive him? – "Good in the service of evil", those words applied to Léon, a Luxembourger in a Wehrmacht uniform, and also the next ones, "The last hope gone", as he hadn't sided with the Americans at Munshausen, God was my witness, he wished them dead and buried, even though he hadn't fired a shot, but then he discovered that Berl was unable to hold his machine gun, that he had to fight for Berl's life and at one point he was on the verge of going down to the nearest German sentry post and telling them he had lost contact with his company in the heat of battle in Munshausen, and then he had tried to find his way home and had put on these civvies because his uniform was in tatters . . . they would receive him with open arms, five or six days – what was that? – it would also benefit his family, no matter what the outcome of the war, because being forced to join the German ranks gave you some kind of protection against guilt, he knew that, yes, the German uniform was his only refuge, a sacred no-man's-land, and here he was in civilian clothes, by God, Agnes, how could I be so blind?! And spurred on by this born-again insight he set off and plodded down the snow-covered hillside back to Escherange, but there for some reason he preferred the Elsens' house to the German command post; the kids were playing on the floor as on the previous day, while a plump, middle-aged woman rose from her chair near the door and looked at him shyly.

"I'm cold," Léon said. There were no other adults in the room, but a moment later the host came in and dragged him resolutely through the kitchen and down the cellar stairs.

"What on earth's up with you?"

"I'm German," Léon said wearily. "I need to find my company again, the regiment . . ."

"Nonsense. They'll grill you alive, it's the death penalty for deserters, regardless of whether you're a Luxembourger or a German, or a Bantu tribesman for that matter . . ."

"I'm not a deserter. I lost contact with—"

"Listen here, young man," the host said, before suddenly assuming a more concerned tone. "What's up with your leg?"

Léon looked down at his troublesome leg. Blood had soaked through his trousers and turned them black from the knee downwards, one dark and one light leg, like those of a circus artiste, and the very next moment he sank to the floor.

But he was aware that the host was dragging him through the cellar passageway and manoeuvred him onto the same "shelf" and that somebody came to tend his wounds, a woman, perfume, but his body began to shake, he was given some brandy and saw Berl's smile when he relieved him of the blood-streaked machine gun, Berl's contented smile, the one a proud father bestows on a successful son, or a condemned man on his saviour, unless the gunner was only acknowledging some good old Prussian fighting spirit. A rearing horse, contorted and screaming between the wooden shafts of a half-buried cart, a rain of splinters, the wound to my hand, he looked at it, saw that it had closed like a clam around a pearl – "That means you're dead," the blind man had said, and not "Good in the service of evil" – "You're dead."

"Leave him there," he heard. "He's one of us!'

In Léon's own language – and he was aware that several other young men had occupied shelves in the cellar, above him and on the opposite wall, young men of his own age.

"I'm from Dorscheid," he said defiantly, and saw the smile on the face above him broaden, a blond fringe over a lean baby-face with wide-open eyes.

"What did I tell you? It's not a trap."

Léon wasn't cold anymore, his feet weren't floating, his eyes didn't ache, the wound wasn't throbbing, he wasn't even hungry, and now he recognised two of the faces from the Wehrkreiskommando in the capital in May, or from the trip to the training camp in Bohemia, Luxembourgers who, like himself, had deserted during the offensive, as they had planned in Slovakia, God had brought them together again on the Belgian border, when the German troops had been ordered to retreat; they had ditched their weapons and uniforms, found help from civilians and travelled on foot, like Léon, all they could do now was lie low until the Americans came, in a week or two, maybe three . . .

"What day is it?" Léon asked.

"Saturday," said the blond fringe above him. "The thirtieth of December."

5

Ortskommandant Heinz Blaskowitz, the local commanding officer, hadn't been stationed in Enscherange for more than twenty-four hours when one of his Truppenführers came and informed him that "three or four deserters were staying at a house with the Elsen family".

"What do you mean by three *or* four?" Blaskowitz growled. "Can't you count?"

He didn't like this war, he didn't like Hitler, his regiment or the much over-rated soldier's life, either, which he called filthy, boring and stultifying, Blaskowitz was an aristocrat, a philologist, a Mozart expert, well-dressed and a lover of literary classics. But neither did he like turncoats, partisans, resistance fighters or whatever they were called, all of those who in the final throes of a meaningless war wanted to save their meaningless skins, and leave the purgatory to others, so he gave the Truppenführer orders to clarify what he meant by "three or four deserters" without delay.

Ten minutes later he dropped his cigarette in his coffee cup, got to his feet and walked the 500 metres through the snow-covered village to the house concerned, where his men had apprehended and handcuffed four men. In the sitting room, apart from the prisoners, the Truppenführer and two guards, was the ruddy-faced Elsen, clearly dejected, as well as an elderly, wizened and self-effacing woman and a blind man with dark glasses who was talking to one of the prisoners.

Blaskowitz stamped his foot and asked for silence, received a whispered briefing from the Truppenführer and mustered the civvies-clad captives, four young men of not even twenty who were making ungainly attempts to stand to attention.

"Deserters!?"

"Luxembourgers!' they answered in unison.

"But well brought up?" he said scornfully with regard to their postures, and told the Truppenführer to remove the chains linking their handcuffs. "And you were taught that by the Wehrmacht. Name, rank and unit! You first!"

"I'm a civilian, Herr Kommandant. Léon V. . . ."

"You're wounded."

"Yes, Herr Kommandant. A bullet wound in the knee. I got it during the evacuation of Hosingen . . ."

"When?"

"The sixteenth, Herr Kommandant. I'm from Dorscheid, but was doing farm work in Hosingen . . ."

Blaskowitz shook his head dismissively.

"Farm work in December?"

"Slaughtering animals, Herr Kommandant."

"But you haven't got any papers?"

"No, Herr Kommandant, my mother has them. She was evacuated to—"

"Find out about him," he said to the Truppenführer. "He's too afraid or too stupid to give his real name – and you?"

At this point the Truppenführer broke in and handed him a revolver he had found on the prisoner next to Léon.

"Look at this, an o.8, and of course you found this in the woods?"

"Yes, Herr Kommandant. I walked all the way here from Stolzembourg, where I was working in a smithy. I'm looking for my family, who have been evacuated from Stolzembourg. I found the gun south of Fennberg and brought it with me in case—"

"How long have they been here?" Blaskowitz asked the host. Elsen hesitated and mumbled:

"Varies. Some five days, one two days . . ."

"Why are they in the cellar?"

"The house is full, Herr Kommandant."

"Indeed. We received reports from one of the girls here that these *Schweine* are deserters."

"I don't know anything about that, Herr Kommandant. They're wearing civilian clothes and they are Luxembourgers."

"Is that so? Well, I have no intention of dirtying my hands. I assume the Sicherheitsdienst will get the truth out of them. Take them to Clervaux on the next available lorry. And clean up this rathole."

He turned and walked towards the door but was stopped by a loud voice.

"Dirtying your hands is just what you're doing, Herr Oberst."

He stared in disbelief at the assembly, went over to the sofa and looked down at the blind man.

"Is that so?" he drawled. "So I'm dirtying my hands, am I?"

"Yes, Herr Oberst. The S.D. know only one truth."

"How do you know?"

"I was in Manstein's general staff before I lost my sight. I know the S.S., the S.D. and the Wehrmacht, and I know they're not the same. I think you know, too, Herr Oberst."

The Kommandant stood rocking to and fro on the balls of his feet, sceptical about this appeal as well.

"Since you're so well informed," he said contemptuously, "you can maybe tell a Wehrmacht officer what he ought to do when he finds a deserter?"

"They're not deserters, Herr Oberst."

"Stop that Oberst nonsense, I'm a Leutnant. And I asked you a question!'

"They're all Luxembourgers, Herr Leutnant. They *can't* be deserters. Unless you force them to be."

Blaskowitz seemed to be struck by a moment of doubt. He put on a dis-believing smile, looked from the bowed heads of the prisoners to Elsen and the old woman's evasive gaze, to the expressionless face of the Truppenführer, who didn't appear to be particularly impressed by the performance, either. The situ-ation irritated Blaskowitz beyond measure. His contempt for Hitler and his stupid war was genuine enough, but so was his fury at this intellectual hair-splitting.

"This war is obnoxious," he said in a quivering voice. "But that doesn't mean that those who have been involved should be able turn their backs on it, wherever they come from. Take them to Clervaux! And clean this place up."

Léon and his fellow prisoners were loaded onto the back of an open lorry and transported the six kilometres to Clervaux, where they were locked in the cellar of the Koener Hotel and had to lie in a heap on the floor, chained to each other, leaving only when summoned for torture or interrogation or to peel potatoes. The one who suffered most was the oldest of them, who refused to say a word, not even his name, and Léon, who had two teeth knocked out and his already damaged knee totally smashed because he insisted that he had not deserted but was just an ordinary German soldier who had lost contact with his unit. A Gestapo officer threatened in his presence that he would soon settle the *Schweinehund*'s hash, but the Major who was in command at the hotel made it clear that this was a Wehrmacht matter and the prisoners would be put before a war tribunal, as was right and proper.

A week later they were transferred to Germany via Enscherange. There they were loaded onto a bus full of American P.O.W.s, and through a fugged-up window Léon glimpsed a group of civilians slogging through snowdrifts at the side of the road and recognised the blind man from the Elsens' house, saw him stop and stare vacantly at the bus, saw him raise a hand and wave, a black angel in the snow, before the bus went on, down the Our Valley and through the border town of Gemünd, to Eisensmitt in the Rhineland, where Léon's knee injury was given some makeshift treatment before all the prisoners were brought before a war tribunal in a disused spinning mill.

The tribunal consisted of twelve officers of different ranks. The prosecution demanded the death sentence. But the defence counsel, the court-appointed young Leutnant with a legal background, pointed out that not one of the four had reached the age of majority, that their actions were manifestations of youthful foolhardiness and asked the court to take into consideration that they could be presumed not to have understood the binding nature of the oath of allegiance, after all they were Luxembourgers.

The accused were led out into the hall and had to wait, Léon sitting on a chair because of his injured knee while the others stood, and none of them said anything because a word can always be taken amiss, and nowhere more so than here, and they could see from each other's faces that they were slowly ageing, that the years were marking them, like surgery, until they became bent and sunken, weary of life, shaking and incontinent, this was the initial stage, but they weren't old, they were eighteen and nineteen, and one of them had to be carried in while Léon, to everyone's surprise, insisted on hobbling in unassisted and also standing up on his one good leg while the verdict was pronounced, there was an angelic expression on his face, as though he glimpsed not a faint ray of hope but rather everlasting redemption in the court's sombre expressions, and maybe that was what they did receive because it turned out that the court had found for the defence, not for the argument concerning their Luxembourg origins however, this went the other way, there was no such thing as a Luxembourger, they were sentenced to fifteen years' imprisonment.

Léon had not been anticipating an earthly reprieve but a chance to be relieved of the unbearable pain, so now his right leg gave way, they had to carry him out, and they were surprised to see that he was still wearing his angelic smile when he awoke, for they didn't know that from henceforth he was a resurrected soul, or an angel, black or white, in ash-grey shrouds with a rook's jagged wings, that kind of thing only appeared in the realm of superstition, and this, by God, is reality.

6

Well, so far this story has been true, so from now on it will have to be considered as pure fiction if it is not to compromise the veracity of the first part, you have to choose, it is either/or as to whether this is a realistic narrative you are contending with or not. Léon the Angel and his three friends were now transported by military escort to a prison in Wittlich and from there to Rheinbach at the end of February. But the Reich was on the retreat, so only a week later they were forced to shovel sand into sacks on the eastern bank of the Rhine, night and day, whether their legs were up to it or not, they had to build defences and run supplies, and all that was left of Léon was his seraphic smile and the hard-earned sympathy of his comrades, they gave him some of their rations, an extra blanket, and developed a system of signals to wake him up and get him on his feet whenever the guards approached.

But then everything went into freefall anyway, and in the chaos surrounding the Allied crossing at Remhagen, the guards were suddenly nowhere to be seen, the prisoners found themselves in empty space, they could escape unhindered, on foot, even Léon, there was no need to make a run for it, only a laborious climb up the beautiful vineyards south of Erpel. He hobbled along with the aid of two crutches which his comrades had made for him, and up in Orsberg they found shelter in a small copse and gazed across the mighty Rhine, lying there stripped of all its bridges from Bonn in the north to Andernach in the south, except for the one at Remhagen which was being defended with titanic energy by the twentieth-century's full range of technological wonders. A historic pandemonium was approaching from all quarters, an unending quak- ing of the earth and heavens, so what now? – for they needed both food and protection, and the four witnesses of this scene were still Luxembourgers, weren't they, at least it was a long time since they had worn a German uniform, but now they were in prison garb and couldn't agree on whether to wait in the forest, go back down to the Rhine towards the advancing Allied forces, move north, south or maybe into the sorry remains of the Reich, because there had to be some possibilities there too – for what? Not even that was an obvious question, and Léon was especially ill-equipped to provide any answers, it was all too similar to the very wrong answer he came up with when he was alone at home in Dorscheid or on the hill above Enscherange and thought he saw the light; but it ended with them parting company: Léon and Benjamin – the blond fringe who had his bed on the shelf above him at the Elsens' house – they went north along the Rhine, on the basis of little more than a gut feeling and the hieroglyphics they saw in the sky, that was the map they had, they walked under cover of night, stole food from farms, slept during the day in haylofts or under the open sky in the forest as Europe's heart thumped and pounded, and Léon thanked God for God knows what, and Benjamin talked about food and described all the details of his childhood home in Ösel, from cupboard linings to horsehair and his left-handed sister and the nightingale that in springtime babbled in his ears, and in Léon's too, like the clearest brook, all the things they would never see again but took with them into the darkness.

One morning they woke up to find themselves surrounded by German tanks, scruffy, exhausted soldiers sitting on their vehicles and smoking and paying no attention to the motley collection of civilian and prison clothes that got up from the dewy grass, open-mouthed and wide-eyed like terrified children. But Léon the Angel had nothing to fear, he was as dead as a dodo, so he approached them undaunted, started up a conversation with an officer who, with complete indifference, told him they were part of Feldmarschall Model's doomed Army Group, in all 325,000 Wehrmacht soldiers who have been surrounded by the Allies and have probably surrendered, who knows, no-one tells us . . . They were given some food, but the victors moved in that same day, and the two friends had to cling to each other to be allocated to the same P.O.W. camp in Sinzig-Käfig, or the Sinzig Cage, as the Americans called this massive internment centre several square kilometres in size, which had been hastily set up on the outskirts of the village of Kripp, leaving lethargy to descend on the Rhineland.

And also Léon's heart.

But what now? In the camp, conditions were more lamentable than anywhere else he had been: there was a shortage of food and clothing and fuel, provisions and tents and equipment and medicine; they had to sleep for weeks out in the open, and after only a few days Léon saw through a heavenly veil that people were beginning to die around him, it was raining, they were drowning in the mud as they slept, there were epidemics and there was a growing barbarism among the prisoners who killed each other over trifles, over nothing. But Benjamin had met a group of veterans from the Eastern Front under the leadership of a young S.S. officer: with unflagging energy, they were busily digging a shelter which was then protected by barbed wire and guarded like a military barracks; Léon was laid on a wooden board under a ragged blanket at the very back, like a religious relic, while the most exhausted prisoners guarded the entrance, and the S.S. officer and a select few went on raids to plunder fellow P.O.W.s and take part in the battle for the supplies the civilian population had smuggled into the camp.

Lying on the board, Léon gathered strength for his meeting with God, but God was great, He sent no relief now either, only more heart-rending longing for home, the Ardennes, with its smells and forests, and Agnes, an even whiter sculpture than ever before, strange words went through Léon's mind, conversations he had with his father about a gold coin he must have stolen and he thought had a face value of thirty-nine francs, which of course was not a unit of currency but a mystery, so he couldn't understand why his father wanted to punish him, I am innocent, Léon said and had to laugh at his own voice, at the hollowness of it; he could mimic his sisters' quarrelling at the dinner table and could be the arbiter because of the age difference, with Leni getting the better deal, and he was appalled to the point of fury that his fellow P.O.W.s kept him alive when he was fated to die – they give me food and blankets, Agnes, which they need themselves, there is no justice in this, how precious I am, Agnes, you are the only person I cannot mediate between, ha ha . . . for there is only one of you, one single person!

7

After four weeks of uncertainty in the badger's den Léon is taken out into the sunshine and laid on a stretcher, he feels himself being showered with hot water, being disinfected, shaved, his whole body, and dressed in new clothes, and is given liquid food and a bed which he never wants to leave, they have to drag him out – well, that won't be much of a problem, he thinks with a smile – and send him by ambulance to an Allied P.O.W. camp in Bavaria, but Benjamin is with me. "You've saved my life," Benjamin says. "How come?" I ask. "They didn't have the heart to kill you," he says, "and I am your friend."

"Yes," Léon says absent-mindedly. "We're friends."

And now there is enough food, it has also become warmer, and Léon can go for short walks in the early-summer sun and appears before a new war tribunal, an Allied one, and they accuse him of taking part, during the Ardennes Offensive, in the attack on the village of Munshausen in the Grand Duchy of Luxembourg, where the Americans suffered considerable losses and where, moreover, summary executions were carried out, which have been documented in two reliable witness statements.

Léon rises to his feet in the provisional courtroom and starts to tell his story, but it won't stand up, it is too implausible, so instead he declares that he can't remember much, a contention he sticks to, even though the prosecutor points out that this will not advance his case, if he has one at all, there are no extenuating circumstances for being a sheep in a wolf's clothing, everyone has to be responsible for their actions, both conscripts and volunteers, could he not have decamped when he was in Schnee-Eifel waiting for Alert Level 1 in December, for we have our own small choices to make within the weightier ones that history makes for us, we all have, G.I.s and generals, that is the wisdom the Americans are there to ordain, Europe is soon to find out, mass movements are dead and the final triumph of individuality will be enshrined in treaties and protocols.

Léon didn't understand much of all this, it confused and irritated him, like a plague of lice, and then his thoughts turned to something else – where was Benjamin? The Americans could provide no answer, they didn't know of any Benjamin, but they sentenced Léon to four years' imprisonment for crimes against his mother country. Together with five other soldiers from the 2nd Panzers (two Luxembourgers and four Belgians in all) and, after a month's futile searching for his only friend, he was transported to Dover, England, whence he was conveyed on a rickety train to a camp outside Edinburgh, where the rain ensured that the seasons merged into one another and time stood still.

But even up there in the north Léon considered that he was making some important discoveries. He began talking to his father again, with a vengeance, both day and night, especially about the missing gold coin with the impossible face value of thirty-nine francs, he maintained in his defence that when a choice had to be made between family and nation then of course you chose the family, the seeds of loyalty germinated in the family earth, nation came second, this insight was what his father expected of him, no, it was not what his father expected of him, neither his father nor anyone else, and Léon was puzzled, didn't he know his own father – *that* was what the conversation about the gold coin was about, and the sun and moon rose above the horizon and united in a black cloud.

Then a fellow P.O.W. told him that the young S.S. officer who had held a protective wing over him in Sinzig had been sentenced to death for the murder of eighty-four Russian prisoners, one of the final Nazi convulsions of the war, and Léon realised he would have to unburden himself, so he went to see the duty officer and demanded to be allowed to testify on the S.S. officer's behalf, he was a good person. But no one knew the case, they dismissed him with a shake of the head and English curses and abuse, and subjected him to various psychological tests, which he couldn't see any point in, Léon was a borderline case, in all of the term's cryptic senses. But here in this field hospital – which they called a sanatorium – he met Leutnant Blaskowitz, who was serving a sentence of fifteen years for the maltreatment of civilians in the Ardennes, he had been unfairly sentenced, too, it transpired, but he confided to Léon that this was a dangerous path they had chosen to tread.

"Which path?" Léon asked.

"Pretending to be mentally ill," Blaskowitz said. "They hate the mentally ill here."

Léon took this in, but then he had to tell Blaskowitz the truth about the fighting in Slovakia, which made him so strong and resilient, fighting in a German uniform, about the Ardennes Offensive and the bizarre days between Berl's death and his arrest in the Elsens' house – he was free then, wasn't he? And the Leutnant was taken aback:

"Why didn't you tell me about all this in Enscheringen?" he asked.

"I wasn't afraid until I got to Enscherange," Léon explained, using the Luxembourg name of the village. "I had never been afraid. But what I'm trying to tell you is that I didn't desert. That was why I went into the town. I had just lost contact with my regiment . . ."

"You should have told me that, too," Blaskowitz said.

"I did," Léon insisted, by now seriously annoyed.

"That's not how *I* remember it," Blaskowitz said.

Some days later the Leutnant was found dead in his bed, strangled and with the name "Hünersdorff" daubed in soot on the front of his prison uniform, good in the service of evil, or the last hope gone when it is least expected. The camp commander set up an investigation, but had to let the matter drop due to insufficient evidence. However, the P.O.W.s were divided up: the so-called *neu-deutsche* – east Belgians, Luxembourgers, Lorrainians, Alsatians – were separated from the genuine Germans, the columns of blood in Hitler's crooked temple, and the guards were reinforced, and Léon felt a growing aversion towards these smug arrangements whereby the *neu-deutsche* were treated better than the pure-blooded Germans and he began to hate the rainy climate – I can't stand rain! – and also the endless mutton, the harsh diet of the Hittites and Pharisees, not to mention his own body, which was a law unto itself all winter, ravaged with fever and illnesses and fits of shivering that made him stammer and say irrational things until he lost all contact with the outside world.

"It's not necessarily a bad sign," a doctor told him in broken German. "You're on your way back to normality."

"Speak French," Léon said. "I don't understand what you're saying."

The man repeated the sentence in German.

"I don't understand what you're saying," Léon said. "Don't they teach you anything on this island?"

He couldn't even visualise the Ardennes, he just saw these sloping, green, Scottish moors that surrounded the camp like the sides of a crater, a funnel to the sky greedily sucking up all its gory sorrow, in a maelstrom. Two winters or two summers, and where were the autumn, the seasons and the sense of time for a feeling human being?

But in late summer 1947 Léon could at last go down on his knees and thank his God. He had been pardoned "on account of his youth and for good conduct", as it said in the papers he was handed and had translated by a fellow inmate, it must have been his terrible knee injury they had in mind – they had kept patching it up, only to demonstrate their ignorance with regard to medicine, too.

Léon grasped the duty officer's hand and shook it ecstatically, thanking him for everything he had learned, here in the middle of the Atlantic Ocean, and he wept like a baby. And less than a month later, on the afternoon of 16 September, 1947, he hobbled off the train in his hometown of Drauffelt after a journey of which he had no memory; in his knapsack he had a sundial, four ashtrays and a round jewellery box with an engraved lid, all made from brass cartridge shells. No state welcoming committee to receive Léon, no fanfares and flags, no post-war compensation or war pension. Léon was as innocent as a child, he was new-born and sentenced to death, he had been granted a life, as a gift or a punishment, who can say what's what with this kind of thing?

He looked askance at the yellowing oaks that cast a faint shadow over the ground, at the horse and cart which his sisters had borrowed from a neighbour and at them, too, Leni and Gertrud in bright dresses, three and a half years older, mature women with summer painted all over their faces, white teeth and curly locks hanging down over their twinkling eyes. They told him that their father had trodden on an unexploded shell the year before and had succumbed to his wounds, but they had not wanted to darken Léon's existence by telling him about this in a letter; they said Agnes had married a bookkeeper from Consthum and had moved to the capital, another thing they hadn't wanted to tell him in a letter, mainly because Agnes had begged them on her knees not to do so. Those were the two pieces of news they had to give him immediately, they thought, otherwise they would probably never be able to do it, one piece of news each. However, they added that the farm was still standing, they had four cows, five calves and a pig, and it hadn't been as difficult to recognise him as they had feared, even though he was limping and had lost a couple of front teeth.

On the road up the rolling hills to Dorscheid, Léon sat as quiet as a clam staring at the horse's mane bouncing up and down, Leni's head resting on his lap; it was a week before he said anything.

"It's hot," he said. "Shall we go for a swim?"

8

A few days before Christmas someone tried to set Léon and his sisters' farm alight. One morning just before Lent he found the word "traitor" daubed on the cowshed wall. At Easter one of the cows died inexplicably.

"It's the war raging in our forests," Léon said as he put out the fire, whitewashed over the vile word and buried the cow. He never went out, neither to Dorscheid, nor anywhere else, he didn't contact any of his old friends, he didn't go shopping, not even for farm supplies, but sat inside reading the Bible, with mounting irritation, until he closed it for good, which, however, did not diminish the irritation. He didn't tell his sisters anything about what had happened and didn't care about anything except Leni doing her homework and keeping up at school. "That's a good sign," she whispered to her sister, and tried even harder to be good at school and patient with her brother.

When another cow was struck down by the virulent epidemic that followed in the wake of the war, the sisters began to nag Léon to get out and about, mix with locals at the morning *Frühschoppen*, go to the market in Clervaux, at the very least attend church, but he just asked them if they had gone out of their minds, and presumably they had, because when he removed all the mirrors he could find in the house, they put them back, for Léon wasn't alone and he had to understand that. He also removed his photos from the family album, but he didn't burn them, and Gertrud pasted them back in. Léon couldn't make up his mind. But the following autumn he sold his father's old wall clock to an antiques dealer in the capital and bought himself a camera and a tripod and developing equipment, set up a dark room in the barn and began to photograph birds of prey. Once a year he went away, by train, without telling anyone where, and returned after three or four days in a slightly more cheerful mood, his sisters thought, but only to sink into despondency a few days later and become absorbed in biblical texts – for the Lord would not release His grip on him – and peregrine falcons and buzzards.

But Gertrud did not shun her sisterly obligations, and now she stressed even more the necessity of her brother having contact with God in the Lord's own house. Léon had to listen to rapturous reports of how lovely the Mass had been today, about the new priest who had arrived from France with a high-pitched voice, *joie de vivre* and encouraging words. One Sunday morning – almost three years after his return home and the day after Leni had finished school in Clervaux with some of the best exam grades ever recorded at the local *lycée* – Léon suddenly appeared in the kitchen wearing his father's best suit and declared that now he was ready to go to church in Munshausen.

He walked through the sparse congregation with a sister on each arm and only now discovered – all too late – that this idea of Gertrud's was not about coming closer either to God or abandoned neighbours but about invoking general sympathy for his tragic figure, so Léon's family could be spared the blighting effects of war.

He stopped, looked from Gertrud to Leni, then down his abject person and at the congregation who avoided his gaze, or turned away, or smiled tentatively, or inquisitively, dressed in clothes that seemed cleaner than Léon remembered, newer and brighter, as though a new era had made its small mark, even in arch-conservative Ösel, and he started to laugh, he kept chuckling all the way through the service and what was more he embarrassed Gertrud by sitting at the front with the women.

He was still laughing on the way home, but this time he was met by his sister's fury, although it wasn't his stupid laughter she berated him for.

"What do you think we actually live off?" she railed.

This caught him by surprise. He answered:

"I don't know, but it must be something."

"Oh, yes, it must be something," Gertrud retorted, stomping up to her room while Léon continued to chuckle and Leni sent him grave looks.

"That was the worst Mass I've ever attended in my whole life," he said irritably, and went to bed.

After that he didn't go to church until he met a German priest whose parish was in the village of Rodershausen a bit further to the west and who had a similar history to his own, either something to hide or something to forget, in other words, probably both. But he continued to chuckle and when the time for him to go away on one of his trips was approaching and he dropped a hint about travelling expenses, Gertrud once again brought up the subject of their parlous finances, their "unnecessary poverty", he should put his brains to some use, earn them some money instead of taking off on mysterious expeditions and otherwise wasting his time – where was he going by the way?

"Nowhere," Léon said, with respect to these short meetings he had with four ex-conscripts, among them Benjamin, who sobbed every time he saw him and always gave him money which he earned from a garage he had established on the outskirts of the capital, because Benjamin did not want to return to Ösel, he also employed two of his old comrades. "I'll do everything you ask." Léon smiled to his sister. "As long as you give me the money. We can call it a loan."

She snorted but complied.

While Léon was away this time Agnes reappeared, with a large suitcase, two nicely dressed boys and a spider's web of tiny wrinkles over her still beautiful face. She was on her way to Hosingen, "home", but wanted to stop here in Dorscheid first, where she had spent her "happiest years". Leni gave her an effusive and tearful welcome and produced her exam certificate almost before the embrace was over, while Gertrud was more restrained. But coffee appeared on the table, the boys were allowed to play with the calves and eventually it came out that Agnes was very unhappy living in town, farmer's wife that she was by habit and disposition, and things were not so good between her and the bookkeeper, she had left him, if the truth be told.

"What!"

"Yes," she said quietly, running her hand slowly over her knee.

"Are you divorced?"

". . ."

Gertrud became sharper and sharper while Leni became softer and softer.

It degenerated into a confused mixture of war and peace negotiations, which lasted until after the onset of darkness, which meant that Agnes had to stay the night. She did not move on the following day either, this time because Gertrud said that she may as well do something useful now she was there, at least while Gertrud was working at the hospital in Clervaux. And that turned into another night, because there was a lot to do, and a new day . . . So that when Léon returned, driving up the hill in a little dust-grey Triumph, and spotted Leni in the yard, busy hanging out the washing, he immediately realised that something was afoot – his sister hurried in, and the next moment Gertrud came out, leant against the house and crossed her arms, without gracing the car with a glance.

"Prepare yourself for a shock," she said sourly, going into the house before him.

Agnes had got to her feet and was standing next to their father's old armchair, staring down at her hands, stroking her knee with one, though not too obviously. From the kitchen came the voices of children, the clatter of cutlery and Leni's laughter.

"Hello," Léon said, and the next moment the guest fell to the floor. He rushed forward to help her but was stopped by Gertrud, who poked at the unconscious woman with the tip of her shoe.

"Don't worry. She's just putting it on."

Léon went outside again and round to the back of the house. He thought this might have had something to do with his clothes, but they were the finest travelling apparel there was, even though they had been his father's, and he only wore them once a year. He went for a walk in the woods, taking care not to get his shoes dirty. A summery warmth hung over the country. The sky was a deep blue, dense and unwavering, as though it had come to stay. He walked up the little hill – with a view of Munshausen and the River Clerve and the hills beyond – where he had placed the sundial he had brought with him from Scotland and watched the narrow shadow fall between the numerals 3 and 4, compared it with the time on his new wristwatch, twenty-five to four, and smiled with satisfaction.

Agnes had recovered, and now she was sitting in their father's armchair looking straight at him.

"Hello," Léon said again.

"Hello," she said.

"Stop that nonsense," said Gertrud.

Leni was leaning against the kitchen door eating an apple. Her brother turned and smiled at her. In the kitchen a plate hit the floor.

9

If anyone had been tactless enough to ask the sisters what they thought had changed most about Léon when he came home, they would at first have been embarrassed and have tossed their heads in irritation, but then they would have said that he seemed so much smaller than they remembered him, almost shrivelled, the way a childhood home seems shockingly small when you return after a longish stay abroad, and Gertrud might have added that he had shrunk in many other ways as well, without being able to define precisely what she meant, except that it was something he could rectify but had no wish to, a form of contrariness. While Leni would not have dared to say that in so many words, and maybe she didn't agree, either. As for Agnes, she wouldn't have answered the question at all, for Léon was not the only man to fight the war on the wrong side in his own country and later be imprisoned by his allies.

After Agnes had been on the farm for three weeks, walking on eggshells, like a timid slave of her former ward, Gertrud, who had never taken a wrong turn in the labyrinths of life, one evening during a conversation over a few too many glasses of wine it slipped out that Agnes had not in fact been divorced by the bookkeeper, he was dead, he had died in a train accident, which they may have read about in the newspaper, this spring . . . and he wasn't insured.

You could have heard a pin drop.

"So you didn't come back because you missed us," Gertrud said, the truth slowly dawning on her, "but because you *needed* us, once again. You have betrayed us not once but twice!"

"Everyone's done something stupid at some time in their lives," Agnes began to explain, but she was rudely interrupted.

"Everyone *else*, yes! The country's full of traitors, but in this house there are none! There never has been and there never will be!"

Léon said nothing.

Agnes made no move to go. And nobody tried to chase her away, either, she fitted in, without fitting in, like Léon, now and then she had to suffer some snide comments but otherwise she worked like a horse to free the farm from the shadow of the war. And she retained her beauty and did her utmost to ensure that her sons did not cause trouble, while adapting to the invisible rules of the house, month after month, until the new roles were so set and ingrained and well-oiled that not even a new war would have been able to dislodge them, for if there is a limit to how far a human being can carry their own cross, then Agnes was not aware of it, she had suffered such pain, now she was home again.

The Baker's Two Lives

Markus told a story. It was about one of five brothers from the East Cantons of Belgium who were all conscripted into the Wehrmacht and sent to more or less exposed posts on the Eastern Front: one ended up in Romania, one in Poland, one in the Sixth Army, one in Hollidt's Army Detachment in the Don Basin, while the last of them was lucky enough to be deployed as a quartermaster in Kharkov. Only two of them survived, the youngest and the next-youngest, the Sixth Army conscript and the quartermaster. In the post-war years they and their wives both had as many children as it is God's wish to bestow upon a good Catholic family: four and six. Their parents also had many siblings, who in turn had children, who eventually married and produced grandchildren, and all these people lived in and around the same small village in the German–French-speaking part of Belgium, close to the Luxembourg border.

But none of them ever asked the two war veterans about their experiences during the great martyrdom, and the brothers were in no hurry to tell them, either. The war was not talked about in this family, the memories were too complex, people had been on the wrong side, whether pressure had been put on them or not, and furthermore they looked upon the Germans with the same deep, engrained mistrust as they looked upon those of their fellow countrymen who had boycotted the Wehrmacht or deserted – as cowards and traitors who were not willing to share their forced burden, suffering or that strange schizophrenia of theirs with their closest neighbours; silence alone could deal with history in a decent manner.

The youngest of the brothers was a baker. In 1968 his elder brother died of cancer and in the summer, five years later, one of the baker's nieces, who studied in Paris, came home on holiday with a Frenchman in tow; they were going to get married as soon as the opportunity arose, straight after her finals presumably, to judge by the looks she sent him.

That summer, as usual, there were some family events to celebrate, a baptism or a wedding or an important birthday, and at some point during this warm black Ardennes night, which they spent in the garden, as tradition prescribed, the niece introduced the baker to her French boyfriend, and the boyfriend to the baker, and announced that her fiancé was a historian and in the midst of a thesis on the war in the Soviet Union.

"Interesting," the baker said with a nod, slightly flattered.

Then his niece asked:

"Do you remember where you were, Uncle?"

He looked at her, perplexed.

"*Remember* – what do you mean?"

Apart from his own six children, she was the one of his brother's children he appreciated most, not least because she was his godchild. Then she repeated the words which were to change his life:

"Do you *remember* where you were?"

"I was in the *Sixth Army*, my dear!' he said, dumbfounded. "Of course I remember!'

But saying this, he realised that the term didn't mean anything to her at all, that neither she nor anyone else in the family, including his wife and children, had any idea what the Sixth Army was, and that this silence which by tacit collective agreement had shrouded these matters for decades did not conceal knowledge of something painful and unmanageable but rather total ignorance. Not even when the Frenchman showed his bewilderment and awe at standing face to face with a living miracle did the niece realise what she had said.

This made such a strong impression on the baker that he decided on the spot to relive the second half of his life. And once again he came home from Russia with head injuries, but this time he didn't go for long walks beneath the beeches to summon up the courage to hand over a letter he carried, he went straight to his parents with the news he had received on the train between Dnipropetrovsk and Kiev, the report that his third brother had fallen too, on the Upper Don, he had lost a leg and both arms, but had lived long enough to be able to dictate a letter to the army chaplain Arno Kumbel – here it is.

After that he served for two years in Normandy, deserted during the

Ardennes offensive, and spent a couple of years in an English P.O.W. camp, as he had done in his first life. Then he returned home and resumed his old profession, he baked bread and *Fladenbrot* and *Schwarzwälderkirschtorte* and in the weeks before Christmas sculpted lovely marzipan figures and in addition contributed to every special occasion with culinary *tours de force* which took the family's breath away. But now he didn't hold back over the war. As soon as anybody asked how he was, he told them the truth, that he still heard the sound of tanks in broad daylight and had the Katyusha rocket launchers' orange-red flashes stamped on his retinas as soon as he closed his eyes and tried to sleep. He told them that he, a rank-and-file soldier, had happened to be in the General Command of the Sixth Army and had seen a tactical map on one of the tables and that on it the south-eastern front resembled a funnel, that the Sixth Army was positioned inside that funnel, in the spout, so to speak, and he had immediately realised that this was not going to end well, the Russians only had to cut off the "spout" and the whole army would be enclosed, and that is what he had told his comrades when he went back to his unit, "We're trapped in a funnel," he had said, "We are doomed," but then the commanding officer had accused him of subversive activity – "You could never trust Belgians" – "It's not subversive activity," he said, and it was only thanks to the fact that we were engaged in battle night and day that I escaped with a reprimand . . .

He repeated this whenever anyone asked, plus a whole load of other things, occasionally even when no-one asked, he told his children and nephews and nieces what he had experienced, at birthday parties and weddings and communion gatherings and Christmas celebrations, about how and where his brothers were killed, what he thought about the old and the new Germany, and he also got his elder brother to break his silence, and when he, the brother, died in 1968 and the baker was the sole survivor, he began to look forward to the day when his favourite niece and godchild would come home on holiday with a French historian who would listen to his story about the Sixth Army and use it in a thesis written at the prestigious Sorbonne.

But when the day came he couldn't see the Frenchman anywhere and, after imbibing some Dutch courage, he approached his niece and asked her straight out: "Where's your Frenchman?" "Which Frenchman?" she asked. "The one you're marrying," the baker said. "The one who's so interested in the fate of the Sixth Army?" "I would never consider marrying anyone who's so obsessed with the war, Uncle. Surely you can understand that," she said, kissing him on the cheek.

There and then the baker decided to stick to his first life after all. And the day after the summer family gathering he went over to see his niece and the Frenchman, who were staying with her mother, his brother's widow, and they received him warmly, the niece both relieved and ashamed, for by now the Frenchman had made her aware of her ignorance: "I'm so sorry, Uncle," she said. "How could I say something so stupid? Pierre says you're heaven-sent . . ."

"Yes, you see . . ." the baker said after sitting down and being served a bottle of Diekirch, for although he was Belgian and proud of it he preferred Luxembourg beer, "we were trapped in a funnel . . ."

The Feldmarschall's Conscience

I

All time machines go backwards, for man has more memories than visions, more habits than foresight, Markus maintains, so whenever he casts his mind hither or thither, the choice is simple, it has to stop somewhere between eleven and half past eleven on the evening of 27 November, 1942, in the sleepy rat trap of a town called Novocherkassk to the south of the Don Basin, a focal point he comes back to again and again, only to get the same answer to his two burning questions; now he will soon be in conversation with Feldmarschall Erich von Manstein, which will turn his already devastated life upside down.

Markus Hebel, an amateur inventor and technical genius, whom the Wehrmacht valued and decorated but didn't promote, had arrived from Rostov on November 21 with the very best of intentions, that is, with four railway carriages brimful of communications equipment and strict orders to set up, double quick, an H.Q. for the General Staff of the newly established Army Group Don, a creation Hitler was expecting miracles from, miracles he desperately needed.

The work had been going on day and night, but because of a lack of staff, especially people with technical expertise – who came in dribs and drabs from Rostov, Taganrog and Starobelsk – and an innate reluctance on the part of the head of the Cossack Guard to speak Russian, which would soon change, a series of major and minor problems had arisen that sapped Markus of his energy and good humour. So when at noon on November 26 his people lined up outside the dismal railway station in Novocherkassk to receive the arriving General Staff, he was on the verge of a breakdown, the breakdown which was to last for the rest of his life and influence his thoughts and deeds until the moment God carried him off in one incomprehensible fell swoop.

General Manstein, who only a few months previously had been promoted to Feldmarschall, was the first to step out into the blinding snowstorm and down the semi-rotten wooden slats which the frost had turned into icy concrete slabs and, unruffled by the howling weather, he immediately took stock of the place with his imposing presence. He was wearing battledress with burgundy General Staff stripes down the legs of his trousers and bore the Crimea Shield medal like a twinkling star on his right breast pocket, the most illustrious of all the General's honours. The second-in-command, Oberst Busse, came close on his heels; this was the man who was to follow Manstein like a supportive shadow through the entire hell on earth which awaited them, and also sacrifice years of his life after the war defending his superior officer against the charges levelled at him, crimes against humanity.

Next to emerge was the Chief of Staff, General Schulz, with Markus' new superior officer, A.D.C. Oberstleutnant Stahlberg, behind him Oberst Eismann, the Head of Intelligence, and the usual procession of technical and military experts who are part of any well-oiled war machine – radio operators and signallers, engineers and drivers, cooks and skivvies – there was even a company of joiners amongst them, which showed some foresight, to patch up the lamentable buildings in Novocherkassk.

Markus had seen Manstein several times before, he had also talked to him, very briefly, during the Kerch campaign earlier the same year, and it was with considerable relief that he had received the news that the General would now be taking over command of the Eastern Front, the most traumatic of them all, for once you have been forced into the service of this barbarism, you prefer, naturally enough, to carry out your duties in relatively civilised ways and especially under a High Command which had the greatest chance of getting you out alive.

Markus spent the afternoon convincing his new commander, Stahlberg, that the work on the technical installations at H.Q. was on schedule, and the Oberstleutnant expressed his satisfaction, was encouraging and friendly in his own punctilious way, and all that remains to be said is that Markus was given orders to report to the General personally, he got up and dutifully went over to the map room which was fitted out how he knew from the Crimea Manstein would want it to be, and found the General there alone, actually an ominous sign, as the General was in the habit of conveying tragic news to his subordinates in private, the death of close members of the family for example, and Markus had not only his Nella and his two daughters at home in Clervaux to worry about but also two brothers in France, not to mention a son somewhere on the Eastern Front, a volunteer, completely against Markus' own wishes and orders, his name was Peter and he was only twenty-one.

Markus greeted him as hesitantly as a raw recruit, and also incorrectly, since of course the General was entitled to be addressed as Feldherr, or Feldmarschall, or Generalfeldmarschall, so he corrected his mistake only for it to be brushed aside with a forbearing gesture.

"*General* will do. Or just Manstein, that's how I sign my name."

Nonetheless this sparse display of joviality still struck a worrying note, Markus reflected, for even though the General was well-known for his biting sense of humour, his refined streak of self-irony and a not insignificant touch of sentimentality (which was mostly used at funerals, remembrances and otherwise on occasions when there could be no doubt about the genuineness of people's feelings, which by the way never clouded his analytical mind), he was not the kind of General to treat matters of etiquette lightly, accept sloppiness or any un-German conduct in his ranks.

Their previous conversation, the only one they had ever had, to be honest, had taken place on the Kerch peninsula, in the eastern Crimea, and had proceeded more or less as follows. With a superhuman effort lasting a whole day, Markus had excelled himself by keeping a running tally of all the positions of every one of the armoured and infantry divisions throughout the whole attack, including details of the enemy's faltering retreat, thereby demonstrating an impressive command of the situation, which the General had taken note of, with the result that when victory was a fact and Kuban lay there like a ripe apple on the other side of the glistening strait, he had, in passing, asked the Leutnant where in the Reich he came from, the General couldn't quite place his dialect.

"I've got two passports, Herr General," Markus had answered.

"I hope by God one of them is German," Manstein said. "Please get rid of the other one."

"That is not within my control, Herr General."

"I'm not talking about official channels, young man. But about what you have inside here."

He nodded towards Markus' uniform and tapped a nicotine-yellow fore-finger on his chest, but did not explain whether he was referring to a visible antipathy towards the National Socialist view of the world or only wanted to urge the Leutnant to overcome the layers of quivering fear which he presumed enveloped him.

"I understand, Herr General."

"Where in all the world do they have such a despicable system that allows people to hold two passports?"

"In the East Cantons of Belgium, Herr General. But I am of German descent. Bad Münstereiffel. The Rhineland."

He didn't mention his marriage to a woman from Luxembourg and his present abode in the same place. And that was that. A trivial exchange of words in the rush of victory, between the Reich's most legendary general and a non-entity without rank, or almost, from a nation without borders and a time that cannot be defined by clocks or calendars or the sun's steady path through eternity. But when they met again, less than six months later, it was natural for the General to take up this thread, if only to show that once he has seen a face he never forgets it, and this became the start of the most important conver-sation in his life, this was how Markus, with closed eyes, presented it to his young friend Robert, his attentive but also extremely critical conversation partner throughout this story, which ought to be of benefit to the material, as Markus is hardly a more credible witness than anyone else; since memory can play tricks on anybody, particularly when events of the nature recounted here are presented. It is 23.30, German time, 26 November, 1942 in the devastated town of Novocherkassk in the Russian Steppes.

"Oh, there you are, Hebel. Have you still got two passports?"

"No, Herr General."

"Good. Only spies have two passports. Don't you agree?"

"No, Herr General."

There was a silence, and Markus saw this abrupt "no" in response to a good-humoured throwaway remark from his superior as a spontaneous flight of fancy, which in the world of reality he would hardly have dared to utter, no matter how exhausted he was, for Markus was no heroic resistance fighter in the wrong uniform, neither in his own nor in anyone else's eyes; he had learned this truth the previous summer when the German troops captured the whole of the Crimea apart from one single town, Sebastapol, "the armoured monster" as Manstein called it, the most formidable garrison on earth, where Fort Inkerman was blown up during the attack by order of the Soviet commanding officer, with the result that thousands of civilians and wounded soldiers who had sought refuge in caverns under the fort (which in more peaceful times served as a storage area for the champagne factories in the Crimea, and now functioned as an ammunition warehouse) were buried under the rubble, before the eyes of the incredulous invading army.

From the start of the campaign Markus had cherished a forlorn hope that an opportunity to desert would present itself, to "go over" to the "enemy" and from there help to put a stop to this German madness, which had also ruined his own country, but that hope vanished here at Inkerman for good, amid swarms of flies and a stench as unbearable as a gas attack. It was here that he changed into a *German* soldier with *one* passport and one heart, to put it bluntly, a resolve which was stiffened when he realised that the Russians' incredible fighting spirit in the Crimea was partly due to Stalin's reluctance to evacuate his decimated armies; only a few high-ranking officers were shipped out at the last minute, while civilians, lower ranks, the wounded, partisans and rank-and-file soldiers were sacrificed, taken prisoner by the Germans or falling victim to a ritualistic suicide instigated by their own officers in the hour of defeat.

With Sebastopol's fall, however, the deafening roar was followed by a strange silence, the whole of the Crimea was in Manstein's (i.e. Hitler's) hands, and a golden, hellenistic peace settled over the peninsula. Markus clambered half-naked over the cliffs near Balaclava, swam in the Black Sea and drank wine with his comrades late into the deep tropical nights which in the summer months caress the Crimea's beautiful south coast. But, with this silence, civilisation returned to him, his ambivalent nationality, if it can be expressed in those terms, although not strongly enough to undermine his resolve to cling to his German identity with a loyalty and readiness for self-sacrifice which shocked him in moments of clarity, but which as a rule he didn't allow himself to dwell on, less and less the further east the campaign went. However, he maintained a streak of his anarchic defiance, a last vesitige of dignity, as he called it, and maybe it was from here that his gruff "no" to the General's light-hearted remark about spies with two passports stemmed, at least that was Robert's view.

"So that's why you've never risen higher through the ranks than your own son," Manstein said with annoyance. "Who is only half your age."

"My son, Herr General?"

"Yes . . ."

The Feldmarschall drew a hand over his face and paused, got up from the chair and stood motionless in front of the map hanging to the left of the black-out curtains, or the "map sketch", where only positions and rivers and infra-structure had been marked in, so no topographical data, which for this section of the front was redundant in any case, it being blessedly flat in all directions. "That's why I summoned you, Hebel," the General continued with his back to him. "To tell you your son is serving in the Sixth Army, on General Paulus' staff. He's fine, from what I gather, with more or less the same function as you have here. In that respect you've definitely had a good influence on him."

Markus felt his backbone straighten and the blood leave the roots of his hair at the very thought of having this information thrown into his face, however true it might be, while his eyes scanned the map upwards, to where the rivers Don and Volga bent towards each other like the tips of two funnels, or two rusty spearheads, or two arthritic knees; the German armies filled the Don knee to the west and the Soviet armies the Volga knee to the east. Paulus' Sixth Army had crossed the Don during the summer near the village of Kalach, on the kneecap, had crossed the flat land between the two rivers and besieged Stalingrad on the west bank of the Volga where the remains of the Soviet forces were still holding out.

The advance was not only very difficult to comprehend, seen through Markus' eyes – even today he asserts he has no idea what Hitler was trying to do in the Volga Basin, even though he is well aware of the official explanations, about the oilfields in the Caucasus, the cornfields in the Ukraine, the water-ways north and south, etc. – it was also fraught with considerable risk, and now the Russians had broken through on both flanks of the German spearhead, which were held by Romanian divisions, and had closed the ring around Paulus. The Sixth Army was encircled! Twenty-two divisions, between 250,000 and 300,000 men, the majority of the German artillery, more than a hundred tanks, 10,000 half-tracks and lorries, 10,000 army horses, engineer units, 600 doctors, planes, trains . . . The Wehrmacht's largest army by far, the one Hitler had plans to conquer heaven and earth with.

It was up to Manstein now to play the role of a modern William of Orange, to open a supply corridor through to Paulus, either from Kalach in the west or from the south, the flat land between the two rivers, where his subordinate Generaloberst Hermann Hoth and his Fourth Panzer Army held their position, while von Richthofen's Luftwaffe supplied the encircled army from the air in the meantime as best it could.

For the time being, no-one talked aloud about the possibility of – as a plan B, if nothing else – securing a controlled retreat for the Sixth Army, over to the west bank of the Don, except for Paulus himself, who had already asked three times to be allowed to break out, only to receive a flat rejection each time from Hitler; Stalingrad had not only tactical but symbolic importance. "All eyes are on Stalingrad," including those of the Allies, since the Russians here had managed to make effective use of the Wehrmacht's own weapon, the armoured pincer movement, and had sown the seeds of hope all over the world that finally it would be possible to put an end to this madness.

". . . In the circumstances," Manstein summed up, "with this in mind, have you got a problem serving here?"

"A problem, Herr General?" Markus stuttered, confused at his concerns being taken so seriously. "What kind of problems were you thinking about?"

The General looked at him with bright, candid eyes.

"We live close to the truth here, Hebel. Does that worry you?"

"No, no, of course not . . ."

"Good. Then you will report to Stahlberg, Oberst Busse or directly to me. Can you write?"

"What do you mean?"

"Well, you have some Russian, I've heard, so I suppose you can write in German, can't you?"

"Of course, Herr General."

"Look at this," Manstein said, holding a dispatch under the glare of the desk lamp.

A letter from the Romanian Supreme Commander, Marshal Antonescu, who launched a scathing attack on the German army leadership, that is on Hitler personally, who had not listened to the countless warnings issued by the Romanians, informing him that the Russians had quietly concentrated huge forces north of the Don, where they had crossed about a week ago, demolished the Romanian Third Army and closed the ring around Paulus.

Antonescu also felt it appropriate to remind them that of all Germany's allies Romania was the most loyal, self-sacrificing and reliable. Now nine of his twenty-two divisions had been crushed, nine put to flight or "missing", while only the remaining four could be termed "still battle fit". This depressing analysis was concluded with a laconic hope that, building on these "ruins", it might be possible to set up a new force.

"I've passed on the criticism to Hitler," Manstein said. "But without comment, even though I share Antonescu's view on all points, as the question of mutual trust between heads of state is a political matter. The Feldmarschall's main concern, however, is relevant to *us* . . ."

He put his finger on the final paragraph: "It is apparent here that some German units, both officers and soldiers, have made disrespectful remarks about the Romanians' performance at the Don and south of Stalingrad. This is not acceptable, even though it is understandable . . . Please remedy this, and look at these notes, they have to be sent to all the General Commands, including Paulus', since he still has two Romanian divisions under his wing . . ."

Markus staggered out into the biting night air, dumbstruck, this was not what he had bargained for, this wasn't why he was here, he needed time, the way every dreamer comes down to earth with the greatest reluctance. But a banal altercation with his superior was after all no great sacrifice, compared with young Peter's fate in the "*Kessel*", the cauldron, the son with whom he had lost an emotional connection when the boy left to study physics in Strasbourg three years ago, after which he had not been home to Clervaux one single time. But he had written letters, evasive and impersonal and platitude-filled letters, so Markus had visited him the autumn afterwards – in 1940 – and in a cramped and shabby room decorated with the new era's regalia he encountered the same evasive attitude that was evident in his letters, the boy who was trying to keep something hidden from his father, it was written all over his face, that awful adolescent mixture of guilt and defiance.

Markus had taken him to a pub and poured schnapps and beer down him and elicited a depressing network of "comrades" and "exercises" and "studies", which he had to take the gloss off if he were to have any hope of winning back his son. In the following months he had sent him pleading and threatening letters, literature of both a religious and humanistic nature, suggested a variety of places where he could emigrate to, England, Switzerland . . . and even dug up a few old medical certificates documenting that the boy suffered from bad eyesight and was unsuitable for military adventures of any kind.

But compared to the magnificent invasion of France, which at that very time was being trumpeted through the propaganda machinery, a lapsed father's circuitous, imploring letters were no more than a creak in the fly-rigging system of a theatre. The last Markus saw of the boy was a photograph he sent his mother just before he went to war and which she – at her son's request – made a half-hearted attempt to conceal from his father but which Markus discovered all the same, and there he was, young Peter, in German uniform, with a decidedly unsure expression of triumph behind the thick lenses of his glasses, my God what a sad sight, this lad who had given Markus such joy, their shared interest in radio transmitters and languages and Catholic saints, especially the Irish St Malachy who on his travels to Rome to learn about continental monastery life had also stopped at Clairvaux where, before his death in 1148, he had related his fantastic life to his friend Bernard, *Vita Malachiae*, the first Latin script Markus had forced his son to plough through – what had he not done to widen the understanding and tolerance in this boy; and then this, his son, dressed in the immaculate uniform of tyranny, so probably it was not inappropriate that he should have the pride beaten out of him in the cauldron, a deep catharsis, together with all the other crackpots on this campaign – and probably on any other – who allowed themselves to be led by the most despicable psychological defect of them all: youthful arrogance!

Markus, the radio technician, got nowhere with writing to all the Commands in defence of the Romanians. After all, what could he write to General-oberst Hermann Hoth, "Papa Hoth", as he was called, the stalwart Commander of the Fourth Panzer Army which had been under continuous fire for months and was at that very moment struggling to keep the Russian "circle" around Paulus' doomed Stalingrad as narrow as possible, in the south? Or to the head of the Army Detachment Hollidt – General de Infanterie Karl Adolf Hollidt – who with inexhaustible gallantry and appalling losses was trying to contain the "circle" in the west?

This was actually Markus' speciality, tolerance and outstretched arms, gentleness; in his youth he'd even had plans to study theology and serve the

Lord, if only that had been compatible with his carnal interest in Nella, whom he met and whose spell he fell under during the Catholic festivities in Trier in the autumn of the great peace in 1918, when he himself and all of Europe crawled out of the gutter with expectations of all that is good: work and peace and starting a family, children being born and baptised and brought up to be well-behaved through example and kindly admonition, since the best qualities, as we know, are passed on while the worst have to be duly forgotten, buried and mourned! But what use was God's wisdom out here in the borderlands, it was enough to make you blush with shame; the fighting at Stalingrad had been going on for three months, more or less continuously, and before that the Sixth Army and the Fourth Panzers had already been in action for three months, a war in the Steppes across six hundred kilometres, this too virtually without a pause, was there even a remote chance that his son could be alive?

Markus pushed Manstein's notes aside, got up and went to the radio room and was enveloped by the hot, sweaty smell of fat Erich Beber, who was leaning back on a folding chair with his headphones hanging round his neck like a rope ladder and his mouth wide open, snoring heavily, his hands hanging on the end of long arms like boiled pig's trotters a centimetre or two above the scrubbed wooden floor. On a divan in one corner half sat, half lay the telegraph and radio operator, Hans Kuntnagel, flicking absent-mindedly through what looked like a bible, both men old front-line comrades of Markus. "Fatty Beber" had been wounded in the Crimea in an embarrassing civilian accident, but not seriously enough to be sent home. Kuntnagel had been with Beber during the Poland campaign, in France and throughout Operation Barbarossa, where Markus got to know him; two ordinary Germans, from Pomerania, a self-taught car mechanic, Kuntnagel, who actually was a farmer and smelt of potatoes and soil to the bitter end, even though he carried around a forlorn dream of being an art historian, with the Italian Renaissance as his area of expertise. And a radio operator, Beber, also a farmer, with few interests other than food and unfunny, vapid jokes. The two of them were inseparable, although Markus had never seen them exchange any signs of friendship.

He made an impatient gesture with his arm, Kuntnagel jumped up and thumped Beber in the chest with the bible. The big man woke up with a snort and both left the room, while Markus sank into the warm chair, perused the latest telegrams and Beber's illegible notes; he had asked Beber to write in capitals but the man could hardly spell and did his utmost to hide it. There were the "cauldron figures", the numbers of Stalingrad casualties, a report by Paulus' General Staff about "enemy activity in the northern part of the cauldron", near the Dzerzhinsky tractor factory, the Red October steelworks, the Barrykady munitions factory . . . the same impregnable bastions, in this city which had housed more than half a million inhabitants when the Luftwaffe embarked on its deadly August offensive, insignificant civilian ants of Markus' modest proportions which the Lord had thrown into the arena between these two new creations of His: Hitler, who wanted "to reach the Volga", and Stalin, who in turn refused to evacuate because "a living town is easier to defend than a dead one".

If his son Peter were sitting at the teleprinter now, in the cauldron, how could he contact him, personally? Markus never found any real answer to this, it was no more than a futile dream, like the carrier pigeons William of Orange sent to Leiden to keep up the population's spirits. He wrote the name of the saint, "Malachy", on a scrap of paper and sat doodling, embellishing the letters, crossing them out and writing them again. The Irish saint whose life story his son had once known inside out – would he understand from the signature "Malachy" that the message came from his father? Or what about his own name, Markus, Mark the Evangelist, who turned back on his first pilgrimage, disillusioned and downcast, and later acted as Peter's interpreter in Rome . . . Or perhaps a tale from his home district would be more likely to strike a chord in his son, Henri le Long and Hervé le Bref? But would his son connect *him*, *his father*, with these names? And if he did, would he really want to know that Markus was here, at the Army Group H.Q., and that his father was stationed at the Command which was now regarded in Stalingrad as its sole hope of salvation.

Markus hesitated.

His vacillation begins here, in this first act of stupidity, in this sick dream, for nothing makes man smaller and more pathetic than war. Nothing makes him greater either, he thought in horror.

2

Markus stumbled out of his austere sleeping quarters at just after six in the morning, having had only a couple of hours' sleep, he couldn't allow himself more if this was to be anything like the reality he was trying to find, out into a new snowstorm, or was it the old one which had set in over the area?

He strode along the icy planks and into the Command H.Q. to present the General with the final written response about the Romanians – and it was approved without any changes. As mentioned, he had turned his back on his Catholic leanings, in favour of the army's usual phrasing: "To maintain troop morale at the front in the south and east and to maintain the bonds of brotherhood that bind our two nations, it is of the utmost importance that no incidents occur between our soldiers and the Romanians, who are fighting on our side for the same high ideals . . ."

The General was in the map room with Oberst Busse, a telegraphist who had arrived the day before, two lower-ranking officers and the cartographer, Jakob Spitz, a man of Markus' age from Berlin, who in the establishment phase of Army Group Don had supplied the place's only civilised entertainment, chess and discussions about the existence of God, perhaps what the Lord must have intended with recent events. Jakob Spitz had red, bristly hair, ruddy cheeks and small, blinking eyes, which were also red, he was a geographer by training, but he had also worked as a railway engineer in the years before the outbreak of war. On one occasion Markus had heard him utter a critical comment about the new Germany's ambitions and expansive plans; it concerned the Luftwaffe's – or more precisely Göring's – claim that it was possible to provide supplies to Paulus' army from the air. Apart from this, Jakob did not complain about the enemy, Hitler, the food or the climate: "We officers live in heaven," he said, "compared with the poor wretches in the field."

The sombre atmosphere of fate and eternity had already settled over the Command like heavy, falling metal dust, the absence of any noise from the terrible things going on only some kilometres north-east of Novocherkassk; nature's eternal voice against the flimsy wooden walls, driving snow and the human pulse, the heartbeat which will quicken from day to day until it finds the rhythm of the battlefield, which Markus knew so well from Kerch and the

Crimea, the stubborn, electrifying buzz which pushes the days forward, one by one, creating a hallucinatory anaesthesia that can be maintained forever.

Jakob Spitz was hanging up a new map-sketch of Paulus' famous "*Kessel*", a cauldron, a red flattened circle between the Don and the Volga, an ellipse, a lopsided jewel, about fifty kilometres from west to east, and forty kilometres from north to south, which gave the impression that the figure was moving, or trying to stretch, westwards, homewards.

To Markus' consternation, the General took the dispatch about the Romanians from him and signed it without reading the contents, whereupon the telegraphist sped off with it. Markus made a move to fall out, but was stopped by Oberst Busse, who handed him a cup of coffee and sent him a faint smile with that broad baby-face of his.

"Did you sleep well, Leutnant?"

"No, Herr Oberst."

"A negative gent, this Hebel," Manstein mumbled with his nose buried in a pile of documents. "Don't let him ruin your mood, Oberst."

"No danger of that."

"What have you got on Hoth here, Hebel?" the General continued, still engrossed in the documents. "His lines, his supplies . . . ?"

"They're open, Herr General, as far as I know," Markus said, keen to display his knowledge, have it approved and if possible also appreciated. "Right down to the Caucasus, he's got his back covered . . ."

"We know that already. But what has he had this last week? It doesn't say anything about that here."

Markus realised that the staff were correlating the information they had received during the night from the Commands in the field with the information that had come in since the Soviet counter-offensive started on November 19. It was not unusual for front lines to report "home" a greater need for supplies than was actually the case, to allow for the time factor and possibly any idiots at Supreme Command.

He walked over to a filing cabinet he'd had put in against one wall and took out the Fourth Panzer Army's transport and supply documents, flicked through them, but gave the whole stack to Busse without comment. The Oberst glanced at the last pages, made a quick calculation and said over his shoulder:

"Fifty-six to sixty per cent? Isn't that on the low side?"

"That's the same figure we got from Finkh last night," Manstein said. "So it is too low . . ."

"These papers are from Finkh too, Herr General," Markus interrupted, uneasy about this discussion of percentages which was intended to lead to a realistic assessment of the strength of Hoth's army; all hope was invested in Hoth here, the line that had to be kept supplied to the hilt if there was to be any chance of breaking the Russian encirclement, history's most barbaric and portentous siege.

"Plus five or ten per cent?" Manstein ventured.

"Given Hoth's confidence in the new army leadership," Markus insisted, "I would not go higher than five, Herr General."

"Is that supposed to be flattery?"

"No, Herr General. It's a mere observation."

Busse whinnied, and Markus was on the point of turning his head in triumph.

"What do we need with Germans, Oberst," the General said drily, "when we've got Belgians?"

"Agreed. Pity there are so few of them. What about settling for sixty-five?"

Manstein nodded and then appeared to forget the whole issue. He got up and stood in front of the map like a Prussian statue. Markus wondered whether this meant he should fall out, but he was still unsure what codes of behaviour the Command had put in place.

"I'll tell Hoth that you're an advocate of the front, Hebel," the General said with his eyes on the map. "He'll appreciate that. From now on, you concentrate on that mystery man, Paulus. Oberst Busse will give you further instructions."

Markus looked in bewilderment from the General to the Oberst, who still had a faint smile on his lips as he nodded benignly towards the door. Markus saluted, turned, looked searchingly at the Oberst once again, who made a gesture for Markus to lead the way out, but they were stopped by Manstein.

"One moment, Hebel. Perhaps you could also update us about Richthofen, since you are better informed than anyone else here?"

Markus turned, thought for a moment, but was then given another nod by Busse and delivered the report which he had learned off by heart and which he has repeated every year since the war and blindness isolated him from the world.

"Richthofen will primarily use the airstrips at Tatsinskaya and Morosovsk for the airlift to Stalingrad, Herr General. Generalmajor Pickert will be in charge of receiving supplies. Of the six strips there only Pitomnik is adequately equipped with lights, a signals system for night flights, snow-clearing facilities, heating devices for the engines and quarters for the wounded . . . Gumrak and Basargino have some of the requirements, but the other three strips can be considered as little more than potato fields, which even the most experienced pilots would shy away from landing fully loaded planes on. The airlift also needs a fighter escort, between ninety and a hundred planes, for now. They will operate from Tatsinskaya and Morosovsk. Generalmajor Viktor Carganico has been given the task of coordinating the whole operation . . ."

Markus drew a measured breath and looked around.

"But . . ." Manstein asked, as if to order.

"I don't know, Herr General . . ."

"Oh yes, you do – out with it!"

Markus savoured the moment even though the ability to foresee the course of events is a poor substitute for being able to do something about it.

"Carganico is a very competent commanding officer, Herr General," he said. "He has also run Tatsinskaya with great skill, but he has never overseen operations on the scale we're talking about here . . . So . . . I would think Richthofen will replace him with someone more experienced in the coming days."

"I see," Manstein chuckled, though sceptical and intrigued.

"So perhaps you could also predict whom Richthofen will choose to replace him?"

"I believe, Herr General, that he will choose Generalleutnant Martin Fiebig, whose work for Hollidt along the Chir Front has already made him a legend. I can't think of anyone better qualified."

All went quiet. Markus looked on with satisfaction as Manstein and Busse exchanged meaningful glances. The only sound there was emanated from the boots of the Chief Intelligence Officer, Eismann, who moved into Markus' field of vision from the left.

"Are you psychic?" he asked.

"No, Herr Oberst," Markus said, prepared for this too. "Fiebig was ordered to Tatsinskaya yesterday, with his whole staff, I assume that was not to have a cup of tea with Richthofen."

Restrained laughter filled the Command H.Q., followed by something that resembled lighthearted but muted relief. Manstein and Busse exchanged glances again, and the latter turned to Markus.

"On our way here we were trying to get an idea of Richthofen's options," he said slowly. "What is your opinion?"

Now Markus struggled to hide his enthusiasm; for good measure he took a piece of paper from his back pocket almost as though he needed something to hide behind.

"I've been working out Richthofen's figures for September and October, Herr General. In the course of these two months he has transported more than 20,000 tons of fuel to the front, 10,000 tons of ammunition, plus 7,000 tons of equipment and supplies. During the same period he has flown more than 27,000 troops for the army as well as shifting 5,000 tons of tank fuel and 2,000 tons of ammunition for them – in addition he has evacuated more than five thousand wounded, a formidable achievement, if I may say so, with the meagre resources he has had at his disposal. But this means that the fleet of planes is run down; the sortie rate for some aircraft is down to 30 per cent. On 9 November – to take an arbitrary example – Transportgeschwader 900 only managed to get twelve out of forty-one Junkers into the air . . ."

"That was a particularly black day," Eismann interrupted coldly.

Markus shot him a quick glance, but continued undaunted:

"Let's look at the sorties which have made it to Stalingrad since the circle was closed. On November 25 it was only possible to land thirty Junkers in the cauldron, carrying seventy-five tons, and that was ammunition and fuel. Paulus has agreed to allow the horses to be eaten, for as long as they last, but in time provisions will take up more of the load, and I would remind you that he needs at least 170 tons of ammunition per day alone. The following day, the 26th . . ."

"Erm . . . Hebel," Manstein interrupted. "I presume all this is leading some-where?"

Markus drew a breath and continued.

"Paulus needs 300 tons of supplies every day, just to stay alive. If the army is to be mobile and operative it must have at least 550. To fly in the 300 tons requires 150 fully loaded Junkers – daily, provided that the planes can be flown every day, which of course they can't, the weather will no doubt be just as much a problem as the Russian air force. From 'Tatsi' and Morosovsk it is 230 and

200 kilometres respectively to the cauldron. Unloading and loading take time, even though Pickert, in Pitomnik alone, has between one and two thousand men working non-stop unloading supplies and clearing the snow. It takes a good hour to turn a plane round, but the ground staff there are already more than overworked, they don't have enough to eat, they can't sleep, so this figure will rise. That means that every plane can make one, maximum two, sorties per day. Thus Richthofen needs at least 800 planes to cover the minimum needs while the whole of the Luftwaffe has only 750 Junkers in service at the moment. Of these, half are in Africa, so the bottom line is that we only have 295 planes available here, of which nowhere near all are operative . . . That is what we have at our disposal, Herr General, to keep Stalingrad alive."

Markus paused, made as if to continue, but instead bowed his head in regal submission vis-à-vis the harsh historical realities, which anyone will now be able to appreciate the full implications of.

"So the answer is no?" Manstein said after a few seconds' silence. "That's what you're saying – it is not possible to supply the army from the air in your opinion?"

Markus sent Jakob Spitz a glance, an appeal almost, this was the cartographer's opinion just as much as his own, but Jakob just looked gravely down at his polished boots without giving so much as the slightest hint of what he thought or knew.

"I'm convinced, Herr General," Markus said slowly, "that von Richthofen has drawn the correct conclusions and communicated them to Göring, Jeschonnek, Hitler . . . and that the Führer will do what has to be done."

"So that's your considered opinion, is it?" Manstein mumbled acidly and turned away. "Alright, you may fall out."

3

Markus felt the sweat on his body freeze. The wretched weather which had prevented the General Staff from taking off by plane brought new, sooty-grey blankets of snow across the Steppes, and there was hardly any daylight to speak of, the horizon was flat and near.

"What was that supposed to mean?" he suddenly heard behind him, like an echo of his own thoughts, and saw Jakob Spitz running towards him, obviously annoyed. "The last thing Manstein needs is all and sundry telling him that the airlift cannot succeed. What we need now is—"

"Oh yes, he does," Markus broke in. "That's exactly what he needs to hear, from all sides, so that he can order Paulus to break out at once!"

He noticed that his pulse was still racing. "Had it not been for that numbskull Hitler," he shouted without restraint, "the army would have been moving west long ago, and as for Göring, do you know what he's been doing these last few days? He's been in Paris, the head of the Luftwaffe has been in Paris to get his paws on works of art while Richthofen and his men have been running themselves into the ground to save what's left of . . . No, forget it." He threw his hands in the air while the cartographer heaved a perplexed sigh and ran a freckled hand through his hair, which shone like a flame in the snowy terrain.

"What's got into the Russians?" he groaned. "It's as if they've been transformed . . ."

"Yes," Markus said. "You may as well take note of the names now: Rokossovsky, Zhukov, Vasilevsky, Yermakov . . . Before you know it they will be banging on our doors in Berlin!"

"My God – you *are* psychic!"

"No, I can see the light, and you ought to be able to, as well. Even a child can see where this is going . . ."

He was interrupted by Oberst Busse stepping out of the H.Q. and walking with his back bent double through the gusting wind. Markus turned his back on the cartographer and signalled the Cossack guarding the canteen door to open up, and as the steam belched out into the cold like singed cotton wool, a whole new question began to preoccupy him: the General must have had something in mind when he told him about his son, some other motive than to confirm that this stray Belgian would give his all to save the Sixth Army, for Manstein didn't take decisions on impulse, and hadn't he himself just lost a son, somewhere near Leningrad? Could his pretty inappropriate information about Peter being in the cauldron be understood as an attempt to create an alliance of suffering between two anguished fathers, a spiritual communion between men who look on as their own flesh and blood are systematically slaughtered, and are themselves to blame? For one tiny moment Markus thought he caught a glimpse of eternity, but as usual this quickly dissipated into hallucinations, there are limits to what you can allow, even in your mind, a thought is not like a sturdy beech tree in the Ardennes, it is not a piece of fertile ground that can be ploughed and cultivated, a starry sky that can be charted and furnished with Greek names and myths; thoughts can handle love and bringing up children, letters of the alphabet and tales and melodies, but they muddle up everything else, thoughts are not clear even though there can be no doubt that this canteen really exists and that it is installed in the only school in the village and that Markus lets the Oberst go in first, to the smell of wet straw, diesel fumes and raw tobacco, nor that the wooden desks are stacked at the back of the room and tables seating six are placed along the outer walls while the dais – on which presumably a teacher's desk used to stand – serves as a buffet table, with cutlery and a washing-up bowl, soap and a dirty tea towel, a tin plate piled with *Schwarzbrot*, a hotplate and a half-full pot of soup, and, my word, there is an apple there, a shiny red eye in a dark night, the Oberst spots it at once, he grabs it and sinks his teeth into it without a moment's hesitation, while Markus stares aghast, unable to decide whether he is witnessing a miracle or a crime.

"I assume we can talk openly with you, Hebel," Busse said to Markus, who could not take his weary eyes off the yellow molars crunching and grinding the juicy flesh.

"Of course, Herr Oberst . . ."

"Let's sit down. Have you eaten?"

"Yes . . ."

"You have a line through to Stalingrad, I understand . . . ?"

This was said before they sat down.

"To that mystery man, Paulus," Markus ventured, now more focused. He felt that the Oberst was eyeing him in an almost shifty fashion; he finished chewing the apple and placed the stalk carefully on the windowsill, again to Markus' astonishment, this time that it was possible to end such a sacred repast with the same casual expression as he started it.

"Although you've been holding the fort here for almost a week," the Oberst said, "we're still not sure what kind of general impression you have formed of the situation. To begin with, I will give you a quick update. Is that O.K.?"

Markus looked at him wide-eyed.

"Is what O.K.?"

"Officially the Sixth Army is under our command, but in practice this is not the case as long as Paulus is at Hitler's beck and call. They're in touch by radio, they listen to one another, but we have only this teleprinter. Hitler and Göring also have control of the airlift. So we can't actually *tell* Paulus what to do as we would have done in a better world, if you see what I mean . . . ?"

Markus nodded. "But hopefully we can help him," the Oberst went on, "by opening a corridor into Stalingrad. Zeitzler has agreed to this in principle and has also promised us two new panzer divisions, as well as an artillery division."

The Oberst drew breath, and Markus thought he heard a sigh. He knew that people everywhere in the field had high hopes of this Zeitzler, who earlier that autumn had taken over as Generalstabschef at Hitler's headquarters and who was thought to be well equipped to influence the Führer with regard to transferring a greater share of the operational responsibility to those who were actually there at the front.

"Where was Zeitzler – or Hitler for that matter – going to get these reinforcements from?" Markus deemed it permissible to ask, for as far as he knew there was a crying shortage of most things on all fronts and also at home in the Reich.

"From Army Group A in the Caucasus or from Elista," Oberst Busse said. "Furthermore, in a few days' time we're getting a division from France. But to get back to Paulus, before we left Vitebsk, Manstein sent strict orders that Paulus should focus his firepower on Kalach and the Don in the west, to cover his back . . ."

"Really?"

"From the positions we were given last night it looks as if he has done the opposite, focused more firepower on the town centre, thus leaving his back open. We don't even know whether he received the order."

This time Markus' jaw dropped. The Oberst continued:

"On the 22nd or the 23rd of November Paulus asked Hitler a second time for permission to break out. This was without doubt a psychological mistake. Paulus has served in the headquarters, knows Hitler personally and knew what the answer would be. On top of that, thirty-six hours passed between him sending the request and receiving a reply. In other words, Paulus had thirty-six whole hours to take on the responsibility himself – as operational commander

– to break out with his army and present Hitler with a fait accompli. Do you understand?"

"Yes . . . er . . . no."

"When Hitler's 'no' came, it was too late. By that time it would have cost Paulus his head to start a retreat although we doubt whether it was that that worried him, nor would it have been much of a price to save a whole army."

At long last Markus saw what he was getting at.

"He doesn't *want* to break out?" he said, dumbfounded.

Busse smiled weakly.

"That's not what we're saying. But the truth is that we don't know Paulus, we don't know how he thinks, nor what he is capable of."

He paused, directed his eyes on the area around Markus' palpitating heart and then slowly raised them until they exploded in his face like shells as he said:

" 'Alethe's white dog' . . . what's that?"

The question was posed in an open, almost cheerful manner, like the rest of the monologue, but Markus felt the blood draining from him, wave by wave, he was filled with shame and fear, gasped, and in his own words looked as if he were having an epileptic fit. He also claims this was the first time he had felt his eyesight fail him.

"An old game," he mumbled. "I was trying to send my son a sign last night, or find out if he's there. *I have to know if he is there!*"

He stood up, then slumped back down. "So I signed off with something only he and I know about, a legend about Bernard de Clairvaux, hoping that he would respond, but he didn't . . ."

"And what was special about this Bernard?"

"Just something I kept going on about, the way fathers do . . . Is *that* why I'm here?" he said suddenly.

"That's why we're all here."

"You want me to ask my son to go behind Paulus' back, his commanding officer, is that what you mean!?"

"Well, the phrasing is not very apposite, Hebel. I think . . ."

"But that's what you mean?" Markus persisted. "You want him to go behind his superior officer's back, inform us about Paulus' real intentions, about his inner soul and what's going on in his head, spy on him in fact!?"

The Oberst went silent and eyed him with the same unwavering patience.

"Are you a volunteer?" he asked doggedly, and Markus was unable to come up with any other answer than that he was there body and soul, at which Busse sighed and said with measured, clockwork-like composure: "There are more than 250,000 men in the cauldron. Our men. They've been fighting more or less non-stop since the spring. Their suffering is already indescribable. Winter is approaching. We know what that means and . . ."

"But I'm not *thinking* clearly," Markus exclaimed. "He's my *son*. Why did you and the General tell me he's there? Of course, you had to, I can see that . . . but if the boy is alive and he fails, I'm sending him straight to his death, me, his own father, there was a summary trial only yesterday, three soldiers were shot because they lost their minds and three others because they had deliberately injured themselves in order to be flown out. Paulus shoots his own when he has to! I can't do it! My son is a naive simpleton, can't you understand that? He would never be able to pull something like this off. He's afraid of authority and also believes in this . . . this . . ."

He was on the verge of saying "Nazi idiocy", but chose instead "vision". . .

"We all do," the Oberst said with a sardonic smile and Markus said: "Very true!"

He is on the ropes now. "Very true!" he repeated, but what he failed to add was that what he now saw as an inalienable truth was that it was not allegiance to Hitler and his madhouse that made all this possible but the soldiers' fundamental and admirable allegiance to *each other*, the same human noble-mindedness and loyalty that hold a civilised society together, keep it at peace and well-functioning – the same ideals that underpin war underpin peace, keep it going, at least once it has started, indeed perhaps they even start it, what do I know? . . . "And I can't accept it . . ."

"But now you're the one clinging to the flag, Markus – not Busse and Manstein."

"What?"

"They want Peter to be a traitor if I understand you correctly!"

Markus' jaw fell and he began to laugh nervously. But after listening to his internal dialogue about the ambivalent nature of loyalty, which had troubled the famous three hundred Spartans at Thermopylae and which has presumably been a continuing depressing theme in every single military analysis since, he suddenly began to wonder who was leading this discussion.

The Oberst got up and went into the mess, but only a few minutes later he was back, with two yellowing porcelain cups and a pot of coffee, then went on as though nothing had happened.

"I can refuse!" Markus burst out. "You can kill me, it doesn't matter, I have no life anyway, at least then I wouldn't be leading my own son to his death!"

He had stood up again, in a desperate attempt to keep his protest alive, partly also to test the Oberst's patience, he now maintains, although it is more likely that he didn't know what he was saying, nor why he was doing it. "That makes it easy for you now!" he shouted, repeating the words several times while his superior officer calmly waited for the powder to burn out and his victim was squarely put into his place by his own inadequacy.

"People like you have always have had it easy," Oberst Busse said quietly. "You observe everything from a distance. You have more information and less fear than we who are in the midst of it. You have no responsibility and no decisions to make. But this is not a court case, Hebel, nor any judgement. Who do you think Hoth is fighting for? He's fighting for his life and his men's, that's what it's all about!"

Markus slumped onto his chair.

"Yes," he mumbled, resigned, almost happy, at finally having got to the heart of the matter. "It's as easy as that."

Markus delivered the lines of this conversation with closed eyes and the gestures and voice of an agitated actor or a spirit medium from the battlefield. But as soon as the Oberst had left him the silence hit him again with full force, like after an unusually demanding performance, while he breathed in the canteen air that stank of cabbage and soot, which closed the circle around a defeated man, the "*Panzerruhe*", the calm which he dubbed his own form of coma, the counterpart to Generaloberst Heinz Guderian's "*Panzerschreck*", which described the state of shock that struck the enemies of the Third Reich as soon as they heard these machines from hell.

But the problem is – as already indicated – that Markus is not necessarily a reliable eyewitness, no more reliable than Father Rampart reporting sins that any believer knows the Vatican could never have committed, not in this life at any rate, and was this high-ranking Wehrmacht officer really sitting here and asking this nonentity of a Belgian amateur inventor and radio operator to spy on another Wehrmacht officer, a general, in God's own army, the Sixth? Believe that if you will. Isn't it far more likely that the nonentity's wandering mind and lack of logic are pulling the wool over his eyes, that he has a modest yet megalomaniacal wish to have a role in history, to steal a trick or two from history to prevent it from repeating its most despicable acts – the way a historian or an Enlightenment philosopher views the past? Or perhaps it is just his very normal desire to save a son without ever knowing clearly how that kind of miracle can be performed. Miracles, as we all know, take a little longer.

The rest of Markus' stay in Novocherkassk is, however, of a far more sober character. War changes you! as he himself says, like the valiant soldier he is. Not perhaps from a Dr Jekyll to a Mr Hyde, but it is certainly Jekyll who is sent home on leave, that is certain and indisputable, home to Clervaux where all his three children are playing beneath the beeches in the farmyard, it would be dishonest of me not to admit this, and yet who is the real you in all the fragments that are floating around in your memory? Fragments moreover that have been smashed to pieces by a war – answer me that, young man!

4

On November 28 Markus sent one message after another to the cauldron, furnished with a range of unmistakable references to the "white dog" – the animal which St Bernard's mother had seen so vividly in her dreams just before her son's arrival on earth and which she immediately took as a sign of his sanctity – but without receiving what he had hoped for: an answer.

Reports were coming in that the Russian armies in the southern part of the encirclement had launched a new offensive on Stalingrad, using tanks, artillery, flak and "Stalin's organs" or Katyushas, which is what they called these fearful weapons of theirs. And a little later Markus picked up a report Paulus had sent to Manstein on the 26th, in which the trapped General underlined the need for him to be "free to make his own decisions – in the worst-case scenario", which Markus could only interpret as a *wish* for an opportunity and an order to break out, if not from Hitler then at least from Manstein, his immediate superior, it was nothing less than a cry from the heart.

The answer was unfortunately not very encouraging, in the eyes of Markus and presumably those of several hundred thousand other soldiers, since Manstein wrote that any attempt to break out at the present time would only drain the Sixth Army's resources, especially their reserves of fuel, and without tanks they wouldn't get anywhere. Any such attempt would have to *wait*, the Feldmarschall pronounced, until Hoth's Fourth Panzer Army had received reinforcements and could then advance towards Paulus from the south – it could take five to ten days – but preparations for a breakout could be made.

Markus appended his ridiculous Catholic codes to this message as well – but five to ten days! – what an eternity that is on the battlefield; he knew that part of the reason for Göring's (and Hitler's) blind faith in the divine powers of the Luftwaffe stemmed from a dramatic event the previous winter, at Demyansk, south of Lake Ilmen, where the Luftwaffe actually managed to supply a trapped army of 120,000 men for four whole months until reinforcements in the spring broke through the "ring" and rescued their exhausted comrades. Stalingrad was, in other words, nothing new, neither in this nor in any other war; in addition, the commanding officer in the Demyansk pocket, General Karl Strecker, now serving under Paulus, was trapped for a second time. Hitler probably saw the experience factor in this ironic fate as an advantage, and Markus could well have done so too, had it not been for the fact that the difference between Demyansk and Stalingrad was somewhere in the region of 150,000 men, besides it having been an *annus horribilis* since then for both the Luftwaffe and the army, while the "enemy" was increasingly assuming the form of a Hydra; the relative strengths of the two armies was probably now 1:3 or 4 in the Russians' favour; moreover Stalingrad dangled at the end of a 2,000-kilometre supply line, thin as a silk thread, far into the world Hitler called Asia. It was pure fantasy, but also the re-enactment of previous blunders: *Victrices copias alium laturus in orbem*, which Markus is wont to chant in a hallowed voice in conversation with his young friend Robert at around this point in the story, the slogan that Charles XII of Sweden bandied around over two hundred years ago when he launched his army against the same vast Steppes: "Ready to lead his victorious troops into a new universe". Has anyone ever won a war? Let alone a war they started themselves and had been waging for some time. It is not at all difficult to point to losers, but show me the proof of a victor.

It was midnight, Markus could walk outside and listen to doomsday and let the cold wake him up under the same sky that covers him at home, God's vast eye of black marble, and he felt calm inside, snow or white ash was falling and history stopped for a moment, it was resting, and he could breathe but not with a feeling of ease, as in the Ardennes forests, his lungs hurt, he grew smaller and smaller, yet was still visible to this vast eye which can lend lustre to even a grain of sand, but he cannot stay here, and once back inside Kuntnagel met him with an earthly grin and an oblique reference to new hard facts.

"You were right."

"About what?"

Markus was handed a telegram, and sure enough, Richthofen had replaced Carganico with Fiebig as the Chief of Operations for the airlifts to Stalingrad.

"How do *you* know I said that?" he asked him suspiciously.

"Jakob told me about your speech," Kuntnagel said. "We do discuss things here, you know. From now on we'll come to you for new predictions and new miracles when things get tough."

Markus forced a smile through his embarrassment and was about to make the point that the art of reading the future was based on little more than a knowledge of the past and all that was needed was an understanding of the customs and traditions ingrained in people, the woeful repetitiveness of human behaviour, which we have just discussed. And then he considered going one step further and revealing that he probably wasn't here but situated some way into the future with all the answers, only he wasn't happy with them and for that reason had returned to the scene of action, to witness everything with sharpened senses and – as mentioned previously, but this can hardly be repeated too often – to search out faults and weaknesses with the intention of putting an end to further recurrences; that he did this like an Enlightenment philosopher, more by leaning than conviction, or rather as a consequence of fate, that was how he lived, both ahead of and after his own time, and don't we all do this, don't we wade around in a turbulent sea of visions and memory, with the present as the most fragile of all the vessels sailing on it, don't we believe that once one mistake has been made that we take care not to repeat it? Possibly, but those are the mistakes we are aware of and security resides in the familiar, in peace and calm; and events don't replicate each other, as we know, they resemble each other, that is the straw we cling to, the small variations between each occurrence; and then Oberst Eismann called him before his thoughts could distil into some kind of clarity and sent him to the airstrip – into reality – to receive a plane from Stalingrad, an envoy from Paulus.

The ground staff had been working around the clock to keep the runway clear of snow, but it was still falling heavily and you couldn't see a thing. They heard the drone of a plane between the blasts of wind and the marshaller wandered along the runway lights before disappearing completely into what resembled a white roar, only to come running out again at top speed in front of a taxiing Junker, guiding it in like a dog, in the snow-swept gleam from the floodlights near the makeshift hangar.

Markus drew a deep breath and braced himself, knowing full well what awaited him, the same as last time, and as usual there was no escape: the plane was carrying twenty-six wounded and a doctor, twenty-six silent gazes searching patiently for something other than the stark face of death as the doors opened down into the swirling powder snow. He could have tried to strike up a conversation with the pilot to avoid the imploring glances, but the Leutnant, a man by the name of Kemmer (which Robert, when he hears Markus recalling this, doesn't think is genuine, but that is his affair), was not amenable to approaches or chit-chat, just stared blackly into space as they ran shoulder-to-shoulder into the Command H.Q. while the doctor went about organising transport for the wounded.

Markus wanted to leave, but Busse asked him to stay to take notes, and once again this was all about the state of supplies and provisions in Stalingrad: the Sixth Army had – according to Kemmer, who debriefed in terse Eastern Front manner – provisions and medicine for twelve days, rations had already been pared to the bone, and as for ammunition they had only 10 to 20 per cent, sufficient for one day's fighting! While the fuel was enough to carry out only short manoeuvres and nowhere near adequate to break through the Russian lines – from Paulus' southernmost positions to Hoth's northernmost ones near the village of Kotelnikovo it was 120 kilometres, a bleak and naked expanse of land packed with Russian fortifications which no doubt were becoming more and more entrenched and better equipped and manned by the hour.

At this point Markus fell asleep, or he fainted, left this world, but as mentioned there was no escape, so he was woken again only a few minutes later by the sound of raised voices. Kemmer had left for the Cossacks' quarters to get a few hours' sleep and Manstein was complaining about the figures: How could Paulus, only four days ago – *so ill-equipped* – report that he wished to attempt to break out?!

Markus fell asleep again and was woken once more by the sound of voices, this time even louder, and realised that Manstein had been discussing the idea of going back to the cauldron with Kemmer the next morning to see with his own eyes how things stood, while the staff were doing their best to dissuade him; a Feldherr can't just abandon the command of *a whole Army Group* and fly into an isolated battle zone, no matter how imperative this might be for his encircled army.

This argument was brusquely brushed aside, as it was an indispensable element of the Feldmarschall's command philosophy to analyse the battlefield at first hand, it was his personal knowledge of every single tiny unit that had enabled them to taste the fruits of victory at Sebastopol, which had prepared the ground for the incredible breakthrough at Perekop and the equally miraculous storming of Kerch – to name but a few successful operations courtesy of the undersigned.

The others nodded patiently at all this, but then Busse again brought up the weather factor: the "Feldherr", as they called him now, risked becoming trapped in the cauldron for two, three, maybe four days with no other contact with his staff than this wretched teleprinter. And at length Manstein began to waver, again and again he ran his powerful horseman's hands over his well-groomed hair while his eyes sought support from the shadowy rafters. Chief of Staff Schulz grabbed the opportunity and volunteered, whereupon the Feldherr gave a grudging nod, and a sigh of relief went through the room.

The following hours were spent drawing up instructions for the mission. Schulz was to visit as many units as possible and get Paulus himself to assess the chances of a successful breakout, as well as establishing as propitious a time as possible, so that the operation could be coordinated with a simultaneous offensive from Hoth's Fourth Panzer Army. The Sixth Army had to avoid "acts of desperation" at all costs, as coordination with the Fourth Panzer Army would then be lost and a catastrophe would be a reality, both for Hoth and Paulus.

Schulz would also have to find out if Paulus was in any position to wait, in light of a conversation Manstein had had with Richthofen the day before when the Head of the Fourth Air Fleet (as Markus now had confirmed) had answered with an unambiguous "no" to the question of whether he was capable of keeping Stalingrad supplied with the necessary tonnage of provisions and equipment.

Schulz would have to judge for himself, however, whether Paulus should be made aware of this unambiguous "no" from Richthofen; on the one hand, the information could make it easier for the encircled General to defy Hitler's orders to dig in for the winter and construct "hedgehogs", as they were called. On the other hand, the information might increase the probability of Paulus wanting to attempt the aforementioned "act of desperation" before Hoth had received enough reinforcements to attack the Russian line from the south. But Schulz would have to form his own judgement, based on his observations of the cauldron, which meant, not least, of Paulus' heart and soul.

5

Markus had hoped to be able to have a few words with Schulz before he left for the cauldron. But everyone seemed to have forgotten about his family matters, and also his minor intelligence assignment, which of course was only fictional: this kind of thing never happens, the little man has to learn this once and for all, so now it was a question of getting it over with if he was to have any hope of keeping up with events.

Kemmer was dragged from under his blankets before daybreak, given a hot bath, a sumptuous repast and a crate of vodka before clambering in behind the controls of the Junker (which the ground crew had filled with fuel and supplies) and returning to hell with the same doctor and General Schulz – and Markus had no option but to stand on the airstrip and watch the plane fight its way through the billowing cloud cover, he stood there until the driving snow had penetrated his clothing, frozen him stiff and woken him up once more when

Fatty Beber came panting over with a dispatch from the cauldron, which in the standard jargon said that "fighting in the city continued with unabated intensity", but it finished with the words:

"Alethe's white dog not understood. Identify yourself!"

Markus felt a tingle in his fingertips and set off at a run. A hope. However, he realised that the telegram did not necessarily come from his son, it could have been sent by anybody, they might even have been in a slight panic if they felt that an important communication from the top brass had gone over their heads.

Markus went to see Stahlberg, and the Oberstleutnant immediately gave him permission to send a reply, on condition that it did not contain anything that could reveal Markus' identity to anyone but his son and which also sent the boy clear instructions that his father wished to remain anonymous, to both his own and his son's commanding officers. Should contact be established at all it would have to be in such a way that made it clear to the "informant" that he could talk "freely".

Markus wrote one sentence:

"Identification of Alethe's white dog: a red stripe along its back. Manstein."

He handed it to Beber, who read it with a furrowed brow and then broke into a smile at seeing the name of the sender before disappearing into the radio room.

Markus got through to Hoth, who was licking his wounds, as he phrased it, after having defended the railway station in Kotelnikovo for days on end against sporadic Russian attacks launched at the panzer division which was beginning to arrive from France, the 6th Panzer Division, it was called, poetic irony, a little brother of the Sixth Army it had come to rescue from the cauldron. The enemy had attacked while they were unloading, but had been firmly repulsed, "a whole cavalry division had been annihilated", as Hoth put it. After that they had been able to concentrate on the new tanks, to their delight, and set to work painting them white; in the next few days – hopefully before the 3rd – they might have as many as 160 Panzer IIs, IIIs and IVs, newly fitted out in Brittany, and also a score of Tigers, the technical wonder that according to Hitler would turn the tide on the battlefield once and for all.

A little later Jakob Spitz came with a letter Manstein had written to Hitler, which had to be sent off at once. And Markus saw to his relief that the Feldmarschall didn't mince his words with the Führer:

"The army has to be brought out of the cauldron," he stated. "They can't survive on the open Steppes through the winter. Above all, it is impossible to continue to concentrate and tie up resources in such a restricted area while the enemy has free rein over the whole 500-kilometre-long front, the Upper Don, from Voronezh to Kalatch, which is not only too long but also too fragile. On top of that, the most critical section is held by the Romanian, Hungarian and Italian divisions, troops which are in a worse state and less motivated than our own. We have to be operational again!"

Incidentally, the previous day the General had delivered the following sermon to Markus about the concept of "mobility":

"Keeping the Fourth Panzers and Paulus' Sixth in the Stalingrad sector for months is contrary to our basic idea of warfare. Guderian's tank philosophy is based on speed, flexibility and élan . . . We can win a quick war against a superior force so long as we keep moving, but not a slow, static one. An army grinding to a halt not only means it cannot conquer new territory, it means that it loses its identity. And you, Hebel, no doubt know what the consequences are."

Yes, indeed, Markus did know what the consequences were, and he would probably have preferred these well-turned phrases to be dispatched to the Führer rather than the more formal ones that were hammered out by the teleprinter. Nevertheless, he happily sent the dispatch off, without the slightest doubt that Hitler would at last come to his senses and order an orchestrated breakout by return, the salvation of the Sixth Army!

Not until several hours later could he take upon himself the burden of also considering the downsides of the letter; Manstein not only painted a dismal picture of the prospects of the German troops surviving the winter, but also insisted that if the two army groups – the "Don" and its neighbour "A" in the Caucasus – didn't coordinate their operations and were not given full freedom of movement then a huge pincer movement from the right across the Upper Don by the Russians, towards Rostov by the Sea of Azov, could cut off the whole of the south-eastern front and make a Stalingrad of all that, too.

It was the first time Markus had seen this clear connection between the fate of the isolated city and the rest of the south-eastern front, it presented both dangers and opportunities, gigantic opportunities, whoever thought he knew what was going on in Stalingrad could think again, no-one knew, least of all a writer who got his hands on it, with his propensity for elaboration and variation, or a relative, with his vivid imagination, unquenchable sorrow and an immense feeling of guilt.

Now Hitler had not only ordered Paulus to dig in for the winter but, while he was at it, renamed his front-line "*Festung Stalingrad*", the Stalingrad fortress, and in addition proclaimed this event across all the Reich's radio stations, which in practice meant throughout the whole world! A new eternity had begun. With untold possibilities.

6

Markus had only had a few minutes' sleep the night before if we discount all his mental lapses, and we do that without trepidation as they did not provide him with any real rest – on the contrary; there was no opportunity to catch up the following day, either; the head of the supplies committee in the cauldron, Generalmajor Pickert, sent a message with the following wording: "Terrible weather over Pitomnik. Visibility no more than eighty metres. Some Heinkel iiis have arrived, an incredible achievement. I salute them all . . ."

But at around eleven o'clock in the evening Markus was sitting with the cartographer Jakob Spitz over a cup of tea preparing for a few hours' sleep, shaking with terror almost, at what his dreams might do to him, when Kuntnagel ran in with the first tangible reaction to his call.

"The white dog: Alethe's dream? Radio Volga," Markus read and felt his heart give a leap; he waved the paper distractedly and intoned in a low, confused and desperate voice:

"It's *him*! He's alive! And he's heard my call!"

It meant nothing that his son might have sent this without knowing the call came from *him*. Nevertheless the gravity of the situation hit him, what was the next step, because there was no strategy for how this "conversation" should proceed, or in what language other than the purely telepathic, and how on earth could they open a channel and at the same time ensure that the receiver did not reveal its existence? Not to mention: was his son – who had been at odds with Markus on every question concerning life and death and decency since he left home in the summer of 1939 – was he at all interested in subjecting himself to a missionary offensive from these quarters when he was in such dire straits?

Markus had already (partly) explained this problem to Jakob, but the cartographer had hung back as usual with the same wisdom that Markus himself had employed in order to survive during his years on the Eastern Front – keep a low profile, make sure you don't know too much and above all ensure that nobody expects anything special from you, no bright ideas, be tougher than most, keep a cool head when others are losing theirs!

He asked to see Stahlberg, but was frostily informed that he was busy with more pressing matters – it had been a black, demoralising day in the Caucasus, and the tank reinforcements meant for Hoth from there were stuck in the mud; there was a railway in the area and Stahlberg was organising transportation by train. While Busse was nowhere to be found and Manstein had probably allowed himself a few hours' sleep?

Not much later, however, General Schulz's battered Junker emerged from the cloud cover, after his recce in the cauldron, and both Manstein and Busse were summoned. The General Staff locked themselves in the map room and Markus was not present at this meeting, but later he was given a superficial briefing by Busse: it transpired that Schulz assessed the Sixth Army's chances if they "waited" as relatively encouraging. He had the impression that Paulus might be exaggerating the losses and underestimating his own strength, but thought that this might be due to a lack of overview rather than panic or deliberate distortion.

Markus was surprised that a top general of Paulus' calibre should have a poorer overview of his army than the visiting – though admittedly very astute – Schulz could glean in less than twenty-four hours. But he, Markus, was too distracted by thoughts of his son, both the fact that he was alive and that it was impossible to talk to him! He needed advice with regard to the "white dog".

Busse was in a hurry, however, and as he was leaving mentioned only that Schulz had brought back with him about twenty wounded from the cauldron and that Markus might find it interesting to talk to one of them, a Leutnant Weber, who had apparently been one of Paulus' assistants.

Markus ran out onto the airstrip, was told that the wounded had been sent to the town hall, which had been converted into a field hospital, and got one of the Cossack drivers, Jaromil, to drive him a kilometre or so through the blacked-out village. Minutes later he was met by a very obdurate reaction on the part of the duty surgeon. Leutnant Weber had severe wounds to both legs, caused by an air attack on the Gumrak airfield west of Stalingrad more than a week ago, the poor wretch had gangrene and it had been necessary to amputate, he was feverish, had been dosed up with morphine and was unable to engage in conversation.

Markus said with set jaw that he had orders from Manstein himself to debrief the Leutnant – immediately. However, it transpired that the surgeon was Manstein's personal doctor and only happened to be here in the town hall to lend a helping hand in his time off.

"If it's a problem," he added sternly," I can talk to Manstein myself . . ."

"I *have to* speak to him," Markus said, stamping the floor like a child.

"He can't speak, I'm telling you!"

"Let me see for myself!"

The surgeon was barely thirty, strong and broad-shouldered like a well-trained soldier, spoke in a refined Berlin dialect while his square face retained an enviable calm. Nevertheless, Markus thought he detected a bristling earnestness beneath his mild exterior, a flicker of emotion, a touch of fear, if nothing else.

"I'm asking you again," he said fervently, "on my knees. I *have* to talk to him."

The surgeon drew a deep breath and deliberated.

"Let me tell you something, Leutnant," he said. "Rats have been at him."

"Rats?"

"He was lying in the ruins of a cellar with four comrades from the 21st – behind the Russian lines. He watched the others freeze to death one by one because they didn't dare to cry for help; he's got frostbite on his back and arms, and rats have left their teeth marks in his wounds."

Markus had sat down. "I can arrange it so that you can speak to one of the others," the surgeon went on in the same business-like tone. "But they will probably only be able to tell you the same thing: that they can't take any more and that if Manstein doesn't get them out soon then we're facing one of the greatest catastrophes in the history of war. It's personal, I suppose – is it something personal?"

He had adopted a more conciliatory expression, and Markus gave a weak nod, almost as if he were acknowledging guilt.

"Yes," he said. "My son's there."

"Then you have my deepest sympathy. There's still not much I can do, but come over here with me . . ."

He led Markus up a staircase and into a dimly lit meeting room where Stalin still scowled from the shadows, with a bayonet hole through his left eye. Along a line of blacked-out windows stood four wide canvas beds with gleaming white linen. An elderly Cossack woman, a volunteer, was sitting on what looked like a milking stool at the side of the bed furthest away and was dressing a wound, the stump of a leg Markus discovered as he approached. The face on the pillow was lifeless, pale, ageless, with black liver spot-like patches around the eyes, a sculpture which time had long abandoned. Markus asked the old woman in Russian whether she had talked to him. She slowly shook her head and continued her bandaging.

"I don't know why," Markus mumbled, addressing the surgeon. "I just had to see it with my own eyes. I have to see everything with my own eyes . . ."

He turned and left. The doctor called after him that he would let him know when the Leutnant regained consciousness, and Markus muttered an inaudible thank you, rushed down the stairs and began to berate Jaromil, who instead of waiting ready in the car had got involved in a game of cards with his friends in the hospital duty room. Once in the car, the man ignored him, even when Markus showered him with a stream of unreasonable accusations, concerning the spirits the Cossacks smuggled into the quarters. Did the fellow have any conception of what was going on out here?!

Jaromil shrugged his shoulders and drove on through the drifting snow, unperturbed.

"I've got four children," he said after Markus had quietened down. "I know nothing."

"No, you certainly don't," Markus said crossly. "One of mine is in Stalingrad."

"Haven't you got any more?"

"What do you mean by that?"

Jaromil shrugged again, and Markus had the impression he was trying to point to more logical paternal feelings than the hysteria he himself had no doubt demonstrated, for example, by saying that so long as the major part of one's offspring are alive then there is nothing to complain about, at least there is no reason to have a breakdown.

"I'd like you to promise me one thing," Markus said. "That the day this place is evacuated you will come to me so that I can tell you how many kids I have . . . By the way, can you get me some apples?"

"What?"

"You've got an orchard. It's you who supplies H.Q. with apples, isn't it?"

Jaromil thought for a minute, then gave an evasive smile.

"I can ask around," he said slowly. "If you're really interested."

"Yes," Markus said, "I'd like some apples, a few kilos . . ."

7

Markus was torn from a dramatic, fireworks-like sleep and felt a ray of sunlight on his retinas, God had opened His eye, that was exactly how he had once planned to regain his sight, now it was happening again, it was summer over the land, a gentle, tender haze, the grace of peace, and Markus thought – quite clearly in fact – that if he'd had faith in an accountable and just God he would have been able to point out to Manstein that his first military tour de force in this war – the "*Sichelschnitt*", the sickle cut, which brought France to its knees in a single month in 1940 – had also hit his forests with full force, Markus' own forests, the Ardennes, and for that reason would haunt the General till the Day of Reckoning in the form of the worst conscience in Europe, and that it was this vengeful yet just force which was now approaching from all the corners of the earth on Russian caterpillar treads. But Markus did not believe in a just God – he thought, also quite clearly, strangely enough – he had a confused, indecisive, unreliable and well-meaning force on his right shoulder, a dove with a falcon's eye, a poppy with iron wings, a medal of snow, like the two streams which flow into one behind his house at home in Clervaux and double both his strength and the pleasure his children derive from making a waterwheel, which spins and spins through three seasons and is locked by ice in the fourth – what? In the distance came the sound of explosions from a lone

Russian plane, of course, a Russian loner who drops his bomb load where it suits him before returning to the other side of the Volga's flat embankments, or maybe it is Fatty Beber sitting on the bunk opposite him and bumbling his way through some contorted prayer.

"What's the time?" Markus said, jumping up.

"Eight," Beber said in surprise, alert now. "German time."

"Has something happened?"

"Nah . . . not really . . ."

It was only now that Markus realised that the fat man was not immersed in his own thoughts but was holding an open letter in his hand, obviously from Germany. Beber was a few years younger than him, but seemed ten years older. In a happier world he would have been a melancholic gardener, a gullible village teacher or a well-girthed butcher. Now he was fully there and doing what he always did at such hours, rubbing his hand to and fro across his broad, pasty face as if to erase his features or perhaps only in a secret hope of avoiding looking at the man he was talking to.

"Letter from home?" Markus said to make conversation, and began to do his ablutions.

"Yes."

Beber was silent again.

"Which you want to show me? You usually let Kuntnagel read them."

Markus knew about this arrangement. Beber had a wife at home in a village in Pomerania and she wrote to him all the time and often at great length about how well things were going for their two sons who were stationed in France and Holland. But during the autumn Beber had begun to suspect she was pulling the wool over his eyes to spare him, since there didn't appear to be any problems with anything at all any longer, although she had been a real whiner all the time he had known her; Kuntnagel had had to assure him that of course what she had written was true, about their sons and herself and all the banal, idyllic life they had the opportunity to lead back home.

"I don't trust him anymore," the big man said gravely. "I trust you more."

Markus laughed mirthlessly and started to dress.

"Why's that?"

"You know more. You know what's going to happen."

"We'll see."

He read out a lengthy childish account about seven or eight hens and a pig, about how she had preserved "tons" of cherries and pears for winter, about how an elderly neighbour was going to do the slaughtering for her and "Hans was doing well in Scheveningen, it was so quiet there by the sea", she hadn't heard from Johann for a while, although in the previous letter she had said everything was fine and they all sent their best wishes.

"Well, what are you worried about?" Markus said, annoyed. "You're sitting comfortably in an office, your sons are equally comfortable and your wife's got enough food. Could things be any better?"

Beber nodded thoughtfully, but at length managed to explain that he didn't like the sentence "it was so quiet there by the sea" – it was completely irrelevant and didn't seem to fit in with the ill-tempered and unpoetic disposition of hers, it was as if she hadn't written it herself, and not only that, this was the first he'd heard about the youngest son being in Scheveningen.

"Have we got anything there?" he asked. "He's in the military police."

"I don't know. But hold the letter up to the light, read it again, every word, and learn it off by heart."

Beber looked at him sceptically and shook his head, but did what he said.

"Well?" Beber asked after a couple of minutes.

"What did it say?"

"Damned if I know – it said the same as what you read, didn't it?"

"Nothing else?"

"No . . . I don't think so."

"Don't *think*?"

"No, there's nothing else."

"Have you any way of finding out any more?"

"From this – no."

Beber was still bewildered. He looked at the letter for a long time, held it up to the pale winter light once more, moving his lips as he read.

"Do you think I should believe all this?" he said finally with a cautious smile, "instead of imagining all sorts of other things?"

Markus shrugged.

"One or the other," he said. "You can't do both."

Beber's smile broadened and Markus turned his back on him, almost in repulsion, and went to get some coffee and an update on Hoth's situation.

It turned out that yet another concentration of Russian forces had been registered north-west of Kotelnikovo, near the tiny village of Poklebin on the Steppes, which Markus had to take out a map to locate. Hoth was expecting an attack at any time, but also assured them he was ready! And Transportchef Fiebig was delighted to report that they "had finally got good flying conditions" over Stalingrad, even though he had to add laconically: "Unfortunately so have the Ivans."

That day Manstein had ordered the trapped General Paulus to move two motorised divisions and a panzer division to the south-west front in the cauldron. In addition, there were a number of technical details attached to the deployment of a supply convoy to follow in Hoth's wake, an armada of lorries with food, medicine and fuel . . . And Markus counted all this as pluses in the calculus of probability which God subjects us to. But still he had no tenable idea as to what to write to his son or whether he should write at all; on the one hand, he clung to the hope that the wounded Weber would recover and give an oracular response – Your son Peter, yes I know him, he is well-fed and active and in the best of health; on the other hand, he was waiting for Hitler's sudden enlightenment, intoxicated by the idea of being able to signal to his son – and all the others in Stalingrad – that an *order* to break out would be given at any moment.

But Leutnant Weber did not come round and Hitler did not answer, an unmistakable sign that the Führer was either at a complete loss, extremely angry or about to announce a decision he knew would hit granite with Manstein.

Furthermore, Markus had begun to wonder why his son – and it *was* him, there was no doubt about it! – had signed the telegram "Radio Volga", that was the propaganda station in Stalingrad which, via Berlin, spread lies and misinformation with frenetic energy throughout the Reich about the great conquests being made here in the east; could it be a cynical sign that his son still shared the official German conception of reality? Or was he trying to tell his father that a channel could be opened up via the radio station?

Markus wanted to believe the latter, but didn't know how to reply. Only late in the afternoon did a solution occur to him, a single sentence:

"Alethe's white dog, I will come to visit you in Strasbourg and are you coming home with me this time? Reply! Don."

But he didn't send it.

He sat looking at it, at his refined and effete scribblings, how insignificant can a man become? He walked around with it in his pocket and slept on it, until Stahlberg started to ask about progress in the "white dog" project at dawn on December 1. Markus shamefully pulled out the crumpled paper again and Stahlberg peered over, read it and demanded to know what the visit to Strasbourg was all about. At first he refused to allow him to send such "an unambiguous message" – what if it were to fall into enemy hands?

Markus doubted it would come as much of a surprise to the "enemy" that Paulus wanted to break out or that Command H.Q. would have no objections at all to him doing so. Stahlberg, however, did not agree, assuming that the Russians listened to German radio and there they would hear that Stalingrad was to be held at all costs.

But half an hour later Markus was given the all-clear, without any explanation, maybe someone – Busse? – had seen that the very unambiguity of the message could either help to confuse the enemy or make no difference at all; unfortunately, Markus suspected it was the latter that was the reason for permission to be given.

He sent the message himself, with his eyes closed, and throughout the day he maintained contact with Hoth, who was extremely satisfied with his reinforcements, the 6th Panzer Division under the command of an exceptionally competent Austrian, Generaloberst Erhard Raus, who was familiar with winter conditions in Russia from the battles around Moscow the year before; his men were taking up positions north of Kotelnikovo, and Markus began to realise that it was also Raus who had been assigned the role of *spearhead* in the attack on the encirclement around Stalingrad.

Then the reply from the cauldron arrived:

"Alethe's white dog. Can I bring my friends along? Malachy."

Markus began to tremble.

"By all means," he wrote furiously, and added: "Do they want to? Bernard."

Less than two minutes later the answer ticked in.

"They do. Are they welcome? Malachy."

Markus got up and ran around gesticulating wildly. Kuntnagel, who had been sitting next to him, munching an apple, gawped in amazement. Markus stopped, put his hand to his head and burst out:

"He wants to know if an *order* has been issued! And I can't confirm it – yet!"

"An order?" Kuntnagel said. "To break out?"

"Yes . . ."

It struck Markus that not even Kuntnagel was aware of the doubt and lack of coordination that existed between Manstein's Army Group Don and Hitler's headquarters, the *Wolfschanze* in eastern Prussia, and between both of these and Paulus, this lethal triangle which God or some other heavenly power would soon have to tear asunder.

"Has such an order been given?"

"Well, yes," Markus said quickly. "But I can't confirm it . . . yet. And of course I can't state a time."

The stocky farmer stared at him in disbelief. Markus sat down and wrote a few words on the back of the paper.

"Send this," he said, embarrassed. "I can't do it."

"Malachy," Kuntnagel read out in a loud, hoarse voice, "'Health? As on your first or second visit to Clairvaux? Bernard'. What on earth is this?"

"I'm just asking how he is, that's all."

Kuntnagel looked at the sheet of paper dubiously, furrowed his brow but yielded to superior force, and Markus went to get some more coffee. When he returned, the answer had arrived.

"Bernard. Same as on the first visit. Repeat: Are they welcome? Malachy."

"Thank the Lord – he is safe and sound, he can walk to Rome and back. Good God, I can't believe it."

"Congratulations," Kuntnagel said drily. "You certainly can't say that of the others in the cauldron. What are you going to answer? He's asking about the order again."

Markus was about to repeat that there wasn't any plan – or order – yet, but then he realised that his son was not asking about orders, he got them direct from Hitler, but about what *Manstein's* intentions were – his *real* intentions.

"They're welcome," he shouted in a eureka-like cheer, for what can humans not make out of even the slightest glimmer of hope. "They're welcome – and sign it Nella or Marion . . . no, no, that's nonsense. Use Clervaux, then he won't be in any more doubt."

Kuntnagel shook his head slowly, and Markus had to go out into the rain thinking that now he had given his son hope, passed on his wafer-thin, bone-dry straw of hope, it was contagious. And he had endowed it with Manstein's pledge.

8

Along one of the outside walls of the old schoolhouse there was a shelf whose purpose Markus had never understood, perhaps the children had put their mittens or lunch boxes or books there when they were playing. Since he had arrived at the village Jaromil had arranged a row of stones on this shelf, stones which presumably he had picked up on his tedious patrols in the neighbourhood; grass and dirt and fallen leaves had gathered round them, later snow and ice, it was as though the Cossack just enjoyed collecting them, but not looking at them, so Markus had got into the habit of keeping this museum of sorts tidy when he needed to find some peace; he swept away the frozen leaves, he cleared the snow and ice and wiped the stones, musing that he had managed to convince his son that Army Group Don really did intend to launch an offensive on the "ring" and that the Sixth Army would have to advance towards them from the opposite direction, but had his son Peter understood that this solution did not mean that they would open up a supply route – as Hitler had ordered – but in fact that the whole of the Stalingrad fortress would be abandoned?

Markus realised that if his son, a nonentity like himself, a telegraphist or a lower-ranking aide, were to have the slightest chance of convincing his commanders of the *true* nature of Manstein's intentions then he would not only have to find himself some allies but also reveal his source, and what kind of credibility does a father have in such circumstances, in a position as he is to dish up the most blatant and sanctimonious lies – contagion?! So the channel to his son was blocked, impotent, a dead end and a sham, like everything else he had been doing these last few unreal years. He moved the Cossack's stones about like pieces in a game of draughts with God. Now it was above all reliable information coming *out* of Stalingrad Manstein was interested in, but Markus couldn't deliver this either, aside from details about his son and "his friends" *wishing* to get out, but with all respect this was just telling him the same as Paulus had written in his imploring letter of November 26.

"I hadn't done a thing!" he usually explains at this point when reflecting on his life. "I had only learned – once again – that my contact with Peter was no more tangible than William of Orange's carrier pigeons."

But then his thoughts were interrupted by Jaromil:

"Barite," the Cossack said in a deep voice. "It's rare in these parts."

He nodded towards the stone Markus was clutching like a rosary in his right hand, barite, rare and as beautiful as the stars in the sky. "Weber's recovered, Leutnant. The doctor told me to say you could talk to him."

Markus erased the musings from his mind and looked at his watch, jumped on board the jeep and got the Cossack to drive him to the "town hall". It was silent there now, no cries of pain and only a few nurses shuffling about in grey woollen slippers, like the sound of prayers being mumbled, a calm of heavenly proportions streamed in on narrow shafts of pale winter light, down on Weber's eyes, dark and watery in the blank face, resembling bomb craters in snow-covered terrain; he had been washed and shaved, an embalmed mummy, but he could move his hands and the old Cossack woman was still sitting at his side on her strange milking stool, busy with some needlework that to Markus looked like embroidery.

He asked her to leave, but she didn't move. He repeated his order in both Russian and German, but she stayed put. Weber's eyes met him at length.

"Leave her alone," he mumbled. "She's adopted me. Her son's in Stalingrad."

Markus nodded reluctantly, he knew that Paulus had not only Cossacks but tens of thousands of Russians under his command, so-called "Hiwis" – Hilfswillige, "voluntary helpers" – who apparently fought just as courageously as the true German soldiers in the Wehrmacht, presumably inspired by their poor chances of survival if they ended up in Russian captivity, Chechens and Ruthenians, Tartars and Ossetians, Cossacks and Ukrainians . . . the same stateless hordes which like the Belgians and Luxembourgers, Latvians and Norwegians, Finns, Frisians, Lorrainians, Italians, Croats, Catalans and Czechs had chosen the right side and thus the wrong one at a strained and chaotic moment in history which will never return with the small solace contrition offers. For Markus, "Hiwis" had become synonymous with the terrified, the foolhardy and the short-sighted, the homeless and the fanatical, for all those who neither wanted war nor were part of planning it but were dropped into it like fresh leaves from a tree in a storm and then were whirled around in the vortex, coping as best they could. Markus was nauseated by it, by this extreme lack of national logic, this Babylonian cacophony where you fought *alongside* your "enemies" and *against* your friends and cried "help" when you meant "attack", or vice versa, Weber would be taking his hand next and lulling him to sleep like the child he was. No, Weber was talking in rolling dreamlike waves about his damnation in Stalingrad, spicing it with a feverish nonchalance which gave Markus the shivers; he had seen a double bass in there, and he had to talk about it, this the biggest and most easily damaged instrument had suddenly appeared from a hole in the ground in front of their positions, on the back of a terror-stricken civilian, and was carried in panic through the piles of ruins, this stout, sanguine negress of the orchestra, a cosmic sound enveloped in the thinnest of shells, a sight which had obviously aroused bewildered laughter in the soldiers and for a couple of seconds caused them to hold their fire, and the man escaped, with both his music and life intact, down into a sewer – and then I'll have to tell you about the postal service, Weber added with a solemn cough, as though he were giving a speech at a funeral: there are more than 250 postal soldiers at work in Stalingrad, they creep around with letters and small parcels, two tons a day are flown in, and how many letters is that? The High Command knows of course what this means for the soldiers' morale. And there are still civilians there, children too, they say they eat corpses . . . no, Weber didn't know anyone by that name (Peter), he didn't serve directly under Paulus, but he had been on Panzergeneral Schmidt's staff, and the various headquarters were a few hundred metres apart, at Gumrak by the way, what, no, we should never have bombed the town, it's easier to defend piles of rubble than houses, now we can't move the tanks, everything is the same as before, the continuous bombardment by Katyushas and the Russian Air Force, it wears you down and what's more you're executed if you don't stand up and fight . . .

It was in light of this moral flaw in the Offizierskorps, which Weber called summary justice, and what Weber related later, that Markus suddenly saw a kind of rationale behind Manstein's antipathy towards Paulus: Paulus had in the critical days, around November 21–23, not only wavered with regard to breaking out, despite strong pressure from several of his generals, he was also hampered by his respect for authority, possibly by some subtle academic doubt, at any rate he seemed to lack the intelligent brutality that made people like Hoth, Guderian and Manstein the true masters on the battlefield, the leap must have been too great for him when barely a year ago he had been put in charge of a whole army, Hitler's largest and proudest.

"Yes, what can you expect," Weber added with weary disdain, "of a man who likes Beethoven and is married to a Romanian, heh-heh . . ."

Markus had nothing against Beethoven or Romanians even though he preferred Mozart and Luxembourgers, moreover he knew that Paulus in addition to the "weaknesses" referred to was also said to treat both prisoners and civilians with humanity, that he showed concern for his soldiers and that his noble and arrogant exterior might well be a cloak for a sincere humility before God the Almighty, all of them qualities which Markus valued, in all other situations except the one the General found himself in at the moment, but of course you can't have it both ways. Then Weber said with the deep indignation of a doomed man that Paulus after his last personal meeting with Hoth – in Nizhne Chirskaya on the west bank of the Don on November 23 – had flown back to the cauldron with crates and crates of first-class wine, champagne, Veuve Cliquot, and a man planning to break out as soon as he can would hardly stock up like this, would he?

"So you think he'd already decided on the 22nd to dig in?" Markus asked, appalled. "Even *before* Hitler declared the town a fortress?"

Weber squeezed his eyes shut. Markus felt dizzy, he began to long for Command H.Q., that was where the answers were, but realised that the most difficult question still remained, which he could not evade this time either, although he had forgotten to ask the surgeon whether Weber realised he was going to die. Markus asked the Leutnant with a forced nonchalance if he had any letters or other things he wanted sent – home?

Yes, Weber had some letters, from the four comrades he had been holed up with, a nineteen-year-old from Darmstadt, a farmer from Hunsrück and a locksmith from the Schwarzwald, three privates and a *Feldwebel* from Linz in Austria. He had also written down a few words himself, which were to be sent to his family in Hamburg. The letters were all sealed, and Markus decided to try to smuggle them out unopened, avoiding censorship, familiar as he was with what it meant to receive unopened letters from the front; an opened letter is a spent letter, it has been robbed of its significance and essence regarding the son's, father's, brother's final sorrowful hours, the relatives feel the final clarifying words have gone and been trampled on – the only words which can give those at home peace; receiving an opened last letter from a dead son is like listening to the mute roar of mass graves.

"I'll be back," he said wearily, tucking the letters inside his belt and adding to the old woman in Russian: "Take good care of him."

At which he left.

9

Important things had been happening at H.Q. while Markus was at the "town hall". A rescue plan for the Sixth Army had seen the light of day on the drawing board. It was called "Operation Winter Storm", and had been drawn up in great detail, though with a great wealth of provisos and alternatives.

Markus was informed that neither Hoth nor Hollidt could count on all the reinforcements that they had been promised. Nevertheless, the plan was not much different from the one he himself had worked out a couple of days previously: on the 8th at the earliest Hoth was to start the nightmare – "with all his might, a massive, frontal attack . . ." – while Hollidt was to "tie up the enemy forces on the western side of the ring" along the Chir Front by the "knee" of the Don.

But then Markus was also shown Manstein's brief to his own staff, a text which was not to go beyond the walls of the dismal village of Novocherkassk, and here it said – categorically – that the Sixth Army's envisaged mission in the Winter Storm could not in any way be reconciled with Hitler's command to hold Stalingrad. The Sixth Army could only contribute to the task of creating a corridor if it concentrated its forces, which would inevitably mean that it would lose ground along the northern and eastern fronts of the cauldron – the enemy, if nothing else, would see to that.

The war's own dynamics would in other words present Hitler with a fait accompli: Stalingrad evacuated. While his generals – Manstein and Paulus – would not have to refuse to obey orders, they would follow them and thereafter merely deal rationally with the consequences.

Markus was impressed, the fact that Winter Storm in both its principal variants demanded a controlled dismantling of the fortress heartened him and in truth the expectant smile that spread across his face reflected the prevailing mood in the H.Q. at this time.

However, he also realised – with muted enthusiasm – that these last deliberations about the war's own dynamics and the enemy's contribution to a happy conclusion of the drama in Stalingrad had to be kept from Paulus' ears. Hearing this would only cause him to radio Hitler, which would prompt immediate counter-orders; indeed, the Führer in one of his famous fits of fury might well go as far as to deny him a corridor. But before these fanciful notions could get out of hand, a telegram came in from the cauldron.

"Mother," it said, followed by a question mark, then the names of Peter's two sisters, Marion and Josephine, each also followed by a question mark.

It had not occurred to Markus that his son might be interested in how things were going at home, either because he assumed his new flawed thinking or the concentrated apathy which eventually afflicts every soldier on the front would preclude this. He sent a reply describing the family's situation in enigmatic terms which he knew his son would understand (and which warmed his heart) and passed on his mother's eternal prayer that "her boy" would return home alive. Finally, he wrote:

"Have you anything to say?"

An obviously ambiguous question, but he had to take the risk. If the son didn't understand he would have to keep repeating it, for as long as his energy lasted. No answer came that day, none from Hitler either, and now it was four, almost five days since Manstein's uncompromising analysis had been dispatched.

Pickert: "150 tons . . . arrived, mostly ammo . . ."

Paulus: "Massive enemy attack on cauldron ties up two motorised divisions and the panzer division which should have been moved to the southern sector . . ."

10

On December 2 there was a hard frost. The previous day's thaw had been but a single breath, the autumn's last, judging by the district's past record. But when Markus stepped out into the frosty air to start a new shift of technical military studies, a little pony stood staring at him despondently, it was tethered to a telegraph pole and munching some straw as it exhaled white cloudlets into the clear air. In the snow at its side sat the Cossack woman from the "town hall" on her ever-present milking stool. She was looking down, immobile, but Markus knew it was him she was waiting for, who else, there was no-one here, so he went over and stared down at her imperiously, she didn't react, she just went on with her embroidery and was no more present than he was himself.

"What are you doing here?" he asked brusquely.

Her face, which she now raised cautiously, resembled a dried fruit, her eyes were filled with a blank, naive expectation, a tame animal's timorous plea, the same pleading expression that Markus wore when he turned his face to the stars: her wide mouth was open and toothless. He shook his head, turned for the canteen and started to walk, but halfway there was struck by a thought – from God? – and walked back.

"He's dead," he said in Russian. "Isn't he?"

She nodded without raising her eyes from the snow. Markus' thoughts dwelt for a moment on Leutnant Weber and his letters, which he hadn't been able to send unopened. "What are you going to do?" he asked; he repeated the question and rephrased it, but still got no answer. Her grey mane of hair looked like the autumn's last cotton grass, her wool-clad body a frosty snowball, her breath was invisible and her feet, like two gnarled tree roots, pointed outwards.

"You can't stay here," he determined. "They'll be after you."

But not even that appeared to worry her. "Are you dumb?" he asked, with growing annoyance.

"My son's in there," she said finally, and Markus couldn't contain himself.

"Whose isn't?!" he shouted. "There are three hundred thousand sons there! And what do you want me to do about it? Go in and fetch them!"

Her wizened face cracked into a broad smile, she nodded eagerly, the cotton grass danced, and Markus turned his back on her again, mainly to prevent himself from committing a more demonstrative act. But once again he stopped in his tracks and repeated curtly: "You can't sit here. Have you nowhere to go? No family? No house? Which unit is your son in?"

"In the 297th Division," she said quickly.

This was an artillery division in the southern part of the cauldron, under the command of Generalleutnant Pfeffer, a man Markus had only peripheral knowledge of, but who he remembered had reported heavy casualties after the Russians' latest offensive.

"I can't do anything for you then," he said abruptly. And disappointment enveloped her wrinkled face, as it had done so often to his own. "What's your name?" it occurred to him to ask, and these words too had to be repeated several times.

"Yadviga," came the hushed reply.

"It's the same name as our Hedwig," he mumbled. "It's originally Polish, isn't it?"

"Yadviga," she repeated. "His name's Oleg . . . Kamenin."

"I see, Yadviga. But there's no-one here who can help you. Take your pony with you and go home. Ask the Lord for help, that's what *we* have to do."

He bumped into Jaromil in the canteen doorway and asked him if it was he who had let the old lady into the compound. The Cossack shrugged, and Markus was about to reprimand him, but was interrupted by wailing air-raid sirens coming from a device Markus himself had installed on the roof of the building.

He ran over to the Command H.Q., which was in a state of relative upheaval. The Russians had launched another massive attack on the cauldron, "concentric" as Manstein called it. And while Markus strove to digest the significance of this information, news came that the Panzerkorps that was supposed to join Hoth the day after from the Caucasus could not – because of heavy snowfall – be certain to arrive before about the 10th. After that Hollidt reported delays from his hard-pressed Chir Front; in addition his scouts had located an ominous concentration of forces behind the very lines he was to storm as soon as Manstein sounded his horn to begin Operation Winter Storm.

"It's uncanny," Hollidt said. "They seem to be able to read us like an open book."

Quite a pertinent remark, Markus thought; all the signs were that the Allies had cracked the Enigma code long ago and passed it around.

In the midst of all this Hitler's answer finally arrived, over five days late and with depressing news: Manstein overestimated the enemy's strength, the Führer declared, the Russians would very soon be facing serious supply and organisational problems, as Stalin had wiped out his experienced corps of officers. Markus took particular note of the following: "They will have problems with their supply lines as a result of their own unexpected success." And so he *refused* to give Paulus permission to weaken the northern front of the cauldron, which Manstein considered a must, not least in order to be able to open a corridor, and for which he had already given the orders, and which Paulus, as far as was known, was now struggling to implement.

Thus confusion began to spread through the upper echelons, both the lower and higher ranks, especially since everyone now realised that if Hitler really wanted to prevent an evacuation of the town then all he needed to do was ensure that the Luftwaffe provided Paulus with more food and weapons than fuel, without fuel he would, as has already been mentioned twice, be going nowhere!

Despite these sombre perspectives there was nothing to indicate that Manstein would shelve Operation Winter Storm. And Paulus himself offered another ray of light as darkness once again sank over the plaintive ruins of his: the army had once again resisted with "bravery, discipline and endurance" this day's "concentric" attacks, the losses had been considerable, but "the enemy had bled more". Furthermore, he put the figures for his stocks *up* by quite a few notches and now estimated that they had reached such a level that he had food and supplies for twelve to sixteen days, though this calculation meant even shorter rations and a continued consumption of the poor army horses, it was water, salt and wood they needed most. However, this presupposed that the good weather would hold and the airlifts could continue as normal. Yesterday 140 tons came in, today 90 . . .

II

Markus dived into bed late at night, but he hadn't slept for more than a couple of hours before he was hauled to his feet by air-raid sirens, aircraft could be heard in the distance and a low boom of thunder shook the earth to the marrow.

He ran over to Command H.Q. and was told by a flustered Beber, who stank of sweat, that in addition to launching fresh attacks on the cauldron the enemy had also unleashed massive bombardments on both Hollidt's and Hoth's fronts. Hoth had managed to regroup for Winter Storm and expected to be able to resist the "partial attack", as he called it, a resolute and convincing tone from Hoth's side, against a background of shelling and frenzied artillery fire, which Markus listened to attentively. Meanwhile Hollidt was on the receiving end of one pounding salvo after another across the River Chir, now also from an unknown number of tanks, the Russians' Fifth Army under General Romanenko, he learned from Intelligence.

But then Markus witnessed a strange reaction on Manstein's part: the majestic figure of the General stood amidst his spiralling cigarette smoke displaying signs of relief, an ever increasing relief as Jakob marked figures and details from the Chir Front on the maps under Manstein's almost cheerful gaze.

Only later did Markus discover the cause of this singular reaction, when Busse, over a cup of Russian tea, slightly elated, revealed that the day's attacks indicated that the Russians did not have sufficient wit or strength to initiate the famous pincer movement across the Upper Don, towards Rostov and the Sea of Azov, which would have created another Stalingrad of all the south-eastern front.

Today's attacks were massive, although they were directed at Manstein's shock troops and if these managed to hold out, the "enemy" could be weakened at these points, which would be so vital for the relief operation when the time came, if it ever did, because here, near the village of Nizhne Chirskaya, stood the only remaining bridge over the Don, the planned escape route for the Sixth Army.

Some time later Markus' mood was further buoyed by the news that the attacks on Kotelnikovo had been repulsed with the help of General Raus' newly arrived armoured division, who thus underwent their baptism of fire, which they sorely needed, as Raus had in fact been assigned the leading role in Operation Winter Storm. And Markus was just about to give the "all-clear" to his fatigued body and soul when news of the definitive collapse of Hollidt's forces came through: Romanenko's spearhead – fifty to seventy tanks – had broken through, advanced twenty kilometres southwards and was heading at full tilt for the vital airstrips of Tatsinskaya and Morosovsk, Stalingrad's umbilical cords.

Markus realised that as a result Novocherkassk would probably also fall, the German nerve centre, where he himself was stationed – the Russians would obviously push across the Chir, the shortest route to Rostov, and not the Upper Don!

With heavy eyes and limbs, Markus watched Manstein as he, in a series of febrile improvisations, moved a panzer division from Rostov and had it speed northwards towards the Russian spearhead; Markus' ears registered that the reconnaissance planes were landing at ever shorter intervals in the driving snow outside; frantic pilots ran in with reports and aerial photos which caused Eismann's face to turn ashen and made Manstein urge on his panzer division with increasing fervour; the Feldherr spent most of the night in conversation with the command tank of the head of this new cavalry, a certain General Balck, who according to what Markus gathered from Stahlberg's terse account had already attained legendary status in the France campaign. And Balck had been given all the numbers, frequencies and data concerning enemy positions when his tanks on the morning of December 8 made contact with the billeted Russian spearhead and immediately went on the attack.

It was a few minutes to six, and only after Markus saw that everyone around him was holding their breath, did he realise that his observations and fears had been well-grounded, everything now depended on this ad hoc night-time adventure only thirty or forty kilometres north of the H.Q., and when he said "everything" he meant everything, from a German perspective, Stalingrad, Kotelnikovo and after that the Caucasus, approximately one million men, the big pincer movement after all, in a different sector from the one Manstein had anticipated, and thereafter the whole Reich, for not even the world's leading military power could sustain blood-letting of these proportions.

Kuntnagel was sitting with his head buried in his gnarled farmer's hands, as always when there was a "radio signals ban" and nothing to do but lose oneself in prayers and fantasies, Fatty Beber was up and down on his chair moving his lips as though reading letters that lied about peace and false idylls at home in Pomerania, while Jakob Spitz was hunched over the maps talking in subdued code with Eismann and Busse.

As mentioned, it was now December 8, a portentous day, Markus thought, but the first aerial reconnaissance reports were nothing special, the crews couldn't see anything in the dark, and there was no word from Balck. Balck was silent. It wasn't until almost ten in the morning that some tersely worded snippets came in, which had to be studied closely and contextualised and queried before they could give any grounds for even the most cautious optimism; less ambiguous reports followed, about advances and more advances, and then unadulterated cries of joy from the telephone and radio lines; everything had gone according to plan for Balck, the Russian spearhead had been smashed to smithereens, sent packing, "annihilated". And in the early evening came the confirmation from Hollidt himself – forty-six enemy tanks up in smoke, the rest in German hands, modest losses on our side, the gap in the line along the River Chir closed, well, *in the process of being* closed.

There were wild howls of joy among the rank and file at H.Q., cautious smiles above the higher-ranking officers' coffee cups and a historic nonchalance about Manstein, who for the last couple of days had also been in constant touch with the *Wolfschanze* in east Prussia. But he no longer spoke to Hitler in person, only with Zeitzler, a point which Markus attached great importance to when he assessed the consequences of these calamities: the Führer was boycotting his own Feldherr on the Reich's most crucial front, no less. However, Zeitzler seemed to accept the analyses coming from the front, at any rate he accepted without exception the operational moves which were made on the Chir and the Upper Don, and did what he could to convince them that the Führer gave his wholehearted blessing.

During Balck's Chir mission Markus sent only one telegram to his son, to make sure he was alive.

"Bernard. Same as the first visit. Malachy," his son replied, which meant that he was not even wounded.

Actually Markus probably ought to have used the opportunity to send him some even more encouraging words, such as that everyone in Clervaux was doing their utmost for the sole purpose of bringing him home, it was only a matter of days now, so hang on! But, imagining the paralysing joy these encouraging words might provoke in an army at the end of its tether, he desisted; messages from the cauldron told of panic on the airstrips, starving, desperate soldiers storming the runway in an attempt to leave, scenes which were made no less appalling by the fact that the German guards had been put under orders to shoot; the frosts no longer only brought death and destruction, but also caused havoc to their equipment: aircraft engines had to be kept running all the time they were on the ground or had to be warmed up over veritable bonfires when the heaters broke down; between ten and twenty Junkers were lost on bad days, planes loaded with the wounded or supplies were shot down over enemy territory. And today Markus considers himself fortunate to have forgotten that more than one thousand planes would be lost in the operation, eleven hundred pilots and so many wounded that only God has a record of the number; Markus recorded all this like a blind machine, wearing headphones and with thoughts as far removed from the action as possible – he was in Manstein's pocket for good, an extinguished civilian light with only one thing on his mind: iron resolve!

In darker moments he possessed a blessed irony that enabled him to put a gloss on the situation; in heaven's borderless name the General was just as stateless – and rootless? – as Markus himself, he was at least half-Jewish, or a quarter, born Lewinski and also an adopted child, a background he didn't hide either when he made fun of Hitler, this Manstein was a multilayered and adaptable personality inside his Prussian armour, split, complex, too intelligent to be morbidly loyal to an Austrian fantasist, but also too loyal – to the Wehrmacht and Germany presumably – to assume the full and total responsibility and do his duty before God and man, unless perhaps he was planning to combine all this in one single operation: Winter Storm?

This, at least, was the straw Markus clutched at, and he didn't share it with his son, no, he didn't, for it was nothing, at most a lethal contagion.

12

When Markus came out of Command H.Q. late on the evening of December 7 – that is while Balck's tanks were rumbling north past Novocherkassk and the fighting by the River Chir was not yet over – he discovered that the old Cossack woman was still on military territory, hunched over the small milking stool like a silent winter monument beside the munching pony, and apparently unaffected by the cold, which had laid a shivering leaden mantle over the Steppes. Markus forgot for a few seconds both Balck and the Chir and strode angrily towards her to deliver a final warning, but before he got that far Jaromil had emerged from the shadows of the barracks and placed himself between them.

"She doesn't want to leave, Herr Leutnant," he said without hesitation.

"Doesn't *want* to?!"

"No, Herr Leutnant."

"Are you telling me you haven't been able to remove an old woman from military premises?"

Jaromil hesitated, but then decided after a few seconds' thought to keep any answer to himself. "You'll have to shoot her then," Markus said coldly. "She can't sit here."

"I can't do that, Herr Leutnant."

"No, right," Markus said with some relief, mechanically registering that if he had been talking to a German soldier this incident could easily have had a more depressing outcome, now at least he wouldn't have to pull rank.

"Have you got any food, Yadviga?" he asked in a sudden friendly tone.

She looked at him quizzically and nodded.

"Can you make me a hot meal?"

She nodded again, giving him a cautious toothless smile and got up stiffly; Markus noticed that the stool was a saddle, with legs which could be slotted into the pockets of a sheepskin over the pony's back. He helped her to strap the saddle on, lifted her up onto the pony's back and walked beside her through the blacked-out village, westwards to a rectangular clump of buildings at the edge of the built-up area. Two young boys darted over the ice-covered farmyard. From a shed with a sagging roof came the sound of horses snorting and stamping the ground. Otherwise all was still, it was dark and a dull starry sky hung above them.

Yadviga led the way into the hovel, which like the other buildings was made of clay and timber beams and half sunk in the ground. She lit a lamp and tried to place him in what must have been the house's seat of honour, a cross between a divan and a child's bed, covered with plush burgundy fabric, as far as Markus could see in the dim light, but he resisted such an undeserved homage and instead began to put logs in the stove while Yadviga struggled with pots and pans and filled the air with monotonous humming.

It was the first time for several months that Markus had found himself in civilian surroundings, the previous occasion was also with Cossacks, in the Crimea, who were evidently better off than Yadviga. When he asked who the various people in the carved wooden frames hanging on the walls were, she answered in monosyllables, she muttered names, maybe a date of birth, but she didn't say a word about her son, perhaps because Markus deliberately skipped the picture he presumed must have been of her boy. But she was keen to talk about her brother, obviously a kind of modern-day Stenka Razin, who had been headman in a village near Starobelsk, fought in four wars and at the age of eighty had also gone off to fight in this one, on horseback with a rifle over his shoulder, only to be ridiculed by the German adjutant in charge of enlistment; later he had been killed in mysterious circumstances which had probably had nothing to do with the war, and now he stared out on the world, cross-eyed, proud and exotic, between a flaking icon and an Orthodox brass crucifix.

Markus had a meal of biblical lentils and Russian kale, in concentrated, solemn silence, while Yadviga chewed with her bare gums at ryebread and what looked like lard; she didn't say anything, but when he thanked her for the food and the hospitality and wanted to leave, she made as if to go with him.

"I can't do anything for your son," he said wearily. "Regardless of whether you stay here or sit outside the barracks."

She allowed him to leave alone, but next morning she was sitting there again, inside the compound, in the same freezing cold temperatures as before. And Jaromil made no attempt to move her on this time, either. Markus saw them talking when he was outside, he heard the Cossack admiring her embroidery with thoughtful grunts and saw him nod to something she had mumbled into her woollen shawl. She made no attempt to talk to Markus, to assail him with impossible demands or annoy him with requests only God could grant. She was just there, day after day, neither desperate nor grief-stricken but subject to her own laws of time, as strong as the force of gravity, and there was a rhythm to this relentless clock that suggested to Markus that not only were the Germans going to lose the war, that the Russian soul could not be vanquished by weapons and western obduracy, but that the breakout operation might fail too, for reasons other than lack of resources, inferior manpower and poor coordination between the supreme commands.

"This civilian nonsense" was therefore what he called Yadviga's endurance outside in the cold. And those evenings he spent with her – three or four in all – he described in terms such as "They only served to obscure facts", and by facts he meant what was happening in Manstein's den, which was close to reality. But he couldn't get rid of Yadviga, and it was one evening when he was showing her how to pray your way through the beads of a rosary that he got his pathetic idea. The background was as follows.

Operation Winter Storm had again been postponed. Manstein sent another written appeal to Hitler. Meanwhile Markus discovered that the Feldmarschall was now also assessing the *positive* aspects of keeping the Sixth Army in Stalingrad, as Hitler wanted: it could have the effect that "the Russians also dig in and slowly bleed to death in futile attacks; Stalingrad could become the grave of the attacking forces".

This terrible thought had crossed Markus' mind too, in the wake of Leutnant Weber's speculations about Paulus' propensity to selfless sacrifice, and it was obvious that Manstein would have to put this idea forward in order to be taken at all seriously in the Führer's bunker, but why play such a high-risk game now, just before Winter Storm was about to be launched? There was still no doubt that this operation was going to go ahead, and Stalingrad was going to be evacuated, as far as Markus could see, but how clearly could he actually see? Wasn't his sight getting worse and worse with every day that passed?

Well, at any rate he could see the absolute ridiculousness of the High Command even considering *attack* – let alone a rescue bid – when the enemy was threatening to break through on all fronts. It was also becoming less and less likely that the Fourth Panzers alone would be able to smash their way through into Stalingrad without the Sixth Army linking up with them, and what was more, who was going to order Paulus to do this?

As there was no sign of a change of heart in the *Wolfschanze*, there was only Manstein who could give the order. But then you were back to square one: Hitler would immediately get wind of the plan over the radio and countermand orders – tell him to stay where he is, don't move! And it was out of this dreadful circular train of thought that Markus' "little idea" came into being. One evening he was sitting over a piping hot bowl of soup at Yadviga's watching her old hands fiddling with the rosary he had been given by his grandmother in his lost youth. Why doesn't someone in the cauldron sabotage the bloody radio line to Hitler? They all want to get out, the soldiers and the generals, too!

The situation was so chaotic there that there had to be an opportunity to do it. But was Markus willing to demand of his own son that he make such a sacrifice, which might not even lead to anything? It made Abraham's quivering knife against Isaac's throat seem like an Old Testament party game.

For two whole days he hovered in fruitless speculation, cast long, searching glances back and forth through history and also had a confidential talk with Jakob Spitz about the matter. The cartographer at first did not want to listen to this "rubbish", but then declared him insane and finally threatened to report him for treason.

"But why has it not occurred to anyone trapped in the cauldron that the direct line to Hitler must be broken?" Markus said vehemently. "They can all hear each other's voices. It's the hearing that counts, not the seeing!"

"They've probably all had the idea," Jakob said. "But where would it all end if people began to put everything they thought into practice?"

"You tell me."

"I don't want to hear another word."

"But don't you have a conscience?"

"I have this uniform. It's an Unteroffizier's uniform. It tells me that I don't have the knowledge to have the necessary conscience. Only Manstein does."

Markus nodded in response to this profundity, but when Operation Winter Storm was postponed for a second time and December 10 dawned to new intensive attacks on the Chir Front, Markus panicked and sent off a message with an apochryphal reference to a Flemish saint who, during the Dutch War of Independence, had broken off his newly established spiritual links with Calvin and returned to the House of the Father in Rome and the Catholic Church. The conversion had cost the man his life but also earned him eternal glory in heaven.

There was no answer.

13

Markus worked steadily with Hoth on December 11. The Generaloberst had finally arrived from the Caucasus with the 57th Panzer Corps, which together with Raus' units would form the spearhead of Winter Storm. The attack was to follow the railway lines to Stalingrad, so they hoped they could use the bridges on the two rivers, the Aksay and the Myshkova, and the whole operation was to be crowned with a convoy of 800 trucks and half-tracks which in an almost industrial tour de force had been brought in, over ten days, by means of the rickety railway to Kotelnikovo, in addition to 3,000 tons of supplies, mostly food and fuel, because if it wasn't possible to open – and keep open – a corridor, then they would at least try, in the heat of battle, to slip some petrol reserves through for Paulus to fill up his battered tanks.

The date was also set – the 12th. And as the moment approached – the evening of the 11th – Markus again felt the acute, unsettling tremors that had afflicted him in the Crimea and Kerch and which he had also noticed during Balck's drive towards the Chir Front. He could see that the same change had been taking place in others, too: Manstein's silence, which became more and more intense, his permanent good humour slightly reined in, even though he still made strained witticisms, you braced yourself, as if to take a kind of leap . . . when, late that evening, at long last Markus received a reply from the cauldron, a standard update – Paulus had only seventy tanks left! – ending with the words:

"Bernard. Don't understand Calvin? Malachy."

Markus wrote the following without hesitation or rather without thinking:

"Malachy. Break with Calvin imperative! Bernard", sent it himself and waited for the next few minutes in a "die is cast" mood of historic proportions. However, this was soon to change because his son repeated the question, first once, then again, and at half past eleven (again German time, the Russians stuck resolutely to their own) Markus sent the same "order" for the third time – "Break with Calvin imperative" – for there was no longer any doubt that his son understood what history expected of him – drop your new faith and come back to the old one, back to your senses – all he needed was a little time to think.

Then Kuntnagel tried to cajole Markus into helping him find Raus' regiment frequencies so that they could listen directly to the voice of the battlefield when it all broke loose.

Markus had staged something like this at Kerch, but on that occasion had been given such a stinging reprimand that he hesitated to repeat the performance; Manstein had no wish to hear of all the ups and downs on the battlefield, where nothing ever runs smoothly, details confuse and blind you to the strategic overview, as they say. On the other hand, the thought of sitting here again with folded hands, begging the Lord God and Hoth for "official" communiqués was not very appealing, especially if it were to go on for several days, never mind weeks, and now it was as if Markus were on his own, that was how it felt, it was a personal matter.

The commanders and the tank drivers communicated openly in the field, occasionally also with their own divisional commanders, they used slang, dialect or some other internal code, but they never gave their names or any other identification, so they had to recognise each other by their voices.

"Maybe we should learn this, too," Markus mumbled with feigned reluctance. "If we're going to make any sense of it. Anyway, it's too far away."

"It's flat here," Kuntnagel countered. "It's possible."

"It would take a miracle."

"Isn't that the reason you're here?"

Markus looked up in bewilderment and started to work his way past the Russian jamming stations, misinformation and insidious offers of surrender and other rubbish that filled the ether between heaven and earth. "Raus is sure to be on the air tonight. You can listen and learn to identify the voices."

They decided to let Beber in on the conspiracy because there was no other option; the new signals people, on the other hand, and Eismann's mistrustful Intelligence Unit, would have to be left in the dark. But Beber wasn't interested in any of this, he had received another alarming letter from home, in which his wife informed him that his son Erich had been transferred to Italy without warning.

"And what have we got in Italy? Isn't that the road to Africa?"

Markus grudgingly read down through the lines of handwriting and had to admit to himself that Beber's wife made no attempt to spare her husband at all, instead she used her pen to unload all the terrible speculation there was on the home front, now she was virtually begging him to prove that all the prattle she heard on the propaganda radio waves was true and correct, letters from the sons were few and far between, it seemed.

"Show it to Kuntnagel," Markus said irritably, and went out into the waiting darkness of the night to have a few moments' peace before the storm. But then he spotted Yadviga again, sitting on her "stool", and the pony, which with closed eyes and bowed head wasn't even nibbling at the clumps of hay she had scattered about in the gleaming snow. Jaromil had lit a fire for her.

Markus waited until the condensation on his glasses had cleared and then went into his sleeping quarters, got ready for bed and slipped between the sheets. But he was waiting for further telegrams from the cauldron which – if they contained the same question – would undoubtedly have the effect on him of a desperate appeal to get the spectacular idea of trying to break through called off, and he would have gladly acquiesced, the "*Panzerruhe*" hadn't sent him into a coma yet, and after half an hour he got up again, looked at the thermometer, which showed minus eight, got dressed and went into the mess for bread, butter, a piece of sausage, and salt, which he took out to Yadviga. He mounted her saddle on the decorated sheepskin, lifted her up and led the pony to the small cluster of farm buildings. There he fed the meek creature, carried Yadviga inside and laid her on the divan, spread a blanket over her and covered the round table with an embroidered cloth, on which he placed two knives and two bowls.

"Soon over," he said absent-mindedly.

Again they ate in silence, he soup, she bread, boiled kale leaves and the lard-like substance she stuffed down with a small spoon. He asked her whether she had any vodka. She nodded towards a cupboard beside a door which presumably led to her bedroom. He took out a half-full sea-green bottle without a label, a medicine bottle with a crumbly cork.

She insisted they should have a glass, they drank one each and finished eating. Then she fell asleep while Markus sat listening to the murmur of the universe, he had another glass of vodka, dropped off for a few moments, thinking that this was the first time he – who had forced himself to live so close to reality – had done anything concrete *not* to comprehend what was happening, he was hiding from reality here, in civilian surroundings, this is what he was doing, with his absence he was saying "no thanks" to further military analyses, to Kuntnagel's eavesdropping, to Beber's letters and Eismann's depressing cauldron reports – the last one he had seen said that Hitler had given Manstein permission to move the 17th Panzer Division from the Upper Don to join Hoth, a manoeuvre which of course would increase the chances of a successful breakthrough. But Markus had also heard the reaction:

"Too late," the Feldmarschall had mumbled, and that might mean, as far as Markus was willing to speculate, that at the moment Manstein was contemplating another postponement, or perhaps a total abandonment of the operation, unless, that is, the monumental Winter Storm had become a matter of sheer moral necessity, a grandiose sacrificial rite to purge the commanders of their bad conscience, or else it was to be enacted for the sake of its place in history, a ritual of honour that was doomed to fail from the outset?

But Markus had put all this depressing military dissonance behind him; weak will lay at the heart of his last supper with Yadviga.

"I couldn't just let her sit there," he says in his defence when Robert presses him on this point. "She was on the point of freezing to death."

"But Jaromil had lit a fire for her."

"That man was not to be trusted. Remember what he said: 'I've got four children,' he said, 'I know nothing.' He just wanted to have control over me."

"Now you're contradicting yourself, Markus."

"I always have done. You have to if you have any ambition to appear decent. But there's another reason I couldn't let her die that evening . . . let me put it like this: as long as there was any life in *her*, there was hope for us all. She held off the insidious bubonic plague that was penetrating our souls from these abominable Steppes – you think you know what flat land is, Robert, since you know Flanders, but the Russian Steppes are not land, they are earthen crust and horizon, it is the planet's vast torso, a sea without a wave, which sucks out every thought and belief as we gaze at them, and our last ounce of energy, and we are reduced to empty reeds through which the wind can sound its lament . . ."

"Did Manstein see her, too?"

"I don't know, but he did of course sleep in the royal railway carriage he'd brought from Starobelsk, so he must have passed her now and then, in which case he can't have done anything to have her removed, and why should he have, he let her sit there for the same reason that he put up with me, even God needs to show some mercy occasionally."

14

Markus did his own personal countdown in the early hours of December 12. He left the sleeping Yadviga and returned to H.Q. at a little after three o'clock in the morning, slept soundly for about an hour and got up feeling refreshed. But while the rest of the staff were sitting with all their lines open, trembling with restrained tension and fear of the battlefield ticking in their ears, Markus' thoughts were still focused on the cauldron, on his own little mission which would have to be carried out in the very near future if they were to have any hope of bringing Paulus under the only command which could order him to break out – Manstein's.

Kuntnagel sat at his side reflecting aloud on why in heaven's name it was that all attacks had to start when the Lord sent His first rays of light over the earth, when the enemy was expecting them, even though they didn't know *which* morning; however, this couldn't be said of Manstein's modus operandi, he knew from France that evenings also have their advantages, those hours when the enemy expects you to take a break, to lick your wounds, which so elegantly expresses how mutilated comrades are dragged out of pools of blood to be counted and to determine whether it is possible to add one more horrific day to the war. "Evenings are like rivers," the General used to intone in fine company, with reference to how a unit in retreat will without fail speed up when it approaches a river in the hope of crossing it unscathed, burning the bridges and forming a new front as quickly as possible; and all the pursuer can do is the same, whether it is midday or evening when he arrives at the river, unless he wants new positions to contend with the following morning; it is the unorthodoxy of evening attacks that occasionally allows them to bear fruit, for war needs light and soldiers need sleep, both sides are agreed on this, and some things have to be more common than others for them to have the advantage of surprise . . . "Sleep, you said, they haven't had a wink of sleep all night – Markus, are you listening?" Kuntnagel said.

Markus looked him in the eye.

"Yes. No."

He was and he wasn't.

"Not that I've heard any voices though," Kuntnagel continued. "There must be a ban on radio contact, but don't you reckon the Russians will think all this silence is suspicious?"

Some minutes after half past four in the morning Richthofen and Fiebig dispatched everything they had that could fly, from Tatsinskaya, Morosovsk and Salsk. Shortly before five Hoth gave his artillery the signal and a purple cardinal's sash began to vibrate on the icy blue horizon east of Novocherkassk

– in Markus' black field of vision. Only a few minutes later a terrified Kunt-nagel picked up a message that "the advance over the bridge north of Kotel-nikovo was going more slowly than anticipated", but at 0520 hours a clear announcement came from Hoth himself to say that all 230 tanks were across, and were storming northwards in a massive frontal attack as the plan prescribed; Raus' 6th Panzer Division was in the middle, the 23rd Panzer Division was on his right flank, Battle Groups Zollenkopf and Unrein on the left, and Markus understood from the din in his earphones – and the staff's reactions – that the attack must have caught the Russians completely off guard, and advances were being made that not even he in his wildest dreams had envisaged: resistance and furious fighting around trenches and anti-tank positions, "total wipe-out", and further progress with every obstacle in their path pulverised. Fiebig even reported – full of enthusiasm from a surveillance plane in the airspace over the battle area – that the "Russians are fleeing, just like in the old days!" And so it went on for the rest of the morning until the more sober members of Manstein's staff felt they had to compose themselves and dampen their euphoric mood: "Where are they?" they murmured. "Have they made a tactical retreat in order to build a new front along the ravines or gullies, or beyond the next river, the Aksay . . . ?"

Markus was told about a new plan that Manstein was working on, which, in line with the army's invocatory christening rituals, had been given the name "*Donnerschlag*" – Thunderclap; at some yet to be defined moment it would replace Winter Storm and include an *order* to Paulus to break out!

In other words, the gloomy H.Q. atmosphere was beginning to lighten. Markus didn't receive any signals from his son, for which he was grateful, but he couldn't help thinking that it was Peter who was behind the exhilarating messages which now began to tick in from the cauldron, as it became clear that Hoth's tanks really were on the move, a confidence without bounds, childish and expectant: "Manstein's on the way!", "We'll be able to celebrate Christmas!", "We're going home!" and so on.

Markus made a courageous attempt to regard these outbursts of enthusiasm as a sign that their brains were still working properly. "Manstein's on the way!" must have been carefully chosen words, calculated to scare the wits out of the enemy if they were listening, as they probably were, or perhaps they were spurring on the Feldmarschall to surpass himself; what low-ranking soldier wouldn't take recourse to this kind of ploy? – with some justification, with the same justification one has for exaggerating casualties, to stay alive; it is the same with communications as it is everywhere else, the most objective message is the most heartless and unproductive, people say that truth is the first casualty of war, and that is fine because what on earth are we going to do with number eighteen? I repeat, eighteen, what do you associate with the number eighteen, Robert? Not a thing, I presume, at most a bag of apples, a feckless stage in our lives when we make mistakes we would prefer not to repeat, whereas for me the number conjures up eighteen dead soldiers, in the same way as I see sixty-nine soldiers when I encounter this number, according to the same linguistic principle which stipulates that the name "Hoth" does not connote to me "an ice-cold Generaloberst pulling off what seemed to be the Second World War's most hopeless relief operation" but rather a living symbol of approximately 100,000 men charging across the frozen Steppes north of Kotelnikovo; and a normal person doesn't think like that, there is peace now and there has been for ages, there is oblivion and sun-filled activity every-where, but I am still in the war, so where others are completely blind to the mathematical figure of 2,991, to me it represents vivid memories of the faces of the 2,991 wounded soldiers we had to leave behind in the field hospital at Feodosia, whom not even the Russians could be bothered to kill off with hand grenades, as they usually did, instead they preferred to drag them into the Black Sea so they would freeze to death, slowly but surely . . . and I could just as easily have mentioned some of the atrocities we committed, not so much the Wehrmacht but the S.S. and the S.A., I might add, so for a brief moment we can drop this ridiculous nationalism, which has nothing to do with numbers, for the simple reason that wars are not waged by nations but by people, stupid, self-important idiots who think they are defending themselves when they attack and are blind to the brutal fact that war scorns everything it purports to defend and tramples over everything it conquers, thereby making us all equal before God, mark my words.

"You're getting carried away, Markus," Robert said.

"Yes, and you would have done the same in my place."

"I've already admitted that. Everyone would have done the same in your shoes, but we weren't in your shoes. That makes us better people than you, freer people, it is peace that has made us, not war. But tell me something. Why did you never write to Nella in all those months? Not a single letter. Didn't you get any from her, either?"

"What do you mean?"

"You're flummoxed whenever I ask that question. And how many times have we been through this? You can never give me an answer even though the question is so simple."

"In order to keep going you have to believe that those at home are safe and sound, Robert. At any rate, that was what ate away at my friend Beber, that his sons were fighting at a different front. No-one can be on two fronts at the same time. We can choose to send letters or not, we can choose to build bridges or not, see or not see, speak or be silent, both alternatives have their uses but they will always be irreconcilable. That's why I didn't write to Nella and she didn't write to me. We don't like to lie to each other and we don't like to hear the truth either. Is that not an answer?"

"Well, I really don't know."

15

By lunchtime on the 13th, Raus' spearhead had not only advanced forty kilometres through enemy terrain but also crossed the River Aksay near the village of Salivsky and from there pushed further north to Verkhne Kumsky, a depressing, half-buried clump of houses midway between the two rivers: "Kampfgruppe Hünersdorff – 11th Regiment – has advanced more than twenty-five kilometres in the last seven hours and established a ten-kilometre-deep bridgehead north of the Aksay. The Kampfgruppe has left the 23rd Division on the right-hand flank far behind. It also appears to have enemy-free territory ahead – towards Stalingrad."

Markus could scarcely believe his eyes. Nor, evidently, could the operation's supreme commander, Hoth; at any rate he sent off a nervous question straight afterwards: "What's happened to the mysterious Russian Third Army? Aerial reconnaissance?" But before Eismann could compose a sensible reply a report came in to say that the bridge had collapsed under the lead panzer at Salivsky, blocking the crossing for the rest – "a new bridge has to be built".

Kuntnagel looked askance at Markus, who read the message again and again and finally mumbled:

"That must mean this Hünersdorff has gone on alone? And that he's isolated at Verkhne Kumsky ten kilometres into enemy territory?"

Kuntnagel laughed nervously, stood up and sat down again.

"There aren't any enemy troops in the area, are there . . . ?"

"There *are* troops," Markus said, and told him to be quiet so that he could catch the next message, which informed them that Salivsky "was under heavy fire from anti-tank guns and artillery". A minute later Chief of Operations Fiebig also reported "extensive enemy troop movements" further north, moving south towards Verkhne Kumsky. Eismann grabbed the piece of paper and said with an inappropriate whistle that this was in fact the "mysterious Third Army" that Hoth had asked about, the first sign that Stalin had woken up, to give the devil his due, for behind the Third, the Second Guards Army was regrouping, they now heard, by the nearest river, the Myshkova, the last geographical obstacle on Hünersdorff's route to Stalingrad.

But everything was going more slowly now, for both defence and attack, Markus could see from the small flagged pins Jakob was pressing with surgical precision into the speck-like dots on the operation maps. Then a full-blown snowstorm set in, which held up Richthofen's Stukas and the 17th Panzer Division, which was meant to be coming to Hoth's aid from the Upper Don – it wasn't even over the river yet! In addition, reports were coming in throughout the day that Hollidt's Chir Front was in danger of collapsing again, the front which was supposed to cover Nizhne Chirskaya where the 17th Panzer Division was to cross the Don and where also wild fantasies abounded that Paulus' liberated army would be able to make their way "home". And if that wasn't enough, the Italian Command on the Upper Don added its own contribution to the chorus of laments: "Enemy troop build-up in the sector north of the Don . . ."

"A terrible day," Markus said, summing up December 13, despite the early advances and Hünersdorff's hazardous push to Verkhne Kumsky, which was enough to make anyone believe in miracles. Markus was also inclined to call it "one of the worst in all my long life". He sent a telegram to his son, and it was no longer a clean break with Calvin that was "imperative" but some tiny sign of life, and while he continued to eavesdrop on Hünersdorff with the increasingly frenetic Kuntnagel, all through the 13th he also had to attend to the 17th Panzer Division, then in the early hours of the 14th there were a few moments of manic silence which Markus grabbed with both hands: he sneaked out and, full of shame, listened to the distant thunder and the idiotic pounding of his own heart.

But, true to form, there was Jaromil, standing at the ready like a tin soldier. He passed Markus a bottle of vodka without a word being spoken and at the same time thrust a Russian Orthodox cross into his hand, a piece of jewellery, Markus saw – made of gold? The Cossack pulled an inscrutable leer, and Markus punched him with all his strength, with the fist holding the crucifix, whereby the man let out a stunned groan, fell backwards and lay writhing in the snow.

Markus took a swig from the bottle until his vision was blurred by tears and noticed Yadviga and the pony. They had camped down in the shelter of a windbreak which Jaromil must have built for her using wooden boards and some old tarpaulins. The Cossack got up as if nothing had happened, pulled another foolish grimace, half turned to Yadviga, before giving a sly smile and triggering another outburst of anger in Markus, who realised that the cross had to be in return for the rosary he had given the old woman a few days ago (which he now claims he never did) – he would find comfort in this crucifix, the Cossack said, a gesture which seemed to imply the man wanted something back, so he dug out a packet of cigarettes, offered him one and they got stuck into the vodka while Markus excitedly held forth:

"Blessed are those who are at the front, Jaromil, who don't have to rot away here sitting on their fat arses – can you hear anything? Have you heard anything today apart from the sound of planes and artillery? It must be the weather . . ." And Jaromil nodded pensively and shuffled his foot, which he continued to do as Markus told him that in his younger years he had, so to speak, *read* his way out of the midden on his father's farm at home in the Ardennes because a teacher had led him to believe that he was a genius and could achieve whatever he wanted in life. "And all I have ever done is invent a kind of glue, Jaromil, a vulcanised solution that can bond two rubber surfaces, which I took a patent out on and which is in huge demand on the battlefield, to patch up the Wehrmacht's shredded tyres. I made a packet, Jaromil, and the glue is probably also the reason they let me keep this stupid rank of Leutnant from the Belgian Royal Engineers, because I'm not a Leutnant, Jaromil, I'm a common soldier like you, a nonentity, and believe me, you can't take your rank with you into peacetime or heaven, it's a millstone around your neck, a bad joke and a shady past that will cling to your stupid name for the whole of the short period anyone can be bothered to concern themselves with who you are, because you are living at a time when all the options are wrong, my friend, I could have touched the stars with my fingertips if I wanted and then I decided to be everything, I almost became a priest and I invented a magnifying glass which could be hung around the necks of old people so that they could read the Bible even when their eyes were failing and some special clips to keep your trouser legs up when you are cycling, plus I've also invented a shoe polish which waterproofs leather, but because of the high rubber content it doesn't shine and so can only be used by foot soldiers, I've got a patent on that too, a certificate, only a certificate, so I am a nothing just like you – how can you be such a proud people, Jaromil, when you are not even a people but Russians and Poles and Crimean Tartars all mixed up, you have neither your own names, land, language nor religion, you borrow the lot from others, like gypsies, no, at least they have their own language, but what has this got to do with me, I'm a Belgian, not even that, so I know what I am talking about, I've got *two* mother-tongues, Jaromil, but only one mother, and on top of that I have Latin and Flemish and the broken Russian I'm tormenting you with right now, which I learned in the trenches, from Cossacks by the way, so I know how you all think, it's your horses, Jaromil, which turn you into the brothers and sisters of the wind and constantly take you away from wherever you are, you have to settle down somewhere, don't you agree, you should cling to the roots of the earth like beetles and maggots and farm your own land, only then can you become a people, a nation, something to go to war for . . ."

"We *do* farm our own land," Jaromil protests languidly. "I've got fruit trees. I gave you some apples . . ."

"Yes, yes, you did give me some apples. You were probably afraid you wouldn't be paid for them. Is that all you think about? Why didn't you give Yadviga apples?"

"She's got no teeth."

"You don't say – stew the apples for her then, you numbskull, use your imagination, and why didn't you put up a tent for her instead of those stupid boards, they only keep the wind off while the frost is just as hard on both sides, there is something fleeting and temporary about everything you do, Jaromil. If only you had been a pilgrim with a spiritual aim to guide you."

16

"Hebel! Leutnant Hebel, can you hear me?"

"Yes, yes, of course I can hear you. What is it?"

Markus had already sat up. And once again he was staring into Fatty Beber's grimy mug, which didn't appear to have seen soap or water since the first day of Operation Barbarossa, but this time it wasn't about mysterious and ambiguous letters from home.

"The General would like to talk to you – at once!"

Markus got up in panic and asked:

"What's the time? How long have I been asleep?"

"We're approaching 1943, I hope," Beber mumbled, then disappeared with that peculiar side-to-side transportation of flesh that is typical of fat men's running while Markus put on his uniform, noticed that a few rays of sunlight were peeping in through the gap in the curtains and ran over to Command H.Q. There, he was informed that Manstein was in the officers' mess, so he rushed over and saw the General standing outside, talking to the head of the guard, the Cossack who had refused to speak Russian to Markus in the first days of the Don campaign and had insisted on German, of which neither he nor anyone else understood a word, the same gobbledygook that he was now entertaining Manstein with.

"At last you're here, Hebel," the General sighed. "Can you interpret for me? I don't understand what this man's saying. He's talking about the rivers icing up. They've been cracking and crunching for weeks now, so it's probably only a matter of days before they're completely frozen over. I want to know what this means."

"Means, Herr General?"

"Yes, at what temperature is the ice load-bearing, normally, after how many days, how *much* can it carry, where, what about the current and so on? – they built a whole railway over Lake Ladoga last winter . . . Ask him about all this and get back to me as soon as you've finished!"

Markus discussed the ice question with the Cossack for almost half an hour. The man answered sullenly in fluent Russian – of course the enemy would be able to cross the Volga over the ice, in only a few days, maybe also the Upper Don, in a week, if the temperatures continue to fall, by laying down branches and planks or pontoons and spraying the lot with water for example, it's an old method, but of course the ice can always be bombed to smithereens, we've got planes, haven't we, ha ha, but sooner or later, before the New Year, I imagine, they'll be able to move a whole army over anywhere they like, by then the rivers will have gone, it will all be steppe, there'll be no difference at all . . ."

Markus mulled on this.

"And the Don's tributaries?" he asked. "The Aksay and the Myshkova, the ones *we* can use?"

"The Myshkova freezes over before the Aksay – the Aksay is . . . well, I don't know . . ."

Markus led him to Jakob's map room and made him put crosses along the rivers on an operational map, on the Volga, the Don, the Chir and also the Don's tributaries, and grade them according to their probable load-bearing capacities. He exchanged a few words with the meteorologist, a short-sighted professor and minor aristocrat from the University of Tübingen, whom Manstein had brought along from Vitebsk and who went under the name of Galileo because no-one else but him believed in the forecasts he dished up. Markus asked him what he thought about the prospects for the coming days – "Frost, hard frost, no doubt about that, the wind will come from the north-east, and as long as there's no frozen mist the weather will be bright and clear" – and then he went to Command H.Q., where Manstein was sitting alone at his desk updating a logbook. From the room next door came the sound of loud voices, Busse and Eismann, as far as Markus could work out, through the half-open door, discussing the impossible situation at Verkhne Kumsky.

Markus handed him the chart and at a nod from the General began to describe the reservations he thought needed to be added to the Cossack's analysis, the Cossack was not from the area although he had an unfortunate tendency to act as if he were, but Markus was interrupted by an impatient growl.

"I wasn't asking for a dissertation, Hebel. This is good enough. Where have you been these last few hours?"

"In bed, Herr General."

"You can't have been doing much there then?"

"Nothing at all, Herr General. Since there is nothing to do anywhere here for a man like me, I have realised that now!'

Manstein seemed to be considering an enigmatic smile, but contented himself with a narrow-eyed, searching look.

"The enemy has blown up the bridge over the Don," he said matter-of-factly. "At Nizhne Chirskaya."

"What?!"

Markus counted his heartbeats, he counted to eight, they were all soul-shaking; he felt more demoralised in the company of the General than anyone; here he had – as he himself puts it – studied his way out of farming's ten tired commandments, adopted the intellectual arrogance necessary to survive with a certain dignity in the higher echelons of society, only to be thrust back into the cowshed at the mere sight of these small, calm eyes, which resembled those of John the Baptist as they stared sadly down at him from the Stavelot altar of his boyhood, and with a similar message, a blown-up bridge, *the* bridge.

"It happened only an hour ago," the General continued in the same flat tone. "And it doesn't seem that this ice will be able to help any of us for now. That means that the 17th will have to cross further south, at Potemkinskaya, we'll lose a day or two – can you deal with this, liaise with Eismann and see to it that . . . ?"

He hesitated and Markus grabbed his chance.

"Does that mean that the Sixth Army will also have to cross at Potemkinskaya on its way out?"

In military terms, an idiotic question, even to Markus, but he didn't give a damn, there was only one thing on his mind, to elicit the General's real intentions, to hear whether in the light of the last day's discouraging developments any changes to Winter Storm had been deemed necessary. Manstein gave a sour smile.

"As long as the ice cannot bear the weight, anyone who wants to cross the

Don will have to go to Potemkinskaya," he said. "Unless they go even further south . . . What happens after that, God only knows."

"I assume, Herr General, that the enemy has had problems navigating the Volga over the last few weeks, with all these ice floes . . . ?"

"Let's hope so – what are you getting at, Hebel?"

"What I'm getting at, Herr General, is that the army has to be evacuated before the ice sets in. Once it has, it is too late – it is too late for anything!"

Instead of answering, Manstein asked – after another unnerving pause – a long question in French, whether Markus had had any contact with his son recently, and if so what had transpired from the conversation. Markus answered in the negative, also in French, and also corrected a grammatical mistake in the General's question before saying:

"Excuse me, Herr General, but I find it regrettable that the General Staff still consider it necessary to test me. French is my mother tongue, just as German is yours. That's how things are and there's no changing them. I now look forward to carrying out the tasks I have been assigned."

But this grandiose pomposity of his made no impression on his superior.

"As far as I remember, you already have a task," the General said. "To guide the 17th Panzers over the Don. And since you show such eagerness to *do* something – keep on your toes!"

The conversation was over. Markus fell out and returned to the mess, had a quick lunch and heard from Kuntnagel that the prospects on the Chir Front were just as dismal, which would probably force Manstein to deploy the 17th Panzers *there*, Kuntnagel said with a lofty, self-important expression, rather than have them join up with Hoth's forces, who by the way were still getting nowhere; Verkhne Kumsky was showing all the signs of becoming a real nightmare, it had been taken and lost and taken again, by Hünersdorff, no less, the 11th Regiment, which fortunately appeared to be made of sterner stuff than flesh and blood.

Markus chose to view all this as a lower-ranking officer's natural tendency to exaggerate, left his friend with a forced shrug, and concentrated on the task of guiding the 17th Panzers south to Potemkinskaya. And as there were no counter-orders when the division – on his chart – crawled past the Chir sector, he concluded that the front was still holding up.

Later that evening it was confirmed that the battle for Verkhne Kumsky, which General Raus in his daily log called "a massive wrestling match", would go down in history as one of the war's greatest tank battles. Kampfgruppe Hünersdorff had indeed been driven out of the village and, after a few terrifying hours of fighting their way round and north-west of the forlorn group of houses, they had managed to retake it, before once again having to withdraw all the way back to the Aksay. Casualties were very heavy, and Markus had to erase from his mind any speculation as to whether the high figures were intended to make Manstein consider calling off the operation or whether Hünersdorff only wanted more reinforcements as soon as possible, in other words that Hoth was again being liberal with the regrettable truth. Kuntnagel's eavesdropping wasn't producing any results, either, Kuntnagel had had enough; moreover, he had his hands full with the setbacks on the Chir Front.

17

At a little after eleven in the evening the 17th Panzers reported that the forward troops had reached Potemkinskaya and found the bridge intact, they were already going over, and Markus made up his mind that this would have to be the last news from the battlefield for the day, it was good news too, something to sleep on, but he couldn't restrain himself, he had to see the figures from the cauldron, it had been good, clear flying weather, but no more than 125 tons had got in, and with a loss of eighteen whole planes! Fighting in the north of the cauldron, dreadful casualties there, too. But there was no sign of life from his son.

Markus considered sending another telegram and decided to repeat one of his earlier messages:

"Malachy. Health. As on your first or second visit? Bernard."

He waited for half an hour, in vain, killed another half an hour looking for Hünersdorff – when did they actually sleep? – but due to the crackling cacophony from the ether he didn't have a clear picture. He played a game of chess with Jaromil, got annoyed as usual at the Cossack wanting to introduce new rules when Lady Luck didn't smile on him and then walked out into the cold night air, where he was struck by the silence and a distant cosmic rumble, which aroused thoughts that had been lurking at the back of his mind all day, especially when he was outside and felt this breath of eternity. They circled around a chapter in Russian history which had made such a huge impression on him during his schooldays, a kind of nightmare, "Charles XII's march from Romni to Gadiatz" it was called, kilometres and kilometres of the frozen terrain north of Poltava, in the context of military history a relatively short march but undertaken in such lethally freezing conditions that the Swedish king's army was halved in the course of a single night. There was a majesty, a kind of national romanticism, about these accounts, illustrated as they were by splendid and pompous masters. The march was called everything from "Charles' definitive defeat" to "the actions of a fool" – as the Swedish King could easily have stayed at Romni – to "the turning-point in Russian history", while the Russians, the poor wretches, were depicted everywhere in an ignoble, unchivalrous light: Peter the Great, who let the winter do the job for him rather than leaving his lavish tea salons and fighting like a man, which he only dared to do at Poltava, when Charles was wounded in the foot and had to hand over command to the indecisive General Rhenskjöld, with well-known results. Markus had learned that the winter of 1708–9 had been an ice age of its own, through all of Europe. The Rhône and the Loire were iced over for months, the fish froze to death in the canals of Venice, the farm animals keeled over in the cattle stalls in the Ardennes, and across the Ukrainian Steppes whole flocks of small birds rained down from the skies. The Swedish invaders sank to the bottom in the Russian eternity like lead in water, as holy Theophan Prokopovich of Kiev observed, for God holds His hand over this people even though many may have secretly wondered why the Lord didn't also use the opportunity to free them from their own tyrant, Peter the Great, but God speaks in tongues, He appears in the guise of a devil and confuses His flock with unsolvable riddles, and moreover, He repeated this exercise a hundred years later when He sent Napoleon into the same abyss, and He was well on the way to doing it a third time, He allowed the ice to take over the place that hellfire had earlier occupied in the European religious consciousness, cold desolate landscapes and a deafening silence which people traverse with bowed, trembling heads, more and ever more slowly, until they come to a standstill and are transformed into sculptures at absolute zero, to blocks of frozen life, where everything is preserved but nonetheless abandoned, where monuments are created by the same inscrutable God who has breathed life into the wild flowers and the leaves and the quails, certainly not by the survivors, who allow their memories to be embellished by the sentimental trumpets of mourning. Markus thought about all this again now, for on this night he saw Yadviga for the last time.

She was sitting as usual on the saddle beside her pony, the fire had died down and she was no longer doing her embroidery, her hands were buried in two great mittens, she had a sheepskin around her body, held together by a coarse hemp rope. Markus went over to her and greeted her with dignity, first in German, then in Russian, to emphasise the foreigner's natural modesty. She responded with a weak smile. The next moment she died.

He saw her final breath, a white cloud that issued from the toothless mouth and disappeared into thin air. No part of her moved. Her arms did not fall to her lap, they were there already. Her head did not sink to her breast, it was held firmly in place by the fur collar, like a crane's egg in a nest of straw. Her eyes did not close and the smile did not leave her lips. Small crystals of ice appeared on the invisible down of her face, the ice's hazy flame made it glisten. Around one of her nostrils a drop formed, but it never fell.

You can say what you like to Markus to get him to admit that this must have happened the other way round, that Yadviga's quiet death stimulated his thoughts on the historic ice and the frozen monuments, in other words, that they occurred *afterwards*. But he categorically denies it. He came out of Command H.Q. and stood still for a few minutes listening to the creaking of the boards beneath his feet while the images of Charles XII's hapless army – and the ice – circulated around his brain – long before he spotted Yadviga's glowing monument to the Cossack soul. So he has also predicted this death, or has seen it coming, prompted by the atmosphere of the war museum that was Novocherkassk, where time has stood still and the war is still going on and will continue to do so forever, and he cites in his defence – after all, it is his sanity which is being questioned here – that he had made this prediction the very first time he looked into her wizened face. This is therefore not a miracle we have witnessed but a realistic course of events, just as Leutnant Weber's demise could not have come as a surprise to anyone who had smelt the stench from his wounds, and we will have to make do with this explanation, or at least desist from claiming that it is not completely true until Markus himself reappraises the issue and turns it on its head.

He lifted the little woman onto the pony and took her home, tethered the animal in the low shed and gave it fodder for a couple of days, then carried Yadviga into the house and laid her on the divan, which henceforth he called the "sarcophagus", with a wry smile, and a vain attempt to drive away the memories. He also maintained that he opened one of the windows so that the frost would tend to her, but he didn't remove her sheepskin, though he did her mittens. At that moment he saw the rosary in her right hand and exchanged it for the Orthodox cross he had been given by Jaromil, but actually by her – he did these things without thinking. Afterwards he went out into the farmyard and knocked on the door of the neighbouring house into which he had seen two boys scuttle on the first evening. But no-one opened up. Everywhere there was this same electric peace, the sky was star-filled, the air was crisp like sandpaper with not a movement anywhere. But on his way back he saw Jaromil smoking a cigarette outside a blacked-out shack, with a man Markus had not seen before, presumably negotiating the price of a new delivery of vodka, Markus' standard explanation of the Cossacks' mysterious behaviour.

He greeted them briefly and carried on towards the quarters and Command H.Q., where Fatty Beber's body odour had made its heavy presence felt in the radio-room atmosphere. Markus immediately wanted to back away, but the big man twisted in his chair and said with a startled grin:

"It's still undecided in Verkhny Kumsky. They're fighting for the third day. What do you say to that?"

Markus was about to ask how things were by the Chir and the Upper Don, the fronts on which the relief operation depended, but stopped himself and went to his quarters. That night he didn't sleep a wink. At just after three he was called by Jaromil, who barged in with a finger to his broad lips while pulling theatrical grimaces – Leutnant Hebel had to go at once and help him out of "a delicate situation".

Annoyed, Markus got up again and dressed, went over to the Cossacks' barracks, which had been set up in the main building of the collective. To the sound of deep grunts and snoring from the rows of bunks on either side, Jaromil led him through the dormitory into the adjacent washrooms, and from there into a coal shed. Here, the Cossack shone his torch on a corpse, clearly one of the guards. The man was lying on his back with a gun in his mouth and his brains blown out over the glistening lumps of coal. Markus bent down and put his finger in a pool of blood and ascertained that it wasn't frozen, which in these temperatures must have meant the tragedy had happened only a few minutes ago – and this right next to the sleeping soldiers?

Markus asserts that he made his decision – suicide – while suspecting that the real cause may have been completely different, it was "a pragmatic decision", as he calls it, for all he knew it could have been the result of an internal disagreement, for example about their accursed vodka, unless the dogs had been scrapping again, the Cossacks who in all wars on Russian soil have fought on both sides, like two nations, and have often changed sides in the process, all according to how the wind blew on the battlefield, or because of other factors that have tempted them; was this the first sign of a new "conversion", back to Russia and the Soviet Union, brought to a bloody end by Jaromil, for example?

Markus asked where the head of the guards was, and Jaromil decided to answer that the man was somewhere in the village – in a civilian house, which Markus took to mean with a woman he was unlikely to be married to.

He asked Jaromil if he'd had any thoughts about why this poor wretch had found it necessary to depart this world. And again the Cossack began to prevaricate:

"I don't know," he mumbled, "but he's been to Stalingrad. He came back today."

"He's been *where*?"

"To Stalingrad."

"In the cauldron? How the hell did he manage that?"

"He's got two brothers there, and about a week ago he went in, he rode north, crossed the Don, to Shebalino, from there he went on foot along the gullies . . ."

Markus had heard about these exploits before, people who went in – or came out – under cover of the ten-to-twenty-metre deep gorges which rainwater cuts into the Steppes in the spring, the only cover there is, but he had regarded it as an element of local mythology, the people's belief that they possessed supernatural powers, the wisdom of the gods.

"One of the guards has been A.W.O.L. for over a week?" he asked in disbelief. "And you didn't report it?"

Jaromil refused to answer. Markus looked him in the eye. "You *did* report it, didn't you?" And the Cossack threw back his head as if invoking some higher power. Markus saw by the sinews in his muscular neck that he was chewing and again felt a deep antipathy, play-acting, he thought, pretence. "You *did* report it, didn't you?" he repeated. "But the head of the guards didn't take it any further. Is that what you're saying?"

"I never said that!" came the abrupt response. "Not at all. But what I will say, Herr Leutnant, is that the head of the guards has a lot to answer for."

Markus thought that if Jaromil himself, or someone close to him, was behind this murder then they had played their cards extremely well.

"What did the poor wretch have to report from his trip to Stalingrad?" he asked sarcastically.

"Both his brothers had been killed, Herr Leutnant. He claimed they died of their wounds because they weren't taken on the planes; he said they only flew out German soldiers. I know it's a lie, Herr Leutnant, but that was what he said."

"And that's why he committed suicide?"

Jaromil nodded.

"Out of grief. He hasn't got any children," he added.

"Let's call it suicide then," Markus said coldly, turning away. The Cossack accompanied him through the dormitory where Markus now felt they were all holding their breath. "Write a report," he said when they were outside, "and see to it that he gets a decent burial."

Jaromil grabbed his hand.

"Thank you, Herr Leutnant, thank you. I knew I could rely on you."

How is it that I can never work out whether I can trust you? Markus thought, and he claims that by choosing not to put the question to Jaromil he was taking another pragmatic decision. The advantage of pragmatic decisions is that rather than passively submitting to difficult realities they try to improve them. Moreover, this gave Markus a reason not to let it go further and also a good defence, should the death, despite everything, reach the ears of his superiors. It was only then that he realised there was something he had forgotten to ask. He went back to the Cossack where he had left him, in deep thought.

"How did he cross the Don?" he asked.

"Ten days ago . . . by boat, I think . . ."

"And today?"

"On the ice. He walked across the ice."

18

The next days have as good as been erased from Markus' consciousness. He "awoke" on the morning of December 18, with the following crystal-clear nightmare images seared into his brain: If Hoth's forces manage to break through it would mean a victory for Hitler's strategy and the Führer would never accept Manstein's contention that it was impossible to keep the Sixth Army in Stalingrad. *Only a failed attempt to break through the lines would make Hitler take a more realistic approach and order a breakout!*

With this catastrophe clearly etched in his weary consciousness, Markus started a new day's work. He struggled through December 18, and he refuses to comment further on "the absence", as though he regretted having brought the topic up at all. And seen in the light of his own plan – to cut the line between Hitler and Paulus – this was perhaps understandable; a blind old man who tells his story to a youthful audience who has never experienced war, even if the listener is his own godson, well, maybe especially in that case, tends to present a mixture of confession, apologia and pedagogical obligation and may not have the energy also to broach those factors which undermine his own version of events.

But in this context something quite different occurs to Robert, perhaps it should have been mentioned earlier, but never mind, it is something Markus told him when he was a child, about all stories being lies, not only because every storyteller, like everyone else, is fickle and unreliable and has his own highly personal manner with regard to sensibility and memory, but also because stories have a beginning and an end, and nothing actually has, nothing stops and nothing begins, it just *is*. This can be illustrated by the fact that if one were to pack all the events which took place, for example, in this year of sorrows, 1942, into one book and call it "1942", it would still be a gigantic distortion of the truth because 1942 also contains remnants of 1941 and 1939, not to mention 1901 . . . It may be that one of the main characters is still alive or a treaty is still valid which the parties involved have to abide by, or might wish to annul, and what about the Ten Commandments which people are still trying to keep, or they show remorse when they break them, and I haven't even mentioned that 1942 was obviously affected by its expectations of 1943, by plans and decisions and ideals and airier notions, about paradise for that matter, or peace, let alone the theories those two English researchers have come up with, that our souls are tiny conch shells, containing the echo of God's voice, which enter our children when we make love to our women, and there unfold as a variation of our own soul and hers; history is a river, Robert, seeing history as a river is the only valid truth, in my view, it roars and bubbles or describes a lazy, sleepy arc of a circle which runs through land and sea and heaven without ever repeating itself, if we are going to be pernickety about it. It is correct to say that what we see and hear and tell is a *fair* representation of the truth, we cannot ask for more, nor can we stomach more, I am afraid, modesty is the greatest virtue, you think about that as I go back to what happened during those two (or three?) days which have become so woefully distant, at least those elements which are important to understanding my further activity as a nonentity in the most formidable High Command in history.

On the 15th we received the following report, written by one of Hünerdorff's company commanders:

> We saw with our own eyes that the Russians were moving towards Verkhne Kumsky in large columns – tanks, anti-tank guns and infantry – without worrying about us in the least, even though they had a full view of us. It was weird. From the village came the sound of fighting, and we were in a very demoralised state, almost completely out of ammunition, unable to make any advances and on top of this the sight of those unending hordes of Russian troops pouring across the Steppes . . .Then two things happened that breathed life back into us. First of all, Oberst von Hünersdorff drove his tanks right up to our group, tore off his headphones and bellowed (I can put it no other way):
>
> "Is this supposed to be my regiment? Do you call this an attack?!

I'm ashamed of this day!" . . . and so on. We were incensed at this outburst, however much we valued and loved his forthright manner . . .

But then there was a new cry for help from Verkhne Kumsky, from Major Löwe, Kommandant 1/Pz. Rgt 11, who had been cut off, and anyone who was familiar with the old warrior knew what this meant . . .We, the commanders, were summoned by Oberst Hünersdorff and Generalmajor Bäke and given a quick briefing regarding the situation. We were then ordered to storm Verkhne Kumsky regardless of losses – our comrades had to be freed, the village purged of the enemy and all the wounded rescued . . . Those tanks that still had ammunition were to lead while the others would be equipped with what was left of the machine-gun ammunition and were to shoot wildly to cause panic. Two companies at the front and three behind. The snow swirled around our caterpillar tracks, our mood was euphoric, and if there had been any sense in it we would have shouted *Hurrah*. We let rip with everything we had, at anything that moved. A Russian tank right in front of mine received a direct hit, Russian infantrymen fled in all directions; they must have thought we were out of our minds. But it worked. In the space of an incredibly short time we were in the middle of the village, without any losses to speak of . . . There we found the men of 1/Pz. Rgt, three of the officers had been killed, almost all the others were wounded, tanks were on fire everywhere, our own and the Russians', all in a jumbled heap, the dead and the wounded lay in the streets, all the houses were ablaze . . .

The rest of the report was a detailed description of the rescue before enemy forces once again broke into the village and Hünersdorff had to evacuate it in a headlong rush, all the bloodstained kilometres back to the Aksay, also completely surrounded by the enemy.

Markus saw from the next reports that while the Chir Front still held, like a drumskin at bursting point, or "like a sieve", as Busse put it, two days previously the Italians on the Upper Don had talked of "partial attacks" and "skirmishes" as well as the discovery of "a *new* army" north of the river, which eventually was identified as Vatutin's' Third Guards, reinforcing the suspicion that the Russians were now finally preparing for the lethal pincer movement – and heading for Rostov.

Markus flicked feverishly through the rest of the reports, the casualties from "the missing days" exceeded his worst nightmares – on December 16 Hoth, Raus and Hünersdorff lost more than 1,100 men, on December 17 close on 600, as well as considerable losses of materiel, which Richthofen and Fiebig also suffered in the air, and at some point the costs would no doubt go beyond what even Manstein could defend, both in the present situation and the critical eye of posterity, if he ever entertained that kind of thought, that is, and we all do, even though we try our best to live in the present.

Early on the morning of the 17th Hünersdorff set off north again, fully equipped with reinforcements, fuel and ammunition, towards the doomed village of Verkhny Kumsky, fought for the whole of this day too, and still there was no clear victor. And then Kuntnagel held up a doctored page from the regiment's war log, perhaps written by Hünersdorff himself that same evening, which Markus read with tremulous eyes:

> Due to continuous fighting over the last few days, which has prevented us from fully rearming, the regiment's combat capacity is considerably weakened. But also the tank crews – who since the 11th have hardly had a roof over their heads or a wink of sleep – are in a state of utter exhaustion. Under the present circumstances the prospects of another assault tomorrow (the 18th) are not good and in the commander's view would only be a waste of effort . . .

"Is it all over?" Markus asked in horror as he solemnly put down the paper.

"No, I don't think so," Kuntnagel said. "He headed north this morning too, and Hoth reported just an hour ago that Hünersdorff actually seemed to be gaining control of the accursed village."

"Did Hoth say that?"

Kuntnagel nodded, both sceptically and encouragingly, at a complete loss as to what to think.

"And that's all you heard from him today?" Markus persisted.

"So far, yes . . . Why do you ask?"

"So nothing from Hünersdorff himself?"

"He doesn't say anything. But what I can say to you is that the front all along the Upper Don has given way."

Kuntnagel tried to conceal his disquiet with a wry grin. "Vatutin – with his new 3rd Guards – crossed the ice during the night. The Italian lines have collapsed, the Russians don't give a damn about the minefields and artillery and 'are charging across the plains', according to the officer I spoke to. It sounded as if he were standing there and watching it happen."

Manstein in his memoirs called December 18 "a day of monumental crisis", which Markus maintains is a gross understatement or a manifestation of military vanity, even though he believes the best lie is the one that is virtually indistinguishable from the truth. He also maintains that he had never seen the General more conscious of the fact that he now held history in the palms of his two hands, and that he was personally sitting beside him when once again – over the telephone – he asked Zeitzler for permission to send Paulus and his army southwards to link up with Hünersdorff:

"The plan can still work!" the General said down the phone. "The 16th Motorised Division stationed at Elista will also have to come to Hoth's aid . . ."

A few moments of silence passed while Zeitzler discussed the matter with Hitler, and General Manstein smoked a cigarette, and the rest of the Command stood around in the crowded Ops room like the Chinese terracotta warriors in their mass grave. Then Zeitzler was back, with his crackling voice, and said that "the Führer refuses". Hitler used the latest developments on the Upper Don as his justification this time; they also affected the Luftwaffe, as Vatutin obviously couldn't be allowed to continue his surge south unopposed, towards Tatsinskaya, the Reich's lifeline to Stalingrad. Manstein received orders to redeploy all the forces which were currently on the move, in whatever direction they were going, to the Upper Don, which was where everything would be decided!

Then Zeitzler asked a question:

"Can Stalingrad still be held?"

Markus gesticulates wildly as he describes to Robert the impact of this question on the officers. It is inherent in human nature, he asserts, that intelligence will always succumb to the tyranny of stupidity because it – *eo ipso* –

accepts it. Confronted with such paralysing incompetence, there was only one thing to do: mutiny, a brutal severing of the umbilical cord, seizing command of the whole front and taking whatever steps were necessary to save as many lives as possible, in other words, performing a macro-version of Markus' own – and for the moment utterly failed, let's not forget that – attempt to steer history into more manageable proportions.

Manstein told his colleagues that *preparations* still had to be made for Operation Thunderclap no matter what Hitler's orders were, and the most propitious moment for Paulus' breakout had to be fixed. In response to Hünersdorff's desperate pressure from the south, the Russians had moved a massive number of troops to the southern part of the "ring", thereby weakening other parts of the front. Eismann had to go into the cauldron to make the final arrangements with Paulus and his Chief of Staff, General Schmidt, the biggest waverer of them all and also the person who had the most sway over his commanding officer.

And Markus was ordered to go along with him.

"Me? Into the cauldron?"

Yes, right now."

He spent a few minutes getting together the necessary equipment, a bag of apples, some bread, butter, salami, a service pistol, which he claims he didn't normally carry, and whatever clothes and blankets he could muster, and he felt an indescribable relief at finally being able to cast off the iron burden of passivity. Kuntnagel organised the reception at Gumrak Airfield inside the cauldron, and a quarter of an hour later the Junker took off from Novocherkassk with Oberst Eismann and Markus, and two pilots.

A veil of cloud hung over the frozen wastes, visibility was good, and Markus listened to the Head of Intelligence's loud discussion with the co-pilot, who was squatting with his legs apart, like a milkmaid, in the gap between the cockpit and the hold, about whether it was possible to fly over Hoth's operational area, an idea which the pilot strongly advised against, until they decided on a compromise, to follow the corridor north along the Don.

As they were approaching Potemkinskaya, where the Myshkova ends, the white expanses in the east were broken up by ever larger black patches – looking more and more like wet newspaper – and scattered columns of smoke, thin red and lemon-yellow tongues of fire burst into the sky, the whine of shells, planes darted around like black fish in a white sea, beneath them a vast mesh of winding tank tracks, spirals and circles, and south of all this a wriggling black dragon as far as the eye could see – the convoy from Kotelnikovo, 800 lorries and 3,000 tons of vital supplies patiently waiting for Hünersdorff to burst his way through.

They crossed the southern lines of the encirclement, a jagged lattice of Russian positions winding round the town like frayed cables. The flak became more intense, the fuselage shook twice, but Markus could see from the pilot's hurried glance at the scratched Plexiglas windows that they must have been puffs of flak, then the countryside – as they juddered into the cauldron and began to lose height – lost the last remnants of whiteness and looked more and more like the glistening pile of coal where he had found the dead Cossack a few days before, with the Volga like a white, rippling band of mourning to the east: not one house intact, no roads, a mining community stricken by an earthquake, with wrecked vehicles, clusters of tanks, horses and tiny human silhouettes in a grotesque flea circus beneath swirling dust and smoke.

Markus saw the pilots smile and realised they were congratulating each other on yet another rebirth as the runway came up to hit them like a battered wall, ten or so bone-shaking bumps before the plane, with a few final snorts, rolled up in front of what had resembled a concrete bunker from the air, but now turned out to be a large military tent with two chimneys sticking out like broken index fingers into the white frosty air.

Markus says what he witnessed there will forever remain imprinted on his retinas, however blind he makes himself, or God makes him, for there is never going to be a reasonable explanation for this blindness of his. What he remembers most clearly is the chaos, the Junker being surrounded by guards before it even stopped, the hatches being flung open and the cheering that filled his body with "exotic warmth", as he puts it – here several hundred thousand men were making supernatural efforts (he ought to have said one and a half million at least, to pay fitting respect to the "enemy" or to be even close to the true figure of all those involved) with only one goal: annihilation. Nothing to gladden the eye, not a second of the cosmic silence that brooded over Novocherkassk, what Manstein called "the truth" presumably, unless he was referring to Markus' next observation, made as he darted across the airfield on the heels of Eismann and an aide, namely that there was a strange kind of order in the chaos: silent, red-eyed ground staff working with a precision and zeal that took his breath away, a rare *esprit de corps* or some innate reflex which at decisive moments transforms panic into death-defying courage.

Paulus' headquarters were in an underground bunker not more than a few hundred metres from the airfield, the only place Markus visited to have any heating at all. Eismann was received by the General himself, who gave an earnest, aristocratic and professorial impression, he was lean but punctilious in his lankiness, meticulously dressed with gleaming boots, face intense and drawn, a tic in his left cheek and, to top it off, restless, haunted eyes.

His Chief of Staff, General Schmidt, was shorter and fatter and seemed calmer, presumably bolstered by the fragile privilege of being next in command, absolved of the ultimate responsibility.

The officers disappeared into Paulus' private rooms while Markus was left more or less to his own devices. He asked the A.D.C. where his son might be, and had to suffer a few minutes of agonising suspense because the man didn't know anyone there by that name. But he was put in touch with an adjutant who nodded mutely and led him out again, a few hundred metres through an ashen mound of ruins and down into a cellar where his son – right at the back of what must have been a makeshift hospital ward – was sleeping on a camp bed, buried in tattered blankets with a tuft of hair sticking out from under his leather helmet.

Markus claims that he immediately recognised him and that the reaction to seeing him will be etched on his face until his dying day, like the expressions on certain icons, though these are rare on Catholic images of saints. And he says he asked the adjutant to go back to the H.Q. while he slumped down on a concrete block to compose himself, though he was in fact feverishly examining the boy for injuries without being aware of it, when he suddenly realised that he couldn't wake him, however long he had been asleep, in other words there was a risk he would return without having spoken a word to his son, and in a moment of weariness he also realised that maybe this was best for both of them; after all, he had no tangible goal with this visit, no purpose, no agenda – his emotions had sent him on a blind mission.

"The Feldmarschall had no more reason to send me there than Dante had to send Virgil to Inferno. He needed an eyewitness, or a surrogate, unless, that is, he wanted to give me the chance to try out my foolish sabotage idea, a means I thought I had found to cut the Gordian knot, just like the one that revealed itself to William of Orange when he was making his way along the dykes at Leiden, an idea Manstein must have known I was obsessed with, and wanted to let me see how stupid or impractical it was. Or perhaps his motive was to give me the chance to get my boy out. But if so, that would have meant desertion and death for both of us, unless Peter was wounded, and of course I had already thought of shooting him in the foot when I took my service pistol before leaving Novocherkassk. In short the Feldmarschall must have left these decisions to me since he obviously couldn't make them himself, and I couldn't bear this freedom, no more than the dictates of reason, I don't even remember the first words we exchanged, but I must have mumbled 'my boy' or 'Petrus', which I used to call him sometimes, at least I remember he said, and I think these were his first words: 'Is Manstein coming?'

"I noticed that the air down there was bad and I remember thinking that sand and gravel must have been blocking the air vent, if there had ever been one, and I said: 'Manstein? Yes, of course he is. Eismann's here with his *Donnerschlag* plan, so you'll soon be out, don't worry. Hünersdorff is ready and waiting by the Myshkova . . .' (He wasn't of course! He was still battling it out at Verkhne Kumsky!)

" 'Is he . . . ?"

"He spoke with such pleading gravity that I had no option but to deceive him, give him false hope, and I felt a sense of relief at doing so, it came naturally to me, this is what I have always done, he was my son; I realise of course that here I was fulfilling the dream of millions of terrified parents sitting at home biting their nails in fear and crying and begging the Lord on their knees to be allowed, just for one moment, to be present at the front to see their loved ones breathing . . . And he didn't even ask if the order had been given, he took it for granted it had been. 'Eismann's here with his *Donnerschlag* plan': what else could this mean to a militarily naive person like my son Peter? I didn't have the heart to elicit his views on the Sixth Army, its chances of regrouping and breaking out, and I doubt if he could have told me much anyway, even though of course he could have given me the official version, and at this juncture I discovered something else – I am digressing, I know, but I discovered that a curious stockpiling was going on in the cauldron, not with the aim of mustering strength for a breakout but in order to celebrate Christmas! Can you believe that? I couldn't. They were looking forward to Christmas, this was the most depressing defeatism, on a par with Paulus' bottles of champagne. Peter also showed me his own little stock, half a bottle of vodka, half a loaf, which fortunately was frozen, some horse meat, which was frozen too, some sugar, and now I gave him what I had brought along, but he didn't want it, he just flashed an apologetic and an accusatory smile and said it would have to be registered with the quartermaster and shared out in the usual fashion (one lousy rucksack's worth!) and even though I obviously could point to the lack of logic in his thinking – he was already doing his own illicit hoarding – I was so incensed by this 'Christmas cheer' that I couldn't bring myself to rebuke him for that, either."

19

Markus also noticed that there was something "inconsistent" about his son: one moment he was in a cheery mood and would laugh inappropriately; the next he was a dutiful, self-assured soldier, bursting with the same idiotic military fervour that had so depressed his father in Strasbourg, only to slump into a dour earnestness, which was very much in line with Manstein's teachings on mobility, armies had to keep on the move, it was being stationary that was the ruin of them, the boy said, as long as they kept moving they could deal with most of what the enemy threw at them, but Jesus Christ, now they were capturing a ruin one day and having to relinquish it the next, the fronts were chaotic and the trenches shallow, snipers, hand grenades, mines, flamethrowers and then those abominable Katyushas, which were now positioned on the west bank of the Volga and made the universe shudder with their sixteen 130-millimetre rockets launched in one single salvo, but the night bombing was still the worst, the Russians had started doing this right back in September in order to operate unmolested by the Messerschmitts – those humming "sewing machines" which crossed the Volga and suddenly went quiet as the pilots switched off the engines and glided silently over the final kilometres, the sole lull in the clamour of the battlefield, the fraught moments of prayers and rosaries, until sharp ears picked up the sudden swish of wings and your brain told you it was too late. Paulus had asked on innumerable occasions for air support at night too, and Markus himself had passed on several of these appeals to Fiebig and Richthofen, but the answer was always the same – the pilots were overworked, the strongest of them were airborne for more than twelve hours a day while for the rest of the time they were bent over operational charts swotting up on positions, eating or catching an hour's nap.

"At one point I couldn't restrain myself," Markus says. "I think it was when he asked after his sisters that I had to mention – as casually as possible – that I could wound him and get him out, it was to show him that I was willing to do anything for him, but he just sneered with affected pride that he would never let down his comrades. 'What's more,' he added, 'You have never been much of a man, Father, you're more like a professor, while I take after Grandad.' This was a somewhat starry-eyed insinuation on his part, stemming as it did from our previous 'hero', my father, who at the beginning of the century emigrated to Belgium, got married there and lived a secluded life on his father-in-law's land in the Ardennes until – when the war broke out in 1914 – he was struck by a bolt of patriotic lightning and abandoned his potato fields to meet his death in the trenches, almost three years before Peter was born.

" 'Grandad fled the clutches of Moltke and Bismarck,' he said, and he said it again when I visited him in Strasbourg ages ago, 'but he came back when the *Vaterland* called!'

"And then Peter had this twitch in his face which was a carbon copy of the tic I had seen in Paulus' left cheek, it really irritated me, as there were no neuroses in the German medical vocabulary, just 'cowardice', which of course was punished by death. And I don't know how to interpret my reactions to the fact that there was something touchingly saint-like about him, he moved about as if surrounded by a divine aura, invulnerable – for example he would show me the bunker of a priest who acted as a doctor in the 16th Panzer Division, and he took me there on a starved army gelding. We set off to the sounds of the thunder of shells and Stuka sirens ringing in our ears at a steady trot to an underground bunker with the regulation three feet of earth and rubble over a thick layer of girders where, of all things, there was an undamaged piano on which the division's commanding officer, Generalleutnant Angern was his name, as far as I remember, performed Bach, Handel, Mozart whenever the opportunity arose, to the soldiers' wails of gratitude.

"Here I exchanged a few words with a major in the 297th Infantry Division and enquired about any *Hiwis* he might know, as if I wanted to help Yadviga and her only son in compensation for my failed mission. But the Major didn't know any Cossacks by the name of Kamenin and was only interested in saying how proud the 297th were at having kept the underground field hospital – which they had built during the autumn – and all its equipment intact; now all he was worried about was that they might not be able to take it with them when they broke out, whereafter he told me that he intended to go and see the Madonna that a certain Dr Kurt Reuber was painting in a bunker a little further east – a great artist, this Reuber, his Madonna gave the soldiers strength and courage; even the ones who broke down at the sight of her would later rise up again as if newborn, now it was only a question of time, further south they were listening night and day for Hoth's rocket-launchers, in the breaks between the shelling, and when the Major heard I was there with Eismann to reach an agreement with Paulus he was beside himself with joy. I scribbled down a few Russian words on a scrap of paper and gave it to him. And as we rode back I saw it, I saw that a calm pallor had settled over Peter's features, his tic had gone.

"Of course it did occur to me that Peter took me there to avoid talking to me, so we wouldn't revert to our usual disagreements, and it is this – as you no doubt understand, Robert – which I remember best, that his tic disappeared. Carl von Clausewitz said that 'war is the mother of all things', but what he had in mind was state building, constitutions, demarcation of borders and that kind of thing, while my attention, however, is directed towards the little man and the invisible lines within ourselves which we never cross but which move like waving, swaying ribbons, first we're on one side, then we're on the other, we keep our word and keep our peace, but the borders move and the words are changed, the interpreters die and our reason fails us, it's almost like sitting down at a piano when all hell breaks loose."

20

When Markus and his son returned to Gumrak, Eismann was still with Paulus. Markus was offered a seat next to the stove in the tent, but he declined and instead stood outside watching the planes land and take off in the drifting snow, beside his son, although they didn't exchange a word (as far as he remembers, at any rate); the ground crews had lit fires in sawn-off fuel barrels and were directing the warm smoke around plane engines through thick, tattered fire hoses; ammunition, weapons, oil barrels, mail and food were unloaded, the wounded were carried out of the enormous tent and put on board the planes . . .

But when the Head of Intelligence eventually appeared there was yet another delay, one of the pilots had severely damaged his hands on the freezing cold propeller, and Eismann spent another half an hour with Paulus while Markus sought refuge in a ruined cellar in order to avoid the stench from the P.O.W. camp he had seen next to the airstrip, where several hundred Russian prisoners lived and died like cannibals in the open air. And after taking leave of his son – with a hug Peter didn't reciprocate – he barely noticed the ashen face of Eismann as he emerged from the meeting with Paulus' General Staff, and nor did he take any notice of the Oberst's silence on the flight back, which included a stopover in Morosovsk to offload the wounded and tank up. They didn't arrive at Novocherkassk until well into the night.

Eismann went straight to the headquarters while Markus went for delousing, wrote a report and called in on Kuntnagel, who was sitting by the controls in the radio room and tore off his headphones as soon as he saw him:

"Hünersdorff has captured Verkhne Kumsky!" he screamed. "Manstein has transferred what's left of the Romanian Third Army to Chir. Now it all depends on Vatutin and how long it will take him to cross the 'Don Bend' if that's the route he takes . . ."

"I know," Markus said with sudden conviction. "We might well lose the war, but we'll never lose this battle."

Kuntnagel looked at him quizzically.

"Good news from the cauldron?"

"It couldn't have been better. Under the present circumstances," he added. "How's the 16th Motorised doing? How can we get them out of Elista?"

"It's too early to . . ."

Kuntnagel broke off with a gloomy shake of the head and Markus hurried out again, went to the mess and got something to eat.

"But on the way back – it was getting on for two in the morning – I bumped into Yadviga. She was sitting on her stool beside the small windbreak staring into the same fire. Beside her was the pony, chewing as always. She had taken off her mittens and placed them like two foetuses next to the flames, her palms and face bathed in the tea-coloured light, her eyes like mica in a clear stream, and I would say I regained my senses by thinking the simple thought that I was either seeing things or else I had dreamt her death; both possibilities demanded further investigation, cold and sober, so I went over and said hello, again respectfully in both Russian and German:

" 'Good evening, Yadviga,' I said, but she started in fright, and I thought it odd that she had not heard my steps, that eternal crunch in the snow, and only then did I notice how cold it was, I hadn't felt it in the cauldron, my feet were frozen stiff in my tight boots, the night pressed against my face like cold iron and prevented me from breathing, but her eyes smiled and I asked her what it was that made her so cheerful.

" 'My son is alive!' she said with the same childlike joy I had felt during the ride from Angern's bunker when I discovered that Peter's tic had gone – Did I tell you, Robert, by the way that my horse collapsed halfway there and we had to shoot it? Peter did it. Strangely enough, the shot drowned the din of battle for a second, all went quiet like when the host at a banquet taps a wine glass with a knife and silences conversation. I walked next to Peter for the last bit, holding the bridle as I used to do when he rode around in the woods at Beaufort on Sundays in his youth. We got hold of a cart in Gumrak and fetched the carcass – have you tasted horsemeat? It's not bad at all.

" 'How do you know he's alive?' I asked. And she told me – reluctantly as always – that one of the Cossacks had been into the cauldron and spoken to him.

" 'It's cold now,' her son had said. 'But it's a good cold. For people like me.'

"From those words she had realised it was him, because he loved winter, the ice and the silence. And at that moment Jaromil slipped out of the shadows and walked up as if he wanted to kill two birds with one stone: to protect Yadviga and to get in my good books.

" 'Was it the same man,' I asked him, 'who went into the cauldron six days ago?'

"But before he could reply I saw she had a sack beside her, I grabbed it without a second thought and emptied it, twenty, thirty apples, frozen solid, bounced around on the compacted snow like billiard balls, and the pony snaffled one before Yadviga could get a hand on it, its yellow teeth chomping into the crystalline apple flesh, and I started laughing.

" 'Sorry,' I said, brightly, 'so sorry.' And of course I helped her to pick them all up. 'Take her home now, Jaromil,' I said, 'and make sure she gets to bed. You can manage that, surely?'

"But he had already gone again. He knew when to come and when to go, but I never learned that trick. I could only grope in the dark . . ."

21

Then everything is silent.

But he woke up once again and everything was just as silent. The din of battle from the cauldron was still there, but only as a scar on his soul. It was bright daylight, a fresh layer of blinding snow spread out in all directions like the frozen waves on a sea, and no tracks of any kind. The radio room was empty; death reigned in the H.Q. But Markus slowly came to and raised the blackout blinds, it was like a flash going off, voices from the General Staff, the tramping of boots, doors slamming and planes on the runway arriving and departing.

Beber came loping up with a cup of coffee and three frozen apples which he claimed he had found outside in the snow, and placed them on the windowsill above the stove. Markus stared enthralled at the gelatinous icy water streaming down the red-flecked peel and collecting to form a black halo on the wood. Then it was gone.

When he went into the H.Q. he found out why Eismann's face had been an ashen grey on the return trip from the cauldron: the Oberst had repeatedly explained to Paulus that it wasn't possible to supply them from the air – the Sixth Army *had* to get out – or die. Paulus, his A.D.C. and Chief Quartermaster had also realised this, that they had reached the end of the road, and beyond! But then the Chief of Staff, Generalmajor Schmidt, repeated with a sneer that a breakout "at present" was impossible, it would be a "catastrophe" and the certain death of all their 250,000 men. "The Sixth Army will hold its position until Easter. You'll just have to make a better job of supplying us."

Thereafter Paulus, his A.D.C. and Chief Quartermaster, backed Schmidt's, in principle, correct line and turned a deaf ear to Eismann's continued warnings. As this news was imparted, Markus caught a despairing, half-stifled sigh from Manstein:

"Can we expect Paulus to succeed in such a difficult and dangerous operation when he himself has no faith in it?"

Under normal circumstances the Feldmarschall would be able to remove such a defeatist general, but these circumstances were not normal, a new man would need time to settle in, furthermore Hitler would object, and Paulus shared the Führer's thinking, obeyed his orders and was living as the acclaimed hero amid the valiant spirit of Fortress Stalingrad, and was clearly also prepared to die there.

In other words, Eismann's mission had been a failure. This was now affirmed by Manstein himself, and Markus once again lost his bearings, that is, he saw that it was all over, but still spent a few confused minutes wondering why the Feldmarschall did not immediately call off Thunderclap and recall Hünersdorff; instead he sat there looking at his manicured hands, in his characteristic wait-and-see posture which Markus knew so well from Kerch and the Crimea and which actually meant that nothing was over yet, it was on the cusp, it could go either way, and only when Kuntnagel had taken Markus to one side and insisted with a patronising grimace that the Command could still continue trying to open a corridor, as ordered, did Markus regain some of his composure; the corridor would force a breakout, whether Paulus wanted it or not, the corridor would open all the floodgates of history and empty Stalingrad of its wretched souls, send them helter-skelter across the Steppes into the hot baths, back to their cosy hearths.

Markus saw to his tremulous delight that Manstein now rose to his feet and ordered some new offensives on the Chir Front, in the name of flexibility, as he called it. And only half an hour later Hoth sent in confirmation that the clean-up operation around Verkhny Kumsky had really begun. Not only that, the next target – the village of Vassilyevka on the Myshkova – would in all probability be in Hünersdorff's hands within the next couple of days – may God be with them! It is incredible! Once they had got to the Myshkova over a hundred kilometres of the encirclement would have been traversed, both rivers would have been crossed and there were only forty-eight kilometres of flat terrain and gorges to cover.

"The race for life and death is entering its final phase," Manstein mumbled, drumming his fingers tentatively on the golden cigarette case lying in front of him on the chart, a gift he received when he was promoted to Feldmarschall. It was now 1435 hours on December 19, and a new appeal was dispatched to Hitler: "Since the last four weeks have shown that it is impossible to maintain the supply lines for the Sixth Army . . . I now consider a breakout by the army – southwards – as the last chance to save the lives of most of the soldiers and whatever equipment is still movable . . ." Manstein emphasised once more the tactical advantages a breakout would provide – it would sandwich the Russians between two fronts – and he ended with a cauldron update: "All the horses have perished, some have been consumed, rations are down to 200 grammes of bread a day while the other supplies – medicines! – will only last until 22.12."

"The case" was addressed to Zeitzler, but was "to be presented to the Führer immediately". And, as usual, no answer was forthcoming.

Nonetheless, at 1800 hours the same evening an order was sent to Paulus to conduct a graduated retreat all along the northern front of the cauldron, to hold the airstrip at Pitomnik at all costs, to fill up whatever was left of the mobile materiel with fuel and wait for the signal, "Thunderclap". But no answer was forthcoming here, either.

On the other hand, Manstein came to Markus with a handwritten note, a message which was to be sent to Hünersdorff in person, via the division, at once.

"Hünersdorff. Congratulations on today's success," Markus read with tears in his eyes. "Expect full follow-up over night. Signed von Manstein."

He sent it, and consulted Jakob afterwards to find the exact location of Hünersdorff. A new push on his own would isolate him again, a new Verkhne Kumsky? And indeed the Oberst's flanks were already lagging a long way behind, in addition to his grenadier regiments under Zollenkopf, Niemann and Küper, it appeared from the charts.

After considerable trouble Markus and Kuntnagel managed to tune directly into the frequency Hünersdorff was using to communicate with his commanding officer, General Raus, who was positioned further south, and Markus decided to spend this "critical night of December 19–20", as he solemnly termed it, with his headphones on and his awareness heightened, in solidarity with the battling angels.

But all he did was pace to and fro with one of Jaromil's stones in his hand, barite, mumbling more or less comprehensible invocations while Kuntnagel, who couldn't sleep either, was listening intently for news and occasionally serving up layman's observations about the painter Raphael, who exhibited such skilful brush technique in "The Three Graces", Kuntnagel had to have something to occupy his mind after all, while Fatty Beber was reading aloud from the Bible, a performance which eventually drained Markus of all his energy:

"Listening to a man who can't read demoralises you, Robert. But we said nothing or we marked time, I don't know, until four in the morning when I had to go for a stroll outside, it had clouded over, although that didn't alleviate the brutal temperatures, it was minus twenty, and I admit that I looked for Yadviga, but the Steppes had swallowed her up, the Cossacks also kept away during these days, I only saw Jaromil once, and the duty officer not at all, he must have been finding solace with the woman he wasn't married to, what do I know . . . ?

The trek northwards from Verkhne Kumsky was unending and unreal, taking place as it did in total silence. The moon rose slowly and the contours of our surroundings were clearly defined. It was a starry night; the snow seemed luminous. Our only worry was that we might lose contact with "the leader". Now and then we sped up and the spearhead slowed down to find the designated route. Since so many tracks criss-crossed the road, it was difficult to find beneath the even covering of snow, even in daylight, and we kept losing our way in the gorges. On these occasions, in order to save time, the commander of the troops who kept the most accurate course took over the role of leader, while the others had to thread in behind. At length Oberstleutnant Michaelis, with a sure nose, led us to our destination, the village of Vassilyevka, where we hoped to find the crossing over the Myshkova intact.

For the last part I was more or less in the middle of the combat group. More gullies and gorges, deep ravines with icy walls in the greenish gleam from the moon. We were under orders not to fire, and I have to admit I never knew where on the map we were. On both sides of the road we suddenly spotted a network of posts which were obviously manned. I was taken completely by surprise, it was getting more and more eerie and the total silence didn't help.

Then we had quite a long stop. My watch showed it was just past 2200 hours, which meant it was past midnight by Russian time. We waited panzer to panzer in close column. To the right of us ran a telegraph line, further ahead I saw a dark area, and beyond that a ridge, with a village perched on top. Ahead of us, stretching across the road, there was an anti-tank ditch with a mound behind it, of roughly my height, and gun positions. It was very cold, and suddenly – I don't know where from – Russian soldiers appeared right next to our tanks – armed! And out of the darkness – to our left and right – more and more of them emerged. We gaped, at least my crew did, hanging out of the open turret hatch, we couldn't believe our eyes. My gunner told me they had weapons and I had to shut him up – Shhh! They think we're Russians!

We expected all hell to break loose at any moment. But nothing happened. On the contrary, they leant against our tanks and tried to strike up a conversation. Not a shot was fired. What were they up to? Couldn't they hear that we didn't speak Russian, only some foreign babble, and couldn't they see the swastikas on our tanks? I wrapped my fingers around my pistol and grabbed a hand grenade from under the seat. Christ, what should we do? Something had to give. I looked at the vehicles in front and behind: the same strange scene was being enacted there.

I still haven't managed to work out how we ended up in this situation, so it is pure guesswork, but they must have assumed we were Russians as we had arrived without any firing of guns, at a steady pace, in the middle of the night and drove right up to their positions – and at least twenty kilometres north of the front! As the Russians were still fighting at this time against the remains of Kampfgruppe

Küper, and were also still engaged with Kampfgruppe Zollenkopf (around Verkhne Kumksy), it had probably escaped their attention that in the darkness thirty or forty panzers had managed to break through and were roaming around deep behind their lines.

We could have shot them down as easy as pie, but apart from the fact that we were under orders not to fire, it went against the grain simply to mow down these inquisitive Ivans. In this way we fraternised for about a quarter of an hour. Then suddenly the peace was broken – at the head of the column. A shot was fired from the ridge, immediately followed by rapid salvoes of machine-gun fire. We ducked down into the tanks, the Russians vanished into the darkness and soon we were rolling slowly but surely towards the village, which we could now see very clearly.

As I learned later, our lead tank was shot to pieces by a T-34 – from a range of ten metres. The enemy tank soon suffered the same fate, but our exemplary commander, Oberstleutnant Michaelis, died a hero's death . . . We stormed the village with our riflemen sitting up top, and at dawn we had taken most of Vassilyevka, and most importantly the critical bridge across the Myshkova, which was still undamaged . . .

22

Markus put down the note and looked at the clock. It was after half past four on the morning of December 20. He had left his headphones, Kuntnagel and the radio and sought refuge in the empty canteen, along with the reports that had come in during the night. It was cold even though he kept stoking the fire, but his hopes had been reawakened, he didn't know whether this was due to his trip to the cauldron, Yadviga's resurrection, Hünersdorff's push during the night or whether a promising pattern was beginning to emerge in Manstein's tactical skills, his famous "flexibility", which made stick-in-the-mud Hitler just as hopeless as the French's unbending belief in the Maginot Line; now Manstein was not going to let Vatutin cross the bend in the River

Don without plans to drive him back at some later point, with forces deployed from elsewhere, perhaps cut off his supplies and starve him out; provided that Hünersdorff accomplished his mission, then the whole situation would be turned on its head!

"Hebel – you have to come. Hünersdorff's on the line!"

Markus left his cup of coffee and the reports, dashed to the radio room and threw himself onto the chair next to Kuntnagel. They waited. Not a sound, a little hissing interspersed with heavy silence. Markus looked at the clock:

"0450 hours: Hünersdorff to Raus. Constant shelling from tanks and mortars. Have been able to repulse an enemy artillery advance from the northwest. One anti-tank post destroyed. Still aiming for target north of the river. Reckon on heavy enemy attacks on 20th. Only twenty tanks left – no fuel."

That was all.

Markus glanced cautiously at his comrade.

"What river's he talking about?" he whispered, in order not to disturb the cosmic silence.

"The Myshkova," Kuntnagel whispered back, also awestruck.

"Are you sure?"

"Of course. This is the second time I've heard him. But what does it all mean?"

"I suppose it means what he says: 'Heavy enemy attacks', and then he has 'no fuel', so we'll just have to wait."

"Do you know what it means to wait, Robert? Of course you don't, but what I like about you, my boy, is that you listen intently to what we've experienced and you don't just turn your nose up at all this, you have empathy and what more can a blind old man ask for? We waited for over half an hour for the next signal. We didn't move, we were dead, for now Hünersdorff was under even more pressure."

"0620 hours: Hünersdorff to Raus. Why's Niemann not coming? Only have eighteen tanks left. I beg you to give the go-ahead!"

"My God, he's lost three tanks in little more than an hour."

Markus put his hands together in prayer, and another hour dragged by until Hünersdorff was back again. 0725 hours: "Still heavy fire from mortars and tanks. Russians surprisingly strong south of the Myshkova, between the German regiment and their support troops; enemy also controls the heights to the north with artillery, anti-tank guns, mortars, machine-gun nests and dug-in tanks. Counterattack impossible, as no fuel. Küper's Kampfgruppe too weak to extend the bridgehead."

Ten minutes later: "Request Luftwaffe support against the enemy in the hills north of the bridgehead. State time of attack." And then Markus had to get up and go for a walk again, away from the trap of field reports, allow yourself to become a slave of the battlefield and you are lost unless at some point you choose not to know, as we have already mentioned several times, cutting the bonds and reading the first book of Genesis, chopping wood, repairing a machine or writing letters for Beber – everything is better than listening, that is like being buried alive. So Markus wandered from radio room to chart table – Jakob had also been up all night listening; how he managed to perform his official duties at this time, God only knows, I don't, if he had any, that is, maybe that is the question – and had his worst suspicions confirmed by the charts: Hünersdorff was in a hopeless situation, way ahead of his support troops, and the front formations as a whole were looking more and more like a punch-drunk middleweight boxer off balance, a desperate slugger trying to ward off blows with his left arm – the Upper Don and the Chir – so that he can hit with the right – Hünersdorff – but with no strength left for either.

At Command H.Q. Markus had the impression that everyone, from the Feldmarschall down to the nail-biting weather oracle Galileo, walked around waiting for the final signal from eternity, the news of Hünersdorff's death: "Hünersdorff annihilated", "Hünersdorff driven back" . . . Some of them were probably even *hoping* for this so that abandonment of the cauldron could be justified and the equilibrium restored!

But all of this meant that everything rested in the hands of Hünersdorff, and was Oberst von Hünersdorff aware, in the fury of battle up there by the Myshkova, that he was keeping alive a perception of the war – whereby, if he failed, the whole front would collapse? In addition, he had carried out orders, and much more besides, after his five crazy days at Verkhne Kumsky, he had performed beyond what anyone could have asked, beyond every order or prayer, he was as free as a bird, it must have drained him of energy, tempted him to return home, where he would have been fêted as a hero and decorated up to his eyebrows. Yes, wasn't Manstein at this moment communicating these very thoughts by telepathy to his wild man at the front? "As long as you keep going you're tying up the whole army group! Just do what is absolutely necessary for the sake of your honour, duty and conscience, then get out!"

"But how do you interpret the word 'necessary', Robert? Didn't the Feldmarschall send a message a day ago saying: 'Expect full follow-up overnight'? Could it be because he was afraid that Hünersdorff's weary brain might tempt him with thoughts of retreat, the irresistible images of made beds and hot baths before the 'necessary' was done? Whatever the truth might be, it makes no difference, in my view, you are yourself and everyone else, part of something and yet you aren't, well, let me repeat myself, Robert – what are we if not small dots of light in the sea of collective consciousness, which light up occasionally and say 'I' as loudly as our voice can carry in the clamour before once again we are mixed up in everything else and become 'he' in someone else's distorted mind, a someone who resembles us, that is why we can understand him and draw up rules for what is 'necessary', that is why the Feldmarschall now knows that there's only one thing that can absolve him, and that is Hünersdorff's *death*, the optimal solution which no-one will be able to contest later, neither Hitler, nor Paulus, nor the thousands of relatives and the legions of researchers and historians who through all posterity will dissect these brutal chapters, illuminate them from above and below and behind with the sterile eye of the peacetime observer – they haven't had the experience, they haven't experienced the war! So I can find no other explanation than that Hünersdorff – as I have already indicated – was really obsessed with transgressing all borders and caricaturing human action and understanding, with liberating himself, through being a person unlike anyone else and therefore doing as he pleases with the joy of liberty in his steely-blue eyes, dying or going home, supreme and untouchable – by the way it is not surprising that he has been kept a secret for all these years because we don't want heroes like this, we want them, yet we don't want them, what use are they and what would we do without them, we can't decide, Robert, no, we can't, and some of this same confused thinking was obviously going on in Kuntnagel's head too – there I go again, thinking others' thoughts – while Beber was becoming stranger and stranger, he was absent-minded and apathetic and grinning like a simpleton, laughing aloud when a pencil fell to the floor and when a fly woke up behind the woodburner and buzzed through the silence as if it were in its own mini-summer, on top of that he was sweating so profusely that the rest of us had some light relief by forcing him to have a bath. But that didn't make the morning pass, it was still there, the morning of December 20, even when at a little past midday a new sign of life came in from the last bastion of hope."

"1315 hours: Hünersdorff to Raus. Enemy strength increasing all the time. However, no new attacks. Still not been able to get the two companies through to the bridgehead. Zollenkopf must be instructed to take buildings by the bridge to allow passage."

Beber's chin fell with disappointment.

"If we only hear something every five hours I won't be able to stand this, especially if things get worse."

"You're used to it, Beber."

"I am not! He's been in there for eight days. In Kerch it only took us three!"

"Kerch was a frontal assault, and if you can't shut up you'd better go and have another bath. You already stink like . . ."

"Fine by me, ha ha."

"What would you give, Beber, to be there with Hünersdorff instead of sitting here?"

"I don't know, an arm maybe, ha ha . . ."

One of Eismann's communications officers came and asked Markus for some help deciphering the aerial photos Fiebig had sent from Tatsinskaya. He went along, somewhat irritated, and became even more annoyed when he realised that the man was incompetent and just needed someone to hide behind. But then he was happy to accept the irritation and the interruption and the incompetence and he started counting Vatutin's tanks crossing the Don Bend – heading straight for Command H.Q. in Novocherkassk! The young man had trouble distinguishing them from half-tracks, truck-mounted artillery and other military vehicles.

"Tanks," Markus said laconically. "They're all tanks. T-34s. They wouldn't move in with their supply vehicles at the front!"

"Thank you," the officer said, causing Markus to think of his son again, reminding him that he hadn't thought about Peter for a few hours and making him wonder why he had given him up or left his fate to more competent powers, to Manstein and God: it was because he no longer had any ideas, solutions, and he remembered what his son had said about his grandfather –

"Grandad" – who turned his back on Moltke's ideas, the great Prussian warrior who knew that a general has only one free choice, whether to go to war or not, after that everything is a crisis solution. But it wasn't Moltke Markus dwelt on but his own father, who couldn't settle in the idyllic Ardennes, he voluntarily sought out the family's roots and thereby his death, and hence the strange fact that he – Markus – had only one photograph of him, taken when the man was a child; Markus' father hung on the sitting-room wall at home in Clervaux, in a picture taken when he was no older than his own son, Peter, who smiled from the frame next to him, while Markus stood, a tower of maturity between them, a rock of experience, wiser and wearier, perhaps also the only one of them still alive. He went to change his clothes.

23

Markus returned to the radio room at half past one in the afternoon, it was still December 20, and at roughly the same time Kuntnagel picked up a message from General Raus to the wild men of the Myshkova:

"Oberst von Hünersdorff. I take my hat off to you and all your panzer gunners and grenadiers and I thank you for your resilience and your resolve. General Raus."

The three of them exchanged glances.

"Is that normal?" Beber wondered aloud.

"It can happen," Markus said absent-mindedly, because of course there was also an internal "battle" going on between Hünersdorff and Raus, and between Raus and Hoth and Manstein, all the higher-ranking officers, as to who should carry the responsibility – or blame – for any collapse that might occur. Hünersdorff, as mentioned, could only be acquitted by the court of history if he died or was ordered to retreat by his superiors. While his superiors could only be found not guilty if Hünersdorff died or was victorious – ordering him back was not an option. Markus had never seen it more clearly than this. "It can happen," he repeated to Beber, "under special circumstances. Manstein sent the same kind of message yesterday, even though it was followed by an order to push on."

"So they want to get the last drop of blood out of him. Because this can't work, can it? Everyone can see that."

"That's enough of that!" Kuntnagel interrupted. "What would *you* do in Raus' shoes?"

"No idea. Probably stay out of it and keep my mouth shut."

"But that's what he's doing."

"He could order him back."

"No, he can't!" Markus broke in, gesticulating. "Hünersdorff can only go one way, and that's towards Stalingrad."

"1415 hours: Hünersdorff to Raus. Still confronted by enemy advances and heavy fire. Can't count on Hauschild before 1700 hours. Request reinforcements in order to advance. Can't go on like this; troops exhausted."

"He wants to *advance*," Beber said with a hollow laugh. "Well, that's something."

"If he gets what he wants, that is."

"What do you mean?"

"There's not much else he *can* say, he needs help, you numbskull, and it's a general he's talking to!"

A good hour passed:

"1530 hours: Hünersdorff to Raus. The enemy's broken through from the north-west. Impossible to contain them without help."

Full stop.

Kuntnagel wrote down this last message twice to be sure and turned to Markus, the sweat pouring off him, his wavy hair plastered to his scalp like motionless breakers on a black sea. Markus grinned and screwed up his nose, then he had to turn away and close his eyes, cover his head and his eyes and the world with his hands, while Kuntnagel got up and pulled down the blinds. The day was over.

"Is this the end?" he asked, with his back turned to Markus.

"No, no . . . or rather I don't know."

Markus had leant forward in the chair and was clasping his knees with his hands. "You'll have to ask someone else. I have no idea . . ."

"1615 hours: Raus to Hünersdorff. Zollenkopf has been sent. Will take Vassilyevka shortly."

"That's impossible!"

"1645 hours: Hünersdorff to Raus. Hauschild has arrived (Panzergrenadier Regiment 114) but not many soldiers. Clean-up starting."

Now Beber had got to his feet as well. He looked as if he was going to make a speech, but was unable to find the words in his huge body, it rumbled like a tombola drum, his eyes were blurred and his mouth gaped like Yadviga's at the moment of death. Markus gave a stiff smile and tried to get the man to sit down again, but Beber had other ideas, his thoughts were elsewhere:

"I've never believed that Erich was in Italy," he said, shaking his head. "I believe he's at home . . . Hebel, will we ever be going home?"

"What's up with him?"

"Sit down, Beber, or go and have a lie-down. Do something else . . ."

Markus got up, took him by the arm and softened his tone: "You have to sleep, Erich. Why did you call your son after you?"

"It's not something you think about," Beber said dreamily. "He's got a savings book. Both of them have, of course. This is not the end of the line, is it? She didn't object anyway. He's the eldest . . ."

"Who's been reading *your* letters?" Kuntnagel asked out of the blue.

"I don't know."

"Yes, you do. You don't trust anyone anymore. Anyone would think you'd turned Catholic. Was it Hebel?"

"But I can't write," Beber shouted. "You have to help me!"

"OK . . . but go and get some rest now. We'll have to take turns to sleep."

Beber didn't leave, he just stood there panting and the next moment Markus was gripped by homesickness, a longing which drained the last drops of life from him, the two absurd children's photographs at home on the sitting-room wall, then it struck him that he had never really understood his beloved Nella, her face disappeared behind thick, green glass long before he had a chance to ask his vital question. "When I met her she was a quiet, innocent soul from the forest, but she sat down beside me with a self-confidence and trust that said: 'I'm your gift from God, take me, but then I'm also your responsibility for the rest of my life' – that was what I needed answering: why me? It doesn't matter who you choose unless you are chosen – I don't know why this question should come up just now, I'm not blaming Léon either for my regarding him as another lost son, but the thing is, he is like Peter, not so much in character but in appearance, like a twin, I thought I was seeing things in Enscherange, Peter has come home, I thought, it was my blindness. Sympathy by the way is not God's work, it is something we have to sort out ourselves, cultivate as best we can in the borderlands between ourselves and the poor children we put on this earth, and the fact that I couldn't do anything for Léon either, not for him or Peter, that is my destiny, and had it not been for this war I wouldn't have known who I am, not that this has been of any benefit to me, that was what I wanted to say about Clausewitz and those notions of his, about war being the mother of all things, that is both true and correct, even if it isn't much of a mother."

"1840 hours: Hünersdorff to Raus. Two of Battalion Hauschild's supply trains have reached the bridgehead. It wasn't possible to get reconnaissance vehicles through the southern front. New attempts will be made during the night. Therefore not possible to do clean-up after enemy breakthrough from north-west. At dawn Hauschild will attack the hills to the north, Remlinger the enemy-occupied southern sector, supported by newly arrived tanks. Plan: extend bridgehead, organise units, replenish ammunition and fuel. Only then can other jobs be done. Need fuel to charge batteries. Otherwise no radio communication. Troops under enormous pressure, no rest, no food, no quarters . . ."

Then the casualties, which Markus simply ignored or left to Kuntnagel, who noted down the figures with an unsteady pen, blotching the paper and cursing, but his eye was caught by "Panzer count: 0/4/2/0/1", which meant that Hünersdorff had only seven tanks left, that he had lost twenty-five in the last twenty-four hours and presumably could be wiped out at any moment, whether he got these reinforcements through or not, they were not nearly enough whichever way you looked at it. And then at last they would be free, Hünersdorff, Raus, Hoth, Manstein – Markus too? I can't imagine it.

24

December 21 had begun. It was just past midnight, 0005 hours in military parlance, German time. In the Soviet Union it was 0205 hours. And Markus, who made it a point of the little honour he had left to keep going as long as Hünersdorff, was on the verge of collapse. Beber, having put the Bible aside, was slumped over the table asleep, snoring like a warthog, and was woken by his body's own exertions. He shook like a holy epileptic and thereby injected new life into Markus too; he gazed at the fat farmer's broad Pomeranian smile, a twinkling naive eye that could never be eclipsed and which actually Markus loved, it reminded him of his father's, even though he would never admit it.

But it wasn't Beber who had called him back to reality, but a distant, audible crackling contact between Hünersdorff and Raus. He rubbed Clervaux from his eyes – it was snowing at home as well – and looked at the clock, it was 0025, December 21, and Beber's soothing smile died as though at the sight of a failed crop.

"Hünersdorff to Raus. Situation even more critical at the bridgehead. Soon out of ammo, enemy attacking concentrically and can only be repulsed in hand-to-hand fighting. Round midnight, Russians in same places, no more than fifteen metres from the centre of the bridgehead. Have dug in under the tanks. Commander has to drive on each and every single one of the completely over-extended, fatigued soldiers to fight back and not give up. Fuel so low that radio has to be used sparingly . . . Have nowhere to put the wounded. Troops are at the end of their tether due to relentless fighting, lack of rest, food, water, heat, quarters, increasingly harsh frosts . . ."

A long series of crackles, the hiss of electric rain, then absolute silence. That was the last they heard from Hünersdorff.

"Raus to Hünersdorff," they heard a few seconds later from somewhere far away in the Kalmyk ether. General Raus was calling his lost regimental commander: "Hünersdorff . . . Can you hear me? . . . Hünersdorff . . ."

Then he, too, was gone.

Beber banged his head against the tabletop and cried like a baby. Then he fell asleep again with a weary sniffle and slumped to the floor.

Markus claims he saw the signs of the inevitable tragedy in the fact that Raus had dropped the formality when addressing his subordinate officer at the moment of death, this is about as far as an Austrian general can go in adapting social conventions. Then came the awful relief, the liberating nausea, the freedom to do what his conscience would not allow him. His heart was pounding like a machine gun, but his pulse plummeted, in sudden jerks, until it subsided into a barely perceptible ticking.

He manoeuvred Beber onto the divan and threw a blanket over him, went out into the cold, starry stillness and pressed his face down into the snow until the flames had engulfed his face, while trying to decide whether he should tell Manstein that Hünersdorff had met his Maker, so that the Marschall and Meister of the battlefield could carry out those plans which all this month he had sacrificed on the altar of conscience, or "necessity", but the Feldmarschall was probably asleep, although a light was on in his railway carriage, there always was, and would he even want this information, unofficial as it was, so Markus made another politic decision to leave it to Raus, or possibly Hoth, woke Kuntnagel and told him the news.

But although his heart was now able to sleep in its own bed, he followed his comrade back to the radio room, rolled out a mattress and dutifully lay down beside a snorting Beber and, in a slow downward spiral, relinquished his resentment towards Paulus, Hitler, Manstein and his son.

But he was woken only three minutes later:

"He's alive! He's alive, Hebel! You've got to wake up! He's alive!"

Markus was up in a flash and at Kuntnagel's side, vaguely sensing that this was too much for him, a new flicker of life now, there must be limits, and what kind of hope is it that is kindled in this pitch-black night sky, a hope for a slower and even more painful death? He hadn't slept for more than a couple of minutes either, that was what his body was telling him, the round clock above the Enigma machines showed it was the beginning of a new day, December 21, seven minutes past five . . .

"Division radio conversation – Raus to Hünersdorff," Kuntnagel repeated with a dry mouth and noted down in large block letters, like Beber at his most clumsy: "Zollenkopf launching attack on Vassilyevka at 0530 hours. Further offensives on designated targets after clean-up at bridgehead."

Markus listened and read, listened and read, staring around him wildly.

"Have you gone out of your mind?!' he screamed. "That's Raus!"

"I heard Hünersdorff as well!"Kuntnagel protested, but feebly.

"How could you do that? His batteries are flat!"

"What do you mean?"

"He's got no fuel, he can't run his generators, he *can't* communicate even if he's alive!"

"No, no or . . . well, yes," Kuntnagel said helplessly, trying to avoid Markus' gaze, "I heard him! Raus doesn't order people to keep going if they're dead!"

"The order is to *Zollenkopf*, you buffoon! He's asking *Zollenkopf* to clean up the ruins by the bridgehead . . ."

"On Hünersdorff's frequency?!"

Markus yawned. Kuntnagel had got to his feet and was wafting the sheet of paper with the ridiculous block letters as if he had found the ultimate proof of God's existence: "Raus doesn't give Zollendorff orders on Hünersdorff's frequency!" he shrieked. "He gives Hünersdorff orders on Hünersdorff's frequency – *because he knows he's alive!*"

Beber was still snoring on the divan with a trickle of saliva running from the right-hand corner of his mouth down under his filthy shirt collar. A tremor ran through him, a gentle breeze, and Markus stared at him with vacant eyes and thought about the winds the Lord occasionally sent across the flat cornfields of Pomerania.

"Who's been listening in to Hoth tonight?" Markus asked suddenly, and turned to study Kuntnagel's reaction.

"I . . ."

"You've been listening in on the division and regiment frequencies!"

"Yes, and Jakob's been here for a couple of hours, while I was writing the report, but I swear . . ."

Markus got up and ran into the H.Q., found an atmosphere there which as usual he had no idea how to interpret, which expressed neither excited expectation nor tragedy, only the same massive, concentrated solemnity that had filled the place the day before and the day before that, no sign of calling off the operation, nor a flicker of hope – necessity; Manstein in an immaculate, freshly ironed uniform, shaven, with a swagger stick lying in front of him on the chart, Eismann in shirtsleeves with his collar undone, leaning over the same chart, Stahlberg with his head in a filing cabinet and Busse with a cup of steaming hot coffee under his good-natured double chin, a team, the war's foremost team, and probably that was how they were sitting and standing on the other side too: Zhukov, Rokossovsky, Yermenkov . . . with their own Hünersdorff in the field, with their own double chins, traditions and cups of coffee; this was a team too, a mirror image which consigned the conflict between Napoleon and Kutuzov to a sideshow in history and likewise the war between Charles XII and Peter the Great to a picnic in eternity.

"Well, Hebel," Busse said, standing in front of him, legs akimbo, "how can we help you?"

Neither Manstein nor Eismann looked up from the chart of the Myshkova region, as far as he could see over Busse's shoulder.

"I'm looking for Jakob Spitz, Herr Oberst. I need some details for the report."

Busse grimaced.

"Is something up, Hebel? You don't look right."

"I've still got my wits about me if that's what you're implying."

"And what have you done to your face?"

Markus was taken aback and ran his fingertips across his swollen cheeks, there was no sensation in them, only this dull, throbbing pain somewhere inside his skull which he had thought was his heartbeat.

"It's the cold, Herr Oberst, that's all."

"As you wish. Spitz is in the mess. By the way, can you ask him to come here? We need him."

Markus heard a brief snort, continued on out and met a blotchy-faced Jakob on his way to Command H.Q., but the cartographer couldn't tell him any more than that Hoth's men had sent reports of the fighting all night, he had no messages direct from division level or lower, but Fiebig had been on his knees begging for reinforcements and . . .

"Fiebig . . . is that the Chief of Ops at Tatsinskaya?"

Markus brushed him aside and continued into the mess, had a quick breakfast, standing, took a pot of coffee back to the radio room and sat down next to Kuntnagel and stayed there, without a thought in his head, he tells Robert, but he had a dark spot on his retina and he was also in the middle of a disagreement with Kuntnagel about Hünersdorff, now they were waiting to hear who was right.

"We're amateurs," he said gloomily.

"Yes," Kuntnagel said. "How can they cope, the Feldmarschall and the others?"

"They don't listen. Now they're probably having breakfast. I wouldn't be surprised if they're also complaining about the food."

Kuntnagel was frowning.

"We should never have started this."

"No . . ."

"Now we can't stop."

"No . . . even though it's over."

"Yeah."

Markus glanced at his Pomeranian friend. Kuntnagel didn't react. They cast envious looks at Beber's peaceful body, closed their eyes and hung their heads . . .

"0845 hours: Hünersdorff to Raus. Remlinger's spearhead at south-east edge of village; Hauschild at the south-west edge."

One sentence. Kuntnagel jumped up from his doze with a perplexed smile, skipped across the floor and admitted in a flurry of words that actually he had been lying through his teeth two hours before:

"But what does it matter now? He's alive! I can't believe it. He's bigger than the Sistine Chapel, Hebel, bigger than Jesus, he's the Leonardo da Vinci of war. I can't believe it!"

Markus laughed nervously and couldn't stop fidgeting, but his body was divided into two halves:

"You're crazy," he mumbled with one part. "I've always known it. One day your brain will shut down . . . How could you lie about something like that?"

"I wasn't lying. I knew it was true even though I didn't hear anything."

"Jesus wept."

Now Markus had got up, too. "It's only a deferment," continued the same half, which was now in full control. "Jesus, why couldn't he have died last night?!"

"What are you saying? He's alive, isn't he?"

"Yes, and what does that mean?"

"That he's alive!" Kuntnagel repeated. "All hope is not lost, Hebel. We can still win!"

"Idiot! Don't you realise that now we'll have to go through the whole thing again, it'll repeat itself, once, twice . . . but then it is definitively finished. We *can't* succeed!"

"Of course we can."

"0905 hours: Hünersdorff to Raus. The first of Zollenkopf's supply trucks is turning into the village."

"What did I tell you!'

Kuntnagel banged his fist on the table and the next minute a telegram from Paulus' staff ticked in, something about "increased pressure on southern front", contrary to all the German hopes and analyses. Markus read it absent-mindedly, made another superhuman attempt to think, but happily gave up. Then Beber was awake as well. Kuntnagel, waving his arms about, briefed him on the glowing prospects, the fat man brightened up like a burnt-out fire and danced a drowsy jig before becoming pensive and asking the crucial question that the other two had held at arm's length all night:

"What about Paulus? Is he on the move?"

"Yes," Markus said before silence killed the little that was left of the good humour, and still with his nose in the telegram from the cauldron. Kuntnagel looked at him in surprise.

"How do you know that?"

"Of course he's on the move!"

Markus irritably rotated the tuning knob, the telegram was ambiguous, like all coded messages; from the front's weary left-hand flank guard – Hollidt – came a constant flow of ominous signals; both Morosovsk and Tatsinskaya were under pressure; there was a drone of planes coming from the airstrip, was this the start of an evacuation from the airfields?

He passed the messages on to Kuntnagel, who took them to Stahlberg and shortly afterwards returned with eyes agog. One of Eismann's people had inter-cepted "something", he claimed volubly, something about a corridor having been opened between Hünersdorff's position and the Don! "Look here."

Markus snatched the piece of paper and saw that the message was not in code, and from the frequency he could see it had passed between two of the 17th Panzer Division's lower units, groups which were trying to push forward west of Hünersdorff. Maybe it was two hard-pressed battalion commanders trying to encourage each other? But during a visit to the Command H.Q. Markus overheard something similar himself, and now he could feel that it was slowly beginning to have an effect on him, with nauseating force, a desper-ate exhaustion caused by the hammer blow that had been Hünersdorff's resur-rection, this pinnacle of soldierly excellence.

News came in from one of Hollidt's units that a Russian Chief of General Staff had been taken prisoner and under interrogation had revealed that Vatutin really did have orders to head for Rostov, which meant the airfields were in their path – including Novocherkassk!

Markus rang up again and enquired in a suitably irritated tone how it was possible to knock the "truth" out of a Russian Chief of General Staff when the information was of such crucial importance, from the German point of view. Are you sure it's not disinformation? No, the C.G.S. was loaded with papers that confirmed his confession, maps, targets, the route and the orders, so Markus wrote a short summary of the conversation, took the telegram and went in to Eismann with them.

"They're not wasting any time," was the Head of Intelligence's only comment. Markus took that as a sign of academic obtuseness.

"Isn't Vatutin on the runway at Tatsinskaya already?" Markus asked peevishly.

"One of his battalions, yes. They are quite near, but we'll know, Hebel, when anything happens, don't you think?"

Markus left him with a covert shake of the head. At 1130 hours Raus was on the air again, this time with an *order* for Hünersdorff to take "the ridge *north* of Vassilyevka, securing contour points 110.4 and 109.5. Make contact with Boineburg heading for Gnilo-Akassiaskaya."

"What's all this about?" Kuntnagel shouted in exasperation, but Markus now noticed that something as absurd as a smile was threatening to creep across Kuntnagel's blotchy face.

"The General is urging him on," Markus said sceptically. "That *must* mean he's got the reinforcements he needs and we're not being bloody told everything!"

"And who's Boineburg?"

"Battalion commander of the 23rd Panzers, Hünersdorff's right flank. Beber, go in and see if you can have a word with Jakob. Get him to track 109.5 and take this to Eismann in case Jakob doesn't like your mug."

"Just as I thought," he exclaimed as soon as Beber was back with a sketch of the location. "109.5, the highest point between the Myshkova and Stalingrad. If Hünersdorff can take that, he can *look* into the cauldron, at least in the dark," he added as an aside.

Beber looked bewildered again as Kuntnagel furiously twiddled the tuner, picked up a message from Fiebig, who wanted an update on Raus' positions so that he wouldn't bomb his own troops south of the Myshkova; they missed Eismann's answer, but what did it matter, Markus had reached the end of the road: he has collected and kept these telegrams and war diaries as incontrovertible proof through all the years since the war, read and sorted them and fingered them like beads on a rosary, these Madonna lilies are stages on his dismal journey to Stalingrad, and now he has achieved salvation, both Hünersdorff's and his own, this general from another world he would never meet, never get to know or even learn the tiniest fragment about, a phantom at the end of a nightmare where only the spoken word could reach him, apart from the images which the great heavenly master cast around in his tortured imagination, and he had to go out into the snow to clear his mind, but as usual he ran straight into Jaromil, the Cossack with the broad, inane features, who besieged Command H.Q. with interminable reminders of his people's bleak fate, were this venture to come to a halt, the people who had fought in two wars and lost both of them, regardless of who won.

"They're coming!" Jaromil shouted excitedly. "They're coming!"

"Who's coming?"

"Paulus! The army's coming!'"

Markus grabbed him half-heartedly by the lapels and pushed him up against the wall.

"And how do you know that, you clown?"

At that moment the door of Command H.Q. opened and Oberst Busse majestically strode out into the freezing weather.

"My God, Hebel. Are you setting about our allies now? What's the matter with you?"

"I'm sorry, Herr Oberst," Markus said, releasing his grip. "This man here told me Paulus had opened a corridor in the west. I wanted to know where he had got his information."

Puzzled, Busse looked from one to the other.

"The Cossacks can read the stars, Hebel. The rest of us have to use whatever we can. Manstein hasn't lost his head once in this campaign and he's not about to do so now, either. Wouldn't you agree?"

"*Jawohl*, Herr Oberst."

Markus thought contemptuously that it was easy to keep your head as long as others lost theirs, but he didn't say as much, he just repeated his facile

"*Jawohl, jawohl*, Herr Oberst" until Busse asked him again if he was alright. Markus composed himself:

"Would it be possible to see the General Staff's recent messages from Stalingrad, Herr Oberst?"

Busse seemed to consider this:

"The last we've heard from Paulus is that he hasn't got enough fuel for more than thirty kilometres. It's forty-eight to the Myshkova."

Markus made a quick calculation:

"Then he'll have to take fifty tanks, and the artillery, and leave the other twenty behind!"

"I completely agree with you, Hebel," the Oberst said with a wry grin, turned his back on him and strode off to Manstein's railway carriage.

"How much do they know?" Markus mumbled.

"Eh?"

He faced the Cossack.

"Can you get me some vodka, Jaromil?" he said. "A few litres, right, shouldn't be a problem, should it?"

"We–ell, I . . ."

"Three litres maybe then, yes, that's the way, Cossacks like clear orders, am I right? Three litres, let's say that then – Christ, Jaromil, how can you go round with a face like that? Looks like you don't know whether there's a war or a party going on?"

The Cossack stared at him sullenly, careful not to attempt a new smile. Then it slowly dawned on Markus that the man didn't care two hoots about what this German Belgian might think about either him or the war so long as he translated what Busse said.

"O.K.," Markus said in a milder tone. "Let's celebrate Paulus' corridor. You can bet your boots it'll all be over soon now, Jaromil. Have you seen Yadviga . . ."

25

Markus read and interpreted the reports with apathetic composure, his hopes neither rose nor fell, when you watch a landslide you don't expect it to stop in the middle of the slope if someone blows a horn, even if he is a general, but perhaps it might run into a rock on its way and change course? But would he ever be able to sleep again? Hünersdorff definitely wasn't going to pull this one off even if God were to bestow on him two or three extra lives, they will be left out on the battlefield, they will become addicted to it and will never come home, they will be transformed into unreal and unlikely ghosts, the bodies will eat and go to work, they will water flowers and kneel before a bowl of holy water, they will look at their children and at an old aunt with warts on her chin, at a mouse darting across the floor and a magnificently decorated birthday cake, and this is the Myshkova, all of it, a river it might be possible to cross, it depends, and in our minds we list all the things it depends on, and finally we are left with all the provisos in the world: stasis.

"Leutnant Hebel, there's some fool here that wants to talk to you. Shall we let him in?"

Markus looked up lethargically and saw Jaromil's eager, frost-reddened face behind the shoulder of the young man to whom he had explained the difference between a T-34 and an armoured car.

"Was I right?" Markus asked.

"Yes," said the young man, "they were all tanks. General Badanov or someone. He's no more than twenty kilometres from Tatsinskaya. It may take them twenty-four hours. Or perhaps twice that. Richthofen has given Fiebig orders to prepare to evacuate."

Markus nodded.

"Let him in," he said. "And he's not a fool."

"Sorry, Herr Leutnant."

Jaromil came in, stamped the snow off his boots and confidently held out a canvas bag, as though expecting applause or a substantial payment. Markus grabbed it, loosened the string around the top and looked down at the three "medicine bottles" containing a relatively clear liquid, buried for the most part under frozen apples. He got up and asked the Cossack to go with him to his quarters.

"Judging by your face, Jaromil," he said with confidence when they were alone, and staring straight at him so as not to miss the slightest movement in this inscrutable Steppes expression, "I would guess that Yadviga's son has managed to escape from the cauldron?"

The Cossack's eyes were evasive.

"She had only one son, Herr Leutnant," he stuttered. "And *he* has five children!'

"I'm sure he has," Markus said. "But so that we don't have any misunderstandings here, let's do it like this: I'll tell you what I believe and you say nothing if there's nothing to say, O.K.?"

Jaromil, after a short pause for reflection, appeared to consider the suggestion a good idea, maybe. "If he's got out," Markus continued hesitantly, "then he's either hiding here in the village or else you've arrested him?"

The Cossack eyed him calmly. "He got out," Markus concluded. "He discovered that his mother didn't need any help, she was dead, and he wanted to go back to the cauldron, but the duty officer was far-sighted enough to arrest him . . . Is that right? And he also made sure he removed his uniform and put on some of your clothing, right?"

The Cossack smiled weakly, but showed no sign of agitation.

"I've got nothing to say, Herr Leutnant," he said with composure, "except that no-one has a bad word to say about the duty officer. He's got a difficult job and . . ."

Markus nodded.

"I know all that. But now I want you to do something for me."

He put his hand in his pocket, took out the cross he had been given by Yadviga and was about to hand it to him, but stopped and stared at it instead.

"There's something not right here," he mumbled.

"What, Herr Leutnant?" Jaromil said, not overly interested. Markus braced himself.

"I want you to give him this," he said, handing Jaromil the cross. "Tell him it's from his mother and she wants him to keep his head down until it's all over. Tell him he's done his duty and that his job now is to concentrate on staying alive – can you do that?"

"That might be difficult, Herr Leutnant."

"I see. Then let's say that I give *you* the cross in memory of . . . whatever you want, of me if you like, and then you can do what you want with it?"

"That's much too big a gift, Herr Leutnant," came the tentative reply.

"If you said no I would be all the more insulted."

The Cossack squirmed but finally took the cross and began to examine it, like a short-sighted jeweller who has just been handed an obvious fake.

"I can give it to my eldest son," he said, testing the waters. "But in that case it has to be a gift, Herr Leutnant, which you have the right to claim back whenever it suits you."

"Thank you," Markus said.

"Nothing to thank me for. What about the apples, if I may take the liberty of asking? It wasn't easy to get hold of them."

"We'll come to that in a moment. First, I'd like you to do me another favour."

Jaromil's eyes wavered again. His sceptical nod was barely perceptible. "I want you to stick around," Markus said.

"I'm always around, Herr Leutnant."

"O.K. That's alright then."

Markus sighed and looked down at the camp bed, the canvas bag and the vodka. "O.K., O.K.," he repeated distractedly. And the Cossack hurried out before the Belgian could get any more bright ideas. But Markus stayed where he was. Lost in thoughts he had never thought before. There was something wrong with Jakob, it struck him, the cartographer's red face in the snowdrifts outside the officers' mess, it was redder than ever, as though there was something he wanted to tell Markus, but then the thought vanished from Markus' mind again.

26

Another night was approaching. Markus had begun to polish his glasses, he did this often and thoroughly, they took turns to sleep and listen even when they were not on duty, but there didn't seem to be any difference. Beber started on a new letter, scribbled down a few reminders about necessary maintenance to be done on the farm, whitewashing, painting, fence posts . . . slowly but surely worked his way into a last will and testament over a transfer of property he and his closest neighbour had discussed, because the man was now in the Balkans, and what if he, Beber, was killed, were his sons bound by the agreement, which was verbal?

It was all a question of the future of the family, Beber said, he had two sons, not one, and it was a crying shame that his writing was so poor. Kuntnagel had to step in and write instructions to the widow, which seemed both easier and more natural – he said with barely concealed contempt – than trying to convince this bonehead that he was not going to die. And at midnight Markus went to bed, without noticing, was woken by Kuntnagel, without having slept, it was past two o'clock – no, his comrade hadn't heard anything, neither from Hünersdorff nor Raus nor Hoth, and Markus took his place at the tuner again, but heard nothing from his fictive saviour either, not even "rumours". He woke Kuntnagel at half past four – it was now December 22 – but remained at his side, silence spread, heavy and inexorable like a shroud, because of course this is how it will happen, once you have been finally lulled into the coma of expectation, and have been made blind to the border between what is and the destruction of what is, and after Kuntnagel had fetched some coffee they said goodbye to their adventures in the snow by the Myshkova and engrossed themselves in Beber's papers – Beber was asleep – began speculating in hushed tones about Pomeranian land law and kept at it until Kuntnagel felt the time was ripe to avow that if *he* got out alive he would transfer the family farm to his sister and brother-in-law without a second thought and head for Italy with the proceeds, a free man, and down there beneath the radiant Mediterranean sun – surrounded by magnificent art on all sides – he would plumb the depths of art history and the human soul, explore the most intricate questions regarding our existence here on earth, roam like a free spirit along hot, sandy beaches while the stars in the sky are lit and extinguished – how, by the way, had a weed like Beber ever managed to get married when *he*, Kuntnagel, hadn't? – that was what he was missing in life, a marriage and offspring to worry about (he didn't mention love), but he hadn't seen himself as one of the others, who in the summer nights of their youth strutted off to dances in the garlanded resort on the Baltic coast, he was a bit above them, he admitted, anyway Beber definitely wasn't a role model for anyone . . . Of course, there would be stirrings in a farmer's body like Kuntnagel's when spring came and the meadows released their fragrances, but that would pass, the smell of seaweed is probably nothing to turn your nose up at, no, Markus had been to the seaside once, to Ostend, on a belated honeymoon with his Nella, the weather had been grey but the sea was no less appealing for all that, and the heavy air redolent of sea-weed and birds and the creatures that from time to time are washed ashore had permeated his memory and later re-emerged in the strangest of contexts, even when he was strolling around in the forests at home and his senses were suffused with soil and birdsong, but he especially remembered the tall posts of the breakwaters sticking upright out of the Channel coast like the smooth teeth of beasts of prey, at right angles to the waves, dividing up the sea into many small seas before it hit land, as it were, so that it couldn't damage the dykes and promenades and buildings . . . By then they had reached a new day, December 22, and a shrill discordant tone interrupted the gentle foregoing musings:

"0635 hours: Hünersdorff to Raus. Enemy attacking from north-east with infantry regiment, from south-east with tanks, have counted twelve so far. Tank attack repulsed, four shot to pieces, am in pursuit."

Markus was asleep.

Kuntnagel was writing. At 0910 hours he was still writing, he was writing down Hünersdorff's shouted communications in Beber-like block capitals: "Enemy still attacking from north-east, now with more tanks . . . Enemy attack from south-east held so far . . . 0915 hours: Urgent. Send air support . . ." And immediately afterwards an order from Raus: "Attack north-east, across Farm 1. Targets must be achieved."

Kuntnagel gave a start and tore off his headphones.

"What's that supposed to mean?" he yelled, and Markus woke up. He could see his comrade only very vaguely through the icy veil.

"Farm 1?" he mumbled drowsily and fumbled with the chart. "Er . . . seven kilometres north-east of 110.4 . . ."

"No, no. The General Command – is that Hoth or Raus?"

Markus thought for a moment.

"Unless it has been sent from here, by Manstein? Have you spoken to Stahlberg?"

"No."

"Anyone else?"

More headshaking. "Then we'll just have to wait and see what he answers."

"If he does answer, that is."

Markus got up to stretch his legs and went into Command H.Q., where he was told by the young man he had helped with the photographs that the cartographer was probably asleep, went over to the quarters and found Jakob bent bare-chested over a washbowl with lather on his face and a razor in his hand, peering at the portrait of Frederick II of Prussia which adorned the flaking wall next to the mirror.

"What were you about to tell me yesterday?"

The cartographer blinked in the mirror.

"I thought you ought to know," he said, drawing the blade across his throat in short, rasping strokes. "Then I thought, what does it matter . . . but Manstein has asked Hitler for permission to withdraw two divisions from the Myshkova and send them back over the Don to avoid a total collapse. He asked him yesterday."

"To call off the relief operation?"

"I suppose that's the gist of it, yes."

"And why didn't you tell me?"

"Because Hitler hasn't answered yet, so nothing has been decided."

Markus shook his head and ran back to the radio room. "1005 hours: Hünersdorff to Raus. Facing heavy attacks from the north-east and the southeast. Holding out only with extreme difficulty. All resources in action. Physically impossible to carry out attacks ordered. The General Command can come and see."

"He's inviting Hoth to the front line!" Markus laughed. "To put a stop to the crazy demands they keep making . . ."

Now Beber was awake, too.

"They're not going to give up now, are they?" he said grumpily. "They were on the point of breaking through."

"When it's 'physically impossible to carry out the attacks'?" Markus bawled, suddenly losing his temper. "Don't be stupid, Beber. Go back to bed. Hünersdorff has to be withdrawn. There's no other way. He has to be withdrawn. He's just committing . . . !"

Beber was breathing heavily and Kuntnagel was shaking his head. Markus put his head in his hands for a moment, turned to the snow-reflected sunlight streaming in through the small porthole and saw a moth stray into the shaft of light and become transformed into a fleck of gold before turning into a moth again after it had crossed through. Markus rolled a lump of barite in his right hand a couple of times and again thought of the Cossacks and *Hiwis* fighting in the cauldron: they must have known a way out but didn't make use of it, the chaotic attrition that has always been at the heart of the Cossack art of war, that is probably how they see their way out, as late as yesterday he had heard laughter in their barracks, pranks and frivolity, a peasant in a kaftan was dancing on the tables and the guards were laughing and clapping their hands.

The only thing left to do was wrap up in a winter coat and go out and see the same cold expanses – my eyes, my valiant eyes, help me across these plains and into a dense forest, give me trees, filtered sunlight and rain pattering down on the thousands of leaves, give me sheltering walls of trees and roofs of boughs and branches, enclose me and keep me whole so that I won't be cut to shreds and whirled away like these hellish snowflakes . . . Markus wanted to speak to Manstein but his feet guided him to the mess, where he had a chat with the chef about the meals, no, can't grumble, this is an army camp, ha ha. "Oh, we'll be alright, I suppose," the chef said after examining Markus' sunken cheeks and grey face. "Haven't you slept, Herr Leutnant? You have to sleep and don't drink the coffee, look, I'm almost ready with the stew." "Mm, nice. Where are you from?" "I've already told you . . ." And Markus stammers, there are too many words and his mouth is too small, like an army that wants to flee over a bridge and becomes easy prey for rapid pincer movements, his honeymoon by the sea, Nella pregnant and careful not to sit in draughts – "Take care of the firstborn, the others will take care of themselves . . ."

"1220 hours: Hünersdorff to Raus. Heavy infantry columns moving towards Vassilyevka from north-west. Urgent, send air support. Critical now. Five kilometres north-west of village. Heydebreck launched attack at 1146 on Birsovoj. Repulsed enemy attack."

"Who the hell is Heydebreck?" Kuntnagel asked in a weary voice.

"23rd Division," Markus speculated, once more at Kuntnagel's side. "That means he's got support from the right flank . . . Birsovoj. Birsovoj – Beber, the map! Oh no, Jesus, that's three kilometres *south* of the river . . ."

"1335 hours: Hünersdorff to Raus. Situation unchanged. Heydebreck's attack on Birsovoj has ground to a halt. Intense enemy aerial activity – rockets."

Markus passed out.

This is the man who wondered whether sleep would ever return and carry him off under its warm wings. But at some point he will wake up and discover that he wasn't lying on his back in the airy boarding-house room by the sea worrying about Nella's welfare as a mother bearing his first child, but on the floor of the radio room, with cold, bootless feet, and that it is the coal fumes from the stove, not Nella's dainty steps, which have awoken him, a dreadful coughing fit, and he can see from the wet marks on the wooden boards that someone must have been outside for fuel, Beber, the floor around his boots is wet, his heaving frame hangs over the back of the chair, patches of dark sweat around each-armpit, like eclipses of the sun, but he is shaking, and Markus hears shouts, voices, and a chill draught sweeps in across the floor, of course it is them coming to grab the big man and handcuff him – him, the man who hasn't even got anyone in the cauldron, it is Jaromil and two of his friends, but it wasn't Markus who sent for them, it was Kuntnagel, and then he sees the envelope containing the letter about the land issue fall out of the fat lump's torn back pocket and flutter to the floor like the wing of a dove, the door slams shut again and Kuntnagel bends down with a snort of contempt, picks up the white envelope, tears it to pieces and scatters them about, he has been waiting for this opportunity – but why doesn't he wake me so that I can help him to get rid of these horrible scraps of paper – they have to go into the woodburner! Now he does it himself, bit by bit, and casts a glance at me, almost ashamed, but why doesn't he wake me, now I will be asleep all day, while he sits there on his own, poor Kuntnagel, the solitary back, bent over the radio, unmarried – such a terrible word, childless . . .

"1900 hours: Hünersdorff to Raus. Targets for December 23: 0500 hours – Hauschild Battalion attacks to take hills in the north-west. 0700 hours – Remlinger Battalion attacks to recapture 110.4. Afterwards regroup to push north."

"110.4 is lost!"

Kuntnagel's unmistakable voice: "He's lost 110.4!" he repeats to himself and God because no-one else is there.

"It happened yesterday," Markus says from behind him. He is sitting on the mattress with a frozen foot in each hand, massaging them to get them warm. He pulls on his boots and gets up with a creak from his back muscles.

"I'm off," he says.

"Where?"

"Nowhere."

27

Let's make this absolutely clear. It is dark again. Some stars, but they go in before Markus can remember their names. He makes a bold foray into the quarters, has a swig of vodka, comes out and is swallowed up by the night, nothing matters anymore, everything is the same, the wind is coming from the north, yes, another snowstorm is in the offing, predicted by Galileo with his usual self-confidence. But then he glimpses a dim light in Manstein's railway carriage, so he heads for that, stumbles up the icy iron steps and feels the brass handle burn against his palm, goes in and finds the General alone behind his majestic desk and readies himself to give an immaculate salute, but is held back by the small brown eyes, which again hit him like jets of hot water.

"So there you are, Hebel. I have to say you have shown yourself to have perseverance."

"I'd like to know what Hünersdorff's chances are tomorrow," Markus said, surprised at the firmness of his own voice, that it could be heard at all. "Herr General," he quickly added, transferring his weight to the other foot.

"He is not alone in deciding that, I'm afraid."

"What are the other dependent factors?"

"Tatsinskaya falling at any moment, the Chir Front not holding, where two of our most battered divisions are up against twelve Russian ones."

"So Stalingrad will have to fend for itself?"

"The airlift will continue from other airstrips. But I have to choose between letting Chir fall – and creating a Stalingrad of the whole Eastern Front – or moving Hoth's troops from the Myshkova to the Chir. Then, the way I see it, we have a realistic chance of keeping the Russians at bay until Army Group A gets out of the Caucasus. After that we will be able to regroup further west, behind for example the Donetz river."

"Will Hitler give permission for an evacuation from the Caucasus?"

"Probably have to, sooner or later. Well, what's your opinion?"

"Me?"

"Yes, you!"

Markus shrugged.

"The decision is not mine to take."

Manstein fixed his eyes on him and calmly said:

"Yes, it is. Read up on the situation, make a decision and come to me as soon as you have decided – and I will do what you say."

Markus' jaw dropped.

"You can't do that, put all the responsibility on my shoulders, an ordinary soldier, a civilian, a poor wretch who is unable to think clearly about anything at all on the battlefield."

He had long forgotten why he was here, as a representative of both eternity and those left behind, to put his finger on the flaws in the Feldmarschall's actions, to find the right address for fury, sorrow and a somewhat more refined quality of human thought, and he realised with limited clarity that this jewel of Enlightenment philosophy was precisely the authority the Feldmarschall's conscience had to invoke in order to ward off the same accusations, but as usual his superior officer came to his rescue:

"That is exactly what makes you the right person, Hebel. I don't need any military advice or suggestions, I have plenty of them, I don't need any more intelligence reports, I need an intelligent civilian, an educated man with his wits about him, deeply rooted in Christian and European tradition, with moral values and an ambivalent attitude towards heaven and earth, a farmer and an artist, an inventor and an ordinary man, I need a common denominator like you, Hebel, with three languages, two nationalities and eternal life, with more empathy than rational thought, a man who is able to show consideration for these horse thieves we're dealing with here in the frozen wastes. You are exactly the man I need."

Dazed, Markus shook his head.

"You . . ." he stammered. "You know I can't stand this kind of pressure, it will blow my brain and I'll be easy prey to my basest instincts."

"What nonsense. You have to keep a cool head and choose between 250,000 men and a million."

"These choices don't exist!"

"As you wish. But Hünersdorff won't get any further, as far as I can see. What do you think?"

I'll wake up soon, Markus thought with a hint of a smile. Then the panic hit him again:

"But I have no guarantee that what I decide will . . . !"

"Of course you don't. You didn't when you got married, either. You have to make a decision based on what you *know* now and what you *believe* will happen in the future, unless you can read the stars. And now you can't fall asleep, seek refuge in a coma or some civilian nonsense or whatever it is you do when you're not here. You will have to write the order to retreat to Hünersdorff yourself, if that's your decision, but don't be afraid. I'll sign it. I'll also take the full responsibility."

Markus could see that the conversation was at an end, unless of course he threw in the towel there and then, but he couldn't, once again he had to see Eismann and Busse's analyses, read Stahlberg's reports, and he thought that if you're awake and want to go back to sleep, you don't pinch your arm, but what on earth do you do then? He laughed at this crazy idea, and as he went out into the storm, for the first time he could inhale the Steppes air without difficulty, God's own breath, as at the dawn of time it had breathed life into the ground he was standing on, except for the Steppes, so he began to walk around in the blacked-out village, watched shooting stars flash through the scudding, granite-coloured clouds, the storm Galileo had solemnly predicted with knitted brow and stiff upper lip. And perhaps the decision is not so difficult, it has already been made, not by him, Markus Hebel, the man and human being with two passports and three languages and a lost son, but by hundreds of others like him, like-minded, in times past as in times to come, it is just a question of fitting in with tradition, of yielding to probability and credibility and experience, yes, the truth, if I might be so bold, but then a new thought struck horror into him: he had spent half his life criticising and despairing over the decision he now had to make himself, and also reconcile himself to it – both futile, for here he stands, having come to the same fateful conclusion as Manstein: a military conclusion, the greatest of them all, at least since Napoleon.

Markus claims that he spent a whole day pondering all this while Hünersdorff held on by the Myshkova, but there is every reason to take this information with a pinch of salt, the aforementioned "half his life" would be a more precise measure of time, and what we have described is only one version of the many thoughts that went through his mind, whether the most credible or the most mendacious, who knows, and what does it matter, the seconds are ticking away, and whether it is done now or at some other time is of no consequence either, yes it is, it has to be done now, yes – there we are, but it is already the evening of December 23, so he runs as fast as his legs can carry him through the drifting snow and finds Manstein at his desk in his imperial railway carriage again, quietly nodding, still showing no sign of tension.

But before the arbiter of history could open his mouth to greet the Feld-marschall, Manstein leant over the desk, his uniform creaking, and held out a piece of paper, wafted it, as a sign to Markus that he should read it and give it some thought, which he did.

"A report from one of Hünersdorff's field commanders?"

On my way to Oberst von Hünersdorff, who had his command centre in a dugout beneath his tank, I was also hit – between the ribs. It was a miracle because the bullet was slowed and deflected by my thick winter gear, my pipe and a cigarette case. I was propelled backwards. Comrades dragged me into a dugout under a tank and a doctor was able to remove the bullet on the spot and bandage the wound. And so I was able to stay with my comrades . . .

Markus looked up quizzically.

"Is that all?"

Manstein nodded.

"This man is pleased not to have to leave the Myshkova," he said. "What does that tell you?"

"I don't think he really means it, Herr General. It's a report. He knows you and Hoth and Raus are going to read it."

"You don't think he would have felt he was letting down his comrades if he had been sent back?"

"Probably," Markus had to concede. "But I still think that's what he really wanted . . ."

"What is it then that we really *want*, Hebel? Can't we make up our minds?"

Markus gave a start and cleared his throat:

"I've made a decision, Herr General."

He put the order to retreat on the desk, smoothed it out with his trembling hands and completed the action with a little bow, as though he were presenting a holy relic. The Feldmarschall held the piece of paper between his fingertips and read aloud:

"Withdraw from Vassilyevka at once. Leave a rearguard, consisting of a Panzerregiment, Kompanie II/ Pz. Rgt 114 (without Hanomag S.P.W.s) and two batteries from Art. Rgt 76 until 2400 hours – under the command of Oberst v. Hünersdorff.

"Destination: Potemkinskaya on the Don.

"Route: 146.9, where you will be met by 17 Pz. Div. . . ."

The Feldmarschall looked up and smiled weakly:

"So Hünersdorff will also form the rearguard?"

"He's the only person able to do it, Herr General."

"You're probably right."

Manstein bowed his head and coughed, and Markus thought he detected signs of doubt in the smooth-shaven muscular jaw. But then the General raised his head and stared straight at him. "I could have written the same myself," he said. "Good. You've done your duty, Hebel. Nothing is more difficult."

He lowered his head again. But after a few seconds' hesitation he lifted the pen and scrawled "Signed by von Manstein", while Markus watched his hand as he wrote, no trembling, but now he noticed that the Feldmarschall's hair had turned whiter than the Russian snow.

"I see you are still here, Hebel," he said, suddenly raising his head again. "And that's good. I have a question for you. Looking back over all these weeks, can you pick a time when we should have ordered Paulus to break out?"

"No, Herr General," Markus answered in the same businesslike tone as when he had held a lecture on Richthofen's work. "Point One: I don't think Paulus would have been able to do it because I agree with you that the prerequisite for success in something as complicated and dangerous as this is that he himself believes in it, and he doesn't, all the signs are that he doesn't, from this distance, and that is how our actions are judged. And Point Two: I don't think he would have done it even if he'd had the means to do it so long as Hitler refused to give his consent."

"That answer is a Trojan horse, Hebel – what's inside it?"

"Doubt, Herr General."

"Reasonable doubt?"

"Reasonable but not enough to invalidate the two points. It's Hitler who has to bear the responsibility, not you. You have done your duty, everyone agrees on that. Richthofen, Fiebig, Hoth, Hollidt, Kirchner, Raus, they all agree. The relief operation cannot go ahead."

"And posterity. Will it be as unanimous?"

"Hardly, Herr General. You will have your command attacked time after time, by critical voices and grieving mothers, hate-filled fathers and aggressive historians, doves and hawks, Nazis and Communists, for the Battle of Stalingrad will be repeated over and over again as long as there are people on earth, and you will feel an unease every time, greater than I have ever encumbered you with because I'm just one painful thought, a nonentity who can be crushed with a glare. You will devote the rest of your days and all your intellect – in the form of your memoirs – to showing respect for the pain and suffering at Stalingrad and defending the decision you have now made. At first, this will not present you with any great problems. As a result of this action, you will be able to save the whole army in the Caucasus. But the man who succeeds will also have to carry with him a suspicion that he not only has the ability to see into the future but that he has also shaped it, and the question of whether you could have succeeded if Paulus had not stood his ground in Stalingrad will always remain. And to that question there is no answer."

Markus had got up. He looked at the General in bemusement, as though searching for his own voice. The old man had leant forward again, either to show Markus his white air or to conceal an enigmatic smile. Markus, at any rate, saw only the hair, and not the smile, it is not his narrative anymore, it is the Feldmarschall's, and for all we know it has been all along.

Vassilyevka, 24 December, 1942:

Evacuation of the bridgehead goes ahead unhindered at 2100 hours. The rear-guard starts moving – as ordered – at 2400 hours under sporadic enemy fire. Destination: Potemkinskaya on the Don. Telegram to say that the Führer has awarded Hünersdorff the Knight's Cross of the Iron Cross. Army Group Don (Manstein), 4th

Panzer Armeeoberkommando (Hoth) and 57th Panzerkorps (Kirchner) commend the efforts of the 6th Panzerdivision and reserve special acknowledgement for the 11th Panzerregiment and its commander, Oberst v. Hünersdorff.

Two Fronts

A good eighteen months after the Sixth Army had been completely destroyed at Stalingrad, on 16 September, 1944, to be precise, Hitler was in his *Wolf-schanze* bunker in Rastenburg, eastern Prussia, along with Guderian, Keitel and Göring. These men were listening to General Jodl's depressing report on the situation in the east: all the fronts had collapsed, production was falling in the Reich, resources were in short supply, all troop reserves were used up and the Russians were in Poland, in great numbers. Hitler's face is ashen, his expression solemn and he doesn't protest as he usually does about "defeatist" talk.

Jodl conscientiously manoeuvres his way through the whole tragedy and eventually moves on to the second chart, which represents the Western Front, and declares that the situation there, sector by sector, from south to north, is almost equally grim; only in one single area is there a ray of light, in the Ardennes, a hundred kilometres of impenetrable forest and steep hills, held by no more than four American divisions, some poorly armed and battle-weary, including troops recuperating from other theatres of war, convalescents and reservists, according to Jodl.

Hitler snaps out of his grey lethargy, raises his hand and shouts:

"Stop."

He lets a few seconds pass before announcing: "I have decided! I'm going to attack. Here, through the Ardennes, over the River Maas to Antwerp!"

A week later Jodl and Keitel receive the general outlines of a western offensive, together with orders to draw up a detailed strategy for the operation. On October 9 they present their assessment of five possible offensives through Holland and Alsace. Hitler tells Jodl to prepare an in-depth operational plan with the aim of driving a wedge between the British and American armies so that (1) the British forces can be driven back to another Dunkirk – "and this time they won't get away" – and (2) we can secure the strategically important town of Antwerp and gain much-needed breathing space in the west before attempting to regain the initiative in the east.

Two days later Jodl sets out Operation Christ Rose, and on the basis of these guidelines on October 27, the Commander of Overkommando West, Feldmarschall von Rundstedt, and the Commander of Army Group B, Feldmarschall von Model, present a plan of attack for the German Army Command West at the H.Q. in Fichtenhain near Krefeld. It is given the code name "Martin" and the plan for Army Group B is named "Operation Autumn Mist".

The generals in command of the relevant armies (Manteuffel, Dietrich and Brandenburger) are also present at this meeting in Krefeld, as well as their Chiefs of General Staff. None of these eight officers believe that the prescribed offensive can succeed and suggest instead a "small solution", a limited attack from Aachen to Liège with the possibility of encircling ten to fifteen American divisions, to give the Allies a fright and in so doing gain some respite.

But Hitler brushes all these reservations aside. It has to be the "big solution" – Antwerp! And the code name is now "Operation Watch on the Rhine", which sounds suitably defensive, should the Allies get wind of the plan. The time of attack is set for November 27, but owing to a lack of fuel has to be delayed until December 10, then December 16. And no military expert, no historian, no-one involved, no relatives, no member of future generations will ever comprehend the point of it. We lack the imagination. We don't know the Ardennes.

Léon's Bridge

I

Basically, we have only one choice to make, the truth or a lie, even if both have so many variants that one can be led to believe that life is complicated. When Jakob Hemmerling, a forester, in the spring of 1894 wrote in his report to Das Königliche Forstamt in Prüm that "there is no bridge over the River Our at Frankmühle", he might have been lying or he could have been telling the truth.

Let's say he was lying: there was a bridge.

In that case, we would presume that Hemmerling's motive for the lie was the footling nature of the case, that he wanted to have it settled as soon as possible; Holper, the miller, had only done what the border farmers had done for centuries, cross the border wherever he needed to, and he was honest enough to admit it. And a man should not be punished for his honesty, even if it borders on stupidity.

This is a plausible explanation. Hemmerling also knows his lie cannot have any negative consequences either for himself or the two affected nations. Everyday life is made easier for a poor miller without it costing anybody anything. It was a handsome, pragmatic and prudent lie which – if it should ever come to light – will only expose and ridicule the legal principle, poke fun at the bureaucratic system and maybe also at the nation state's fragile borders.

However, it is quite feasible that something else may have motivated Hemmerling. He could have been standing on the bank of the Our one bleak, rainy day in mid-winter, staring at Holper's ramshackle bridge, which was within a whisker of being rushed away by the roaring masses of water, and he may have thought: Is that thing really a bridge? And he may have smiled at the thought because in fact he has been commissioned to identify, and if necessary remove, "a bridge", not a pile of junk.

Well, it is a bridge, in the sense that it enables a relatively sure-footed person to walk from one bank to the other, two banks which happen to be situated in two different countries. But it is unlike any of the other "bridges" which span the same river and the same border between the two nations, so if the common features of these other "bridges" constitute a kind of definition, then the Frankmühle bridge definitely does not fall within it. Jakob Hemmerling can therefore happily return home and write in his report that there is no "bridge" at the place in question in the Our Valley, and he is able to return home with a clear conscience.

But, as the quick-witted reader will have noticed, this can then no longer be classified as a lie. This latter interpretation – which excludes the Frankmühle bridge from the category of "bridge" – challenges the very distinction between the truth and a lie.

Strangely enough, the other possibility, that he was telling the truth, leads to a similar conclusion. Let's imagine that there *wasn't* a bridge there, neither a bridge nor a "bridge", so to speak, and that in other words Jakob Hemmerling was standing on the German side of the river and could see only water flowing and not some man-made link between the two nations, then his report is as truthful as it can be, within the broadest possible definition of the concept "bridge".

This might mean that the miller, Holper, did *not* build a bridge and that the first person to inspect the bridge, Krebs, the land surveyor, was therefore seeing things or had gone to inspect the wrong bridge, for instance the one in Gemünd, which is also a bit of a rickety construction. But we know that this is not the case, we made it clear that the miller lost patience with the two countries' small-minded bureaucrats and built a bridge himself, which we even briefly described. Which means that the truth must be either that the autumn's high waters swept away the bridge, at some time in the period *between* Land Surveyor Krebs' inspection and Forester Hemmerling's, or else that Holper, the miller, dismantled the bridge in this same period so that the river would *not* destroy it, and put it into winter storage. In both cases he has every intention of re-erecting it as soon as the level of the river allows.

If this is the case, Hemmerling, the forester, also has truth on his side. But only with respect to the letter of the law, not with respect to its spirit. The spirit of the task obliges him to use his brain as well as his eyes, and if his brain (matured and sharpened on these very border issues) did not tell him, by analytical means, that the bridge would undoubtedly reappear, then a simple question directed to the miller himself, or a new inspection in the spring, would have convinced him. In other words, the case is such that if there had *not* been a bridge when the forester carried out his inspection, neither a bridge nor a "bridge", then Jakob Hemmerling was concealing the fact that there *has* been and *will* be a bridge at Frankmühle. His report is both true and untrue, what is true one day is a lie the next and vice versa, just like Schrödinger's cat.

2

On the morning of 22 January, 1945 Lieutenant Edward B. Fitsch (plus crew) took off from the Le Perron airbase in northern France in his B-26, and only minutes later he was at the head of two squadrons of American bombers, thirty-six B-25s and five B-26s in all, on a raid over the Ardennes to put paid to the German retreat. Hitler's Ardennes Offensive had ground to a halt, as predicted by even his own generals, and now his troops will not to be allowed to return home unhindered and gather strength for more stunts.

Visibility is good, there is a light wind and Fitsch has specific orders to "take out" all the bridges spanning the Our, and trap the fleeing German soldiers in the Luxembourg forests so that the advancing American ground forces can "destroy" them there, or at least force them to leave behind their heaviest materiel.

But as Fitsch leaves French airspace and enters the Grand Duchy of Luxembourg his radar and some of his radio equipment packs up and the navigator has to struggle with a number of unsolvable problems in the skies. As a result of these difficulties, ten of the bombers lose contact and abort the mission. But Lieutenant Fitsch has got good eyes, good binoculars and also good maps, so he decides to carry out the operation nonetheless.

The squadron flies in along the Our Valley from the south while Fitsch and his men count and plot the bridges for all they are worth and communicate the positions to their comrades in the formation behind. They go into a wide bank north over Luxembourg and then Belgian territory, "Raum St Vith", as the Germans call it, and come back along the Our Valley again from the north. Straggly clouds have come between the Americans and the European landscape, and moreover the German flak batteries have spluttered into life in the white, snowy forests on both sides of the black river. Fitsch, however, has had experience of winter days in the air, so he sends orders to ignore the artillery and break off, which was the plan – the plan he had himself concocted during his sweep north – and at 1202 hours precisely he drops his load on the bridge at Dasburg, immediately afterwards reporting back to the base in France "an excellent and surprising hit", whereafter one bridge after the other is blown to pieces, all down the *Westwall*, the Siegfried Line.

But as the Lieutenant starts climbing again he spots a bridge which isn't on the map but obviously does still exist, a thin, white line across the murky Our, which now flows in an unbroken line from Lommersweiler by St Vith in the north until it is absorbed by the River Sauer in the south.

"We'd better have a closer look at this," he says to the navigator, who has finally sorted out the radar equipment, so the German fighters, which incidentally they have not seen a sign of throughout the raid, now pose less of a threat. The Lieutenant banks over Luxembourg, veers northwards, brushes Belgium and once again comes in along the Our Valley from the north. This time he dives lower. He flies lower than he has ever done before in a B-26, and he has to because the cloud cover has become denser, as has the German flak. But he can't make up his mind:

"Is that thing there a bridge or not?"

"It's impossible to say," the navigator answers with binoculars to his eyes. "If it is, it's very small."

Lieutenant Fitsch reflects in the few seconds he has available before making his decision:

"It's not a bridge!"

But the artillery fire has become ferocious now, as though it is the Führer's bunker in Berlin itself they are defending, and this arouses the Lieutenant's suspicion, and even though he stands by his decision, this suspicion takes the edge off the satisfaction he feels on this historic day as he heads south-west again, "home" to the base in Le Perron, safe and sound.

3

Two weeks later the ground forces have advanced up to the German border as it existed before 10 May, 1940, along the River Our. But there they find the bridge across the border at Dasburg has been blown up, so they have to rig up a temporary one as fast as possible, a Bailey bridge they're called, a British construction. And the easiest way of doing this is to attach cables to the other side, so the commanding officer of the 25th Armored Engineer Combat Battalion of the American 6th Division, Colonel George W. Mitchelson, casts his eye along the line of weary soldiers to find a volunteer to send across the icy torrent of water. Then he notices a civilian standing next to him in the freezing cold, a boy of eleven or twelve, in shorts and German army boots, with a peaked cap and otherwise no clothing apart from a filthy, ragged shirt.

"There's a little bridge south of here, *monsieur le commandeur*," the boy says in French.

This sentence is translated by a G.I. from Louisiana. Colonel Mitchelson searches his pockets for some chewing gum or chocolate and orders one of his soldiers to give the boy his lined jacket and then follows him through the forest along the bank to Frankmühle.

"Do you call this a bridge?" Mitchelson says.

The man from Louisiana translates:

"The Colonel is wondering whether you call this a bridge."

"*Oui,*" the boy says.

"Yes," says the man from Louisiana.

Twenty men cross the Frankmühle bridge with drilling equipment and walk along the German side up to the remaining piers at Dasburg. They throw the ropes over, the cables attached to them are dragged across and secured, and that same night the project is complete, a Bailey bridge, the 6th Armored Division can roll their trucks across and bring the war to an end.

4

Then the bridges remain untouched.

For many years. It is peacetime. And they are barricaded off. The German properties on the Luxembourg side were confiscated by the exiled Luxembourg government in London in 1944 and they stayed confiscated well into peacetime. The German land in Luxembourg is sequestered, as it is known, which means it isn't shared out among Luxembourg farmers, like war reparations for example, but lies fallow, which may be good for it. And since a war doesn't end in a draw, but has at least one winner and one loser, the Luxembourg land on the German side is *not* confiscated. There is some divine justice in this.

This means that the Luxembourgers have to cross the river, they need to mow the grass over there, they need to milk the cows, and since the poverty is greater there than here, they are likely to have to do some business and carry out the odd job or two. But there are no bridges. That is, the bridges that do exist are rickety, they are makeshift constructions or the battered remains of Allied engineering and, what is more, access is regulated by Luxembourg border guards who demand to see a passport and a border pass from their defeated brothers on the German side, while they let their own through without raising an eyebrow. They do this by agreement with the French occupation forces, who at present are in administrative control of the Rheinland Pfalz and who with peevish indifference ensure that the Germans stay at home, in Germany, which is now called the Bundesrepublik.

And you don't get bridges if only one party wants to cross. Even a child can see that. Nor does it help that the mayor of the Luxembourg village of Rodershausen sits down to write a letter, as has been done many times in the history of this border river, to his German colleague in Dasburg/Daleiden, wondering whether it isn't time, now that almost five years have passed since the war, to build a new bridge in a joint venture so that civilian traffic can return to its normal levels, in the same way as the River Our has always been able to follow its normal course without interruption. All this leads to is that the local council in Dasburg answers citing the resolution of 27 November, 1949:

"This is not our bridge."

The bridge belongs to the French and the Luxembourgers. They can keep it.

But if this German land is no longer in Luxembourg, God still is. And God lets His church bells ring out in Rodershausen and broadcast their dulcet tones across the world, also over the River Our into Germany. On 15 August, 1951 the editor of the German *Trierische Landeszeitung* has had enough: "There is something amiss when the villagers on the German side who belong to the Rodershausen parish want to go to Mass in the Luxembourg church and cannot do so. They would rather not wade across the river in their Sunday best, and they are not allowed to use the bridge at Eesbisch, a kilometre further down. It is prohibited by law."

The priest in Rodershausen, Father Rampart, preaches brotherhood and conciliation in one and the same breath and comments that the farmer on the German side who now has his land lying fallow in Luxembourg is not identical with the soldier who under the barbaric command of General Manteuffel plundered and burned like a man obsessed, no, the farmer who has his land sequestered here, Uncle Franz, that is, who with chattering teeth and trembling limbs sought refuge in this very church in Rodershausen, along with his terrified family, when Hitler marched in, the first and second time, indeed also when the Americans came, may God be with them, the first and second time, and God let Franz come unto Him and protected him, look, there he is, to this day, but his legs are wet, he is wet all the way up to his crotch, it is a shame for all of us.

5

So once again the bridge at Frankmühle has to support people on its unsteady shoulders, the boldest of them, that is, and those with the best knowledge of the area. But it is as it has always been both too small and too big, if it is there at all indeed, and it probably is, for while the two nations interpret the new pact – of 10 January, 1950 – between Luxembourg and the French occupation force in wildly differing ways: the Luxembourgers think it opens the way for free traffic in both directions and across all the bridges, while the Germans think it only opens the way for "limited traffic", while the French for their part are convinced that if there really is to be a new bridge built here it certainly shouldn't be them who finance it – the people who use it should, and we don't want to use it, we want to go home to France, furthermore we have certain demands to make regarding the technical specifications of this potential bridge, we reserve the right – in our capacity as the highest military authority in the region – to determine that it should be equipped with an explosives chamber.

"An explosives chamber?"

"Yes, filled with dynamite so that it can be blown up at the touch of a button if there is any more trouble here, from either side."

This conversation took place between the Head of the French Gendarmerie in Kreis Prüm, Colonel Henri X. Thibault, and the mayor of the German town of Dasburg. But it was interpreted by a fifteen-year-old Luxembourg boy who crossed the river every day, using the Frankmühle bridge, to earn some money by doing just this, as the Germans don't speak French and the French don't speak German but the Luxembourgers speak both, in addition to the language they speak among themselves which no-one understands – this is the same boy who earlier informed the American Colonel Mitchelson about the exist-ence of Frankmühle. Now, of his own accord, he asks the French colonel the question the German mayor has been dying to have answered but dare not ask – the mayor himself is an advocate of the new bridge; it is the financing side he doesn't want to have anything to do with:

"The mayor was wondering," the boy says, "if *le colonel* has considered on which side the detonator would be situated."

The Frenchman's jaw drops and then he roars with laughter:

"And he dares to ask me that!"

"I thought so," the boy says.

"Thought what?" the colonel says.

"The mayor says he thought you'd say that," he translates and then trans-lates everything back to the mayor, who heaves a deep sigh. The boy, however, reminds him that since the French have dominion over Germany but not over Luxembourg, and therefore presumably will only make things difficult for their German subjects, if not out of sheer revenge then maybe as a result of their normal French contrariness, thereby presumably also making things difficult for the Luxembourgers, then it may be best to do our own negoti-ations, as we always have done.

"You're a smart lad," the mayor says with a wry smile. "I would never have thought you were from Luxembourg."

6

And so begins a new phase of hectic correspondence. It is all about money, not about goodwill, so when the Germans decide that perhaps they do want a bridge, yes, apparently they do, Kreis Prüm public works department has to be brought into the picture and they have to draw up plans. But they are unadventurous plans which envisage recycling steel girders from Hitler's defunct *Westwall* line of defences, one lane of traffic and a total budget of a measly 15,500 Deutschmarks. And that is too little. It is not even enough for a decent construction at Frankmühle, and that is already built, if we are to believe the rumours coming in from down the valley, but as we know we have to be wary of them. Das Staatliche Hochbauamt in Trier, however, has more money, more responsibility and higher goals, so they draw up their own plans for a bridge with two lanes, no scrap from the *Westwall* and at a guaranteed total cost of 36,000 Deutschmarks.

In the late summer of 1951 *Der Trierische Volksfreund* writes: "When will the Dasburg bridge finally be rebuilt?", "Important border crossing still closed!", "Bridge necessary for everyday traffic", etcetera.

Over in Luxembourg they have already been campaigning for a while to have the link restored, and on 18 February, 1952 the Luxembourg Minister of Public Works, Dr Bodson, summons representatives from the regional authorities on the German side to a meeting in the Luxembourg border town of Vianden, at which it is decided "to build a huge, two-laned bridge over the Our Valley without delay".

But there are many dissenting voices raised against the German plans. From the Luxembourg side. An engineering company in Diekirch, Luxembourg, is commissioned to draft new plans, which it does, and another company, on the German side, in Konz, adds the finishing touches. These plans are approved by both countries, after some debate. The job is put out to tender and won by an engineering firm from Trier, where poverty is highest and prices are lowest, with a stipulation, however, that they also use Luxembourg manpower according to an agreed ratio, after some debate.

The costs are to be covered solely by the Germans, by Dasburg Council, which has no money, but which will not be thwarted for that reason, for now is the time, cost what it may, so the council immediately starts negotiations with its own regional government in Trier about financial support, negotiations which, four years later, result in the sum total of 110,000 Deutschmarks. Dasburg – or the Bundesrepublik – thereby gains full ownership of the bridge and consequently also bears responsibility for its maintenance. There will *not* be an explosives chamber; that is a matter of trust.

7

The demolition of the provisional army bridge and the sinking of the two new concrete pillars can therefore begin on 26 September, 1952. And this is where Léon comes in again. For three years he has been driving himself (and Agnes) mad at home in Dorscheid, hearing the cries from the holes in the ground at Sinzig P.O.W. camp, they won't stop, so his sisters Leni and Gertrud have got him into the quota of Luxembourg workers as a hodman and cement labourer on the Dasburg Bridge Project. And Léon's reacquaintance with the world is not as painful as he has been convinced all these years that it would be. He is hard-working and unsociable and, moreover, has forgotten all his German. His French is not much use, either, because now bridges are being built and reconciliation is being promoted, and the time is approaching when the French actually ought to leave, so Léon speaks Letzebuergesch and has a seventeen-year-old from Rodershausen to interpret whenever problems arise, not that he says very much, but the little he does say he would prefer not to repeat, however trivial it may be.

The work progresses quickly, at an incredible speed, as if all the time that was wasted sitting on each side of the narrow river staring longingly across at each other has to be recaptured by force. And the site manager, an efficient, goal-orientated engineer from Frankfurt an der Oder, wants more men, more and more all the time, because he lives by the motto that two work twice as fast as one, while the local Catholics, both the authorities and the workers, both the Germans and the Luxembourgers, are more inclined to believe that two men often work just as slowly as one, but then the quality might well be 50 per cent better, all depending on your point of view, so the work progresses in fits and starts, some things go quickly and some things slowly, including Léon's return to civilian life. He thrives on the work with a wheelbarrow, spade and cement mixer, but not on being surrounded by all these people dressed in more or less the same way, and who slave away to the roared commands from a German foreman. So when night falls over the site and the fraternisation usually continues, for all the others, in Dasburg's only bar, Léon strolls down the Our bank on the German side in silence, to Frankmühle and across the small bridge there, "home", to sit in Father Rampart's library in Rodershausen and talk about God and also less weighty matters, such as the bridge he is trying to construct at home in Dorscheid, between him and Agnes. He can never bring himself to bring up the subject, but Father Rampart can see what is going on inside his mind and gives him a helping hand with remarks such as:

"You know, Léon, that both men and women are indispensable in God's design, *non est bonum esse hominem solum.*"

And Léon would answer:

"Indispensable to whom?"

"Well . . . to us all, we are all indispensable, to humanity no less, *you* too, Léon."

Léon gives this some thought and says:

"How do people actually know they can trust each other?"

There are in principle two answers to this question, as with so many others, and Father Rampart has tried both. The first goes as follows: "You *feel* it." But as Léon does not have feelings he can rely upon, in his view, and for that very reason tries to find more tangible proof, here from his friend the priest, this conversation ends with Léon saying no more and Father Rampart understanding from his silence that he has given the wrong answer, at least if it is his intention to bring together these two no-longer-so-young people whom the war tore asunder.

The second answer goes as follows, and Father Rampart is inclined to think that this is the truest answer he can give: "You can never be absolutely sure that you can trust someone, but it is a social duty nonetheless to behave as if you can."

To which Léon says it wasn't himself he had in mind but the other party, and moreover he doesn't know how to behave in a way which would inspire trust without it being misunderstood.

This remark is also followed by silence. Father Rampart has twice tried to follow up with casual gestures and a few words about Léon brooding too much, he should just watch and wait, take the first step and make a decision. And then Léon leans forward in his chair and looks down at his hands and says he will do one day, he can feel it, he can't live without the notion that one day she will be his, it is there at least, this thought, even though he is trying to cast it out of his mind, anyway it doesn't matter.

"What?"

"Nothing, it doesn't matter."

Léon is on his feet. "To think that I should have bothered you with this again," he says. "Goodnight, Father, and I'm sorry I let my tongue run away with me. This won't happen again."

8

By the end of October the bridge pillars are ready and they can start on the job of putting in place the enormous iron girders that will carry the road linking the two countries. A committee has also been set up for the official inauguration, with a master of ceremonies, a band, treasurer, priest and event organiser. The priest is not Father Rampart from the nearest parish. It is Father Claesen from the rival German town of Daleiden, and the explanation given is as clear as the water the bridge spans: it is the Germans who have footed the bill, every Pfennig, while the Luxembourgers have only contributed with the minor achievement of not allowing themselves to be tempted by the absurd French idea of explosives chambers and detonators on their side, and that is too little, it is nothing in a civilised world, but they are very welcome to join in the festivities and the procession, which starts at the bridge – as soon as Father Claesen has consecrated it – and moves up the hill on the German side, to Daleiden, where the man resides who will declare the bridge open, Saltin, the provincial mayor.

But then tragedy strikes the area, a one-year-old child is found dead in a field on the German side, and since Léon is away that day, driven by a sudden need to sleep in his own bed in Dorscheid, the suspicions of people in the district fall on him, this strange, introverted Luxembourger who lives there, deep in the woods, and says "Doosber-Breck" instead of "Dasburger Brücke", on the rare occasions he does open his mouth.

But that same evening Father Rampart is visited by one of the building workers, a young, agitated man of German descent who confessed to the crime, the child had been crying so much, he said, tears streaming from his eyes, day and night, it was a nightmare, and an accident, no, it wasn't his child, he didn't know who the father was, he just slept with the child's mother on the quiet, a German girl he went to see in the dark and left again in the dark, and he did this because his wife lived in Ernzen, which is a long way away . . .

Father Rampart received the young man's confession on God's behalf and told him to confess the murder to the French gendarmerie, too; people were going around with the mistaken belief it was someone else, they thought it was Léon.

The man promised to put his fate in the hands of the law. But it transpired that instead of Father Rampart giving the sinner an admonition he gave him a good idea, he didn't confess, he returned home and went to bed, and at work the next day his mouth was sealed with seven seals.

When Léon also showed up at the building site, of course people thought it strange that a criminal would come back so brazenly, but that is what criminals do, they want to admire their handiwork, they want to study its effects, it is a mixture of curiosity, conscience, vanity, *Schadenfreude* and presumably also further vices that drive the criminal back to the scene of the crime. But no-one said anything, and Léon was not even told that a crime had been committed, you don't say to a murderer: "Hey, have you heard? A child was killed here yesterday?" So Léon went about his business in blissful ignorance of both the murder and the suspicions; in other words, there was nothing conspicuous about his behaviour, he was as he always was, reserved and extremely private, people noted with disbelief and disgust.

The gendarmerie arrived in force and carried out its investigations, and even though people in border regions know how to keep a secret there were enough Germans who didn't like a Luxembourger getting away with killing a German child, so it wasn't long before Léon's name was mentioned, it was a relief to have it out in the open, now it was done.

Léon was arrested at work and at first didn't realise what this was all about, then he put up a furious resistance. He had to be clapped in irons, and three officers carried him down to the provisional jail that had been established in the Dasburg bar. Late that afternoon the news travelled over the river to Rodershausen, where it reached Father Rampart's ears.

"Léon has been through enough," Father Rampart thought, and then added on his own behalf: "I have, too." Before he crossed himself and left, over the Frankmühle bridge, to break his oath of silence to God, for borders are not only there to separate friends from enemies, one language from another, me from you and neighbours from those who are not necessarily good neighbours, or to prevent someone moving from one narrative to another without warning, they are also there to be crossed at the appropriate time.

"You've arrested an innocent man," he said to the inspector in charge, who was vainly trying to bribe Léon with some friendly chat and a cup of cold coffee – Léon was sitting dejectedly, half out of his mind, on a spindleback chair, refusing to say a word.

"Oh no," mumbled the inspector, seeing the clergyman. "That was all we needed. Having this case further complicated by a priest from Luxembourg."

"I'm German, young man," said Father Rampart. "Come with me and I'll show you who the perpetrator is. He has confessed to me."

All the inspector could do was go with him along the bank to the bridge, where Father Rampart poked his forefinger in the chest of the culprit and said:

"Him. He did it."

But then he, too, mounted a furious defence, he hadn't done anything wrong, nothing at all, so they had to clap him in irons as well and carry him on their shoulders, down to the provisional jail, and seat him in a chair next to Léon.

On the way, Father Rampart was struck by a terrible disquiet, partly caused by the miscreant's genuine surprise and violent resistance, partly by his own clear breach with the Lord, which had set his stomach in ferment, he hadn't even hesitated, but his agitation was mostly caused by the words the inspector had come out with . . . *further* complicated, he had said, and what was that supposed to mean, didn't he think he had the right man when he had Léon?

Father Rampart asked him point-blank: "What did you mean by 'further complicated', Herr Kommissar?"

"What seems odd to me," the inspector said slowly, "is that now a day and a half has passed since the child was found murdered, yet – as far as I can judge – none of the people we've interviewed considers it as strange as I do that no mother has come forward. And we have two suspects, a youth from Germany and a war cripple from Luxembourg – as far as I can judge – who both stubbornly deny the charges. In addition, we have no forensic evidence and no witnesses either, except for you, whom I doubt any court on earth would trust, if I may be allowed to say so, Father, for a priest who breaks his vow of silence has no credibility, neither in this world nor the next, he does not speak the truth, he does not tell a lie, what he says is quite simply of no value.

Then Father Rampart woke up from his bad dream and stared down at his large body, dumbfounded, and felt his insides churning, as though he had received all the sacraments at once, a short life, life is so short, and what do we do with it, we throw it away, no matter how sacred it is, he thought, before getting up and going to the window, where he gazed down at the morning-grey garden and behind it the peaceful Our, which meandered through the dewy meadows with such heavenly calm, if only life on earth were like that. Borders are scars, they say in the Ardennes, don't allow them to develop into sores, allow them to heal, build bridges and share the expenses like brothers, don't divide them up according to who has most use of them, or who gains most from misusing them, for "use" and "misuse" are like lies and truth, they have many interpretations, which in the end has ramifications for other rivers, with or without a contentious bridge project.

He went down to the kitchen, where the housekeeper, Madame Gören, reigned supreme, but now she was asleep, so Father Rampart took a bottle of cognac and sat at the sitting-room table by the large window overlooking the garden and gazed down on the peaceful Our as he had a glass or two while concluding that the reason why people from time immemorial had been allowed – on both sides – to wade over but not necessarily cross on a bridge was that God created the river whereas man created the bridge, and man has to be on one side or the other, you can't be on both, and man does not necessarily like the person on the other side, and as there are two there is a conflict, and now this new bridge is going far too fast, it is happening too soon, for there is a time for everything. As he was thinking this, day broke.

9

It was a special day.

The River Our rose. It broke its banks and roared like a dragon with all the rainwater it had collected on its winding journey through Belgium and Germany. Then the rain arrived here, cloudburst upon cloudburst, the river swept along with it twigs and branches and grass and soil and sand, and the Frankmühle bridge and the shuttering around the bridge pillars at Dasburg disappeared in a turbid maelstrom, foaming as yellow as the froth around the devil's mouth, one look was enough to tell you that there would soon be no bridge. Work has to be suspended and the workers are told to go home, they stay in their rudimentary lodgings smoking and playing cards and drinking beer and writing letters in three languages, because it won't be better tomorrow, it will be worse, the whole week through, until it begins to affect their spirits, what about pay, now they have to go on the dole, and you have to do that in your home district because Dasburg hasn't got the means to bear these expenses as well as those of a bridge that will never materialise, so the workers go back to their respective homes, the river has reached a level it will retain all winter, the winter when they removed the Bailey bridge and when for once, after all these years, the Frankmühle bridge was no longer there, as far as we know. In Rodershausen only half the congregation attends church and between the empty pews Father Rampart's voice rings hollow. But he is not beaten.

10

Not until late spring do thoughts of the other bank re-emerge. The sound of muffled hammering is heard from the bank, not at Dasburg but at Frankmühle on the Luxembourg side, the mayor of Rodershausen has got an eighteen-year-old to sink some oak posts in the river bed where the old ones were, Holper the miller's posts are no longer there, the mayor is only doing a site survey, to see whether the place is stable enough to bear anything anymore.

But for the eighteen-year-old it means a great deal more. He returns a day later with two friends and a horse which he rides through the water, with a rope between his teeth, because now he is sick of living beside a river he can't cross, he lives in a free country and can move at will, westward as far as he likes, mile after mile in a Europe without let or hindrance, Bastogne, Dinant, Namur, yes, even Antwerp, Manteuffel's distant goal, is at his feet, but he chooses the obstacle, like Manteuffel, he chooses to settle here, not that it is very far, he carries posts over to the German side, as well as tools, and drives the posts in there, and his friends secure logs to the top, they start from opposite ends with hammers and nails and attach boards to the logs and meet in the middle, so it was done, that was all he had wanted, to make sure he could get home dry-shod with the horse wading in the river alongside him. But this is what is needed, the time is ripe, the Our has been tamed, and work at Dasburg can be resumed, it is March 1953.

11

The universe is mild and warm. When the sun is in the south it shines as brightly on both sides of the river, on the workers who flock to the site again, from hither and from thither. But it doesn't shine on Léon. Léon is lying in his attic at home in Dorscheid, in pensive mood. He has just been musing about something that happened to him in the P.O.W. camp near Edinburgh. A fellow inmate came up to him to pass on a greeting from a blind man Léon had met in Enscherange when he was arrested and sentenced to fifteen years' imprisonment by a German war tribunal, there was no message, it was just a greeting, a token that someone outside his family remembered him. And yesterday he had seen this blind man again when he dropped into Clervaux for a new camera lens, he was sitting next to Leni's old Latin teacher in a patisserie, eating cake. Léon had also taken this as a sign, because he knew there were no coincidences in this world, every life is planned and predestined according to an inexorable pattern, like the circles buzzards describe in the sky, and we have only to make sure that we don't go off course, that is all we can do, that is why Léon is at home today, for safety's sake, and now in a couple of days it will be the weekend, so he might as well stay at home until then. He walks round in the forests, which have begun to attract birds again, they swirl around him making an infernal racket, but then who should come along the path but Father Rampart, as broad as a barn door and clearly irate. "Get back to work, Léon," he says. "You made a contract. You have to keep your word. We're building a bridge and you know as well as I do that, beside the alphabet and weapons and borders, bridges are mankind's greatest invention, whereas if you stay all alone in your wilderness you will go to the dogs, *non est bonum esse hominem solum!*"

Léon defers to this childhood wisdom, and on Monday morning, shame-faced, he returns to his work by the Our, produces some plausible explanation for his absence and is let off with a sullen grunt and three days docked off his pay.

12

Léon works. And now he no longer goes to Father Rampart every evening, but sits with colleagues and plays cards and drinks beer in the Dasburg bar. And in the few months it takes to construct a decent bridge he notices something strange, he notices that more and more of his countrymen have begun to talk Letzebuergesch, and not only to each other, no, they also insist on being understood by the foreman from Frankfurt an der Oder, and perhaps it has been like that for some time, perhaps it is not a figment of Léon's imagination, perhaps it was the war that had given the impetus to this new code in the

Ardennes, or revived an old code so that these forests could be separated from the neighbouring ones in more ways than by a narrow river, across which there will soon be wide-open bridges. And all this means that life is about to return to Léon. He has noticed that he is not so different from others.

Buried Alive

I

Sometimes God holds me between His forefinger and thumb and lifts me into the sky so that I can see the earth as birds see it, or bomber aircraft, and then I spot Léon down there, who finally has a plan of action for "the reconquest of Agnes", as he calls it, because he has possessed her before, in his mind.

And I can see Robert, too, he has left Clervaux and is in the Belgian university town of Leuven – imagine having the luck to study in Leuven, his mother has always said, and Father Rampart has also nodded in approval at the mention of this prestigious institution. Robert studies history, then psychology, then he goes back to history, half-heartedly, for none of what he spends his time on is worth dying for, it is knowledge, in his view, not a skill.

But he is part of the new movement sweeping Europe, a wave of academic criticism of existing practices and values which has barely risen from the dust, and that half-heartedly too, so he joins a small group of anarchists, where the need for rigour and objective thinking is not a top priority. And now his finals are approaching, his dissertation on Charles XII's diplomatic hocus-pocus to bring Poland to its knees in the light of Voltaire's famous historical analysis. Then his mother rings and orders him home, it is urgent, she says in a way only a mother can, but don't panic, she says again in the way only a mother can, it is not life and death.

It is mid-January. Robert gets a lift with a friend to Bastogne and catches a bus with ambitions of crossing the border to Clervaux. But half a metre of snow has fallen in the Ardennes and the flimsy vehicle can only make it up with difficulty and down through the narrow valleys and backwaters to collect small fleeting shadows that scuttle from their pink and pale orange brick houses carrying brown paper packages under their arms and shabby suitcases, short, thickset Ardennes peasants with ruddy faces and rough hands who know how to keep their moods and their bitterness to themselves – they have their own invisible paths here, Robert thinks excitedly every time he returns home and hears this language which is so distinct from all the languages it resembles; where his neighbours have yielded to the universal "*Soldat*", for instance, Luxembourgers say "*Zaldot*", and people who change "*Soldat*" to "*Zaldot*" to retain their distinctiveness, that is Robert's people, a sturdy rock of yeomen, diplomats, interpreters and customs officials and the caricatures of modesty portrayed by their neighbours, because "*Zaldoten*" is in fact what they were, both Markus and Léon, and not "*Soldaten*", yes, Father Rampart was probably a "*Zaldot*", too, despite his German origins.

But at that moment a shudder went through the bus, and also Robert's body, a quivering suspicion that his mother had finally found the time right to shed light on the mysterious circumstances of his birth, to break her wondrous silence and tell him over a glass of red wine or schnapps that his father, the Pianist, did not head towards Vianden when he left her on that unhappy day at the end of January, but directly east, over the Schwarzenhügel hill and down into the Our valley and across the border at Dasburg or at Frankmühle, probably the latter, because the Dasburg bridge had been blown up, just like all the other serviceable bridges, and there he read, with an ambivalent smile on his lips, the sign which Colonel Mitchelson's Armored Engineer Combat Battalion had just nailed to the shaky bridge pillars: "You are now entering Germany! No fraternization with the Germans!"

A dazed, wounded American might well have chosen this route, a confused jazz pianist, but equally a German soldier might well have done so too, such as a paratrooper who, in his attempt to sabotage Allied communications in the first days of the Ardennes Offensive, had strayed from his company and was wandering around in the snow and the forests, with frostbite, starving and on the verge of a breakdown, until at the will of the Lord he met a Belgian beauty, who due to the shifting military fronts at the time picked him up and took him in for a while, out of pure compassion, and then fell in love with him, for she discovered that he, too, hated the war, he was from Saarland and used to travel to Luxembourg as a child, to the River Sauer in the summer to do some fly fishing with his father in idyllic surroundings, a father who incidentally fell at Kursk eighteen months earlier. She also became pregnant by this German straggler – it is not even certain it was love, loneliness is enough, or fear – before the fronts blurred once again and for the soldier it was time to go back home, double quick, across the only bridge still standing in those days, Miller Holper's chicken ramp.

Robert, for obvious reasons, had never aired these absurd and not least hurtful reflections to his mother, who'd had such a struggle to provide him with a decent identity, it has never been an easy decision, he hasn't taken it yet, he sits over there in Leuven speculating about it every day, for who can honestly claim his own identity is irrelevant? No-one, to be sure. What otherwise is the purpose of birth certificates and confession boxes and nationalities and forgiveness, or all this new science about blood groups and D.N.A. tests, not to mention the morbid tendency people of any "significance" have always had to make geneological tables and family trees, their "significance" lies in their origins, in their passports and language and blood. Unfortunately this goes for the vagabond and charcoal-burner too, for perhaps they are actually the son of a prince or a general and not of that pitiful, destitute bungler who drinks and lies and is as brutal to his wife as he is mortified in front of his children, and it is not only the possible heritage which is in their minds, although that would be very welcome, but there is also some innate self-confidence, a realistic hope that one day they can wash off this charcoal-burner's grime and employ a servant and be respected by those who scorn them now, sit on a board of trustees and teach their children Latin and to play the flute, it all comes from your origins, the worldly and the spiritual, from behind and beneath, the way the top leaf on an oak tree has its origins in the branch beneath, not the roots.

And, Robert continues to ruminate in the jolting bus, what about the even murkier heritages that are handed down from generation to generation, "from father to son", which is what those who have a son say, all the tales which are told by those who can talk and have lived to those who still haven't begun to do either, the magic and the folklore and all the authentic accounts of our forefathers' wars and sufferings, their fleeting love stories and valiant crusades and blunders for nation and empire? It is in the light of this that Robert looks upon Markus, his spiritual font, the voice he listens to and the man he imitates, while the American and his despairing jazz in the castle ballroom only become apparent through his mother's evasive reminiscences, her determined fight to put the past in a coherent, rosy light, because what people say, that one story is as good as another, is not true.

2

Maria received her son with open arms and a big smile, as robust and feisty as in her prime when she crossed swords over the Latin books and won. She served a sumptuous meal and told Robert that Markus wanted to meet him at his home on the new farm, it was urgent, Léon and Father Rampart had also been summoned and would pick him up tomorrow morning, then she excitedly announced that she had a new job at the Maria Goretti School in St Vith, across the border in Belgium, which meant she could "go back home" to the village of her childhood, Wallerode, and settle in her old home, but not to worry, she wasn't going to sell the house in Clervaux, because she knew that Robert wanted to be here for the same reason that she wanted to go to Wallerode, but that was none of her business, he was grown-up now . . .

Robert smiled at these familiar evasions of anything to do with Leni and his fragile bonds of affiliation, Leni who now, by the way, had behind her one of the town's most successful divorces, not only because she was one of the first women to take such an unnecessary step but because she had "managed", nonetheless, managed to get somewhere decent to live and hold on to her academic career. But what was she waiting for, the local gossip wanted to know, because time is no friend to a beautiful woman, and now the young men of the town are growing up and entering the danger zone, for Leni is no nun, it is written all over her face. But nothing happens, the years go by without anyone taking the gym teacher's place and, consequently, also without her losing her self-assured smile and well-deserved good name.

Robert was given an update on the unattainable woman every time he was at home, music to his ears, but the melody was sombre, for after a year or so in Leuven he began to think that Clervaux was too small for him, too restricted, quiet and, yes, narrow-minded, and he began to loosen his ties, with Leni too, he put off writing letters, forgot messages, had a lot on, that kind of thing, but that kind of thing continued, now and then there was Christmas and the summer holidays, which gently returned him to his place in Leni's body and soul, and he realised that for every year that Leni walked around with her reputation intact down there in the cool tranquillity of the small town, parading the eternal question – "What is she waiting for?" – that the noose was tightening around his own future, he was twenty-five and ravaged by a greater uncertainty than ever.

"What's the hurry?" he asked his mother, referring to Markus' urgent summons.

"Probably thinks he's going to die again," Maria smiled. "Maybe you'll be left something. You've been his son after all."

"Didn't he lose everything in the war?"

"We all did," she said in her familiar, weary expression, and Robert again had to acknowledge her incredible ability to make him think that he had grown up in affluence. But when did he actually begin to doubt her? Is this something that everyone does, regard the accounts of one's origins with greater and greater scepticism, or was this his own private failing? Last autumn he was sitting in the reading room one day and leafing through some past editions of *Life* magazine – to brush up his English – and he had seen in black and white, in an article about the Battle of the Bulge, that Manteuffel's troops really did come across a piano-playing G.I. in Clervaux's chateau ballroom, it even said he was the sole survivor.

At a pinch, he could imagine that his mother at some point in the distant past had read the same article and lifted the bizarre idea from there, you don't make up that kind of thing, it's either true or it doesn't exist! And of course she was aware of this. But would this ever end, this toing and froing, from one to the other, still not being able to ask her straight out, it might ruin her life's work and presumably also be an act of sacrilege against the absolution Father Rampart must have given her, apart from the fact that this type of plain speaking never took place in this house. Now, for example, now he gets up and thanks her for the meal and kisses her on the cheek and says:

"I'm going for a walk to see Leni."

"That's very frank of you."

Yes, he could be frank for he has no intention of going to see Leni. He just wants to stroll around town, which he always does on the first evening he is at home. He puts on a coat and goes out into his town, which, behind shutters and lowered blinds, is preparing to go to bed. Snow is still falling from leaden clouds which are low in the valley now, on the football pitch the goals stick up like enormous croquet hoops from the virgin expanses while the chateau is bathed in light from the three new projectors, and the hills around are swallowed up by the dense night sky.

He crosses the square where the tourist buses usually park and heads for the narrow alleyways, chooses a bar at random, but spots his old principal in there, Crookneck, who had once hesitated to give Maria the requisite approval for her Latin primer, their eyes meet, two nods, but Crookneck looks down, he is old now, there is an empty glass on the bar in front of him, it is refilled and Crookneck laughs too loudly at a remark the landlord makes. Robert goes out again and walks towards Leni's house, yellow light steals out between the shutters and the window frames on the ground floor, so she is awake, but he doesn't go in, why doesn't he go in and find out who he is once and for all, she must know?

There is no answer to such questions. But there is no point leaving now, so the crux is whether he is closer to his or Leni's house. He is closer to Leni's house, right outside it, then he turns and goes home, but once there he turns on his heel and goes back to Leni's. Now the ground floor is dark, but there is a light on in one of the windows upstairs. He stands motionless until it is switched off, then he goes home and thinks no more about why. Crookneck haunts his thoughts, the incomprehensible conversation he once witnessed between him and Markus, as well as Markus' reluctance to do anything to help Maria in the Latin primer dispute, which was resolved as it had to be, there was probably some kind of explanation, but Clervaux has gone to bed.

Robert has, too.

He cries in his sleep, tosses and turns between the sheets, his heart thrashes around and his limbs shake, but he doesn't notice. The next morning he doesn't notice either, or else he has forgotten, sleep has taken it and now it is light and there is more snow, and of course tonight he is going to see Leni, once and for all, if only Markus can find peace.

3

Markus and Nella had moved out of Clervaux to a simple farmhouse with no land on the outskirts of the village of Doennange, in the hills to the west, where there was even more snow. But something else was to make this day extra special for Robert. His mother had gone to meet a solicitor in Meyerode about the inheritance in Belgium, but he found her diary which was usually under lock and key in the bureau in the "library" and was only taken out when her tears could not be stemmed in any other way; now it was in a no-man's-land between him and her, on a little pedestal table on the landing between the two bedrooms, where Maria in the spring and summer months placed a vase of flowers and otherwise just covered with a cloth. It was impossible to determine whether she had forgotten it in her haste – after confiding to her diary her plans to move? – or whether she wanted him to find it and read it, in the same indirect way that she normally informed him about things that cannot be said, as if to give him a choice as it were, and thereby absolve herself of the possible consequences; and he found himself reacting in exactly the same manner by placing the book unread on the top shelf of the cupboard next to the bathroom, behind some old towels and frayed cloths, to be retrieved if she said it had gone missing, as innocent as an undivulged secret – Here it is, Mama – and to read it only if she *never* asked about it, whenever that might be.

In a good mood, but also slightly despondent about this eternal game that no-one can win or lose, he had a quick breakfast, dressed and was ready by the time he heard the squeal of the tyres on Léon's "new" car as it pulled up in the yard.

There weren't two men in the vehicle but three; the third got out and introduced himself as Erich Beber, Professor of History and M.P. for the German S.P.D. Party, Hamburg, a robust, thickset and lively man in his fifties with an eager handshake and military history as his area of expertise, it soon transpired, as he talked constantly about all the time he had devoted to the tragedy of Stalingrad, the most myth-laden of all catastrophes, that was also the reason why he was here, after having corresponded with Markus Hebel on the subject over a number of years, particularly as there were some unclarified issues regarding Beber's father's "war neurosis" . . . And the others realised in the course of the first two or three kilometres, which took them a good half an hour, that Beber must have put a lot of pressure on Markus to have this audience; Robert was more interested in his mother's diary and irritated that the foreigner was like "most Germans", a common response in these parts when you meet someone looking for something he already knows, and Father Rampart may have felt the same, at any rate his contribution to the conversation soon lapsed, into a pious smile, and if there was one thing Léon didn't want to hear about it was the war, so he kept quiet too, and anyway he had his task cut out keeping the vehicle on the road, it was an old army jeep that he sometimes used to relieve the tractor at home on the farm.

So Robert was the only one left to keep the conversation going and he asserted that no-one knows anything about Stalingrad anymore, his peers at the university think it was the war's turning point, finito, as do most Europeans nowadays, those on the mainland at the very least, while the Americans tend to claim it was Midway or D-Day and the invasion of Normandy, and the British probably think the Battle of Britain was the deciding factor or Montgomery's El Alamein and the subsequent Sicily landings, and of course here in the forests we have our own little version of the events, of the Ardennes Offensive in 1944 and Manstein's and Guderian's Blitzkrieg in 1940, it depends on what kind of turning point you are talking about, that was all there was to it . . .

Robert didn't notice the irony in his own voice until Father Rampart gave a polite cough and commented on the dreadful weather and how it might spoil the whole excursion. But it upset Beber that universities were now filled with youngsters who knew nothing about history and who were only interested in unbridled freedom, they would end up making the same mistakes all over again. Why don't I like him, Robert mused, after all Markus is German too, even though he has managed to cross a few borders in his life, so is Father Rampart, he is from Paderborn and it wouldn't surprise me if I was from Saarland, in addition to my Belgian half, and that leaves only Léon, no-one knows where he is from, he is from here.

And as for Stalingrad – we were stuck in the snow anyway – Beber contended it was the Sixth Army's demise that gave Stalin the necessary authority at the Yalta Conference to gain acceptance for the Soviet Union's role as a superpower, and now we were well and truly stuck. We had to get out and push. But Léon was not much of a hand with the American vehicle, the wheels spun and turned the packed snow into mush and the gear changes required a much bigger man, so the party decided to park the jeep and cover the last two or three kilometres on foot.

Robert knew a shortcut, a firebreak that cut straight through the forest-clad hill like a broad avenue. And Father Rampart had the opportunity to reprimand him for his surly treatment of their guest – "We are not in the habit of saying what we think, think your thoughts, think whatever you like but don't say it, besides he is not your guest . . ."

They plodded up through the thick snow for the first kilometre and into the open countryside, into a huge field that led to the other fields that covered the whole landscape, divided up by low beech hedges and the odd hazel tree or a bent oak along the boundaries, and the wind howled across. Father Rampart was panting, his heavy body leant forward into the gusts, his black cassock-tails flapping like raven wings. Beber had briefly put the war on hold and produced a bottle of schnapps, which they took turns taking swigs from.

"What a beautiful country."

"Yes," said the others. But Robert was nervously eyeing Father Rampart's face, which was only very slowly regaining its naturally ruddy hue. The old fellow said he might have to sit down for a minute, but by then he had already toppled over and the others had to drag him to his feet, they stood motionless, gazing across the fields and panting in unison, there wasn't much to see because of the iron-grey clouds drifting through the valley and obscuring the view of the hills to the north and east where, on the next ridge, the village of Eselborn resembled tiny mounds under the snow and the smoke was snatched from the chimneys like fluttering ribbons and dissolved into nothing.

They started walking again, it was snowing more heavily now, and they made slow progress. Father Rampart did not even have the energy to be annoyed by his own frailty, he had to be half carried and was occasionally given schnapps by his new friend, but as they were squeezing through the last kissing gate in the last hedge before Doennange, Léon suddenly announced from beneath the arm of the panting Father Rampart that he had got married. In the registry office, in the capital last summer, only a civil marriage, halfway between a marriage, which the Lord prefers, and living in sin, this was the compromise that Léon thought he could manage, a halfway house, but now he hoped that Father Rampart could arrange the religious side of the matter some time in the spring, although Agnes had been married before, many have been, she is a widow.

"Congratulations," Beber said, proffering his hand, while Robert burst out laughing and Father Rampart angrily tore himself free of the supporting arms and gasped for breath. "She's also expecting," Léon quickly added, as if to get it all out in one go. "A boy."

"How can you know?" Beber asked.

"Of course it'll be a son," Rampart sighed after recovering his breath. "May God bless you, Léon. You're a good lad. And, if not, it'll probably be a girl."

"Yes, that's a possibility too."

As they came to the first farm a farmer appeared from the cowshed and eyed them with a sceptical expression, Father Rampart in particular, who was on his last legs, seeming to hold his attention.

"Oh yes, old Hebel bought the house over there, called Hammer, a year or two ago."

Father Rampart had to summon up his last reserves, and with the help of Léon, who was thinking about Agnes and that now there was no way back, and Robert, who was thinking about the diary and his mother and Leni and lots of other unclarified issues, he covered the final two hundred metres at a snail's pace, also assisted by Beber, who dreamily repeated that he hadn't had the slightest inkling that coming here would be such a wonderful experience, he never went anywhere except to party conferences; true enough once he had gone to Stalingrad and allowed himself to be photographed in front of the grandiose memorial to the battle there, it had been a terrible trip, and it was a terrible monument . . .

4

There was great confusion as they came into the long stone house, which in a telephone conversation with Robert the previous year Markus had called his "final hermitage", he was no longer a Cistercian monk, he had to rise from the depths of Clervaux up to the higher land.

Nella received them all of a fluster and with a lot of drama, it was in fact not Markus but she – and Maria – who had summoned them, and Beber hadn't been invited at all, at least not by her, but just sit yourselves down, it's too late now, all the roads are snowed under, well, the thing was that Markus had changed beyond recognition, he went out at nights, slept during the daytime, didn't eat and had all but given up talking; he even claimed he was getting his sight back, and it all started a couple of weeks ago when a small parcel arrived from Russia with a strange cross in it, there must have been a curse on it, at any rate it didn't look like the ones she had hanging in the house – there was also a letter with it, but none of them could read it and who knows whether it had anything to do with his son again.

Father Rampart took the cross and looked around for a chair, slumped down on the bench next to the stove and announced amid much huffing and puffing that this was a Russian Orthodox cross and therefore harmless, to Nella's relief, but what about the letter, and where is he?

Markus was out, as usual, often he didn't come home until after it was dark, it didn't matter, he said, for blind men can see where the rest of us can't, but she didn't like it all the same.

She started making coffee and setting the table, Léon was sent out for some briquettes, and Beber, who didn't have the ability to talk about the war in a casual way or keep quiet about it in the Ardennes way, tried again to involve Father Rampart, who had focused his attention on the bottle of wine Nella had put out, while Robert donned his coat, went outside and found Markus and Delila's tracks in the snow. He followed them across two broad fields until he reached the beech forest stretching like a white cathedral into the sky as far as the eye could see, where he found the old man sitting on the bottom rung of a *Hochsitz*, a hunting tower, staring into a bonfire like Prometheus watching over his most precious spoils. Whimpering and dissatisfied, the treacherous and immortal Delila was running around her master and the fire in ever smaller circles until she curled up and settled between his feet and the fire. Markus raised his eyes and stared straight ahead.

"Is it you?"

"It is me."

Robert offered no explanation as to why he had appeared out of nowhere like St Hubertus' stag, nor was he asked for one, it was a repeat of the meeting at the ruined mill when the German balloonist took them on board. Markus was living somewhere between dream and reality. He had received yet another confused letter forcing him to turn back time; a Cossack had, through his wondrous circle of acquaintances, come across information about his son's – Peter's – fate; the boy had survived all the ordeals of Stalingrad until January 31, when he was taken prisoner along with the other 91,000 soldiers still alive. Paulus and many of his generals had converted to the Russian creed, they wrote fliers urging German soldiers to capitulate and desert and these were dropped over Manstein's fleeing armies, out of bitterness towards the Führer presumably, towards Göring or Richthofen, or towards Manstein . . . and were rewarded with a few anonymous years in East Germany; by then Paulus' Romanian wife had long since died, from grief no doubt, both sons had fallen in battle and he himself held out until 1956, they must have been long years.

"But I've already told you all this . . ."

Markus paused, gave a forlorn smile and rubbed some snow on Delila's belly to stop her coat being singed by the flames, she growled quietly and licked his hands, and he said: "It's not cold enough here, it never gets cold enough here, that's why we don't know what ice is, Robert, despite all this snow. But now I've been told by my friend Jaromil that Peter declined the offer, he would not desert his Führer and Fatherland for the 'Red nightmare', he would sooner perish. And he did, ironically enough not of cold or hunger, like most of the others, but at the hands of a bunch of Romanian fellow prisoners, as there was war in the camps too, and there was me, waiting for this news all these years, receiving mountains of letters from people who believe they know something, and then it is Jaromil who convinces me, not that it came as a shock, it is more than ten years since the last poor wretches came home, only 5,000 survived, and I had resigned myself to the fact that he wasn't alive, but this, the fact that he wasn't able to turn his back on Hitler, even beneath the very portico of death, even when his own commanding officer did, I just can't comprehend that."

"But you've never trusted this Jaromil before," Robert said. "Why now?"

Markus sprinkled more snow over Delila's wet belly, watched the steam rising from her coat and smiled a faraway smile:

"He's given me the names of all of his five children, and his grandchildren too, as well as all their birthdays, maybe to exult, maybe he expects a present or he just wants me to send them a thought on May 5, February 12, October 10 . . . or else it might be a ritual, I don't understand the Cossacks, you don't know where you are with them, I only know it's him, this fool Jaromil, and that he is telling the truth, whether he realises it or not."

Robert had found some twigs and laid them on the fire, then he sat down and began to think about the diary, whether he would ever read it, and now he knew, he wasn't going to read it, not until the time came when whatever was in it would no longer have any significance, he was going to keep it, have it and own it but not read it, she would not get any apology from him, or understanding, this was a fitting revenge for her well-intentioned deceptions, for who of us can understand our parents no matter how much we read, and who isn't a fictional character when it comes down to it, war is not only the mother of all things, an explosion that sends its shrapnel in all directions, but also the whining stepfather of rootless pariahs, and who am I, other than a nomad in this country, driven here by love and not war, but afflicted all the same by these resurgent faces and improbable stories and incapable of forgetting them, for everyone has a memory which may not be reliable but which is almost indistinguishable from a dream that one day it must be possible to . . . No, perhaps not, these are uncertain times, they always have been.

"We'd better go back," I hear myself saying. "You've got guests."

"What?" Markus says distractedly, lifting his head and staring at the massive swaying forest of beech trees, which is snow-covered on the windward side and as black as a raven on the other.

"Léon and Father Rampart, and someone called Beber. Nella thinks you've been driven mad by the Russian cross."

But then Markus says something I definitely don't understand:

"One belief is as good as another. It's got nothing to do with the cross, or

Peter, but last week I had my request to be buried in the memorial cemetery at Daleiden rejected. They don't bury soldiers any longer in German soil, especially not Belgians, they give them everlasting life, the dead can go wherever they like, and I'm not going back with you. This Beber only wants to hear about his father, and yet he doesn't, and Father Rampart is asleep, or he is drinking my wine, good for him."

"We'd better stay here then."

"Yes. Now it's beginning to snow again. It's coming down thick."

"Can you see anything?"

ROY JACOBSEN has twice been nominated for the Nordic Council's Literary Award: for *Seierherrene* in 1991 and *Frost* in 2003. In 2009 he was shortlisted for the Dublin Impac Award for his novel *The Burnt-Out Town of Miracles*.

DON BARTLETT is the acclaimed translator of books by Karl Ove Knausgård, Jo Nesbø and Per Petterson.

DON SHAW is a teacher of Danish and author of the standard Danish–Thai/Thai–Danish dictionaries.